MY HAND AND MY HEART

Isabel Huntoon

ISBN: 978-1-7348620-0-3

For the most wonderful husband in the world. Thanks for your unwavering support, my love.

1

As she slipped out the door and carefully closed it behind her, Nime shivered in the chilly damp of midnight. The air was heavy and salty from sea spray. She breathed it in and blinked away drowsiness. If she wanted to uphold her wisp-tag win-streak, she'd need to be alert.

She flexed her fingers and stretched her arms as she hurried down the gently swaying walkway toward the Academy. Her muscles were a little tight after physical training earlier, but that was fine. A game of wisp-tag with her friends was never as strenuous as Nime's PT. Sess could hold his own against Nime, but he wasn't competitive. Rem was too afraid of getting caught to pay attention and only came for Miel, anyway. Miel was crafty but slow. And Chi only cared about having fun. It was hardly challenging for Nime to win against them.

Haven was quiet, only the ever-present hum of the generator and the whipping wind disturbing that quiet. As she made her way through the Residential area, the gentle slap of waves against the sides of the settlement faded. The Academy was near the center, bordering the square along with Botanics, Maintenance, and the Clinic. This late, even Botanics was dark.

Nime's friends waited for her in front of the Academy doors. She sped up to a jog. Of course they had waited for her instead of breaking in themselves.

"We've been standing here forever," Rem said. He rubbed his arms and shivered. He'd tucked his chin into the high collar of his sweater and his hands into the sleeves. Sometimes he reminded Nime so much of Navi. Her little sister always preferred extra-long sweater sleeves so she could keep her hands warm. "It's freezing." No one else shivered, but then Rem and Nime, cousins, shared the same thin frame, and the wind coming off of the Endless Sea was sharp as always.

"I showed you how to circumvent the scanner," Nime said. Handing her lamp off to Sess, Nime knelt on the lite-crete walkway, cold and damp. This tablet scanner was normally off—what need would the Academy and library have to be locked?—but the archivists, in an attempt to keep students from doing exactly what Nime and her friends were doing, had blacklisted all tablets registered to students after hours. "You could have gone in already." Nime pulled out her multitool and switched it to a flat head screwdriver. Rem scowled at her while she pried the cover off of the scanner and reset it. When it came back online, they would have about a second to open the door without having to use their tablets.

"I'm not a delinquent, unlike some people." Rem looked away and pressed his lips into a thin line.

Chi snorted. "And yet here you are, breaking into the Academy at midnight," she said. Nime watched the lights in the scanner's circuitry. When they blinked off for a second and then on again, she grabbed the door with one hand and slid it open. Her other hand slapped the cover back on, and she waved her friends through.

"I'm not breaking into anything." Rem crossed his arms and stomped through the door into the entrance hall. It was pitch black inside, but Nime's lamp showed enough of the room that Rem wouldn't trip over anything, at least within a few feet of the door.

Miel followed and raised his eyebrows at Nime while addressing Rem. "Of course not," he said. "You're simply existing in the same place while other people break in, and then going inside with them. Totally different." Rem turned around, jabbing a finger in Miel's face.

"I'm only here because you all don't know how to keep out of trouble without me, and for some reason, I don't like it when my idiot friends get stuck doing service for breaking the rules, leaving me with no one to hang out with." Rem huffed and turned back around. Miel looked over his shoulder at Chi and made a face. They giggled. Sess followed them quietly, and Nime came last, letting the door close behind her.

By day, the Academy entrance hall was full of people, teachers and students alike, studying or relaxing between classes around the scattered tables. Branching off the room were hallways leading to classrooms and offices, with more on the upper floor. By night it was eerily silent. Or it would have been eerie, maybe, to Navi, easily scared as she was. Nime had snuck in so many times it was almost routine. She stepped around her friends and led the way across the room to the stairwell and elevators, unpowered like the rest of the building.

"Do you want to complain all night, or do you want to play?" Nime asked. Sometimes they played wisp-tag in the classrooms, but this time, her friends followed her down the stairs to the library. The library and archives were what Haven had been built for: to protect books, art, and data from the flooding that had turned Aht Carina into the Endless Sea. The database, saved mostly in the rows and rows of memory banks in the storage beneath Haven, held the aggregation of almost every piece of knowledge and culture from before the Fall.

Nime turned right at the landing and stepped into the first level of the library. B1 housed the common and durable books made in the century or so before the Fall, along with post-Fall literature. The most important pieces, the most delicate manuscripts and art, were further down. A few feet away from the stairwell, Nime stopped at a wide table and set her bag on a chair before placing her lamp in a groove on the surface. The others crowded around the table and dumped their bags on it.

"Standard rules?" Sess asked. He stood quite still next to Chi, who bounced on her toes in impatience. Standard wisp-tag—the game students of the rebellious variety had been playing since Haven was built—was simple. Each player got a lamp, broken just enough that the bioluminescent bacteria inside could slowly leak out, and hid somewhere dark. The goal was to find and tag the other players with the wisps and be the last person standing.

"Too easy," Nime said. "How about we only count fatal touches?"

"Anything that would kill a person?" Rem said. "Fine, maybe I'll win this time, since nobody pays attention when I talk about anything medical." Nime smiled.

"I call Rem for my team," Miel said, grabbing Rem's arm. Rem elbowed him away to get some space.

"Free for all," Nime said. Miel dropped his arm and pouted, but Nime knew he wasn't going to give up that easily. If Miel wanted to team up, he would, regardless of the rules. "Boundaries are…" looking around, Nime hesitated. "How about from the stairs to the seaward wall, excluding the private study rooms and bathrooms?" The others nodded.

Digging through her bag, Nime pulled out a small wisp-lamp with faint, branching fractures that had been sealed to stop leaks. She carefully pried the sealant off of the crack and handed the lamp to Sess. He pressed his fingers against the thick, glowing liquid now seeping from it. Nime did the same to four more lamps, passing them off to Chi, Rem, and Miel, and keeping one for herself. Her lamp leaked its sticky, sweet-smelling liquid into the palm of her hand. The five of them now glowed faintly with green-blue wisp-light.

"Anything else?" Chi asked, practically vibrating with anticipation.

"No." Nime gripped her lamp tighter and stood up on the balls of her feet. "Ready? One minute to hide, starting now."

* * *

I'm in a city in my head where the lights never go out. The city is familiar; I've imagined it so many times that I can name the streets I see below me, dark lines between glittering steel and glass buildings. They tower over those streets, stretching into the sky like trees. Skyways trace between them through the air. There are so many people here, more than Haven, more than I've ever seen in real life. This, I imagine, is what it was like before the Fall.

I'm alone at the top of one of those towering buildings, a wide window framing the city below like a painting. The room I'm in reminds me of the luxury of pre-Fall royalty. Everything is gold and white and beautiful.

Once, I told Athis-nin, my counselor, about this room at the top of this tower. I told him about how I could never seem to leave, even if I wanted to. He thought it was my mind's representation of my loneliness, and that I couldn't leave because I fear rejection.

I'm not sure he's right, because how would that explain the people who come and speak to me, who call me by a different name than

Navi? I didn't tell Athis-nin about them, because it seems a little silly to tell him that these people assure me of how important I am. Mostly it's the priestesses: they tell me again and again that I can do great things, that my shaping will save the world. I'm not sure what shaping means, but it has something to do with creative Potential. No one in Haven can use Potential, which people used to call magic. According to the priestesses, that's why I can't leave; my shaping and I are too important. That seems silliest of all, but for some reason, I always believe them.

And then every time I come back to reality, I feel smaller than ever because it's not true. When I blink and see the Endless Sea instead of an endless city, the belief in my own importance fades away, and I feel stupid for ever thinking I could change the world.

Now, there's someone else in the room with me, not a priestess or a politician. It's not anyone who's ever been here before. I can barely see them; they stand just beyond the light, and something obscures their face. I take a step closer. It feels right that they're here, like the room was missing something vital, and now that this person is here—I step closer again, light glints off of something metallic—I'm finally comfortable. They look up, and long, smooth black hair slides away from their face and—

A click brings me back into my bedroom. I open my eyes, and my heart pounds against my chest. That was new. And then I scramble out of bed, my foot landing in yesterday's leftover ink. I wipe it off on my other leg. I forgot I left that there. On go some socks. I wiggle my toes. They were starting to get cold. I grab my shoes in one hand and a wisp lamp in the other. Hurry, Navi, I think. Nime will be long gone at this rate.

And I'm right; I can barely see the bioluminescence of her lamp bobbing along the walkways. My chest starts to hurt as I run to catch up. Prime peeks out of the clouds enough to show me the edges of buildings and walkways, and even Secondary and Tertiary show themselves to give me more light. It makes the darkness less scary, but there are things other than the darkness that scare me.

Haven is terrifying at night, with the wind sneaking between walls and the spray of salty water from waves hitting the edges of the floats. Without other people to distract me, the Endless Sea seems so impossibly huge and Haven, floating on it, so tiny. I swallow and run faster, and my legs burn. I should have just asked Nime if I could go with her.

But if I asked her for help, then she'd have asked why I need to go to the library at midnight and I... I take a deep breath and hold it for a second. When I let it out, there's still a lump in my throat. It's probably for the best if Nime doesn't find out that Aeri, my classmate, dared me to meet her and her friends in the sculpture gallery.

I want to turn back. But I also want to be brave, like the me from my dreams. Like Nime.

And anyway, I'm already close enough to watch Nime open the Academy doors and walk in. She does it casually, kneeling for a minute in front of the scanner and then standing and rolling her shoulders. She holds the door open as four people I didn't see before step out of the shadow of the building. My breath catches.

And then releases. It's just her friends. Even our cousin Remy, who normally yells at Nime for breaking the rules, is there, and he looks annoyed. I run to catch the door before it closes fully, escaping the dim green light of Prime. I press my hands over my mouth to keep from breathing too loudly and look around, trying to make out shapes in the darkness. The entrance hall is filled with shadows too deep to see through.

I am not afraid, not even when I hear footsteps moving away from me, echoing against the lite-crete floor. My eyes sting with the threat of tears, my stomach twists, but I tell myself I'm not afraid. The footsteps tap rapidly down the stairs now, so I breathe and walk forward. It's so dark, I feel like I'm walking into nothing. I brush past a chair and grab it, like it's the only other thing in the world.

When I can't hear their footsteps anymore, I pull out my wisp-lamp and rub my hands over it. The wisps must be colder than I thought because it takes a while for them to fully wake up. But there's enough light to see by, so I head for the stairwell near the back of the entrance hall. The world turns a ghostly blueish-green from my lamp. I wish wisp-light was on the warmer end of the spectrum. As it is, it casts a haunted glow over everything I pass, like the light below sea level, blue and wavy and distorted.

What floor are Nime and her friends going to? Hopefully not down into the archive. I lean over the railing by the stairs. I can't see anything, not even a hint of light. It's like they disappeared, like they sank into the sea with nothing to mark where they were. I take a step down.

This isn't so bad. Even in this odd lighting, the Academy is familiar. My heart slows and my shoulders relax as I descend, and I realize no one knows I'm here.

A series of rapid, slapping thumps make me freeze on the last step before B1. I don't blink or even breathe. The lights move around through the shelves; I cover mine with my sweater.

Once I stop moving, I can hear more running footsteps. It must be Nime. I recognize her voice, along with Chi's laughter. I step down fully onto the floor. I never thought to wonder what Nime and her friends do when they sneak into the Academy.

Nime runs past the stairwell, weaving between tables. She doesn't see me, but she does see Sess, I think, farther ahead of her. I step up close to the archway separating the stairwell from B1 to see better. Yeah, that's Sess. None of Nime's other friends are that tall. He disappears behind a shelf, and Nime chases after him, holding a lamp out in front of her. She disappears too.

Chi comes out from between two rows and sits down at one of the tables by the stairs. She's glowing? Wisp-light is smeared all across the top of her chest and stomach and down one side. There's even a couple of splotches on her neck and face. She's laughing and craning her head to see what Nime and Sess are doing. I can hear a scuffle, and Chi kneels on the chair to get a better view. She cheers at whatever she sees, and then covers her mouth and laughs. Soon, Sess comes into view and plops into a chair. He's covered in wisps, too. They're in his hair and dripping down the back of his neck into his collar. He smiles at Chi and rubs at the stains before leaning his elbows on the table. She stands on the chair, using his shoulder for balance. Sess says something to her, and Chi hops back down into her seat.

I can hear Remy and Miel somewhere, too. A larger light moves down a row to my right, and there they are. Only their hands, the ones holding their lamps, glow. Chi and Sess turn to look at them. Chi scoots forward, until she's on the very edge of her seat, and grips it with her wisp-speckled fingers. Miel winks at her, and Remy elbows him. Sess rests his head on his hand.

Remy and Miel creep forward, along the line of shelves. They stop when Rem holds his hand up and listens. I try to listen, too. I don't hear anything, but I do see Nime crouching at the end of a row on my left. Well, I see her lamp and her head. The rest of her seems to blend in with the shadow of the shelf. She moves almost imperceptibly slowly. It doesn't seem like anyone else sees her.

I look back at Nime, but she's gone. I blink. She was right there, moving like a barnacle. Where did she go? And then I see a tiny flash of light that doesn't belong to Remy or Miel, and there she is, on top of the shelves. They definitely don't see her, not until she jumps down behind them and slides her wisp-covered hands along both of their necks before they can react. Chi cheers again, and this time she doesn't cover her mouth. Remy shushes her and scowls all the way to the table. Miel says something, and Nime responds by wrapping her hands around his neck again, but they both laugh.

When Nime walks over to the table, she's smiling and lifting her chin. The light on her hands is starting to fade.

"So that's 1 win, 4 tags for me already tonight," she says, leaning an elbow on Sess' shoulder. "You guys need to work a little harder, or I'll beat my own record."

"How are you always able to sneak up on me?" Remy asks. He crosses his arms. "We need to give you bells or something. But congratulations anyway."

"Maybe you would've heard me if you and Miel hadn't teamed up. By the way, that's a unique tactic in a free-for-all," Nime says with a sarcastic smile.

"She didn't sneak up on me," Chi says. She laughs again. "Or Sess. You should have seen it, Rem. It was like a teeny-tiny, little biter swimming after a, a whale or something, the way she was chasing him." Chi laughs so hard she can't talk, and Nime sighs.

"Not sneaky at all," Sess says, and it makes Chi laugh even harder. Nime pokes Sess' cheek and tries not to smile. The corners of her mouth turn down, and she would look stern if I didn't know she was about to laugh. She and Remy look a lot alike when they suppress a smile. I try out the expression. Would I look the same?

"Teaming up to defeat a more formidable opponent is a perfectly acceptable strategy," Miel says, simultaneously serious and silly. He flutters his eyes and loops an arm around Remy's neck. "Nyrem and I are simply intelligent enough to realize that neither of us can beat you on our own. After all, you, great Nime—" Chi snorts "—are a celestial being of amazing capabilities who—" Nime rolls her eyes "—is so far above our own level—"

"Miel." Remy draws out the second syllable. Miel stops and turns to face him. He looks like he's about to start talking again, but Remy beats him to it. "Shut up." Miel pouts. Remy covers his mouth, but I hear a laugh.

The five of them make an interesting picture, with the wisps on their skin starting to fade but still illuminating them in the surrounding darkness. I would love to paint it, if only there were a pigment to mimic the glow of wisps right where it meets their skin. It's white in the middle, but translucent blue on the edges. And where the wisps have died there are shiny smears that reflect a small amount of light.

"Let's start another round," Nime says, and I jump a little. I need to meet Aeri and the others still. Looking back at Nime one more time, I hug the lamp to my stomach and keep going down the stairs. The sound and light fade the farther down I go.

* * *

As Chi got ready to give the signal for another round of wisp-tag, Nime bounced on her toes in excitement. The thrill of winning had her heart racing and her energy spiking. She barely blinked as Chi counted down to one.

And Nime was off, counting the seconds in her head. She followed the glow of a lamp, unsure of who it belonged to. Technically, this was an unfair way to play; players weren't supposed to follow others during the one-minute hiding period, but Nime was impatient. Moving quietly, she closed the distance between herself and the person ahead of her as the minute came to an end.

Tensing her legs, Nime rubbed at the crack in her lamp. Her hand came away gooey and glowing. Time was up, but she'd give whoever this was a few seconds to make sure there'd be no argument about cheating.

And then she struck, sprinting toward the person, not caring about silence anymore. She recognized Rem a moment before she pressed her wet hand into his back, just below his left shoulder blade. Her momentum pushed him a little bit, but Nime stopped herself from crashing into him.

Rem turned around and looked at her. He crossed his arms.

"Seriously?" he said. "The game just started. I haven't had a chance to play yet!" Nime shrugged. Rem shook his head but started heading back, lifting his chin and raising his voice. "I'm out!" There was a surprised noise from somewhere nearby, and Nime turned her head toward it. Rem clicked his tongue at that. "Truly, Ni, you're like a robot." Then he turned a corner and disappeared into the darkness.

Heading in the direction of the noise, Nime came to a break in the shelves where her lamp revealed a few comfortable chairs and a database access point. The access point's backlit screen gave off its own glow. It looked a little spooky, sitting in the darkness. Navi wouldn't have liked it. She'd have probably been scared but pretended she wasn't. Nime smiled. Or maybe Navi would have liked it. There were times when Navi stopped and looked at the strangest things for inspiration. Maybe this would have been one of them.

The person who had been there was gone, but Nime didn't let herself relax. They could be close. She curled her arm around the lamp, blocking some of its light. As she turned to move on, a speck of light outside her circle caught her eye. She squinted at the drop of wisps on the floor. She'd found her next target.

The question was: who was she following? A trail left behind could have been carelessness, or it could have been left to lure her into an ambush. If Nime was following Chi, it was probably not a trap. Chi didn't do traps, they weren't fun enough for her. If it was Sess, he might have not even noticed he was leaving a trail. But Miel…if it was Miel, then this was definitely a trap.

Nime wrapped her sleeves around her lamp and managed to block out most of the light, leaving her with barely enough to keep from smashing into things. But she could see the little trail of wisps along the floor more easily. The droplets were long and splattered, like the person had been running.

She followed the trail regardless of whether it was a trap or not. It wound up and down rows with no apparent destination. Once or twice it almost disappeared, but Nime found it again each time. The trail kept well away from the open areas beyond the shelves, and Nime was losing track of where exactly she was. Had she left the modern fiction section already? Or was she in a different part of the library entirely?

"I'm out!" Chi yelled from somewhere on the opposite side of the floor. Nime paused. The trail must have belonged to Sess or Miel, then. Nime grit her teeth and kept going. Following was not her style. She'd much rather have been on the offensive than trailing an unknown quarry with no better plan. At least she was catching up with them. The droplets were brighter, fresher now. Bigger, like the person was slowing down. She stepped softly, still concealing her light.

And then the trail ended, and Nime stilled for a second to think. Her neck tingled. Turning, she came face to lamp with Miel. Her arm came up to protect herself as Miel lunged forward. Nime jumped back and tensed her arms and legs. Too bad for him he hadn't gotten her while she'd been distracted. There were very few ways he could win now.

Miel didn't let the miss catch him off guard; instead, he lunged again. Nime dodged backward. She couldn't get past him, but she was faster than him. If she could just get far enough away, she'd be able to regain control of the situation. He kept pressing forward, his hand—glowing with a small puddle of wisps—uncomfortably close to tagging Nime's head. Nime moved back, looking for an opening to touch him with her own wisps. And then Miel faltered a little, landed a little wobbly on one foot, and Nime took her chance to run. She turned, planning to circle back around, and—

She found a bookshelf directly behind her, blocking her escape. Nime whipped back around. Miel was right in front of her, hand gripping his lamp like he was afraid he might drop it. He smiled.

"Aww, come on, Ni, I expected better of you," he said. "I was planning on catching Rem or Chi like this, not you." There was an indignant "Hey!" from the table, probably from Rem. Miel laughed. Nime laughed too, though she eyed his hands and the shelves surrounding them at the same time. Now it made sense. Miel had led her through a convoluted maze, into an aisle in what looked like the medical reference section. An aisle that inconveniently ended at the wall, trapping her. She clenched her fist. Such a stupid mistake.

"I should let someone else win sometimes, right? It's the nice thing to do," Nime said. Miel opened his mouth, his face playful. And then the open mouth turned into a shocked one, and he turned around. Now that his body wasn't blocking the light, Nime could see Sess standing behind him, lamp in hand. Miel had a splotch of glowing blue in the middle of his back.

"What in Moeth's salty—" he said. He looked back at Nime and then at Sess again. "I was just about to tag her, how could you?" Sess blinked and stepped aside so Miel could get past him. Miel grunted and hit Sess with his shoulder as he passed. Sess rubbed his arm and looked at Nime.

And then she was on him, her glowing hand headed for his chest, neck, head, whichever she could tag first. Sess responded in a split second, blocking her arm and looking for a chance to strike. He was surprisingly quick, Nime knew, from years of sparring with her in PT. She had wanted to learn to fight when she was twelve, and since they'd done everything together, that meant Sess had learned, too.

Now, the need to win burned her up inside. She had to quickly, or their friends would think she hadn't earned it, that Sess had given it to her. The thought made her chest tight.

Her hand pressed against the left side of his chest half a second before his grazed her face. They both stopped, and suddenly Nime could hear her heavy breathing. She swallowed against her dry throat and pulled her hand back. Sess stepped back and nodded once.

"I'm out," he said. Nime blinked a few times, rapidly, and she smiled at him. She touched the side of her face, where he'd left wisps, and started walking back toward the table. Sess didn't even have to try to catch up with her, with his extra-long steps. "I didn't hurt you, did I?" he asked. Hurt? He'd barely touched her. Okay, so the skin under the wisps would be red for a bit, but it'd take a lot more than that to get Nime to admit pain. She took a second to answer.

"Me?" she said. She scoffed and pushed his arm before looping hers through it. "Please." He hummed and didn't respond. "You startled me there," Nime continued. "I didn't hear you coming." At that, he looked down and nodded.

"Miel was distracted. It was a good opportunity." Sess looked ahead as they neared the table where the others were waiting, and Nime let out a breath. Fine. As long as he didn't think he was rescuing her, that was fine. Nime relaxed the muscles of her neck and shoulders. She didn't remember them tensing up.

Rem, Chi, and Miel all looked at them when they emerged from the shelves.

"Who won?" Rem asked. Miel sniffed and looked away. Nime gestured to herself and plopped into the chair next to Chi.

* * *

I stop on B3, the top floor of the archive. The sculpture gallery stretches out to the left of the stairwell and far past the walls of the Academy. The archive takes up a huge amount of the storage space beneath Haven, and I've never been able to make it all the way through in one go. I lean against the wall. My head falls back against it, and I wince at the thud. Rubbing the back of my head, I start looking for Aeri. Why did I ever agree to do Cera's challenge with her? I want to be braver, sure, but I know she doesn't like me.

"You'd think Navi would just get genius Nime to do the work for her, like she does everything else," Aeri had said earlier, during class, quietly enough that our teacher, Midra-nin, couldn't hear her. But I could.

"Don't even say that, what if her crazy sister showed up?" Aeri's friend Danan had said.

"Remember that time Nime broke Erden's arm?" That was Curra, Aeri's other friend. "And Navi just cried about being bullied? Truly? She wasn't the one who got her arm broken over nothing."

I'd pulled my hair over my shoulders, forming a copper curtain, and tried to ignore my hot face and stomachache.

So. They don't like me. Which made it weirder when Aeri came up to me after that and asked, "Navi, have you heard about Cera's Challenge?"

Of course I have. Everyone has. You spend the night in the sculpture gallery, and Cera will possess one of the sculptures. If you manage to see her and not get caught, you'll do well on all your assessments. Why the Celestial Warden of Luck would help with assessments, I don't know. It's not true, anyway. The Wardens are just personifications of abstract concepts meant to inspire and comfort us. They're not real.

But for some reason, when Aeri asked me to come with them tonight, I nodded and listened as Aeri, Danan, and Curra walked away laughing.

And now I'm here, walking down a tightly packed and stabilized row of 23rd century statues, trying not to look too closely at any of them. They all cast strange shadows in the wisp-light. I don't know which ones are worse, those that have defined shapes, like people or animals or objects, or the abstract ones, shaped like the things that float behind my eyelids when I close them. Both make my heart jump when their shadows move as I walk. I blink fast. I chew my lip. Do not cry. Don't cry, not when Aeri is waiting. I swallow and keep walking. I try to distract myself.

The moving shadows merge into the shadows of my imaginary city, and for the first time ever, I'm outside of my tower. I'm on the upper skyways, and even in my imagination, I'm afraid of looking down. But there's someone by my side, and I feel less afraid with them. It's the black-haired person from earlier, only now I can see her face. She reminds me of Nime for some reason, even though this person has metal running down her neck. When she raises her hand to point something out I can see that her arm, from her shoulder down to her fingertips, is metal, too.

I look where she's pointing. In the sky, taller even than the other buildings, a huge tower looms. Atop the slender, curving trunk of it sits a golden mass in the shape of a lotus flower. I shiver when I see it. I've never seen my tower from the outside before. I wonder if I could see my suite's windows, somewhere in the lotus' spreading petals, from down here. The cyborg touches my arm with her human hand, and I tear my eyes away from the tower. I don't know why I'm out here, but I want to enjoy it while I am.

I keep walking through the sculpture gallery, but my surroundings blend into the shadows of the city in my head. The city is hectic, teeming with people; I can feel the activity around me like a buzzing under my skin. It seems so real, like it's not just a figment of my overactive imagination.

I slip between two massive funerary urns to get to a different section of the gallery, making sure to stay close to the stairwell so I can hear if Aeri and her friends come in. In the city in my head, the shadows get thicker, darker. It's always hard to tell how much time has passed when I'm daydreaming, but it seems like it's been long enough that Aeri should be here by now. But the only other shapes in the gallery are the sculptures. I frown. I'm not late, am I? I didn't bring my tablet, so I can't even check the time, but I was pretty sure the clock at home said fifteen minutes to midnight when I left.

But what if it didn't? What if I spent too much time in my head, and I'm late, and they already did the challenge and left, and they're going to think I didn't come. Or maybe I'm early, and I'll have to wait here in the dark for who knows how long. What if there's another, hidden, sculpture galley I don't know about and I'm in the wrong one? I glance back and forth, but I can't see anything outside of my light. I hold the lamp tighter.

It's fine; I can wait. I press my lips together and stand up straight. Not a problem. My lamp fades a little, and I almost drop it trying to wake the wisps back up. I swear I see something move in the corner of my eye; my head whips up just in time to see…nothing. There's nothing there, nothing behind any of the statues, especially not a Celestial Warden. That doesn't make my chest any less tight. I feel cold and clammy, even through my thermals and my sweater.

It must have been my imagination, a shadow moving behind me, because the shadows in the city crowd around me and the cyborg. I move closer to her, and my skin prickles like I'm being watched.

There's a noise in real life, a squeak, and I don't want to be here anymore. I start walking, jogging, away when I hear a voice. I stop. Aeri? I almost call out. But that's not Aeri's voice, or Curra's, or Danan's. I step behind a sculpture—a marble woman leaning on her sword, head bowed—and cover my lamp. My other hand comes up to cover my mouth. If it's not them, who is it?

"—better than to believe a couple of Intermediate trouble-makers." The person is a woman, old I think, carrying a lamp. I crouch and get as close as I can to the statue, as close as its shadow. I can see her face, though the wisp-light makes her look pale and blue. It's actually a nice blue, now that I look closer. I wish I could recreate it. I bet a mermaid would have that color skin. And the way it sharply drops off into dark, dark blue in the shadow of her nose… "Teenagers," she tuts.

I blink, and the elder's face is a face again, not layers of colors and shapes. It's Ko-nin, one of the archivists. I press harder against my mouth, against the noise trying to escape it. I hide even further behind the statue. When Ko-nin passes me, I half-crawl, half-walk in the other direction, back toward the stairs. My heart beats hard in my chest. I hope I'm not making noise, but I can't tell over the rushing in my ears.

In my head, the cyborg and I run along the skyways of the city. The shadows chase us, close behind. My heart is in my throat, because if these shadows catch me, something terrible will happen. My chest feels hollow at the thought of them, and I know what the priestesses have told me. They warned me that this could happen if I left my tower. That there were people, destructive and cruel, who wanted nothing more than to stop me from saving the world. These must be those people; they must be. But the cyborg is with me, and I know she'll keep me safe. Even so, my hands shake.

The skyway we're on ends at a housing complex with a security gate. We could go through it—my biometrics could get me into any building in this city—but if we do, the priestesses will know where I am. And that scares me as much as the shadows chasing us. But the cyborg says something to me, a soft mumble that I can't quite decipher. Imaginary-me knows what to do, though: the cyborg's presence makes pulling a thin spike of rock from the creative Potential at our feet as easy as breathing. The spike climbs the building, and my cyborg grabs on, hauling us both up with it. A giddy laugh bubbles out of me. The priestesses never let me shape anything fun. As we reach the top of the building, I shape the spike into sand and watch it fall back to the skyway.

In real life, I make it to the safety of the stairwell. I let myself breathe again. Ko-nin's light is barely visible, somewhere in the maze of sculptures. I hope Aeri and the others aren't in there somewhere as well. I creep back up the stairs.

At least now I have an excuse to not be there. No one wants to get in trouble over Cera's Challenge when the whole point is to do better on assessments. I can go to class tomorrow and tell Aeri that I tried, but Ko-nin, terrifying guardian of the archives, was waiting there, so I left. Aeri will probably understand.

When I get to B1, I lean against the railing. Nime and her friends are still playing, though it looks like their lamps are half empty. If Ko-nin comes up here, Nime will get in trouble. I don't know about her friends, but Nime is already in cold water with the archivists. And the librarians. And the teachers.

I chew my lip. I should warn them.

I start to step forward, and then stop. Nime will want to know why I'm here. I don't want her to know about this whole, stupid thing.

I press my hand to my forehead. What would Nime do in this situation? Easy. She would go out there and tell them and not worry about getting caught.

Unfortunately, I'm not as brave as Nime. Not even in my daydreams.

Footsteps on the stairs below me. I stop breathing. Ko-nin is coming. There's no more time for me to think about it. I run up the stairs to sea level, only this time I don't try to be quiet. Under the stairs up to the second floor, there's a small, dark space. I stuff my lamp underneath my sweater and crawl under. It's dusty, but at least I'm hidden.

Nime should've heard me, surely. I hug the lamp to my stomach and wait.

2

A noise on the stairs made Nime's head snap in that direction, and everyone else froze. She lunged over the table to scoop everyone's lamps into her bag. It glowed a little, especially at the bottom where the wisps collected, but it concealed most of the light.

"Stay here," she said, feeling her way over to the stairwell and peeking up and down. It had sounded like footsteps, but she wasn't sure which direction they'd been going. Either way, the game was over for the night. She headed back to the table, her friends' faces barely visible in the dim light. They still had glowing spots all over them, and Rem's eyes were wide enough to shine. "We need to go. Come on." She shushed whoever pushed their chair back too loudly, and they all crept over to the stairwell.

Nime paused. She couldn't see any lights from above, so it was probably safe to leave. She stuck her head out over the railing, and the question was answered for her. There was a light coming up from below. Maybe two floors down.

"New plan." Nime turned around to look at everyone. "You four head up and get home. I'll stay to make sure you don't get caught." Rem shook his head and glared at her. But she knew how afraid he was of disciplinary action, even though it was usually just having to work in Sanitation for a few weeks. Miel edged toward the stairs. Rem turned his glare to Miel.

"And what about you?" he asked Nime. "You're already on a warning; they'll ban you from the library for a month for this." Nime sighed and peeked back over the railing. Her friends needed to have left already.

"I'll only stay long enough to distract them; if I go back to Residential through storage, they won't be able to find me." Nime pointed toward the stairs when Rem didn't move. "Go, please. The more of us there are, the more likely we are to be caught." Chi looked down and pulled her hair over her shoulder. She tugged on Rem and Sess to get them moving. Rem huffed and followed her, Sess only a second behind.

* * *

Miel pops up from the stairway and runs for the door. A breeze follows him, and it brushes my hair against my face. Chi follows, though she sticks around to wait for Sess and Remy, who climb up a second after her. They jog toward the exit, not looking back. The door slides shut with a thump. It's silent for a few minutes.

Where's Nime? They were supposed to all get out together. Could she have not heard me? I stick my head out, trying to see down. Maybe I could make more noise? The doors open again, and I pull my head back so fast it hits the underside of the stairs. I clutch my head and cover my mouth. Are they back? They're supposed to go home, not stick around and get caught.

But I hear more sets of footsteps than four people should have. And those voices are definitely adults. One voice stands out to me, one I've heard every day of my life. This voice is unmistakable as it draws closer: it's Mom.

* * *

Nime moved away from the light coming from the stairwell. As the footsteps and light approached, she rubbed her hands all over the lamp and rolled it toward the stairs. The footsteps stopped on the landing, and Nime slid back into the shelter of the shelves. Placing her feet carefully, one after the other, she backed down the row. The light moved closer, and she let out a slow breath.

That should've been enough time for her friends to get away, but just in case, Nime set one foot down with a little more force. It hit the floor with a soft tap, and the person with the light made a noise. Nime hurried to the end of the row.

Now that they were on her, all she had to do was lure them away from the stairs, loop around, and make it down to storage. It would be like she was never there.

The cracked lamps in her bag were either out of wisps or asleep, and Nime stumbled in the dark. She reached out a hand, feeling for the edge of a shelf. The light and footsteps reached the other end of the row, and she paused for half a second. She could almost see who it was.

They turned down the row and Nime's fingers found the corner of the shelf. She slipped around it and moved a little more quickly past the aisles.

"Whoever is in here, you are violating the library code of conduct by remaining in the building after hours without clearance," the person said. Their cold voice carried through the air, and Nime clenched her jaw. That was a voice so used to imperatives that its owner probably hadn't asked a real question in years. She knew that voice, and suddenly she was fiercely glad the others hadn't stayed. Her mother wasn't exactly lenient on rule-breakers. Nadra had always given Nime the most severe punishment available, even when the rest of the Board would have been happy with less. There was certainly no risk of anyone accusing her of nepotism. "Come out now, or this matter will be taken to the Advisory Board." Why was Nadra there? Nime narrowed her eyes and glanced back in the direction of the light. It was already odd for anyone to have been patrolling the library; that person being on the Advisory Board was even more unusual. Shaking her head, Nime kept moving.

She could've made a run for it then, headed for the stairs while Nadra was searching the maze of shelves, but the area between the shelves and the stairwell was open, and Nime couldn't see well enough to avoid all the study tables. She needed to get a better idea of where Nadra was.

Nime made her way to the wall near the stairs, sticking to the safety of the shadows, and crouched behind a chair with a good view. Nadra emerged into the open area and approached the stairwell, shining her lamp in every direction.

"Ko-nin," Nadra said, speaking into her tablet almost too quietly for Nime to hear. "The meeting is starting, but there's a student on the first floor." She paced as she spoke, and Nime missed what she said next.

Nadra tucked her tablet away and headed up the stairs. Meeting?

Nime managed to keep the burning desire to follow under control until Nadra's light wasn't visible anymore. And then curiosity drew Nime out into the open and up the stairs. Not all the way, just enough to look over the edge of the floor. Several adults were seated around a table in the entrance hall. They'd turned on only a handful of lights, which left the hall dim and strange looking. Nime shouldn't have stayed —it was stupid to stay just to eavesdrop—but the fear of being caught was nothing in comparison to her desire to know.

Nadra was saying something. Leaning forward, Nime tried to slow her breathing to hear better. Looking at the group, she recognized most of them from the Advisory Board. Why would they be meeting in the Academy in the middle of the night? Maybe they'd expected the Academy to be empty. Thoughtless of them. Didn't they know about Cera's Challenge? Wisp-tag? Rebellious Intermediate and Advanced students? It might have been against the rules to be in the Academy after hours, but that had never stopped a student before. That was obviously why Nadra had been making sure no one was there. Nime smiled a little, knowing she was doing something her mother would've been furious about.

"I know this is not the usual meeting spot for the Board, but this matter is both pressing and sensitive," Nadra said. A murmur spread through the group. Nime leaned back a little. The Board meeting room auto-broadcasted at all times to tablets, so anyone could watch the meetings if they wanted to. Nime's eyebrows pinched together. The Board members were supposed to be upstanding members of the community, not sneaking around like this.

"The most recent status report on the generator has not been positive," Nadra continued. "Ciril-nin, please."

Ciril-nin was the Head Engineer. Nime stilled. She didn't know much about the generator. No one did, thanks to the Architects using some relic from before the Fall, instead of something sensible like solar or tidal power. The relic was dangerously full of Potential and so powerful that it needed to be sealed away.

Potential had been everywhere in the past. People had used it all the time, at least according to the history texts every Intermediate studied.

Magic, the ancient peoples had called it. Later, when the Technological Revolution had spread across the planet, they'd called it Potential, and its users shapers or breakers.

The relic and its Potential provided more than enough energy for Haven, but if it ever failed, the engineers had no way to fix it. Maybe it would've been better for "magic" to have been left behind with everything else when Aht Carina flooded. It wasn't as if anyone in Haven could do anything with it. All it was now was a source of unknown danger.

"There's a leak," Ciril-nin said. "Sometime over the past week, one wall has ruptured badly enough to release a steady stream of Potential, and I only noticed it today during a routine check. I don't know what caused it, and when I tried to cover it, I couldn't get closer than a few feet without this—" he paused, and there were gasps and distressed comments loud enough for Nime to hear "—happening. It's not responding to any treatments, and it was almost unbearable before the anesthetic. I don't think I need to tell any of you what this could mean."

Nime swallowed. No one had ever been exposed to the relic inside the generator before. Some of the engineers had speculated that it would outright kill anyone able to get close to it. Ciril-nin's presence was proof that it wouldn't. But whatever injury he'd gotten was concerning enough.

Could Potential spread? If its effects extended beyond Maintenance, people could get hurt. They could die. Nime's mind raced, flashed to Navi. Chi, Sess, Miel. Rem, Uncle Kel, Aunt Iloa. Her dad. She clenched her fists. They had to fix it quickly. Several Board members said as much.

"How exactly would we do that?" Nadra asked in the tone she normally reserved for the very stupid. "Who is going to volunteer to risk getting close enough, only to find out that we don't have the materials or the ability? Everything the Architects used to build and contain the generator is at the bottom of the sea. The artifact contains Potential, and they used Potential to seal it. So if anyone has somehow rediscovered a way to use it after all these years, now would be the time to let me know."

"What can we do?" someone asked.

"Nothing," Nadra said, and Nime wanted to scream. "The fact of the matter is, if the effects don't spread beyond the generator, then the solution is simple: we close off the building and leave it as is. And if it does reach beyond, there's not enough time to do anything. We would have a matter of weeks. I suggest keeping this quiet. There's no need to cause a panic over something we can't control."

Nime had to stop herself from running up there and demanding what in the Endless Sea her mother was thinking. Do nothing, because it might be fine? And if it wasn't fine, they should just give up? Resign themselves to death, and even worse, not tell the people? Her skin felt hot all over. She breathed out through her teeth. For a second she couldn't think over the anger. Nime clenched her fist and swung at the wall. Her hand slowed an inch away, and she pushed it into the wall quietly. She turned and shook her hand loose. She wouldn't get caught now. Because unlike her mother, Nime never gave up.

It took effort not to stomp back down the stairs, but Nime managed. She needed to think about what she'd heard, needed to come up with something if the Advisory Board wouldn't, but first she needed to get home.

Since she didn't know where Ko-nin was, Nime took the circuitous route through the database server rooms and kept her lamp low. The storage below Haven held several mazes worth of hallways and passages, so she stuck to the routes she knew already: from the B1 server room, the entrance to which was tucked away in the library stacks, down to the B4 server room and into the lowest level of the archive. She emerged into the manuscript storage rooms and shivered, hurrying toward the main hallway. She rubbed her arms. Only the offices, reading rooms, and bathrooms on B4 were heated. She had her thermals on, of course, but the chill so far below the water seeped into her bones and made her fingers stiff.

The hallway was long, with offices and reading rooms on one side and manuscript storage on the other. Nime could see all the way to the stairwell at one end of the hall in the light of the glowing nameplates next to each office door. At the other end of the hall was a door into the rest of Haven's storage. She turned toward it, touching one hand to the wall as she walked.

Ira's office was on B4 as well. It shouldn't have been; he was a tutor, and the rest of the tutors and teachers had offices in the upper levels of the Academy. Then again, he was still only an apprentice tutor, even after three years, and there was limited space above sea level. And Ira had always had bad luck, with this and everything else—things breaking when they shouldn't, avoidable injuries and illnesses he got anyway. He was even still living with his family because the genetic counselors hadn't found a match for him yet. And most recently, a failed psychological evaluation that had kept him from being advanced to a true teaching position. The results were supposed to be secret, but nothing in Haven ever truly was, not when all 217 people knew each other so well. Unstable, was the rumor. Unfit for such an important position.

Nime frowned. She couldn't see how anyone would think Ira was unstable. He'd been working so hard to become a teacher, tutoring Nime, Rem, Chi, Miel, and Sess for two years. And he was still stuck down in the archives and denied by the Education Board.

As she passed Ira's nameplate, Nime's hand ran over a stretch of empty air. She froze. Only then did she notice the faint light within. She tensed, getting ready to run again. Peeking in through the opening, Nime let out a breath. Ira wasn't inside.

His door was partially open, and his lamp was still awake, sitting in a holder on his desk. It looked like he'd been there not long ago, based on the brightness of the lamp. Papers were strewn about in no particular order on the desk, crumpled and often smudged with something. It was a good thing Ira wasn't actually an archivist because his clumsiness would not work well with one-of-a-kind manuscripts.

Far off footsteps made Nime jump a little, and she tucked her lamp under her sweater to block its light. That had to be Ira. Nime hurried down the hall. It would be better if he didn't know she was there. The last thing she wanted to do was make life harder for him.

The door to storage was locked, but Nime disabled the tablet scanner in a moment. Who would have guessed she'd become so proficient at getting through locked doors? She snorted. Everyone who knew she knew how to disable the scanners, that was who. Thankfully, that group didn't include her mother or anyone else with the power to reprimand her. It was a good thing she and Sess had wanted to explore the defunct ships when they were Intermediates, just twelve or thirteen. She'd gotten a lot of practice breaking into the abandoned docks without alerting anyone.

Closing the door behind her and pulling out her lamp, Nime paused for a second before moving farther into the massive room. Back when Haven was new, storage had been filled with boxes upon boxes of food and clothes and luxuries. Now, most of the boxes that sat on the open shelves were empty. There were some clothes left, mostly pieces that must have only been useful just after the Fall because it hadn't been warm enough to wear something that thin and that short in hundreds of years.

She reoriented herself and started walking along the wall, passing rows of what used to be food storage. All that was left were a few barrels similar to the ones that had been repurposed for water storage up in the Distillery ages ago. If she remembered correctly, hugging the left wall would eventually bring her to a hallway separating Botanics storage from Academy storage. There, she could take another set of stairs back up to the surface and finally go home.

Before she could get too far, the door slid open with a squeal. Nime stepped into one of the aisles to block line of sight and wrapped her lamp in her sweater again. She grit her teeth and let a long breath out her nose.

"I'm checking storage right now, but I don't think there's anyone here. I haven't seen anyone down here or on B3," said Ira, a little too loudly to be covert. A dull thud echoed. "Ouch." Frowning, Nime moved to the other end of the aisle she was in. As annoying as it was, she was just going to have to wait him out. "I'm sorry, I'm not trying to make noise, it's just dark in here and bins keep jumping out at me," he said, and then a little quieter, but not enough to make a difference, "Oops, sorry." Nime shook her head. He was going to injure himself like this. What was he doing here? Obviously, he'd been sent to search for her, but what was he doing in his office so late in the first place? Nime's thoughts trailed off when she heard him coming closer. Her eyes widened.

How did he know to follow the wall and turn right at the branch only two rows away? Nime could see his light, trapped by the things on the shelves, not reaching her. Turning at an intersection, she moved a little faster, but his light still followed her. She ran on the balls of her feet to keep quiet and took another turn.

It was a dead end. She'd walked straight into a dead end. For the second time that night, she was trapped. The feeling pressed down under her skin. Her pulse raced in her ears. And Ira's voice was loud enough to hear again, insisting that he couldn't see why anyone would hide down here, after all, it was cold and uncomfortable. Through it all, Nime's stomach dropped more and more. She didn't know if Ira would turn her in or not; more importantly, she hadn't wanted to get him involved at all. She backed up to the shelf at the end of the row.

Turning, Nime skimmed over the shelves and their contents, looking for a way out. The row backed up against two walls, and bins filled the shelves. She could move some out of the way and crawl through the side that wasn't against a wall, but the noise would give her away for sure. The back shelf, though, was a little farther away from the wall than the others, and there was one less bin on the bottom shelf, leaving about a foot of space. If she could squeeze in behind them, that would be a decent hiding place with minimal noise. Hands trembling, she pushed the bins farther down the line to make the opening bigger. She ducked into the space she'd made, shoulder scraping against the frame. It was tight, but she managed to get through and shove the bin back into place with her foot.

And then she fell backward into empty space, not the wall that had appeared to be there. With no light, she couldn't tell how far back the space went, but the fact that it even existed was odd. She didn't have time to question it further, not with Ira getting closer and closer. Nime breathed in sharply and turned back around, and Ira stood in front of the shelf with his tablet out, still speaking with someone. She squinted against the light from his lamp. Could he see her? Or did it look like a wall to him? He moved the light down so she could see his face, and yes, he could definitely see her. They made eye contact through the shelf, and Nime's chest constricted. Ira raised his eyebrows.

* * *

I breathe out through my mouth. Footsteps leave the library. When I can't hear anything else, I stick my head out of my hiding spot. My lamp barely makes a dent in the dark. My legs wobble a bit when I stand, but at least I don't hit my head this time. I walk outside. The door slides closed behind me with a click. It's raining again.

It's raining again, and we could all die.

My eyes burn hot, and with no one to see me, not even Prime, I cry. This time next month, I could be dead. Nime could be dead. Dad and Mom and everyone else in Haven could be dead. Everyone in the whole world. I trip over something and keep walking. The darkness isn't even scary anymore, but my hands still shake.

I don't remember the walk home. My arms open the door to our unit, moving the shoe I wedged there to keep it open out of the way, and my feet carry me to my bedroom. I stand in my room and stare at my ceiling. I'm dripping on the floor. My sweater is soaked. And we could all die.

Sweater off. Wet socks off. When I'm lying in bed and my lights are off and my blankets are finally starting to warm up, I press my face into my pillow. The fabric underneath my eyes gets hot and wet. After a while, I roll onto my back. I pull the blanket over my head.

What would it be like? Whatever happened to Ciril-nin didn't sound good. And even though Mom said the Potential might not spread far enough to cause problems, the Architects sealed it away for a reason. I can't help but think the reason was that it *would* spread.

I don't want to die. I don't want it so much, I feel it like a hard thing in my stomach. Thinking about it makes me feel awful. I don't want to think about dying anymore. I'm not supposed to have to, not for another 80 years at least. I grab the blanket in my hands and squeeze. How could this happen, how could the generator be leaking Potential, and no one knows how to fix it? And no one knows about it at all? No one but the Advisory Board, me, and Nime, whose head I saw peeking up from the stairs for a minute during the meeting. I wonder for a second what exactly she heard, and then I frown into the blanket. The Advisory Board should tell people.

Maybe if they did, someone would be able to come up with something to save us. Instead, I'm one of the few people who know, and I can't do anything. I'm only 13. I don't even truly know what Potential is. Only that it used to be a source of magical power, that people used to do incredible things with it. Only that it feels like a rush of warmth through my skin when the imaginary-me uses it. Like everything in my daydreams, it feels as real as the blanket on my chest, as true as my real life. Sometimes it feels more true.

Why do my daydreams show Potential as a beautiful thing, like paint or sunlight, when the reality could kill me? I'm sure Athis-nin would have something to say about that. My hands loosen. I pull the blanket off my head and close my stinging eyes. I lie there and let my mind wander until I'm somewhere else, somewhere that isn't Haven.

The city isn't still—it's never still, and I don't know how I came up with something so *busy*—but it is quieter than I've ever heard it. I am close enough to the ground to breathe in the smoggy late-night air, so much thicker than the air up near my tower. My chest burns from exertion.

I can't see the cyborg anymore. I don't know where she is, and panic sticks in my throat and stomach. The shadows that were chasing us have caught me. They close in around me, faceless human shapes. Dark fingers and hands reach out to me, and I can't move. This is everything the priestesses warned me about. Even worse, I know what their darkened fingers mean.

They're not black, they're dark, dark blue. The blue of the night sky, though I can't see it beyond the brightness of the city. The corruption starts at the fingertips, staining like ink, and creeps further up over time. And it only starts when someone regularly practices breaking.

The realization makes me shiver, both versions of me. The priestesses have told me all about breaking. About the destruction it's capable of causing. Breakers are the type of people I'm supposed to save the world from. But all I can do is freeze up and hope that the cyborg will save *me*. Some hero I am.

A shadow touches me, a sharp pinch on my upper arm. The world sways and fades around the edges of my vision. And the last thing I see for a little while is hands, dark-tipped hands, surrounding me.

When I can see again, everything is soft and distorted, like in a dream. I sit up and hold my head. It hurts every time I move, so I don't. Whatever was about to happen with the shadows, I'm glad that the cyborg saved me. She must have saved me, even though I don't remember it, because how else would I be back in my tower?

I blink, and the world clears up enough for me to look down at my bed and realize it's not my bed. I'm in a bed, but it's not the one in my tower suite. My eyes widen. I look around, wincing when my head pounds. This is not my tower.

This room is much less nice than mine. Instead of clear glass, the walls are made of concrete. The bed has no soft white blankets or gold pillows, just a yellowed mattress and a flimsy thermal blanket. A glass cup sits on the floor next to the bed with what looks like water in it, but I don't touch it. Cold air pricks my skin into goosebumps; that's not something I'm used to in the daydream. Smog coats the bare walls, the way I'm told is common in the lower levels of the city.

I take a deep breath to keep calm. Just because I'm not in my tower doesn't mean I'm in trouble. The cyborg might have brought me here to keep me safe. Maybe we're hiding from the shadows. Where is the cyborg, exactly? She's not nearby; I'd be able to tell if she were.

I don't panic. Navi, in the real world, would definitely panic. But imaginary-Navi doesn't. I swallow and take another look around the room. A light on the ceiling shows rough, brown carpet and a tiny window near the top of one wall. Light spills under the door from outside. I can't hear anything beyond it. Swinging my legs over the side of the bed, I stand up. My shoes scrape against the carpet, and I look down. Even if I would have been able to get back to my tower without the priestesses knowing, they'd be able to tell I've been out by the state of my shoes. The marble floors of my tower are kept so clean I can see myself in them. And my shoes, not meant for the dirty streets and skyways, are ruined. They used to be white. Now I'd say they're about the color of the Endless Sea on a cloudy day. That is, gray.

I move over to the door and open it a crack. I don't see anyone in the hallway beyond, low ceilinged and as dirty as the room, so I take a step out. And now I do hear something: voices, somewhere to my left. I follow them. A staircase leads up, the voices coming from above. None of them sound like the cyborg.

At least now I can make out what they're saying. I hear them speaking in the way people do in memories: not the words themselves, but the meaning. Someone mentions the priestesses and my tower. These people want to do something to the priestesses. Something bad.

"Without the Lif, the creator cult won't be able to do much," one of the people says, and I hear those words more distinctly than anything else. That's me. I'm the Lif. I don't know if that means anything in the real world, but here in the imaginary city, it's something the priestesses have called me before. Something to do with shaping, with magic, with a golden light that fills my veins.

My breath sticks in my throat. Without me? But the cyborg, she would never let anything happen to me. But she's not here right now. And she let them take me.

I back down the hall, toward the room I came from. I need to get back to my tower. And the cyborg isn't here to help me. Pushing the door closed behind me, I slip back into the room. I pull my hand across the door, and liquid metal spreads from my palm. It forms a bar, molding seamlessly into the wall on either side of the door like it belongs there. And then I turn and look at the small, high window.

The world gets fuzzier, more dreamlike again, and the last thing I can remember is the sight of my tower from the ground in pale, morning light.

* * *

"Ko-nin," Ira said. Nime stood frozen. "There's no one down here." She smiled and let out a silent breath, and he gave her a knowing look. "I'm sorry, I just looked in storage, and there's nobody here." Nime could hear Ko-nin through Ira's tablet, and she didn't sound pleased. Nime never would have asked Ira to cover for her like this, especially not if he was going to get yelled at. He pressed his lips together and straightened his glasses. Eventually, Ko-nin stopped, and Ira ended the call with a sharp tap on his tablet. He looked at Nime and rubbed the back of his neck. "That could've been close, hmm, Nime? I'm glad I saw it was you."

"I hope she's not too angry with you." Nime pulled out her lamp and looked over the edges of the shelf. Ira laughed a little, waving off her worry.

"It's fine. Nothing like the trouble you'd have been in," he said.

Nime tugged at the edge of the shelf. It didn't move. "Are you stuck back there?" Ira peered in. He looked at her again, and the corners of his mouth turned down. "What in the Endless Sea?"

Turning, Nime saw that the space behind the shelf was bigger than she'd first assumed. It was more of a nook than a room, but to find even that hidden behind a shelf was a surprise. She looked back out toward the opening and swept her lamp over it again. *Someone* had wanted to hide the little room. Shelves didn't tend to move on their own and block off open spaces, or disguise those open spaces behind an image of a wall. She leaned in close to the back of the shelf and scanned it. There, in the approximate middle, was a projector the size of her thumb. Sticking her arm through, Nime looked up at Ira.

"What does it look like from out there?" she asked.

"Like the wall, but transparent. If you were farther back, I probably wouldn't be able to see you," Ira said. Nime turned the projector off, and it detached from the shelf, landing in her palm. She dropped it into her bag. No sense in wasting good parts. "Why would someone make the effort to hide this?" Ira continued.

Nime turned back around, an "I don't know" on her lips, and then shut her mouth. The large machine in the back of the nook was probably the reason. Pieces of it lined the floor. She looked back at Ira and nodded toward it. "Maybe because of this." Ira leaned in as close as he could and narrowed his eyes trying to make it out. Nime tried moving the shelf from the inside one more time, but it was likely locked into the floor, like most furniture, and needed to be moved from the front.

Kneeling, she pushed one of the bins over and wriggled past it, sliding out into the aisle. She stood and rubbed her arms. That metal was *cold*. Ira looked at her.

"Oh, are you heading home already?" he asked. He sounded disappointed. Nime shook her head and gripped one of the shelves.

"I assume you want to have a look at it, too?" she asked. He nodded. "Then I'll have this open in a second." The first pull only wiggled the shelf, and Nime shifted her feet for better leverage. The second pull was successful, and the shelf slid outward like an ancient door. She pulled until she nearly stepped on Ira's toes. Her lamp, forgotten, slid out of the crook of her elbow and plopped onto the floor.

Nime glanced down and sighed. It was broken, a spiderweb of cracks filling the dent where it had hit the floor. The glowing wisps seeped out, one spreading tendril touching her foot and soaking into her shoe. Ira didn't seem to notice, moving around Nime and into the little room. She followed.

Ira's lamp lit the small space, and Nime could see the full extent of the machine in front of them. Dust coated the disassembled parts, but despite being stored improperly, it was in decent condition. Whoever hid it had stacked the pieces in semi-neat piles and labeled the largest two sections. Ira bent over one pile of parts, a mess of disconnected circuitry and metal. He leaned in, poking a finger into the mess of wires and then pulling it out with a wince. Blood welled up on the pad of his finger. Nime frowned and kicked the bottom of the largest piece. She glared at it for good measure. And then Ira stood back up and Nime barely had time to read "Transporter platform" on the side of it before he tugged on her arm and headed for the opening. Transporter? She pulled back a little, and Ira let go. He rubbed the back of his neck.

"I just realized how late it is," he said, sighing. "This is all very interesting, but I think we should both go home for the night."

"But—" Nime said, and then she looked at Ira. He normally looked pale and thin and unwell, but now his blue eyes were shadowed and ringed with dark circles. He pulled his glasses off to rub his face.

"I'm curious too, but I'm also exhausted, Ni." He hardly ever called her that. Nime's heart twisted and she looked down. "It's nearly two in the morning, so why don't we call it a night?" She nodded, and stepped through the opening to wait for him before closing it again. He passed close by her, a little wobbly. He seemed so fragile sometimes that Nime couldn't help but want to protect him the way she did Navi. But Ira was her tutor, and even though they'd been close for years, she could only do so much for him. She couldn't intimidate the Education Board into seeing his value, or the teachers and archivists into being nicer to him. She scowled.

Ira gestured for her to follow him, turning back when she paused at the broken lamp and puddle of now dark liquid.

"Don't worry about that, I'll ask Sanitation to clean it up. I'll say I dropped it while searching for the mysterious intruder." He smiled, and Nime's heart lightened a little.

The walk to Ira's office was short and silent.

"I'll make sure Ko-nin's gone," he said when they arrived, ushering Nime inside. He disappeared with the lamp, leaving Nime in darkness, before she could respond. She wondered if he knew about the secret Advisory Board meeting. She couldn't leave until that was over, too.

She stretched her hand out, searching for the edge of the door frame. Ira's office was cramped and messy, the floor strewn with books and papers and things that belonged in Recycling. It was only a few steps to the couch, and—something felt soft under her foot. She leaned down to touch it and found a pillow. Had Ira been sleeping in his office?

Nime moved her leg forward until it hit the edge of the couch, then sat. The word *transporter* ran through her mind. It sounded similar to tech that had been used for travel pre-Fall, but she didn't think Haven had access to something like that. They only existed in diagrams and data now, she thought. Where would it transport to? She breathed in sharply. If it went somewhere safe, that could be the solution to the potential Potential problem. First thing tomorrow, she would come back and investigate further.

The door slid open, and Nime squinted in the sudden light. She heard a soft "Sorry" and a thump as Ira tossed the lamp onto the couch next to her and sat down with a sigh.

"Were you sleeping here?" Nime asked. She was still holding the pillow, so she set it down beside her. Ira slumped a little. So that was a yes. "Why?" She couldn't help asking, though she could guess the reason.

He shook his head. "I had some work to finish up, so I didn't see the point in going home for a few hours," he said. His jaw tightened, and Nime chose not to press. His family, just like everyone else, probably wanted to know why he'd failed his psych eval.

"Anyway, I think we're the only people left in the building, so you're safe from Ko-nin's wrath," Ira continued. He gave her a look. Then he glanced down and pushed his glasses up. "In the future, it might be best to *try* not to draw attention to yourself when you're here after hours.

However," he paused and looked back up at her with the smallest hint of an amused smile. "If you find yourself being pursued with the threat of banishment again, you can just hide in here, you know. You may be violating the code of conduct, but I think you deserve a little leeway." Nime smiled so hard her eyes crinkled at the edges. A warm feeling filled her chest. "I'm not particularly attached to the rules."

"Neither am I," she said, watching for the exasperated shake of his head and laughing at the look on his face, somewhere between amused and annoyed. Nime stood. "I'll let you get back to sleeping."

Ira nodded. "And, Nime," he said, as she opened the door. She turned to look at him. "If you heard something tonight, I don't think you should tell anyone just yet." Nime's eyes widened. So Ira knew, too.

When she left, she closed the door behind her and leaned against it. Now that the danger of being caught was gone, fatigue made itself known. The thought of climbing up four flights of stairs made her groan and rub her heavy eyes. She tried not to drag her feet along the way.

By the time Nime got to her front door, she had just enough energy to be annoyed. On top of the game of wisp-tag getting cut short, the near-miss with her mother and Ko-nin, and the news about the generator, Nime didn't have her tablet, so she couldn't just unlock the door and go to sleep. She gripped the scanner tightly, leaving lines in her skin from the edges. Her other hand rifled through her bag, first checking the pocket near the top, then digging past the lamps and the projector and all the other bits and books from the day until she touched her multitool.

Residential doors used the same tablet scanners as the rest of Haven, though resetting the scanner often left the door unable to close fully. Strangely, the scanner on this unit had been malfunctioning on and off again since around the time Nime was given her multitool at age twelve. No one would notice.

She slid the door open and slipped her shoes off. Before going into her own room, Nime slowly opened Navi's door, checking on her. It was something Nime had done since Navi came home from the nursery when Nime was five years old. Sometimes more than once a night, when something sitting heavy in her chest wouldn't let Nime sleep.

Navi was always safe, always sleeping soundly. It calmed the tight feeling, like the relief of new air after holding her breath. This time was no different. Navi was curled up in a ball, one foot peeking out, and her blanket rose and fell with steady breaths. Nime's mouth turned up at the green ink that stained Navi's sock, crumpled on the floor.

This was why Nime needed to find a way to keep Haven safe, starting with the machine in storage. Navi deserved to live, not just survive for a few more weeks until what amounted to magical radiation got to her.

"Don't worry," she said. "I won't let you die."

When Nime finally settled herself into bed, her sleep was anything but restful.

3

The sunrise wakes me, coloring the inside of my eyelids red. I sit up and open my eyes. My room looks the same as it did yesterday—small and messy, the inks I brought home from the art room cluttering my desk, the ceiling and walls covered over with drawings—and I wonder if last night was a dream. Well, the ink stain on the floor is new, but not exactly unexpected. Ink stains dot my floor like freckles. This one is shaped like a foot. My foot. That would be because I stepped in it, of course. I scrunch up my face and let the embarrassment wash over me. Stupid. In the bathroom, I scrub at the ink residue on my foot with warmed-up cleanser.

Dad makes actual fish for breakfast instead of heating up nutrient formula. The Fishery must have harvested a surplus yesterday. He and I sit together at the table in the main room with steaming plates of salted fish in front of us. Mom must be at the admin offices already. I hear her voice at that secret meeting again. Or maybe she's still asleep. Nime probably is. She was up even later than I was last night.

I poke at the fish. Memories of last night twist in my stomach. I need to think about something else.

I look up at Dad. I focus on the nice, honey color of his eyes and how they crinkle in the corner when he smiles at me, and his hands, on the table, holding his fork. They're big compared to mine and rough from the chemicals he uses in Sanitation, but they're very warm. When I tap the back of his left hand, he flips it palm-side up and closes his fingers around mine. He has lighter skin than Nime and I do—we got ours from Mom—but his and Nime's share the same cool undertone. I lean over my plate and sniff. Salt, seaweed, that indefinable smell of water in sunlight. It smells good.

Tastes good, too, when I start eating. It's been a while since I've had food other than nutrient formula. I smile at Dad, and he smiles back. His eyes do the crinkle thing, and I love him. When I'm done eating, I stand up and kiss the top of his head, right in the middle.

* * *

Nime practically had to hold her eyes open when she woke up to Navi standing beside her bed. Nime smiled a little and opened her eyes wider.

"What time is it Sunshine?" she asked with a yawn. Light streamed through her window onto the wooden floor between Nime's desk and her bed.

"Almost second light," Navi said, giving a sheepish smile. Nime groaned, scrubbing a hand through her hair, which stuck up in short, orange tangles. No time for a warm, relaxing cleanser soak, then. She'd have to deal with a quick, cold spray instead. She rolled out of her blankets, landing lightly on her feet. Navi hugged her before she'd even stood fully upright. "Sorry Ni, I didn't think to wake you up earlier," Navi said. She sounded guilty.

Nime tensed. "It's my fault." She pulled away and looked at her little sister. Navi seemed well-rested, at least. No darkness under her amber eyes, and her skin faintly simmered the way it did when she was well. It was a little like the golden iridescence on a fighting fish's scales, only not so bright and obvious. Navi deserved the nickname "Sunshine," both in appearance and personality. "Don't worry about it," Nime said, smiling and stepping around her to head for the bathroom.

Navi followed her out and skipped toward the main room. "Breakfast for the late-risers today is nutrient formula," she said in a sing-song voice. Nime gagged loudly and stepped into the bathroom with the sound of giggles behind her. She caught herself falling into routine and starting to heat the tub that took up most of the room. Grimacing, she stripped instead, perching on the edge of the tub. She pulled out the cleanser dispenser, braced herself, and sprayed cold cleanser all over, rubbing it into her skin and hair until she could feel it tingle. By the time she finished, she was shivering and feeling barely cleaner than when she'd woken up.

A yell from the main room hurried Nime's actions, and she pulled on her used clothes and jogged back to her room. Clothes went into the sanitizing cupboard, from which she pulled out another pair of thermals and a thick sweater. Dressed, Nime hurried out into the main room.

Navi laid with a cushion under her stomach near the heater in the corner, drawing on her tablet. Nadra stood in the front doorway, drinking something steaming hot. And at the cooker, Ild stirred half a day's worth of nutrient formula and a stimulant into a cup of water. Nime's nose wrinkled at the sight. *Centuries* people had lived on Haven, and still, no one had managed to make nutrient formula taste anything but gross. At least the stimulant would make her headache go away.

"Welcome to the day, Nime," he said with a kiss to her forehead. She took the offered cup and looked inside at the smooth, gray liquid.

"Don't complain," Nadra said. She didn't even look up from putting her shoes on. Nime clenched her jaw and gripped the cup tightly. Anger heated her more than warm cleanser ever could. She glared at Nadra until her glare was met by an equally fierce one. And Nime had to leave, for Navi and their father's sake, stalking back into her room to grab her bag. She took a minute to breathe. As much as she wanted to go out there and accuse her mother of being a horrible, lying coward, with the audacity to treat Nime like a child, Nime also hated the way Navi shrank into herself whenever Nime and Nadra lost patience with each other.

Tipping her head back, Nime swallowed the thick nutrient formula in one go. It tasted like chalk and slithered down her throat in a way that had her swallowing again and again for a minute. She pressed the cup down onto her desk with more force than necessary and grabbed her tablet from its charging platform. It buzzed with a reminder that her Advanced Tutoring Group would be meeting in five minutes. She shut it off before sliding it in her bag.

When Nime left her room, calm enough, Navi stood waiting by the front door, peering out at the beginnings of a light rain. Nadra was gone. Ild had gathered up the breakfast dishes into a stack for the sanitizer, and Nime balanced her empty cup on top of a plate. He gave her a look that dissolved into a small smile.

"Before you go, can you fix the door again? It's the same problem as always," he said. Nime didn't look at him as she nodded and stepped outside to fix what she'd broken. Navi waited just inside the open doorway, sticking her hand out to catch the mist. After a quick reset of the scanner, Nime and Navi waved at Ild as they set out for the Academy.

Navi looped her arm through Nime's, breaking through the thoughts of Potential and death and transporters that circled their way through Nime's mind. She struggled for something to say.

"How are your lessons going?" Nime asked. "Are you making any progress on that calculus problem set?" Navi sighed, and Nime frowned a little. "Midra-nin should be helping you if you're struggling." It would've been inappropriate for Nime to pay a visit to Navi's classroom, but that had never stopped her before. Navi would be embarrassed, though, and that did stop her. Nime would leave that as a last resort.

"She did try," Navi said, scuffing her feet against the walkway. "It didn't help. No matter how many times Midra-nin explained it to me." Navi trailed off. Nime wished she could help, but previous attempts had ended with frustration on both sides. Nime had never had to *learn* things in Intermediate, they'd just made sense. She didn't have the slightest idea of how to go about explaining them to someone who didn't understand, and the last thing she wanted to do was make Navi feel stupid.

"You should go to tutoring after school," she said.

Navi made a squeak of protest. "I can't go to tutoring, people will think I'm stupid," she said, her eyes wide. Nime wanted to tell her that no one would think that, that people understood students sometimes needed a little extra help, but it would've been a lie. A particularly egregious lie, considering the number of times Nime herself had thought the same about her classmates who had been unfortunate enough to need it.

"No one would dare to call you stupid," Nime said. That, at least, was the truth; not with Nime around to correct anyone brave enough to try. Navi chewed her lip, unconvinced. "I'll go with you," Nime continued. At that, Navi's eyes brightened a little bit. "And, Ira is one of the tutors this afternoon." The final blow. Navi perked up for a split second before self-consciously restraining herself. Nime fought to keep the corners of her mouth down.

"I'll go if you think I should," Navi said. She turned her face away from Nime, but pink ears peeking out from her hair gave her away. Nime didn't say anything else about it while they walked, just enjoyed the peace of listening to Navi chatter about anything and everything that came to her mind.

* * *

"Sorry I'm late," Nime said as she stepped into the sparse study room her tutoring group met in every other day. The oval table and chairs filled most of the room, and only a tablet-synced screen covered the gray walls. She sat down in the last seat, between Chi and Sess, and glanced around the room. "I had a late night." Her gaze passed over Ira, who looked, at most, mildly curious, to meet Chi's. Chi smiled like she knew a secret.

Miel grinned, his dimples appearing for a brief moment. "Not to worry, Nime, you're worth waiting for," he said, blinking his long eyelashes at her. His voice was meant to be smooth and charming, but Nime had heard it too many times to care. Rem rolled his eyes and elbowed Miel. Miel grabbed his side in mock agony. "Now that you're here, are you sure you and Rem are genetically related? I can't believe someone so mean shares the same genes as you, the nicest, sweetest person in Haven." Someone in the room snorted, and Ira cleared his throat.

Rem rolled his eyes again. "Morning," he said. Sess, on Nime's other side, nodded slowly, his eyes half-open. He looked like he normally did: on the verge of falling asleep. The previous night probably hadn't helped with that.

Chi raised an eyebrow. "A late night doing what, exactly?" she asked. Miel's grin widened.

"Do you truly want me to answer that?" Nime asked. Ira was lenient with Nime because they'd been close since *he* had been in Advanced, and that leniency didn't usually extend to the rest of the group. Chi pouted and opened her mouth to respond. Ira cleared his throat again, this time a little louder and accompanied by a firm readjustment of his glasses. Chi closed her mouth, and Nime relaxed.

"I'm sure you're all aware that Nytherial's Day is the day after tomorrow, so perhaps we could move on to the actual purpose of this meeting?" Ira said. Chi at least looked scolded, though that lasted only a moment before excitement took over.

"I'll go first," she said. Ira nodded, leaning back into his chair. "I'm just about done with my offering, but I'm going to have to frame the collection as more of a 'truth can be found even in obscurity' type of thing. I talked before about how The Mothers of Aht Carina was a fairly common subject in the literature throughout pre-Fall history, but we don't know anything concrete about it. I haven't been able to find any specifically religious texts from the Sacred Valley—the seat of the Children—only ones that mention the Mothers in passing. Unfortunately, other civilizations barely make any mention of it in their literature, at least not what was preserved. Some literature from Zhumia *does* discuss it, but the difference in theology is almost to the point where it seems like a different religion with the same name." Chi shrugged. "So, I figured I could work around the absences in recorded history and present what little I did find as an invitation to continue searching for the truth. Everybody normally loves that."

"Will you have enough evidence to support your theories?" Ira asked. Nime grit her teeth over a yawn, blinking slowly and pinching herself to stay awake. But the next time her eyes snapped open, she'd already lost the thread of the conversation.

"That's true," Chi was saying, sitting up straighter. "We know the general tone and beliefs from personal accounts. We know that the Mothers were a duality, the opposing forces of creation and destruction, and that an important aspect of it was the Cycle of Rebirth." She cupped her chin. "But I couldn't find a single document defining that cycle or listing out specific tenets. It's weird how little detail there is, almost like everything with the specifics was left out of the database."

Nime frowned. She knew Chi wasn't serious, but the suggestion still unsettled her. When the Architects built Haven, they'd filled it with all the knowledge and art in the world. The database held everything from advertisements for ancient food to the DNA sequence of every species of beetle. Nothing was too small, or too obscure, or too useless. Nothing had been left out. Certainly not something that had actual historical importance like religious texts. If something like that could be missing, what else could they have forgotten?

Chi shrugged. "Anyway, I'm ready to present my findings at the festival." She sat back and Ira nodded.

"Sess?" Ira said, and Sess looked up from his hands and blinked.

"My algorithm is ready," he said. After a second of silence, Nime nudged him gently with her foot. He looked at her. "Oh, do you want a demonstration? It's kind of a long process; it needs a lot of data to accurately predict a person's preferences." Rem listened politely, but Chi and Miel weren't even trying to hide their bored slouching. Nime looked at them until they straightened up, Miel with a sigh and Chi a little more apologetic. "Um, it's been collecting my data, so I guess I can tell you it works well with the lights and temperature in my unit, but not as well with predicting when I want to sleep, um, but I'm not sure if that's because I have unusual sleep patterns or if there's something else," he said. "You can look at the code if you want."

"Are you ready to show it?" Ira asked, hands folded on the table. Sess nodded, and Ira moved on. "Miel?"

Miel leaned forward and smiled in his most charming way. "I'm keeping my plant a secret until the festival, but she is magnificent, trust me." Ira raised his eyebrows, unimpressed.

"Can I assume you're ready, then?" he asked. Miel nodded and leaned back in his chair. "Nyrem?"

"My salve has been showing good results in the clinic," Rem said. "I still have to finish up the report, but it'll be ready on time."

Finally, Ira turned to Nime. "Nime?" he asked. She was suddenly very awake, and she looked at Ira, at a loss. Her project for Nytherial's Day, an AI-controlled robotic bird meant for over-sea exploration, seemed like a waste of time when a catastrophe needed averting. How could he be so *normal* about this?

"I—" she started. She looked at the group. "I'm going to pull a Miel and keep my progress a secret for now." Ira frowned at her, but Nime couldn't tell them that she was abandoning the project and the presentation to work on a dismantled transporter, not unless she wanted them to know about the generator leak. And, looking around at them, that was the opposite of what she wanted.

* * *

"I heard someone got caught in the sculpture gallery after hours," Aeri says quietly. I look up from my literature assignment and frown. She stands by my desk with her arms crossed and a not-very-nice smile on her face. I don't respond for a moment. Does she mean me? Because as far as I know, I didn't get a reprimand this morning. Or did someone else get caught down there when Ko-nin came? Aeri rolls her eyes. "I heard an archivist caught someone who believed that stupid challenge and went down there last night." Stupid challenge? Yesterday she talked about it like she believed it.

"Um," I say. "I didn't see anyone else when I was there."

Aeri looks confused. "What?"

"I mean, I saw Ko-nin, but I didn't see any other students, so I don't know who would have gotten in trouble. Unless one of you…" I trail off. Why would she be telling me this if one of her friends got caught? Aeri still looks confused. I turn to look at her friends. Their desks are clumped together near the back of the class—Midra-nin encourages "cooperative collaboration" by letting us work with others if we want. None of them seem upset. In fact, they look like they're having a great time, even though we're supposed to be comparing the cultural significance of funereal poetry in various early pre-Fall civilizations. I look back at Aeri. She narrows her eyes. I glance over at the rest of our class so I don't have to make eye contact.

"So you're telling me that you didn't get caught in the archive last night?"

"No?" I tug on the end of my sleeve. Aeri frowns and turns around so fast her hair floats a little, stomping back to her friends. After a second they all look at me, and I try to smile. They look away. I go back to my work. I guess I know how Ko-nin knew to look out for students last night. I swallow and blink away tears that sting my eyes. Aeri and her friends were never going to meet me there, and I can't understand why they would go to the trouble of pretending they were.

I just want to forget about last night entirely. It won't do any good thinking about Potential or secret meetings or people who don't like me, because it's not like there's anything I can do about it anyway. It only makes my stomach hurt.

And, Nime knows about the leak, which is comforting. At least, I think she does, so I don't need to worry about it. She won't let anything happen to me. She's always saved me whenever I needed it. Now is no different.

* * *

"And Navi, are you ready for your role as Nytherial?" At the sound of Midra-nin's voice, my head shoots up, and I drop my stylus. It lands on the floor next to me. Some of my classmates laugh quietly, and my face heats up.

"I think so. I know my lines," I say. I spent a lot of time going over them again and again. Nime even got her friends to help me and ask me questions so I could practice more outside of class. And I don't have to do much, just stand up on the stage, say my lines about blessing the festival, and then walk around and answer people's questions with profound-sounding but vague sayings. Even so, I still feel like I have a school of fish living in my stomach. It's so soon. Only a couple of days away. For a moment, darkness closes in around the edges of my vision, and all I can hear is the sound of my own breathing.

"I'm confident you'll do well," Midra-nin is saying. She smiles at me and pats my shoulder as she passes between desks, and I nod through what feels like water in my head. And then it passes, and I can hear and see again. Midra-nin has started talking about the importance of Nytherial's day to Haven.

Nytherial, Celestial Warden of Truth, the one Haven likes the most. None of the others get a festival this big, though we get their days off work, too. I understand, even though Iridis, Celestial Warden of Life, is my favorite; she's supposed to live in beehives and spend most of her time playing with babies, which sounds like a nice life to me. But Truth is the most important, and that's why we have Nytherial's Day.

Truth, and by extension knowledge, Midra-nin says, is the reason we're here in Haven instead of lost to the Endless Sea like everyone who wasn't chosen by the Architects. Our library and archive hold all the knowledge and culture of the world before the Fall, the most important things in the world. They were more important than the hundreds more people who could have fit on Haven if it wasn't full of artifacts. I frown. I've never liked to think about that.

I look up at the walls, at the art and educational posters previous students made and Midra-nin hung up. I wonder if any of the ruined, ancient schools at the bottom of the sea still have things on their walls. If they even have walls anymore. The Architects were trying to preserve humanity through information. They decided it was fine if that meant less people survived. Making sure future people could have a good life was worth it, maybe. Though I don't think the Endless Sea will ever go away.

When I was younger, I thought Nytherial would come down from the stars and make me tell the truth if I left even a little bit out. But that was when I believed the Celestial Wardens were real, before my Basics teacher explained it to me. I almost wish Nytherial were real right now. She could come out at the festival and tell everyone about the generator leaking Potential. Then people would know, and I wouldn't have this stupid secret taking up space in my heart.

Everyone would believe her, and no one would make fun of her or get her in trouble because she's a Celestial Warden, not an Intermediate student with low assessment scores and a tendency to cry at everything.

Midra-nin keeps mentioning Truth, and every time she does it feels like the slap of a wave in my face. I pick up my stylus and continue my drawing of a tree. No one would believe me, so there's no point in trying to tell anyone, I tell myself. No point in risking it.

* * *

Nime lingered in the stairwell as her friends headed back up to sea-level. Once they were out of sight, Nime's smile dropped. It took too much effort when all she could think about was the night before. In a way, her earlier fatigue had been helpful. It made it harder to think about things that weren't present. Now that the stimulant had kicked in, and she was fully awake, visions of the people she loved, dead, were harder to avoid.

Pressing her hands through her hair, Nime blocked out those thoughts. She had to figure out what exactly was going on; the secret board meeting hadn't been extremely informative, and if Nime wanted to find a solution, she needed more information. She stood at one of the database access points dotted around B1 and typed out her request. But "Haven generator blueprint" didn't yield any good results, only information about the cooling mechanisms outside the sealed generator. Nime narrowed her eyes and tried again with "Haven Potential safety." A few news articles about the construction of Haven popped up, but not nearly as many as she would have expected, considering Haven had been humanity's last hope. At least the articles gave a name to what was inside the generator: a "Destructive Potential Core" or DPC. Nime found no plans for Haven or the generator, and no guides for safe operation of the DPC.

She tried again with her newfound information. "Haven Destructive Potential Core" brought up just one new result: a short article arguing against the appropriation of religious relics in the newly-constructed Haven. Nothing about what exactly the relic was, or what it did, or how to contain it.

Tapping her foot, Nime exited the article. Why was there no information? The Architects would have had some kind of plan, surely, considering the danger. And she would think they'd have wanted it to be repairable in case of this exact scenario.

Nime frowned. The lack of information was odd, yes, but more importantly, it wasn't helping her come up with alternative plans for saving Haven. She shook her head and moved on to the other things she wanted to search.

"Destructive Potential Core health effects" yielded few relevant results. It seemed like the name referred specifically to the relic in Haven, and if there were other things like it, they hadn't been tested and researched. One result looked promising, even if it was a personal blog post on "magic." No credible source after the year 4000 used the word magic to talk about Potential.

Nime read it anyway. With so frustratingly little information to go on, she was willing to take any scrap she could find. And, surprisingly, the magic post had some relevant information. Titled "Destruction Magic and Its Effects on Bystanders," it was a response to a speech a politician had given. Nime tried to grab the transcript of the politician's speech, but nothing came up. Pausing, Nime tried again, only to get an "Entry not found" error. Her mind went back to Chi that morning, talking about missing information. The thought formed like a lump in her throat. But there were more pressing things to worry about at the moment, so she shook her head and focused on the blog post.

Apparently, as long as there was a balance—the post seemed almost purposefully obtuse about what that meant, probably because of the assumed context of the missing speech—users of destruction magic would be fine. Without that balance, the magic would begin to break down the user's body to fuel itself. Nime skimmed the lines, searching for some kind of timeline or symptoms. "A week for the vulnerable, two to three weeks for someone with a higher capacity for creation magic." She stopped there and read the previous sentences. The author referred to a person by name, unfamiliar to Nime, and stated that contact with them was dangerous. Nime stopped, downloaded the post, and sat down in the reading room off of the stairwell.

Apparently the author of the post advocated against putting the named person in prison because of the danger inherent to being around them. It would be cruel to the other prisoners, who would only last about a week around this person before they'd start dying. The post didn't describe how, but if Nime assumed "destruction magic" was equivalent to destructive Potential, she could guess.

If she could equate this person and the core, that would mean that the Potential could spread beyond Maintenance, and that Haven would have about a week before people started dying. If they weren't equivalent, well, then Nime would have wasted her time and no one but her would suffer for it.

One week. It was such a short amount of time.

Maybe someone on the Board was also trying to fix it. Maybe Nime was wrong for assuming that no one else was making an effort. But even if they were, Nime wasn't going to assume that and wait for a solution when there was a potentially viable one in the dismantled transporter. If someone else was also trying, then they would have two solutions instead of one. Though, she couldn't see any other possibilities, not with a deadline of one week.

Her tablet vibrated in her hands, and she jumped a little.

Navi. She breathed in. She had promised to take Navi to tutoring. Part of her itched to get to work on the transporter, on what could be Haven's last hope. But it was Navi. Nime didn't think she could say no to Navi if the world were ending that day, let alone in a week. She would work on it as soon as Navi was done.

Nime slipped her tablet into her bag and went to meet Navi by the stairs.

* * *

I'm only halfway through with my tree when my classmates start standing up from their desks and leaving. I look up. Midra-nin is walking toward me with a gently concerned look on her face. I already know what she's going to say, what she has to say in private. I shut off the screen of my tablet and hold it to my chest like it will shield me.

"Navi," she says, and I meet her eyes for just a moment. "I've been looking over your work on the calculus assessment, and I wanted to talk to you about it." She frowns a little. I swallow. "I thought maybe you never asked for help because you had the same aptitude for math as your sister, but it seems that's not the case. Why haven't you? I want to help you understand the material."

"Um," I say. I keep my eyes on the table. I like Midra-nin. She's always nice, but I can't get myself to ask her to explain again when the answers she gives make no sense to me.

"Would you be more comfortable with one-on-one teaching, instead of with the class?" she asks. I chew on my lip. Probably. I nod. "In that case, how about we set up weekly meetings to make sure you're understanding everything, and in between you can go to the tutors for extra help." I nod again. That's two people now who have suggested it. I try not to let it hurt. Nime and Midra-nin aren't trying to call me stupid, they just want me to do well.

And Nime was right. When I leave the classroom, I lean against the gray hallway wall and check the list of tutors available this evening. Ira-nin is free still. My heart beats a little faster. I almost tap the schedule to make an appointment, but instead I message Nime and head down to the library when she responds.

Nime makes the tutoring appointment in her name, and I follow her to one of the smaller study rooms like a duckling. Ira-nin looks up as we enter, and his eyes slide from Nime to me and back. His eyelashes are so long and dark.

"Ah," he says, leaning back in his chair. Nime sits down opposite, and I stand in the doorway. "I was just wondering what you would want tutoring for, Nime." Nime looks at me and saves me from myself because I don't think my voice works anymore. Ira-nin looks at me, too, and pushes up his glasses. Oh, Seas, am I dying? My face feels hot, and I'm 90% sure human hearts aren't supposed to go this fast.

"Navi's been having a little trouble with calculus," Nime says. Ira-nin nods and smiles a little. How does Nime do this every day without having a heart attack?

"Have a seat, Navi." He pats the spot next to him. "Math is my specialty." He smiles wider, and his eyes almost close. He's just so beautiful. I sit down. Nime slides my textbook across the table, and I have to stop staring at Ira-nin to open it up and find my spot. My fingers are a little clumsy, but I get it eventually.

Focusing on the questions is difficult. It's that school of fish in my stomach again, swimming and fluttering around. I read the problems, but the words and numbers don't mean anything, which isn't all that unusual for me. Ira-nin walks me through the problems and doesn't seem to notice when I stare too long or stutter. It's nice, once my heart slows down a bit. Nime never tries to make me feel stupid, and Ira-nin is a good tutor. I even get some questions right.

But then Nime leaves. I'm in the middle of asking a question, and Ira-nin's eyes follow her until she's out of sight. Suddenly, my chest tightens. I take a deep breath, and Ira looks back at me.

"Something wrong?" he asks. I shake my head. I feel cold. I finish asking my question, and he answers it well enough, but he's as distracted as I am.

It's hard to concentrate again; my head feels like I'm underwater, all fuzzy and dulled. This isn't like the heart-racing nerves I had before, though. This feels worse, and it doesn't make sense. What's wrong with me?

Nime is gone for what feels like forever. When she finally comes back, the weight on my chest seems to lift. My head still feels fuzzy, and I'm still cold, but at least Nime's back. Whatever that was, I just want to go home.

"Um," I say. Nime turns to me. "I think we should probably leave soon." Her eyes widen, and then she nods and stands up. Ira-nin tenses next to me, but he rubs the back of his neck and smiles.

"Sure, we're at a good stopping point," he says. He doesn't look at me when he says it. "Feel free to come to me if you need any more help." This time he does look at me, for just a second. The fish swim around again. I swallow and stand up. My legs wobble.

"Thank you, Ira-nin," I say. Is that what I'm supposed to say? I don't know, I've never been tutored before, but I should be polite, right? Nime holds the door open for me, and she waves at Ira-nin. I was too formal; I seem weird now. I chew my lip.

I stop worrying about my choice of words when we start walking down the hall. For the first few steps it's fine, but the closer we get to the stairwell, the lighter my head gets. I can walk, but my legs feel slow and unresponsive. The world starts going black around the edges, getting worse as we start climbing. And then the blackness covers everything, and I faint.

* * *

Nime only left for a few minutes, just to find blueprints for the transporter, just so she could be ready to fix it that night. But when she came back, Navi looked pale and anxious, arms wrapped around her stomach.

They made it halfway up the stairs before Navi stumbled and nearly knocked Nime back down. Only Nime's quick grab for the railing kept both of them from falling. Helping Navi get her balance back, Nime checked her over. Navi didn't seem injured, but she was very quiet, and her hands shook. She clung to the railing and looked down at Nime.

"Sorry, Ni, I don't know what happened there," Navi said, her voice weak and wavering. Nime shook her head, helping Navi up the rest of the stairs. When they reached sea-level, she guided Navi to the nearest chair and hovered next to her. Navi leaned back and closed her eyes.

This is it, Nime thought. This is how it ends. Why Navi, though, and why so soon? For a second, she rubbed Navi's back and blinked rapidly. She didn't cry, hadn't since Foundations, but it was a close thing, and that snapped her out of her worrying. Crying solved nothing. Instead, she messaged Rem, and her fingers only shook a little. Action solved problems, and the only way to solve this was to figure out exactly what was wrong with Navi. It might not have even been related to the leak.

Faced with the prospect of Navi in danger, Nime found it much harder to think about leaking destructive Potential. It couldn't be that. It was too soon; they should have had a few more days at least. But there wasn't much else it could have been. People didn't just get sick in Haven, except for Ira and the elderly. When the original survivors had been chosen, they'd been screened for any genetic predispositions to diseases, and every generation since then had been as well. The genetic counselors always selected the genes that led to stronger immune systems and overall wellness, as well as intelligence and physical capabilities. Every person in Haven was designed to be the best that they could be given their DNA. The clinic existed more for injuries and reproduction than illnesses. Ira was a disease-prone outlier.

"I'm fine," Navi said, and Nime blinked. "I just need a minute." Nime sighed. Navi looked so different from that morning. Her skin had a pasty undertone, and she leaned against the back of the chair like she couldn't support herself.

A hand on Nime's shoulder startled her, and she turned to find Rem looking between Navi and her with concern. He had a small smudge of cleanser on his arm, which meant he had probably been at the clinic working when she messaged him. It should've made Nime feel better, him being there, but it just made her feel useless. She watched him stoop next to Navi and hold her wrist in his hand for a moment, counting under his breath. He frowned and pulled out his medtab, passing it slowly over her.

"What happened?" Rem asked while he waited for the results of the scan.

"She fainted on the stairs," Nime said. Her voice sounded far away.

"Can you think of any reason for it?" A chart popped up on the screen, and Rem started reading it. For a moment Nime stared at him. Yes, she could. There was one possible, terrible reason. She opened her mouth to tell him. And then she closed it. For some reason, she couldn't say anything. And maybe that was for the best. Rem didn't need to know. Nime would make sure the leak was fixed, for Navi, for Rem, for everyone she loved. And the rest of Haven, too.

"No," she said. Rem looked at her out of the corner of his eye while he listened to Navi's breathing. His eyes narrowed. "What is it?" Nime asked. Rem looked up at her, his face guarded.

"I'll be honest, I don't know what this means." He paused and looked at Navi. Her eyes were wide and glassy. "You should let me take you to the clinic," Rem said. Navi shook her head and then pressed her hands to her temples.

"Remy, I'm fine, I don't need to go to the clinic," she said. Nime rubbed Navi's back again. "I'm sorry for worrying you, but nothing's wrong with me." Nime lifted her eyes but didn't scoff at Navi like she would have anyone else. Rem pressed his lips together.

"Technically, that's true," he said, and Nime's eyes snapped to him. He showed her his medtab. "I can't find anything that would have caused the fainting, but that doesn't mean you don't need to be checked out by someone with more experience than me." Nime barely heard the second half of his sentence. Surely any damage caused by Potential would show up on the scan. And Rem would have said so, at least to Nime, if it did. Something like relief filled her chest, along with a new worry. If it wasn't that, what had caused it?

"Navi needs to rest at home," Nime said. Rem made a noise of protest. "If she gets worse, I'll take her to the clinic right away." Rem clenched his jaw but looked away and nodded.

Navi started to stand up, and Rem and Nime both took an arm to help her. Rem walked with them, supporting Navi until they got to Residential. He left them there and headed back to the clinic with one last disapproving look and click of his tongue.

* * *

I truly am fine by the time Nime and I get back to our unit. Fine except for embarrassment. I'm just glad Remy didn't insist on taking me to the clinic. He's as stubborn as Nime sometimes. Dad's worried of course; that's normal, even though I don't like worrying him. He presses the back of his hand to my forehead and fusses over me. Mom sits at the table, working on paperwork, and her lips thin into a line when she sees me.

I don't feel like I'm going to faint anymore, but my legs are heavy and hard to lift, and all I want to do is sleep. I step around the clothes and art supplies on my floor, flop onto my bed, and sigh.

Tomorrow, my class starts setting up for Nytherial's day. The day after that, I'll be acting as Nytherial at the festival. I hope I feel better by then. Everyone would hate me if I messed up the festival.

I picture it. The perfect performance. I remember my handful of lines, and how I'm supposed to stand, and I don't hesitate or mess up at all. Celestial Wardens don't hesitate or mess up, especially not Nytherial. I stand up straight and my voice is steady, and by the time I've gotten to the end of my blessing, I realize that it's not me anymore, playing Nytherial. It's Nime. I roll over onto my stomach and curl up my legs.

Nime would do a better job than me. She's confident and smart and strong. Nime wouldn't even be worrying about doing well. The scene in my head changes. Nime-as-Nytherial is amazing. Everyone loves it. And after the blessing, before she leaves the stage, Nime-as-Nytherial tells Haven about the Potential leak. I pull my blanket over my head. It's warm inside.

That would definitely mess up the festival.

My daydreams used to be more varied. I imagine the massive city, of course, and my golden tower. But just as often it'll be jumbled together with other daydreams, other adventures. There's one I particularly like, one where I live in a valley filled with trees, with streams, with deer and turtles and hawks. Just me and the planet that breathes beneath my feet. There's a temple in that valley, made of iridescent marble, and a sense of peace fills me when I imagine it.

So it's a little surprising that I've been going back to the city, when all I truly want is the peace I find inside the temple. Whatever the underlying psychological reason, as Athis-nin would say, I imagine what would happen if I were this Navi, braver and smarter than the real one.

I'm back at the top of my tower, my stained shoes leaving smudges on the shiny, white floors. I'm in the priestesses' wing, and I can feel familiar anxiety swimming around in my stomach. I don't knock when I enter—this Navi never knocks—but all of the priestesses look up when I do. Most of them are sitting or lying on the same kind of white couches I have in my suite, eating fruit and drinking something that smells bitter and warm. Pink dawn-light streams in through the huge windows and blinds me.

And because the priestesses are so important to me, because they've raised me and taught me and loved me, I am brave enough to tell them. I tell them about leaving the tower, about the shadows. I tell them what I heard in that other place, the plan to hurt the priestesses. I tell them about the dark blue fingers and hands and faces.

I don't tell them about the cyborg. I wasn't supposed to meet her yet, and if I tell them about her, I'm afraid they'll stop her from coming to see me again. And the thought of that makes my chest hurt.

Heavy silence sits in the air for a second after I'm done, and then the priestesses surround me, all talking at once. A few of them dust me off and bring me a seat. Others ask me for more details. But the High Priestess doesn't say anything. She's a warm woman, kind and wise, like a mother, and guilt for leaving eats at me. She told me it was for my protection, but I left anyway.

The High Priestess clears her throat and kneels in front of my seat. She takes my hands in hers and looks up at me. She thanks me for telling them, tells me that she understands I must get restless up here. The priestesses nod and murmur. And then she tells me how we can stop them. I was so brave to come forward, she says. If I could be brave again, they could catch the shadows.

They don't only want to hurt the priestesses, she tells me. They want to hurt me, maybe even kill me, to stop me from saving the world. That scares me, of course it does, but I can't help the relief I feel in the real world. It's stupid that this story I made up in my head makes me feel better, but it does. Don't worry about that real-life problem, Navi.

I shake my real head against my real pillow. There are no priestesses who will believe me without proof here in Haven. It's silly to think that telling people would cause anything other than trouble.

* * *

Navi went to bed, shutting her door behind her, and Nime was lost. Ild asked if she wanted to have dinner, but Nime shook her head. What she wanted was to fix Navi, to fix the leak, to stop anything worse from happening. What she wanted was to do *something*. She made an excuse about having more work to do and slipped out into the rainy evening, headed for the library.

As she walked, she planned. A week or two, that was how long she had to either fix the broken transporter or prevent more destructive Potential from leaking. The transporter looked similar in construction to the other machinery in Haven—it had probably been built by the same people—and Nime had disassembled and reassembled most of them for practice in the years she'd been an apprentice maintenance engineer.

Since the pieces were organized and in good condition, Nime hoped it wouldn't take too long to rebuild. With the biggest components still assembled, she estimated she could do it in a week, faster if the blueprint she'd found was usable, fastest if she chain-stimmed and didn't sleep until it was done. Rem would yell at her if he knew, she thought. Even so, she stopped by a dispenser on her way to the library and requested as many stimulants as it would give her. She received a double handful, the entirety of a month's worth. More than just Rem, everyone would disapprove, but that had never stopped Nime before.

She chewed one and grimaced at the bitter taste. Maybe as she worked on the transporter, she'd be able to figure out why it had been taken apart in the first place. Disassembling and recycling old, broken, or unneeded machinery was common practice. Disassembling and then hiding machinery in secret nooks was not. Whatever the reason was, it had to be something more than just a broken part.

4

Nime shook her arms in the Academy entry, and a drop of water slid down the back of her neck and into her collar, tickling her spine. She shivered. The heaters above the door opened, sensing moisture, and blew warm air down at her, leaving her sweater damp and her hair frizzy.

Ignoring the people waiting out the rain in the entrance hall, Nime headed for the elevator. The elevator landed with a ping on B4, and Nime strode out. She checked her tablet as she walked past the archivists' offices. She had a good five hours to work before she even needed to worry about the library closing.

The air in storage chilled Nime's damp skin and hair as she hurried through the maze of shelves to the secret nook. Now that she could properly see it, the nook seemed even smaller than it had the night before. She left the shelf shoved open just wide enough for her to slip through.

Nime spun her multitool between her fingers as she compared the parts before her to the blueprint on her tablet. It looked like the body had been split in two, and the platform, the largest and most important component, was mostly untouched. That was a relief. The platform alone would've taken more time than she had. But the frame, the control panel, the power supply, those would be easy with the blueprint. Nime nodded once to herself. She sorted the parts into piles by type, and then she was silent for a long time.

Hours flew by. There was nothing in the world but her hands and the blueprint and the machine in front of her. A buzz pulled her out of the intricate work of reassembling the computer that controlled the transporter, and Nime huffed, setting the circuitry down gently before tossing her multitool at her tablet. She slid down onto her butt and rubbed her knees. Kneeling on the floor had been a fine idea until the stimulant wore off and left her with an aching head and sore knees.

Nime grabbed her tablet and opened the new message that'd interrupted her. Then she groaned, tipping her head back.

I expect you to be home tonight, read the message from her mother. Nime grit her teeth. It was already late. Another message popped up. *Someone has been sneaking into the library after hours. It would be unfortunate if you were to be caught up in that.* Nime looked away from the screen. Nadra must've suspected it was Nime the night before.

She shoved her tablet into her bag and stood up. Looking at the parts laid out on the floor, she ran a hand through her hair. Most of them wouldn't fit in her bag, and while Nime had never been opposed to heavy lifting, she didn't exactly want everyone in Haven asking her what she was doing. As much as she hated that the Advisory Board was keeping the leak a secret, Nime didn't want to tell anyone yet, either.

The control panel was small enough, though. Nime picked it up carefully and checked to make sure she had all the parts. She needed a different set of tools to continue working on it anyway, so her mother's message wasn't terrible timing. Nime stopped and scowled at the ceiling. She needed the electronics tools she'd returned to Maintenance two weeks ago. And she wouldn't be able to get another set quickly enough.

Resisting the urge to kick something, Nime considered her options. She could steal a set from Maintenance, though the building was probably locked at that time of night and was more difficult to break into than a residential unit or the Academy. She could request one and wait. Or, she could borrow Sess'. Since he was apprenticed with the electrical engineers, he had his own set of electronics tools. She opened her messages with him.

The last thing he'd sent her was a video of several baby seabirds following their mother through the water. Nime laughed softly. She could ask him for his tools, and he would give them to her. That wasn't the problem. The problem was that he would be curious, and he would want to know why she needed them when her Nytherial's day project was supposed to be nearly done.

Finally, Nime sent Sess a message. She'd rather not involve anyone else, but her options were as limited as her time. It helped that Sess was the least likely of her friends to ask questions if she made it clear she didn't want to answer them.

After a short moment, he agreed to drop the tool kit off in her room. Nime didn't respond to his message asking why. She rubbed her eyes and stretched. Her fingers found a stimulant at the bottom of her bag, and she chewed it quickly, swallowing before she could taste the bitterness. At the very least she could finish the control panel up that night in her room, and maybe even get an hour or two of sleep. She pulled the shelf back into place, her arms and legs heavy with fatigue.

By the time she reached the B4 hallway, the stimulant was kicking in, filling her with that first burst of energy that always made her limbs itch to be moving. It carried her, running, toward the elevator. The doors blurred as she flew past them.

And then an office door opened a few feet in front of her. Nime couldn't stop in time, could only register that it was Ira she was running into as her face slammed into his arm. She fell backward, landing on the floor. Ira stumbled, and Ira's face went from furious, truly furious, to concerned in a split second when he looked at her. The initial anger shocked her for a moment through the pain that radiated from her nose; Nime didn't think she'd ever seen Ira angry before. He reached out and pulled her up. She held her nose and grit her teeth.

"Nime, are you okay?" he asked. She pulled her hand away from her nose. Blood stained her fingers. Ira stared at it for a second, his face unreadable, before looking away. Nime frowned.

"It's nothing," she said. "Are you alright?" Ira nodded, but he was glancing between her and anywhere else, distracted.

"Here." He gestured inside his office at the couch and told her to sit. She sat, leaning forward and cupping her hand under her nose and the slow drip of blood. It ached. She wondered how her face looked. It must have looked bad because Ira stood in the doorway for a moment, swallowing. She should have gone to get towels to keep from making a mess, but when she tried to stand and go to the bathroom, Ira stopped her.

"I'll go get you something to clean that off," he said. Nime sighed as well as she could without the use of her nose. Of course she'd get a nosebleed in front of someone afraid of blood. There was no mistaking it, that kind of reaction. Navi was the same, though she would go pale and close her eyes when she saw blood. Ira couldn't seem to look away.

Nime tried to keep any blood from spilling out onto the floor, so when Ira walked back in holding several towels, he stopped short in the doorway, freezing at the sight of Nime using both hands to contain the small puddle that had grown in his absence. His eyes darted back and forth between the blood and Nime's face, and he held his breath while he handed her the towels. His hands trembled.

Nime carefully grabbed one with the hand that wasn't cupping the majority of the mess and started cleaning up. Ira closed the door behind him and adjusted his glasses. He seemed better now that the blood wasn't visible.

"Are you sure you're okay?" Nime asked from behind the towel now pressed to her nose. Her voice came out muffled and nasally.

"I should be asking you that," Ira said, letting out a shaky breath. Nime didn't get it. It was just a little blood, not even from a serious injury, and it was *hers*, not his.

"It's almost over, don't worry," she said, and pulled away the towel to check if the bleeding had stopped. Ira's eyes widened again at the red-spotted cloth, and Nime turned her wrist so that most of the color was hidden. One of the towels was wet with cleanser, so she grabbed it and rubbed it in circles all around her nose, mouth, and chin, trying to keep it away from the inside of her nose. Cleanser stung on broken skin. Next, her sticky hands. Then she wiped it all off with the other end of the towel. It came away a dirty reddish color. At least she felt cleaner now. "How's my face?" she asked.

Ira grimaced. "Ah, well, you look like you were in a fight," he said.

"Perfect." Nime balled up all the towels and stood. She took a metallic-smelling breath through her nose. "I'm sorry for that," she said, and Ira put up a hand to stop her.

"Hold on," he said. "First of all, let me take those." Nime hesitated but held the wad of towels out for him. "Second of all, I have to ask:

are you planning on violating the code of conduct by remaining in the library after hours?" He laughed as he said it, and Nime gave an exaggerated sigh.

"No." She patted her bag. "I'm taking my work home with me tonight." Ira cocked his head. "I was just in storage, trying to fix that machine we found last night."

"Oh?" Ira said, his voice light. "Which part is that?" He gestured to where a corner of the panel pressed into the fabric of Nime's bag. "Can I see?" Nime nodded and pulled it out. Some of the unattached components fell onto the floor, and Ira stooped to pick them up. As he spread out the parts on his hand, Nime saw a tablet memory chip poking out from the mess. Where had that come from?

"It's the controls," she said. "I'm going to finish it up tonight." Ira nodded. Nime held her open bag toward him, and after another second he let the parts slip in. Nime slid open the door before turning back to him. "Sorry again for all of this."

Ira straightened his glasses and smiled. "Nothing to worry about, as you said." He joined her in the doorway and leaned his shoulder against it. "I'm sure you'll want to sleep tonight, though. After last night you must be exhausted, and this won't help." He touched her cheek near her nose very lightly.

"Come on," Nime said, lifting an eyebrow. "I'm tougher than that." She started to say more, but approaching footsteps startled her. She pulled her bag close to her body as she turned to see who was coming. Chi and Miel stopped walking when they noticed Nime and Ira in the doorway. The four of them stood silently for a second. "Hey," Nime said. Chi smiled and came closer, slipping her arm through Nime's.

"Hi," she chirped. Her eyes darted between Nime and Ira. Ira rubbed his neck.

"Was there something you needed?" he asked. Chi shook her head.

"We were actually looking for Nime," Miel said, "and thought we might ask you since someone—" he leveled a look at Nime "—isn't answering her messages." Ira smiled tightly and leaned forward a little.

"You looked in the right place," he said. And then he stepped back —until then Nime hadn't realized how close they'd been standing— and tapped the door once. "But all three of you need to be getting home now, so—good night." He closed the door, and Nime stepped out of its path. Miel and Chi stared at her.

"What?" she asked, and started walking back toward the stairwell. Miel and Chi didn't respond until the elevator door closed the three of them in silence. Only then did she notice the obvious curiosity on their faces as they sidled up close to her.

"Nime," Chi said, drawing out the 'i'.

"What?"

"Did you happen to get rescued by Ira last night?" Chi asked.

Nime bristled. "I didn't get 'rescued' by anyone," she said.

"I knew it," Miel said with a smug smile. Nime rolled her eyes.

"What exactly do you think you know?" she asked. "And why do you care?" She did her best to keep her face neutral. Obviously, they didn't know what had happened the night before, but the fact that they were trying to figure it out was not helpful. Miel was perceptive and persistent when he wanted to be, and he and Chi loved gossip.

"I don't think, I know," he said, pausing for effect, "that you spent much longer here last night than we did."

"And that time was spent with Ira," Chi said. Nime furrowed her brow. She didn't get where they were going with this.

"And how did you two come to that conclusion?"

"I was talking—"

"Flirting with," Chi added helpfully.

"*Talking to* one of the archivists about an unrelated matter—"

"Middle-aged women fall for his 'such a pleasant young man' routine too easily."

"And she mentioned that Ko-nin was in a bit of a mood today because—"

"All it takes is a little flattery, and they tell him everything."

"Chi! She was bitter because some student was in the library after hours, and Ko-nin couldn't find them, even though she enlisted the help of a tutor who was working late." Miel paused for a second as if expecting Nime to respond. When she didn't, he continued. "And since Chi and I were already curious about why you were so tired this morning, we connected the dots and figured it out." He looked at her like it was obvious. Nime just stared at him. "We know what's going on between you and Ira." He grinned at her. Oh. Now she understood.

The elevator opened up onto sea-level. Nime waited until they'd left the Academy and were in the relative privacy of the outdoors before she turned on Chi and Miel, eyes narrowed.

"What are you talking about?" Nime's voice was incredulous. "Nothing's going on with Ira and me!" Chi rolled her eyes, and Miel snorted.

"Okay, sure," he said. "That's definitely what it looked like just now."

"What did it look like?" Both of them stared at her like she was stupid, and she took a deep breath to keep from getting angry.

"Ni, did you not see yourselves? You were standing in the doorway, facing each other. Romantically." Chi emphasized the word with hand gestures that didn't make any sense contextually. "He touched your face. Romantically." Nime shook her head.

"Yes," Miel said. "Believe me, I know flirting when I see it. And I couldn't see *you* clearly, but Ira was into it. He was not happy to see us." Nime frowned. She shook her head again.

"You two are being ridiculous," she said. She looked around, but it was late enough that few other people were out. "You realize that it would be a serious violation of ethics for him to...to have anything other than a scholarly relationship with any of us?"

"Come on!" Chi said. "It's obvious you two have a more-than-scholarly relationship." Nime tipped her head back. This was nonsense.

"Okay, yes." Nime held up a hand to keep them from interrupting. "You're right; Ira didn't report me last night when he saw me, but that was it. And we weren't flirting just now. He touched my face because I had a nosebleed earlier. I'm not interested in anyone 'romantically,'" she said, emphasizing the word the way Chi had, "let alone *our tutor*." Chi and Miel looked at her doubtfully.

"That can't be all of it," Miel said. "What were you doing in his office, with the door closed?"

Nime clenched a fist behind her back. "Am I not allowed to go to Ira's office?" she asked. Chi just raised her eyebrows like that proved something. Nime let out a breath. "Not only am I not in some kind of secret relationship with Ira, I also don't *want* to be. And you two need to stop saying things like that. He could get in a lot of trouble." Neither

Miel nor Chi said anything for a moment. Nime walked toward Residential, and they followed on either side of her.

"We won't tell anyone," Chi said. She touched Nime's shoulder. "It's just, you've been acting weird, and we want you to be honest with us."

Nime looked at her with her mouth open and thought about what would happen if she told them the truth. Then she turned her head forward and kept walking. Who would want to know something like that? Who would want the constant pressure weighing down on them, the inability to do *anything* without wondering when it would end. Who would want to know when they would die? Nime wasn't going to put that burden on anyone else.

Chi and Miel picked up some silly topic of conversation as they walked, and Nime played along. That was the whole point of keeping the leak a secret, after all: to keep them from worrying. She had to act the part, at least. At the edge of Residential, she expected them to split off and go to their own units, but instead, they kept pace with her.

"It's not too late, we could go to Recreation?" Chi asked. "Or are you heading home for the night, Ni?"

Nime sighed and rolled her shoulders. "Yeah. I wasn't as stealthy last night as I should have been."

Miel raised his eyebrows. "Got caught?" he asked.

"No," Nime frowned. "Not exactly."

"And now you're in cold water with your parents." Miel nodded seriously, and Nime made a face at him. He looked at Chi over Nime's head. After a second they both nodded decisively. "Don't worry, we'll take care of that."

Nime squinted at them. "No you *won't*. I don't need you making my mom more suspicious."

Chi waved her hand. "You took the heat last night, so let us cover for you for once," she said. "Please?"

"Fine," Nime said. "Just act like I was helping one of you with something and lost track of time."

"Sure, sure." Chi grinned and bumped arms with Nime.

Nime's hand wandered to her bag as they walked, and she traced the shapes of the parts through the fabric. She ran through the transporter blueprint in her mind, distracted enough that she almost jumped when they reached her unit.

Chi and Miel stationed themselves just behind her as she opened the door.

"Thanks again for all your help yesterday," Chi said. Nime stepped through, and Miel leaned on the doorway. Nadra, sitting near the heater, didn't look up from her tablet, but Nime could tell she was listening.

"Yeah, sorry for keeping you out so late, but I, at least, am finally ready to present," Miel added. Ild walked into the main room and smiled.

"Chiri, Miel, nice to see you," he said.

"Hi," Chi waved. "We're just dropping Nime off." She turned to Nime again. "If you end up needing help with yours, just let me know. It's the least I could do after you stayed up all night for mine." With that, she and Miel said good night, and Nime closed the door behind them.

"It's good of you to help your group members," Ild said. "Sess was just telling us about how you helped him last night, too. He's in your room right now." He looked at Nime with a mix of suspicion and amusement. Nadra finally turned her head to fix Nime with a soul-piercing look. Nime paused for a second. Of course Sess had. Not that it mattered, anyway. Her father had no other reason to be suspicious, and if her mother wanted to voice her doubts, she'd have to explain why she had been at the academy in the middle of the night, too.

"Yeah, thanks," Nime ended up saying. She kicked off her shoes and clutched her bag close. Ild patted her shoulder as she passed him, and Nime gave him a short smile. She ignored Nadra. When she finally got to her room and closed the door behind her, she sighed. Sess sat on her bed, bag on his lap, and he perked up when she arrived.

"I brought the tools," he said, pulling a small box out of his bag. Nime nodded and placed it on her desk. "But why—" Sess continued, and she stopped him.

"If I ask you not to ask questions will you listen?" She immediately regretted her choice of words; the almost hurt look on Sess' face was unbearable. "I'll tell you in a few days," she continued, and he hesitated for a moment before nodding.

"Sure," he said. After a moment's hesitation, he looked at her. "Do you need a second pair of hands for anything, though? If I don't ask what you're doing?" Nime stalled for time by pulling off her bag and setting it on the desk chair. The help could be useful, but Sess would be able to figure out what she was repairing. And he wouldn't need to ask questions to start getting ideas.

"Thanks, Sess," she said, "but it's pretty simple. I'll be fine." He nodded once, and she sat down next to him. On any normal night, Nime would spend some time with him before he left. Any normal night, she'd have already been hanging out with him. But now she leaned her head against his shoulder for a second before sighing and stretching her arms in front of her. "I should probably get to sleep soon." It wasn't technically a lie, she probably should. But she said it knowing it would make Sess leave the fastest.

And he did, after a quick good night and a worried look.

With her bedroom door locked behind her, Nime got back to work.

5

Nime ran her hands over and over through her hair as she looked around. The control panel was missing a piece. Her room was torn apart, her things scattered about and any semblance of organization ruined. But the CPU was not there. She'd turned her bag inside out and emptied its normal contents onto the floor. She'd even moved her bed and searched under it, shaken out the blankets.

Sleep had caught up with her before she'd finished repairing the control panel, and now, in the dim gray light of a cloudy morning, a piece was missing. Nime closed her eyes and squeezed her fists until her nails left marks on her palms. It was fine. She'd probably left it with the other parts in storage, or maybe it had fallen out of her bag in Ira's office. Straightening, she gathered up her tools and the panel, chewed up a stimulant, and got ready for the day.

Nime blinked when she reached the door to Maintenance. She hardly remembered walking there, too busy thinking about the leak, the transporter, Potential. Even now, it was hard to concentrate on anything else; this hyper-focus was just the first symptom of too much stimulant and too little sleep.

Her stomach growled. And too little food. At least she wasn't shaking. Yet. The last time she'd chain-stimmed, she'd gotten shaky and dizzy after two nights of no sleep. So that gave her at least another day of steady hands, which should be all she needed. When it was all over, she could sleep for a whole day without waking up worrying every hour.

Before all of that, though, while Nime waited for a more reasonable time to search Ira's office, she needed to check something. She waved her tablet over the scanner, and the door to Maintenance slid open with a rush of cold air from inside. The cooling mechanisms required to keep the generator from overheating made the whole building as chilly as the depths of storage. Nime pulled the sleeves of her sweater over her hands, and the door slid closed behind her. Only the hum of the generator disrupted the quiet. Just after sunrise, no one was working yet, which was another reason she'd gone there first. Ciril-nin, the head of Engineering, had been at the secret Board meeting, and probably wouldn't let Nime get close enough to see the damaged wall. She wondered if he'd let anyone else near it. She wondered if it was a good idea to try to get near it at all.

Normally when Nime walked into Maintenance, it was for work, and she let herself get drawn into the crowded shelves and disorganized bins full of old things broken beyond repair. They littered the space, centuries-old machines she only knew from history, long-dead people's gaming equipment, anything and everything the original survivors had brought into Haven that hadn't stood the test of time. But their parts were still salvageable, so there they sat, gathering dust and waiting to be dismantled.

She turned her attention to the generator just feet away from her. Her hand pressed against the wall that contained it. The metal was warm, even with the coolers. Keeping one hand on the wall, she followed it around. It went in a circle, a cylinder through the heart of Haven, with Maintenance surrounding it. She wasn't sure what she would find, but she needed to know. Needed to see what had happened with her own eyes.

A temporary wall blocked Nime's path. It stretched across the narrow, shelf-lined hallway, and a projector stuck to it warned: "CAUTION: RENOVATION IN PROGRESS." Nime took a second to shake her head.

The nearest shelf was only a few inches from the temporary wall, and Nime easily climbed up it and stepped across to the other side. She shook her head again. For someone trying to keep people away from something dangerous, Ciril-nin didn't seem to have tried that hard. The shelf wobbled as she climbed down, but it held until she got her feet on the floor.

She turned around to continue following the wall and saw it. A gaping hole torn through the material of the wall, right at the seam. It had been bolted shut and sealed tightly. Nime stepped closer. She was already risking injury by being so close, but she needed to see. Though now that she thought about it, nothing felt off or painful. And checking her hands showed nothing out of the ordinary.

Nime slowly reached out, preparing to pull back if something happened, and ran her fingers over one buckled edge. A thin, oily film coated the seam, almost like machine lubricant. The residue on her fingers was the color of the night sky, but she had never seen blue oil before. Rubbing her fingers together, she leaned forward to look at the hole again. Her eyes traced the marks, deep striations going in toward the gap. And on the other side, there were dents along the edge, matching up with the others.

Almost like a tool had repeatedly been shoved at the seam until it broke.

Nime couldn't breathe for a second. She couldn't hear over the pounding of her pulse in her ears. Her hands twitched. Her vision narrowed in on the hole, and then she turned and kicked the temporary wall again and again, until the bioplastic cracked. She stood for a moment and panted.

She was going to kill whoever had done this.

* * *

Nime stalked into the training hall, ignoring the other people getting their recommended PT in early. Hardly anyone used the punching bags in the corner near the lesson rooms, which was good because Nime wasn't sure she could stand to even look at another person. She had never been so furious before, so filled with the urge to destroy something. She didn't want to punch a bag, she wanted to punch something that would break. She wanted to tear the bag apart and burn the filling. She settled for her regular practice, though the thought of someone purposefully causing the leak gave her warm-up punches more force than usual.

Activity did not calm the rage that boiled under Nime's skin. The sound of her fists hitting the punching bag echoed through the high-ceilinged room, every ounce of anger she felt behind each punch. She could feel the impact compressing the bones of her hands, her muscles tiring, but she couldn't stop. If she stopped, she'd explode. The heat inside of her needed some outlet, so she kept punching, even as her fingers started to ache and her lungs burned from the effort.

The skin on her knuckles split, and finally, the fury drained away, leaving Nime gasping and exhausted.

In the changing room, she winced as she unwrapped her hands. That had been stupid of her. She needed her hands to be in working order, and reckless aggression like that could have easily led to a serious injury. She straightened her fingers and sucked on her teeth. There wasn't any time to waste on uncontrollable rages; Nime had to be better.

* * *

Only the soft tap of Nime's shoes broke the silence in the B4 hallway until the buzz of her tablet made her jump. She pulled it out and ignored how tired her arms were. Her knuckles ached at the movement.

The message was from Ira. Nime stopped walking and opened their conversation, scrolling through the last few days' worth of messages. At the top, the newest message was outlined in blue.

Found something you might need, it said. "Stop by my office today." Nime sighed. She tilted her head up and thanked the Wardens. One piece of good news, finally. The CPU could have been gone forever, maybe dropped in the Endless Sea, maybe recycled into some other piece of tech. But it wasn't. Ira's office was only a few feet away, so she stepped over to it and knocked on his door. A distinct crashing sound came from within, and Nime pulled on the handle. It was locked.

"Ira?" she said, loud enough to be heard through the door. Heavy steps clattered next, and then it was silent. She frowned. As Nime considered taking drastic measures, the door slid open, and Ira looked down at her. His hair was disheveled, his clothes rumpled.

"Good morning," Nime said. Ira looked blank for a second, and then he nodded and opened the door wider.

"When I said, 'stop by,' I didn't expect you so soon," he said. Nime stepped into the office behind him. She paused in the doorway, looking around. His office was almost as bad as her room. Or, rather, it looked like it had been as bad as her room, and that banging and crashing had been Ira trying to put it back together. The cushions on the couch were loose and misaligned. Pieces of paper and things Nime couldn't identify covered the floor, though some had been pushed under the couch. A small mound of dirty fabric sat half-hidden behind the desk. Nime looked closer, and Ira walked back to his desk, kicking the pile fully behind it as he went.

"What happened?" Nime started straightening the couch cushions, and Ira laughed a little.

"Nothing," he said. Nime looked over at him. "I didn't know it was you, just now. I was worried it might be one of the heads." His smile dropped, and his eyes narrowed. "I wouldn't want them to have another reason to tell me I'm not fit to be a teacher." His voice rose a bit at the end, and Nime was angry on his behalf, a fraction of what she'd felt half an hour before.

"You're the best teacher I've ever had," she said. She punched a cushion back into place and regretted it when the fabric scraped against her knuckles. Ira stared at her for a second, leaning back in his chair.

"You're the best student I've ever had," he said. Nime started to smile. After a moment, Ira leaned forward. "I found this last night." He placed a small square down on the desk. "I assume it's yours." Nime let out a breath. She moved to his desk and picked up the missing CPU.

"Thank you." She turned it over in her fingers. How could she have been so careless with something that important? Closing her fist over it, Nime looked back up at Ira. "I'll get back to work, then." She turned to go.

"You should work in here instead," Ira said. Nime turned back to him. "Then you won't have to freeze in storage." She opened her mouth to protest but stopped. He was right, it would be more comfortable to work someplace with heating, and Ira already knew about the leak. So she nodded. Ira smiled. "Good. Well, I won't keep you, you'll probably want to start moving things in now."

Nime nodded again and tucked the CPU into a pocket in her bag.

* * *

The day before Nytherial's is almost as exciting as Nytherial's itself. Setting up for the festival, the offerings and exhibitions, all of it. The square that sits near the center of Haven transforms from open space and bare lite-crete to a miniature city of tents, stalls, and canopies.

We technically have class today, but Midra-nin gives up on trying to get us to settle down and takes us to the square to set up our exhibits. Other groups have already started to put up the tents and stalls, and I can see the structure of the festival taking shape. Something warm and happy bubbles up from my stomach and into my throat. If I could paint this feeling with ink, I think it would be the light pink color of a coral bass. A breeze blows my hair across my face. I don't mind, though I wish the sun was out. I wish it was warm enough that we wouldn't have to wear sweaters for once. A festival like this should be sunlit and flower-scented, like the festivals at the temple in the valley in my mind.

I blink, and I see white petals floating in the air, hear the murmur and hum of a distant crowd. I blink again, and they disappear.

"Alright, let's go pick up our supplies. Head on over there," Midra-nin says, pointing, "and start setting up. I'll be with you in a moment." Then she turns to me and takes me to a small tent near the raised platform at the edge of the square closest to the Academy. "You'll get ready in here today and tomorrow. Ibbi-nin will help you." She pulls open the tent and gestures me inside. The space fits two people and a chair comfortably. Ibbi-nin is already there, brushing off the costume. She looks like she could be Nime's friend Chi's older sister, with the same curly, black hair and wide nose.

"Navi, honey, glad to see you," she says. I've only met her a few times, but I remember that she's an archivist. That's why she's here, besides me needing help to get this costume right; she works with the delicate fabrics and textile arts stored in the archive. "Now, let's turn you into a Warden."

It's not as intimidating as I expected, dressing up as Nytherial. I was almost afraid I would ruin the ancient robe, but like everything else the Architects made, it holds up well despite its age. And Ibbi-nin has taken great care of it.

Somehow, with some folding, tucking, and tying, Ibbi-nin takes the bunch of silky white fabric and turns it into the same robe every other Nytherial has worn. The fabric is like nothing else in Haven, light and airy and flowy. The breeze chills my exposed arms, but I love it. I feel almost like I'm in some myth from before the pre-industrial era, thousands of years ago. Dressed like this, I can imagine myself as outside of time. But I think if Nytherial were real, she would choose an outfit more fitting for life in the stars. Something warmer, probably.

The lantern and the mask Ibbi-nin gives me next aren't very practical, either. The lantern is all glass, with real, actual fire inside. I can't stop staring into it. It flickers and dances and changes from yellow to orange to red. I've never seen fire this close before, and it's so much different than any painting or sculpture or written description. It's beautiful, but at the same time, it scares me. Something so pretty can destroy so much. There's a reason we don't have fire anymore.

The mask is plain, white bioplastic that fits itself to the upper half of my face tightly. When I look closer, I can see tiny, raised designs in the same shade of white covering the surface.

A light to symbolize the power of Truth to expose things in the dark, and a mask because—well, I'm pretty sure it's just to make the role seem less like a person everyone in Haven knows already and more like someone who could be Nytherial, but Ibbi-nin says it's because anonymity encourages honesty. It's the same reason people wear masks to the nighttime festival. It seems to me like an excuse for the adults to party without worrying about any judgment.

And the final part of the persona: a girl. Me. Nytherial is always a girl, always an Intermediate student. I think Midra-nin said it was because youths aren't burdened by the social pressure adults are that keep them from being honest, and that this age is full of questions and discovery. I'm not sure how true that is, considering how often I have trouble speaking my mind.

Ibbi-nin nods her head when everything is on, adjusts the length of the hem around my shins, and then we take the costume off, sooner than I expect. I'm not sad to be warm again, though, and I feel more like myself in my own clothes. When I step out of the little tent, the square looks like a half-built city. The white bones of tents are packed in close together, some as wide as a Residential unit, some only big enough to fit one person. My classmates are working on our section of the Intermediates tent, setting up their displays and tables. Midra-nin is with them, holding a handful of loose wires next to a boy with his back to me.

As Nytherial, I don't have anything to offer for the festival, so I head over to the glass dome of Botanics, right next to the square. Last year's Nytherial's Day was spent tired and anxious in the Basics tent with my paintings. The people walking through said nice things, but it's easy to tell when someone's only being polite. Art never gets much attention at the festival, so I didn't expect anything else. Still, the idea of having to stand there while people look at and critique my art again is almost as bad as the thought of standing there in front of everyone as Nytherial. It could be worse, I guess. I could have to do both.

That light pink feeling is heavier in Botanics, in the humid air and green smell. It's so drowsy and quiet, with the buzz of bees and the sprinkling of the irrigation system. The only other people here at this time of day are elders getting their walking in, and I smile at Sigua-nin and Zad-nin. I know them as well as I know anyone in Haven, which means enough to say hello. Zad-nin did an amazing sculpture out of salt a few Nytherial's Days ago. I remember standing before it in awe of the movement he'd managed to capture; I hope that made him happy.

Sigua-nin takes my hand. "Navi, sunshine, lovely to see you."

"Here to keep the bees company?" Zad-nin asks with a smile. I laugh a little and nod. They keep walking around the perimeter, and I head in toward the apiary.

I haven't been sleeping well recently, even though I've been sleeping a lot. It's my daydreams, especially the city; they've been seeping into my real dreams and the space between asleep and awake. The city and the shadows seem so real that sleep doesn't feel all that restful. I fall asleep, dream I'm in the city, and then when I wake up, it's like I truly did spend the last few hours running around with the cyborg. It's been getting scary lately, a change from the usual boring quiet of my tower.

A few bees buzz around my head as I walk up to the hives, and when I hold out my hand they land on it. I sit down on one of the benches. I don't know what the Architects were thinking when they added benches around the apiary. They're always empty, because Emira-nin, the apiarist, isn't sitting when she's working, and I'm the only one in Haven who likes to sit near the bees. I think I'm also the only one who hasn't been stung by them, so that's fair. More bees fly over, and I lie down and close my eyes. I can feel their little fuzzy bodies land on me and crawl around.

I start to drift off to sleep, lying there in the warm and the quiet. Please brain, I think, take me somewhere nice.

Behind my eyelids, I start to see the outside of my tower, the golden petals and glass. I open my eyes and blink hard a few times. Let's try this again: I close my eyes and imagine the green, green valley. Much more comforting. Even if I did somehow get transported to the valley in my sleep, it would probably be as relaxing as actually sleeping.

I start to drift again, my head cushioned on something soft and long and green. Blue sky peeks out from between the trees, and fluffy clouds gather above me. It gets darker under the gathering clouds, darker and colder. I blink, and the valley gives way to the crowded night of the city. I can feel the mass of people down here in a way I normally can't up in my tower. Some part of me, back in Botanics, wants to open my eyes and try again, but the vividness of this dream makes it hard to remember that there is another me.

The cyborg is with me. She isn't as happy as last time. There's something wary about the way she treats me. Before, she would have been relaxed with me. Before, she would have touched me casually. Now, she barely looks at me, and she definitely doesn't touch me. As we pass under a streetlight, she turns her face away from me. I catch a flash of metal on her face where there wasn't one before. It makes me wonder why she has the enhancements, what was wrong with her old arm, and now her old eyes. But I don't ask because I'm afraid. Not that she'll leave me, never that. She wouldn't, not unless the priestesses made her. I'm afraid that if I push too close to her, the priestesses *will* make her leave. And I'll be alone again.

So, to stay together, we stick to what we're down here for: finding the shadows and bringing them to my tower. The priestesses didn't want me to go, but I insisted, and how could they say no? I am the Lif after all. And sitting alone in my tower while my priestesses try to save me makes me feel useless.

I stop moving, and the cyborg does too, holding out her metal arm in front of me. I can feel something wrong in the air, the destructive Potential that makes it hard to sense the people around me. It's like a hole in the world, a missing spot. That's my only clue that we've found them, but the cyborg seems more certain. She turns her head this way and that, and now I can see her new, silvery eyes. Something in my stomach twists at the sight, but I don't have time to think about it before a shadow emerges from a nearby building and moves toward us. The person speaks to us, something about trying to save us. I don't believe them. Saving us from what, after all? Themselves?

The cyborg looks at me, and it's hard to meet her eyes. But there's a question in them: should we do what we came here to do? I nod, and she springs into action. For a moment, I wonder why I'm even here; the cyborg is more than capable, and there's only one shadow. And then there's a brief flash of light near the shadow's hands. Flames stretch out and lick at the cyborg, scorching her metal arm and catching on the fabric of her shirt. She cries out.

My heart sticks in my throat. I can't put out the flames with my shaping, and I'll just get in the way if I move too close. Before I have a chance to panic, she pulls back, smothering the fire on her clothes. And then in one swift motion, the cyborg pulls off one of her metal fingers and shoots something out from the joint. The shadow staggers backward, pressing a hand to their neck. With a groan, they sink to their knees.

I hurry over to the cyborg and reach for her side, where a hole is burned through her clothes. The skin there is red and shiny and blistering, but when I touch my fingers to her skin the blisters fade, and the redness grows into the pink of new skin. She itches the spot and nods at me.

Together, we approach the unconscious shadow, and when we get close enough to see their human face, I pull back. It's a boy. Not a shadow, just a boy, maybe 15, his face soft and young underneath messy hair. There's a red spot on his neck, and the cyborg leans down and plucks a tiny, shiny dart out.

A twitch of his fingers draws my eye, and I frown. The cyborg picks him up and tosses him over her shoulder, and we head for my tower. One of the boy's hands dangles near my face, and I keep looking at his fingers, stained dark blue from his breaking. He hasn't had decades to use it, so it's only affected the tips.

How did someone so young come to be a part of something like this? He's still a child; he can't possibly have the kind of cruelty and hatred needed to be a breaker, can he? Guilt sits heavy in my stomach. I hope the priestesses can help him see the light. We're taking him back to them so they can question him. Maybe while he's in my tower, we can show him kindness. We can show him a different path.

This will be good for him.

My hand slips down, knuckles smacking into the ground, and I'm sitting up before I realize I'm awake. I blink and move my fingers. They're not scraped, only a little red and stinging. The sky is gray and cloudy outside of Botanics, and I have no idea what time it is.

I try to put the city and the cyborg and the shadow-boy out of my head. Sometimes it feels like I have no control over these imaginings, especially lately. Maybe Athis-nin is right, and I spend too much time escaping into my daydreams. Maybe it's finally affecting me. Or maybe it was already, and it's just now starting to show.

Once, I didn't respond to my name in class because I didn't recognize it. Once, I looked at my hand expecting to see one much larger and darker than my own, and I kept looking at it that day to reassure myself that my hands were still mine, the ones I've always had.

Once, I saw a blood-filled Endless Sea, and it reminded me suddenly of war, brief flashes of red and white faces, of dead and dying people floating in a river. I've never even seen a dead body, let alone a war. That one left me crying in my room for days. Dad and Nime thought it was because of the dead shell whale and the smell, but truly it was because I couldn't forget those faces I shouldn't have remembered.

This isn't something normal, I know that much. And Athis-nin hasn't explained it for me because I'm too afraid to tell him about the times I look for people who don't exist, the times I expect there to be only two moons in the sky instead of three.

I look down at the ground and swallow. A handful of bees crawl around aimlessly, and I watch them closely. Some are still wandering all over me, but most are gone, maybe off to pollinate our food. A bee near my foot flutters her wings and then stops moving. I frown and lean over her. When I touch her gently with my fingertip, I expect her to move again, to wriggle or fly away. She does nothing.

The rest of the bees on the ground have stopped moving, too. I stand up and walk over to the hives, making sure not to step on any of the bees. Up close, I can normally hear them buzzing away inside. Now, the buzzing is faint. Something's wrong.

I've watched Emira-nin inspect the hives before, but I've never done it myself. Still, I open one up. I can't get past this off-feeling, this fear that slowly grows up through my lungs and heart. When Emira-nin opens the hive, there is a swarm of activity. The workers are everywhere, crawling and flying around the comb. When I open the hive, only a few are. The rest are motionless. The workers still moving drag the bodies of their sisters out of the hive, but there aren't enough to keep up with the crowding dead.

My heart sinks, and tears sting my eyes. I know it's normal for bees to die. I know they only live for a month or two. But this many? All at once?

I hoped that Haven would be fine, that the leaking Potential the Advisory Board talked about would stay confined to Maintenance and the generator. Mom and the others seemed to hope for that, too. That night, they decided to wait and see if the problem would spread; no one offered another plan, or said they were going to try anything else.

I swallow against the lump in my throat and close the hive. Would the Board act now? Would Nime? When I saw Nime's head peeking up from the stairs, I assumed she knew. I assumed she would try to fix it.

Maybe I shouldn't assume. Maybe she doesn't know. Maybe I'm the only one who knows the Potential is spreading. If the bees are dying already, how much longer will we have?

6

It didn't take long for Nime to move the transporter from storage to Ira's office, but it hurt. Her whole body shook by the time she was done. Maybe she should message Rem, ask him for some of his experimental salve. Would it work on sore muscles and bruised knuckles? Even if it would, the lecture Rem would give her was not worth it, she decided.

Ira wasn't paying any attention to Nime as she set up in the corner of his office. It *was* easier to see with the main lights on. Her eyes drifted over the neat piles of parts. She would skip the control panel for now and work on something shaky hands could do. As she fit one structural piece to another and started securing them, Ira looked up from his tablet.

"By the way, what happened to your hands?" he asked. He seemed curious, not judgmental. It wasn't the first time he'd seen Nime with fighting injuries.

She clenched her jaw to keep the anger from coming back and gave her multitool a sharp twist.

"The leak in the generator," she said. "Someone did it on purpose."

Ira's eyebrows rose. "Who would do something like that?" Nime shook her head. After a moment, he spoke again. "That doesn't answer my question, though."

Nime spread out her fingers and looked at the backs of her hands. "I got angry," she said in a tight voice. They were quiet for a while. The metallic clinks from Nime's tools drew her into a focused state, and when Ira spoke again it startled her.

"What do you plan to do once this is fixed?" he asked. Nime kept working.

"Find out where it goes," she said. "Move everyone in Haven out of here."

"But what if it doesn't lead anywhere?" Ira's voice was soft. Nime's hand loosened on the tool. She swallowed. She hadn't allowed herself to dwell on that, but suddenly the possibility was all she could think about.

"I haven't—" she broke off. She swallowed again. "This was the best plan I could come up with." Saying it like that, she sounded so helpless. Ira didn't respond. Nime leaned her forehead against the transporter. "I don't know if this will work, but I don't know what else to do."

"I'm not sure there's much you or anyone else *can* do." Ira leaned forward over his desk.

"Yeah." Nime's shoulders slumped. Earlier, she would have ignored a statement like that. But hearing Ira say it, the low odds and high risk of failure loomed large. "That's probably true. There's not enough time, we don't have the materials or the ability to block the Potential, and I don't think the rest of Engineering knows about the leak. If they knew—" She wasn't sure how to finish that sentence. Ira was right. What could they do if they knew? About as much as her. "I have to try, though," she said. Giving up would be a failure of its own.

"Yes," Ira murmured, a slow smile spreading across his face. "I suppose you do."

* * *

I need to talk to Nime. I need to tell her what I know. Once I do, she can take care of the rest, whether that's telling someone else or fixing the problem. She'll be able to do a better job than I would.

This morning, before she left the house in a hurry, Nime told me she'd be working down on floor B4 of the archive if I needed her. In the nearly empty Academy, I take the elevator down and try not to think of dead bees. When the doors open, I step out into a long hallway, with restricted manuscript rooms on one side and offices on the other. Where would she be working down here?

I can't get into the manuscript rooms to check if Nime is inside, but I also can't see any light around the edges of the doors. I walk farther down the hallway, reading the name plates as I go. If I've ever explored this far down before, it was a long time ago.

As I walk, I hear Nime's voice and turn toward it. It's coming from one of the offices, and she's talking to someone else.

"—Don't know if this will work, but I don't know what else to do." Her voice wavers. What is she talking about?

"I'm not sure there's much you or anyone else *can* do," says the other voice. As I get closer to the door, I realize it's Ira-nin's. My eyes widen.

"Yeah," Nime says. Her voice sinks low. "That's probably true. There's not enough time, we don't have the materials to block the Potential, and I don't think the rest of Engineering knows about the leak. If they knew—"

I turn and walk back down the hall. Nime doesn't—I suck in a breath and blink rapidly. Nime doesn't say things like that. Nime would never agree that she can't do something. Nime doesn't stop or give up. Nime is too obstinate, Mom says. I take the elevator up to sea-level, step into a bathroom, and sit on the floor with my back to the door.

Too many thoughts tumble against each other in my head: tiny bee bodies littering the ground in Botanics; the secret meeting, Mom's suggestion to keep this quiet; why can't Nime fix it? My eyes fill with tears.

There's this tightness in my chest that makes me clench my jaw and grab fistfuls of my sweater. Is anyone doing anything? I know Mom said the leak couldn't be fixed, but is anyone on the Board even trying? When are they going to tell Haven?

At least imaginary-Navi is willing to do something when her home is in danger. After the boy-shadow, the cyborg and I found more shadows, all stained dark blue somewhere.

The lights of the city blur and diffuse through the glass of my tower as we deliver another unconscious shadow—a middle-aged man with blue spreading up his arms this time—to the priestesses. I feel good, I feel like I'm doing something important. In this world, I'm doing something to save myself and the people I care about, and I feel useful in a way I rarely do in real life.

And if we can help these shadows, these people, especially the boy, even better. I haven't seen him since we caught him, and as this new shadow is taken away to another part of the tower, I ask one of the priestesses how the boy is doing. She looks to the side and frowns as she tells me he's being rehabilitated. Something about her answer makes my cyborg squint her silvery eyes and leaves me feeling unsettled.

Hours later, the cyborg and I walk through a rooftop garden. I am tired—maybe something from real-Navi bleeding into this one—and I barely even see the shadow before they grab me. They wrap their arms around me, only they're not arms, they're branches, wriggling and growing. I freeze. The shadows shouldn't be able to grow something living like this. They lift me and move me backward, away from my cyborg.

With a press of my fingers, the branches shift and become paper, and I break free. The shadow behind me clicks their tongue, and the grass beneath me climbs up my leg. The cyborg rips at her own branches, and I wince a little when they wither and die. I don't understand what's going on; a breaker can't tap into the creative Potential needed to grow trees or the soil that begins to slowly pile up at the cyborg's feet.

The grass pulls away on its own when I remind it to be still again, and I turn around. The shadow stands near the glass fence at the edge of the garden, their hands cupped around their mouth. I think I see a small spark of gold escape from between their lips. But that's impossible, and I need to know how they are doing this.

I blink, and a sheet of ice encases them. The dirt piling up around the cyborg keeps coming, so I wrap ice around the shadow's mouth and then, finally, everything stops. I slide the shadow toward me as the cyborg kicks away the dirt and the branches. She starts to pull off her finger to tranquilize them, but I shake my head. I have to know how this could be.

The shadow, up close, is no shadow at all. This is a woman, old and delicate, with papery skin and thin, floaty hair. I touch her and make sure she's unhurt, and as I do, I see through the ice that her mouth is gold, gold spreading down her throat like some kind of bird, reaching down under the collar of her shirt. If she opened her mouth, I'd be willing to bet I'd see gold inside, too.

"Please stop," I say, and when she nods the ice around her mouth evaporates. She speaks—not with creative Potential filling the words, but normally—and she tells me how this is possible. She is a shaper—the gold on her throat is evidence of that. And she is one of the shadows who have been trying to destroy me, the priestesses, and my tower.

I turn around and lean against my cyborg. This isn't right; it can't be. I know, I *know* that only a breaker could do something like that. Shaping doesn't allow that kind of hatred; that's what the priestesses say. And yet, this woman, a shaper, is one of the shadows. She doesn't seem to hate me, though.

And then, "The others are dead," she tells me, her voice impatient and somehow full of pity. I can't turn around. If I look at her, I'm afraid I'll see that she's telling the truth. When I ask who, she scoffs, tells me my priestesses aren't as merciful as I am. I can't believe that. "You will be, too, soon enough," she says. And I believe her even less. The priestesses are raising me for the slaughter, she says, like an animal, and it will be soon.

One look at my cyborg's face stops me from ordering her to sedate the woman and carry her to the tower. Her eyes are low, and her lips pressed together.

"Tell me," I say, and she has no choice.

I smack the real floor with my real hand, and I am in the bathroom in the Academy again. My hand stings, and I shake it out. When I hold it in front of my face, it's shaking. Why do I keep drifting off like that? I hadn't even realized I was doing it until my heart started beating so fast I could feel it in my throat. I take a deep breath. Now isn't the time to be daydreaming, especially not about that. I shake my head as if I could dislodge the city from inside and it would leave me alone. Hiding out in my mind isn't going to help anything. I can't help anything.

Well. I could. I swallow. Nytherial always tells the truth, all of it. Tomorrow I'll be her, standing and giving the blessing in front of everyone. If Nytherial was going to tell people, it would be then. And maybe no one will believe me, and maybe no one can do anything, but shouldn't they get the chance to try?

I stand up and look at myself in the mirror, leaning against the cleanser dispenser.

Every other time I need her, Nime swoops in, like a sea bird diving for fish, and saves me. She fixes things for me. And just like in my daydreams, the people that normally fix things can't or won't. Aren't daydreams supposed to be escapism? Aren't they supposed to take me into a world better than my own? Right now, I'm stuck in two worlds that are ending.

I need to think, to take all of this jumble, all of this mess and emotion and put it somewhere else. My fingers tap against my arms. The art rooms will be empty right now. I take the stairs up to the second floor and turn right at the first corner, stopping in front of Art Workroom 2.

The room is empty and dim, cloud-filtered light coming in through the windows. I look around at the tall work benches, ink-splattered and chipped, and at the brushes, ink bases, and other materials organized on shelves in the corner.

I scan sealed packets of pigments with my tablet to see what color they are. Chlorophyll green and red. Too happy and lively, respectively. I need something that will mirror this chaos in my head and heart. I grab some basic black, which doesn't match my chaos, no matter how angry and sad I am. But there's a darker green that's dull enough. My hand hesitates over the golden-yellow I often use. It's sunlight and honey and gold. I grab that, too.

I drop the packets on a table and head over to the paper racks. Scan tablet, wait for a beep, take the large roll of paper I requested. This paper is thicker than book-paper and smoother than the recycled stuff we use for cleaning. I love the feel of it, the texture of the fibers. A flash on my tablet catches my eye. "Monthly resource limit reached." Like nearly all resources in Haven, the use of paper is limited to keep our long-term supply stable and renewable. I eye the rack, dozens of rolls of paper in various sizes lined up on it. It feels unfair when so few people even want to use these supplies. I'll just have to make this count, then.

I carry the paper over to my table. It catches the air as I unroll it and clamp it to a frame. I start to lean it up against a stand, but then I remember that I'm alone, and no one will complain if I sit on the table.

I smile a little as I slide my hand up the wall to bring up the lights, and then turn back to my pigments to mix them into ink. I find myself humming a song. It's slow and wistful and happy at the same time.

When my ink is ready, I climb on top of the table and lean the frame against the wall, facing the light. I cross my legs and sit in front of it.

White. Not pure white, there are some beige-y bits in there from extraction, but it's still white by anyone's standards. Once in art class, Mio-nin told me that sometimes you just need to make a mark somewhere on the white, to make it less perfect, less intimidating. Some people are afraid of messing it up. But blank paper has never been intimidating to me. It's waiting for me to make it into something else. Waiting for color and life.

I look down at my tray and grab a clean brush. Black first. The ink is thick and dark. I dip the very tip of the brush in. My mind is always clearer when I'm making something.

I am scared. Sad. Alone. Frustrated, with the Advisory Board and with myself. I was relying on Nime again, like I always do. I was going to tell her about the bees and give her all of the responsibility, all of the worry. I was going to pass everything off to her and never think about it again. If she knew, I thought, she would fix everything. But she knows, and she's trying, but she said herself that there's not much she can do.

The ink seeps into the paper slowly as I trace my brush over it. I wonder what it is Nime's doing. What it is she's not sure will work. I take a thicker brush and spread thin green across a sky full of gray and black swirls and waves.

I could ask her. I could go back downstairs and talk to her, like I meant to earlier. But hearing her echo the same things the Board said that night was unbearable. I can't keep assuming she's going to save me or anyone else. That brings another wave of tears to my eyes. Nime always saves me.

The image in front of me is a conflicted, roiling mess. Like the sky during a storm, like the underside of clouds when light filters through, turning the world green and sharpening shadows.

I frown. The storm looks too angry. Drops of golden-yellow ink fix that. There are nice things in the storm, things that bloom like flowers.

The storm becomes the thing out of which the flowers grow.

If Nime's not going to save me, to save us, doesn't that mean I have to do something? Doesn't that mean I have to tell Haven about what's coming?

I spend hours painting, until, finally, I'm done. It's finished, and my head isn't bubbling over with thoughts anymore. I hop down from the work bench. I don't feel happy, exactly, not like I was earlier, but I do feel better. I'm not going to start crying again, at least.

I turn and take one last look at my creation. Stormy is a good way to describe it, and for some reason, the longer I look at it, the more familiar it seems. Not the colors, not the exact composition, but it reminds me of…something. A memory that I don't actually have. It's unsettling, and goosebumps prickle my arms and legs. I'm missing something, I'm forgetting something important. But what is it?

Swallowing, I turn my back on it. The lost feeling sticks in my chest, though, and trails along behind me as I leave.

* * *

Nime's head ached by the time she closed up the last panel in the body of the transporter. It snapped closed with a click, and she sighed. Leaning back on her feet, she pulled out her tablet to check the time. Sunset. And the next day was Nytherial's. She sighed again.

She didn't regret the last couple of days spent fixing the transporter, but something in her felt like a failure. She was going to let down her friends. They were supposed to meet tonight in Botanics to make sure everyone was ready for the festival. But Nime probably wasn't going to be there to present her offering or to watch Navi's blessing. The whole point of fixing things secretly was to keep the ones she loved safe and happy. How could Nime do that if she ignored them to spend what could be their last days working?

She clenched her fists. These wouldn't be the last days for anyone, that was why she was doing this. And the transporter was so close to being ready. All that was left was hooking up the control panel and configuring it. She stretched. Ira looked up from his tablet. He'd been reading something all day.

"Oh, before you leave, I found this last night as well." He pushed a memory chip to the edge of his desk.

"Have you checked it?" Nime asked. She craned her neck and leaned forward to grab it. If it had been with the parts of the transporter, it might have answers to questions she hadn't given herself time to truly ask. There still wasn't a clear reason for the machine to have been disassembled, or hidden. She turned the chip over in her fingers. It was tiny, the size of her pinkie nail.

Ira propped his head on one hand and looked at her. "Yes, I did." He paused and tilted his head. "And when I did, I remembered something about myself. Does the word 'Unlif' mean anything to you?"

Nime shook her head and then stopped. "Unlif," she said quietly. Images flashed through her mind, gone too quickly to process. They left impressions behind: blood, flames, a huge rift, emptiness. Her head spun, and she pressed a hand to her temple.

Ira smiled. "Interesting." Stretching his arm out toward her, he said, "Come closer, Nime." She did. "Actually, go over to the door." She did. "Now come back?" When she came back to stand in front of his desk, Ira's smile stretched wider. "Hmmm. Forget I said anything about it."

Nime blinked. Her head was pounding, and for a disorienting second, she couldn't remember where she was. And then she shook her head. Ira looked at her with concern.

"Sorry, I forgot what we were talking about," she said.

Ira brought a hand up in front of his mouth and coughed. "You need to get more sleep. I was telling you that it might be a good idea to take your friends with you when you try out the transporter tomorrow. For safety."

Nime looked down. Why hadn't she thought of that before? She could meet her friends in Botanics and convince them to come with her. It could be dangerous, wherever this transporter went, but even that had to be safer than what waited for them in Haven. And if it was dangerous, Nime could protect them. She always had.

Nodding, Nime stepped toward the door. "Yeah," she said. "I'll do that." She nodded once again and waved at Ira. It was only when she slid the door shut behind her that she paused, confused.

7

Nime ran her thumb and index finger over the memory chip in her bag again and again as she waited under the big tree in Botanics for her friends. Was this a good idea? Ira was probably right, but it seemed wrong. Would it truly be safer to bring her friends to an unknown location? And if it was, shouldn't she bring Navi, too?

Chi yelled something close by, and Nime dropped the chip into her bag. She looked up as Sess walked toward her, Chi on his back. A few moments later, Rem walked in one of the doors with Miel on his heels. Based on Rem's annoyed expression, Miel was saying something ridiculous. Nime took a breath and smiled.

* * *

The night outside is dark and busy with people, but home is quiet. Dad sits on a cushion in front of the heater, reading. He looks up when I close the door and pull off my shoes.

"How was your day?" he asks, standing up and coming over to me. He smooths my hair back from my face. I close my eyes; his are too concerned.

"Nice," I say. It was, for the first part. "I was painting."

"A new piece? Did you finish?" Dad smiles and heats some water on the cooker.

"Yeah, and sort of." I think back on it. I was finished for today, definitely. There wasn't anything more for me to add. But when I try to remember what it looks like, it feels like I'm forgetting something again. He unseals the nutrient formula jar and scoops some out into a cup. Then he turns around and leans against the counter. "I'm out of paper for the rest of the month," I say. I try not to sigh.

He frowns. "You're one of only a few people who use the art supplies. They should expand that limit."

"Don't we need it for other things? For the archive?"

"We also need art. In the future, we'll have records, sure, but those only explain the facts, not the culture or the atmosphere of a time period." In the future. I blink and swallow. Dad doesn't know, then. Mom hasn't told him. I try not to cry, but I can feel it building up, so I step forward and wrap my arms around his middle. If my face is hidden, he won't know I'm crying. He hugs me back, and I have to stop myself from crying harder.

"We have too many scholars and not enough artists in this place," he continues, rubbing my back. I sniff and try to calm down so my voice doesn't wobble.

"But knowledge gave us life." I can't make anything louder than a whisper come out. He hears me anyway.

"And creativity gives us soul. Both are important," he says. I rub my forehead into his thermal shirt. The cooker beeps. Dad pulls his arms away, and I do too, slowly. I wipe my eyes, but he's already seen. For a minute, he just stirs together the powder and hot water. My tears stop, and I clean up my face with my sleeve. Then he looks at me over his shoulder and smiles. "The world needs people like you, who see things differently. Otherwise, we would be doing the same things in the same ways as we did thousands of years ago. Nothing would change, because the academic types get too caught up in the established rules and boundaries and ignore the possibilities outside of them."

He pulls a jar of honey out of the cupboard and scoops a dollop into the cup. It falls like an amber stream, like sunlight. It turns the light gray drink tan. I can smell the sweetness from where I stand. I don't understand what he means.

He turns back around and hands me the cup. "What I'm saying, Navi, is that sometimes it's good to work around the rules if it's that important to you. I'm sure there's some way you could get more paper." I wrap both hands around the cup and bring it up to my nose. I'm not sure Mom would want Dad to encourage me to work around the rules, since I think that means breaking them. Maybe Nime takes after Dad when it comes to this. I take a gulp of the drink and feel the warmth slide down my chest and into my stomach. I sigh.

"How do you always know when I'm sad?" I ask into my cup. Dad laughs and puts away the honey and nutrient formula.

"Same way you know when I am. Your mom and Nime aren't as good at that as we are. They need people like us to remind them that they have emotions at all. A lot of people here have trouble with it. It comes from Haven prioritizing other types of intelligence over emotional." He pauses. "You and I have different strengths. That doesn't make them any less strong."

"Thanks," I say. Nothing has changed, nothing is fixed, but I feel better. Being around Dad is like being around Nime. I feel safer. Warmer. He nods, and I head off to my room.

I sit down on my bed and lean against the wall, pulling my blanket up over my head and shoulders like a hood. I breathe in deeply. I am surrounded by people I love. Dad, Mom, Nime. Everyone in Haven. They all deserve to feel warm and safe—to *be* warm and safe. And me, sitting here in my bed, waiting for Nime or someone else to do something and save us, I'm not giving them what they deserve.

I have the chance to tell everyone about the leak, and maybe it won't fix anything. Maybe it is hopeless. But at least I'll have tried to help. I breathe out. I press my lips together and nod. Tomorrow at the festival, when I'm dressed as Nytherial, I'm going to tell everyone about the leak.

* * *

Nime didn't pull out the chip when the group met under the big tree. She would wait until Botanics emptied a bit, and they could talk without being heard. Her smile felt tight on her face as she greeted Sess and Chi, and then Rem and Miel.

Sess sat down with his back against the low wall Nime sat on, and she gently tugged on a shaggy lock of dark hair. He looked up and smiled.

"Busy day?" he asked. Nime frowned and leaned back.

"What makes you say that?" she asked. Sess' eyes widened.

"You've been working on your secret project, right? You have oil on your hands." He touched one stained finger and then hesitated. Nime knew what he was going to say before he said it. "And you just look kind of tired."

"Kind of tired?" Rem said. He escaped from between Chi and Miel, and they followed him over to the wall. "You look like you haven't slept for a week." He narrowed his eyes and crossed his arms. Nime looked back at him. Her face dared him to keep going. And, of course, he did. He glanced down at her hands. Nime shoved them under her thighs, gritting her teeth at the sting. "Did you get in a fight, Ni? Who was it this time? Give me your hands."

Nime gave in and let him pull her hands toward him. It was inevitable; bandages would have given it away, and Rem was too observant to miss it. She was just glad that nothing worse had happened when she'd investigated the leak.

He pressed careful fingers into the bones of her hands, watching her face. Nime already knew nothing was fractured, but Rem tested her fingers gently and inspected the broken skin of her knuckles.

"I didn't fight with anyone," Nime said. Rem looked at her, unimpressed. He let go of her hands and reached into his bag.

"Sure. Here, hold still," he said and twisted open his jar of salve. Nime almost laughed. She should have asked him for it from the start. It was cool where he dabbed it on her reddened skin.

"Tomorrow night we should all take a break. Just have fun, no work or school talk allowed." Chi said, glancing between Nime and Rem and smiling brightly.

Miel grinned. "This year is the year we stay for the party," he said.

Chi nodded and spun in a circle. "With the masks on, no one will know that we're not supposed to be there!" Rem shushed them and looked around.

"They will if you keep yelling about it," he whispered. Chi laughed. Rem looked at Nime again. "I don't think I need to tell any of you how important it is to get an adequate amount of sleep, and that stimulants are not a replacement." Nime glanced away, but Rem continued. "I'm sure all of you know that using stimulants excessively can have awful side effects. I don't particularly want to see you in the clinic for heart palpitations or hallucinations."

Nime looked at him, and neither of them glared for once. Rem's glare was worry hidden in annoyance, but he wasn't hiding it now. Nime's was a warning, all anger. But she couldn't be angry at Rem for caring about her, so she looked at him and didn't say anything. She would sleep when they were safe. Until then, she wouldn't waste the time.

Miel looked around and pursed his lips. "Anyway," he said, and Rem shot an annoyed look at him from the corner of his eye. Nime relaxed, and Chi sat down next to her. "Anybody have any secrets to confess tomorrow?" He smiled charmingly and pushed his blonde hair away from his face. "You can always get them out of the way early; I've been told I'm a very sympathetic listener. If it's about how jealous you are of my hair, don't worry, I already know."

Nime laughed along with the others. She stood up and stepped close to Miel, leaning in like she was about to whisper. He smirked and tilted his head toward her. She took a breath.

"Your hair isn't that great," Nime said, her voice loud enough to make the nearest couple turn their heads. Miel gasped, pulling away and looking at her with exaggerated betrayal. Chi giggled. Rem sat down next to Chi with a short laugh and shook his head. Even Sess laughed, though he tried to cover it up with a cough. Miel raised one eyebrow and stalked over to the wall, where he sat down and spread his arms and legs out like a starfish. Rem pushed at him to make space, but Miel only spread out more.

"No, this is her punishment. There's no room for you," he said, glaring at Nime. Rem sighed. Nime grinned and stood over Miel for a second. And then she turned and flopped down on top of him as heavily as she could, mimicking the way he was sitting. "Get off!" he yelled, or rather, tried to yell. It came out as an exhale as the breath was knocked out of him. Nime ignored him, stretching out and leaning back to muffle him.

"Hey, does anybody know where Miel is? He just disappeared," Nime said in her most innocent voice. Sess laughed again, and Rem and Chi groaned. Miel sighed as well as he could given the circumstances and tried to shove her off of him.

"Your jokes are awful, and you are *way* heavier than you look." He flailed around with his arms and legs, but all he ended up doing was knocking into Rem.

"Muscle tissue is more dense than fat," Sess said. "Nime has a relatively low proportion of body fat to muscle mass, so she's heavier than the average person her size." He glanced at them out of the corner of his eye, barely visible behind his hair.

"Thank you." Nime smiled at Sess and his mouth turned up a little.

"Yes, thank you, genius. I know," Miel said, now worming his arms in between himself and Nime. "But what you have failed to calculate is how long I have before I asphyxiate under the weight of all her muscles." When he was finally able to push her off, Nime went without protest, moving over to sit near Sess.

Nime could see the nearest glass wall from her spot, and in between the breaks in the clouds, the sky was pink from the sunset. It looked like something Navi might paint. She sighed and closed her eyes, which felt like they'd been open forever. Chi, Rem, and Miel talked about something that had happened earlier, some gossip, but Nime only listened enough to nod and agree at the appropriate times. Sess nudged her foot, and she looked up. He tilted his head; he didn't have to open his mouth for Nime to understand that he was asking if she was alright. She smiled at him, but he didn't seem convinced. Nime stood up and leaned against the tree.

Outside Botanics, people were walking, and Nime watched without truly seeing for a minute until Navi passed by and turned to wave at her. Nime returned the wave, pushing the smile back on her face for Navi's sake. Because Navi didn't look happy. She was calm, but something sitting just under the surface had obviously upset her. Nime considered going out to talk to her, but Navi turned and kept walking. Nime lowered her hand. She looked back at her friends to find Chi watching at her curiously. Nime cleared her throat.

"Navi," she said, and Chi nodded and turned back to the conversation Rem and Sess were having. Miel tried to get into it, but then Sess said something about probabilities, and Rem talked about the learning algorithm used in the medtabs, and Miel just looked bored.

When Rem noticed that Nime was paying attention again, he looked at her. "And I was wondering if Navi might be a similar case after she fainted the other day," he said. Nime had no idea what Rem wanted her to say. He waited for a second and then helped her out. "Has she been feeling alright since then?" Nime nodded, and Rem pressed a hand to his cheek. "Good. I was worried she might need more serious medical attention."

Nime stared at him, and then she cleared her throat. "Why would that be?" she asked.

"If you were listening, you would know that a few cases cropped up in the past 24 hours where the patient was brought to the clinic with vomiting, headaches, and some dizziness. Enda-nin, the head of Medical, took them all on herself and won't let anyone get close to them, so everybody is concerned." He pursed his lips. "It would be irresponsible of me to say this is a new disease, but I have no idea what else it could be." He shrugged. "I'm just glad it's only been a few people so far." Nime stared at him and bit the inside of her cheek to keep her face neutral. Rem looked at her sympathetically and went back to talking to Sess, but Nime didn't hear it.

So soon. She'd thought they would have more time. For a second she thought, maybe this was why the Board decided to keep it a secret. Less than a week, and already people were getting sick. There was no way they were going to make it through this.

As soon as she thought it, she squeezed her hands into fists until her nails dug into her palms. They were going to make it through this, every last person in Haven, because Nime would never give up. Nime wasn't some coward, hiding behind secrets so she didn't have to do the hard things. And she had a way to do it, to save everyone.

She looked at the group in front of her, where Chi was braiding a chunk of Sess' hair. Miel plucked a flower from one of the berry bushes behind the wall and handed it to Chi with a flourish. He picked another for Rem when Rem rolled his eyes.

"Stop hurting the plants," he said, but he took the flower anyway.

Miel waved Rem's concern away. "It's fine, I work here." Sess sat quietly with a peaceful look on his face as Chi wove the flower into his little braid. Nime's heart squeezed in an unbearable way normally reserved for Navi. She loved them.

Nime had to get them all to safety as soon as possible. If any of her friends—or even worse, Navi—were hurt, she wouldn't deserve to get to safety with them.

"I—" she said, but she stopped when they looked over at her curiously. Rem scooted over on the bench to make room and patted the spot beside him. Nime bit her cheek again as she sat down. "I want to show you guys what I've been working on." A chorus of "Oohs" surrounded her as she pulled her tablet out. She grabbed the memory chip, too. Loading up a diagram of the transporter, she held it out for them to see. Sess sat up onto his knees. She told them an abridged version of how she'd found it, minus the secret meeting of course, and all she got in return was an excited Chi and Rem, a skeptical Miel, and a professionally curious Sess.

"How do you know it's a real transporter?" Miel asked. Chi scoffed, and Miel scoffed back. "Seriously, if she's presenting it at our tent tomorrow, I want to know." He turned back to Nime. "And if it is real, how do you know it's going to work?"

"I don't." Nime's voice was sharp. "But it's almost ready to test, and I wanted to give you the chance to be the first to see a new place." She pinched the memory chip in her fingers and held it up. "Also, this was mixed in with the parts."

"A memory chip?" Chi asked. "Have you looked at it yet?" Nime shook her head. "Let's see what's on it!"

Nime popped open the latch that hid her own chip. After dropping it into a pocket in her bag, she pushed the mystery chip into place. Her tablet darkened for a moment, then brightened with a chime. The restart progress bar crept along for a good minute, during which Miel kept sighing impatiently, and Sess listed the various things that could be wrong with the chip. Finally, the main screen opened up, and everyone went silent.

It was different from Nime's, from everyone's, the icons in the wrong places and the interface unfamiliar.

"HICOS version 4.02," she said. It glowed at them from the top left corner of the screen. She frowned.

"What operating system is that?" Chi asked. Sess touched his chin and then looked at Nime. His eyebrows scrunched together.

"Um," he said. "This operating system hasn't been used for ages." He shook his head, and Rem asked how long. Sess looked down at his own tablet. "We've changed OS's probably ten times since this was phased out. It was released about a hundred years post-Fall."

"This thing is supposed to be two hundred years old?" Miel said. He turned to Nime and patted her arm with a sympathetic frown. "You've been scammed by someone with a lot of time on their hands."

Nime started exploring, ignoring Miel. It seemed real enough; the fitness tracker had data, the calendar had reminders and appointments, everything seemed like it had been used by a real person.

Chi reached over Nime and tapped open the messenger. "If it's fake, whoever set this up is incredible," Chi said. She gestured to all the different conversations in the app. "They clearly have a lot of dedication. Maybe it's a psychological experiment." She opened the most recent conversation.

Rena-nin, you are summoned before the Advisory Board at midday on the 23rd. Your judgment will take place in the Board meeting room.

What is this about? I haven't done anything wrong

This isn't a punishment. Your actions regarding the Dome transporter may well have saved us all, and the Advisory Board wishes to discuss a reward. Please remember to bring your tablet.

"What does that mean?" Rem asked, frowning.

"The transporter was disassembled when I found it," Nime said. "The owner of this chip must have been the one to take it apart." The rest of the message didn't make sense, though. Why would that have been something worthy of a reward?

"But why was it disassembled?" Chi asked. "And why did they leave the chip with it?" Nime didn't have an answer for her. "This seems too convenient to be real."

"Or," Rem said, "It truly is 200 years old, and we're uncovering history."

"It's fake," Miel said. He sounded confident, but he kept glancing at the messages and then away. "If this transporter went anywhere, we would know about it. And there would be no reason to have cut contact.”

Nime opened up the documents. Her fingers moved slowly. “‘OPEN ME,’” Rem read, and Nime blinked. There, surrounded by other, normally named folders and documents, was one labeled in all caps. She opened it, and Chi sucked in a breath. It was full of documents, named in detail and organized by subject.

“The Mothers of Aht Carina,” Chi said. She pulled the tablet from Nime’s hands and started skimming a document. She switched to another one, and another, and then she lowered it and turned to look at the group. “This is everything I’ve been looking for.” She turned the tablet to show them. On screen were the words ‘The Cycle of Rebirth and Its Economic Impact.’

“You’ve been looking for a boring essay about ancient economics?” Miel asked, his voice light and teasing, but Chi looked at him seriously.

“This essay does not exist in our database.” She opened another document. “Neither does this. I don’t think I’ve seen anything on here before. Not in the library, not in the archive, not even in the manuscripts.” She raised her eyebrows and tugged on a piece of hair by her shoulder. Nime took the tablet back and looked through the documents in the folder. There were a lot of them, even some about the construction of Haven. She stopped on an image labeled “original plans for floating and dome sanctuaries.” She opened it.

“This is—” she didn’t finish the thought. This isn’t possible, was what she was going to say. The floating sanctuary must’ve been Haven. So what was the dome sanctuary?

“Are you sure you didn’t just miss it?” Miel asked.

Chi shook her head. “I’ve done tag-searches, I’ve done word matching, I’ve searched for specific phrases and words throughout the entire database and gone through the results one by one. I’ve even hand-searched the manuscripts to make sure there weren’t any translation errors. The Mothers are my chosen specialty. I have spent years searching for any scrap of information about the religion, and trust me, these are not in our archive.”

Rem frowned at the tablet. “How could that even happen?” he said. “This all clearly existed after the Fall, so that means that it had to have been uploaded to the database. Where would it have gone between then and now?" Nime had a sinking feeling in her stomach. There was nowhere for it to have gone, and no one in Haven would have removed it. The destruction or concealment of knowledge was antithetical to everything Haven had been built on, everything it had been designed for. It was not possible.

Except—"Data doesn't delete itself," Nime said.

Rem's eyes widened at the word delete. "Who would do that?" he asked, his voice soft. Even Miel was quiet for a minute.

"They would have needed administrative access," Sess said.

"And the ability to make everyone in Haven forget about an *entire other* settlement and everyone inside it," Miel said, having finally recovered. "It seems unlikely. It was probably some kind of bug." He nudged Sess' shoulder. "That's possible, right?"

"Um, to remove or corrupt such a specific subset of data? It would be possible, but improbable." Sess turned away when Miel looked at him.

"Wouldn't people find out? Wouldn't someone have said something? Wouldn't whoever was responsible be banished?" Chi asked. She scrolled through the folder slowly, her eyes sad as she looked at all of the nearly permanently lost information.

"Not if everyone in Haven was in on it," Nime said. Someone would have talked, someone would have told their child or grandchild about the lost data, about the atrocity that had been committed. Chi's shoulders slumped, and if Nime weren't so busy pretending everything was fine, her own might have as well. Two hundred years before, the entire human race had decided that the best course of action was to delete irreplaceable information from existence.

"Why?" Rem asked. He sounded so upset, Nime pulled him into her with an arm around his shoulders. "It doesn't make sense, why would they delete all of this?"

Miel leaned back with his arms crossed. "If, and I'm still not convinced, this is real, the only logical conclusion is that everyone in Haven wanted to forget about this information. About, again, an *entire* settlement."

Nime took a breath. "The truth is probably on the other side of the transporter," she said. If curiosity was what drew them away from danger, then she would use it gladly. Besides, when all of this was over, they would need to restore the missing data. "We could present this for Nytherial's Day if we find more evidence."

Chi nodded. "Yeah," she said. "I think we should all go there tomorrow morning, before the festival." She looked around at the group. "I, for one, would love to have more to show than the collection of implications my essay is currently. And, if there are people there, maybe we can reconnect with them." Sess blinked and nodded slowly.

Rem narrowed his eyes. "It seems a little reckless to wander into an unknown place on our own," he said. "But I'll go."

Miel sighed, and all of them knew that if Rem was going, Miel was going to go, too. Nime smiled, pretending that it was excitement for the adventure and not relief.

8

When the sky outside her bedroom window lightened enough to be considered morning, Nime took another stimulant and went outside. Too many things were rattling around inside her to stay in a stifling home filled with people she was either mad at for concealing the truth or concealing the truth from. So she waited outside until her fingers shook from the stimulant and there was enough gray light to see by, and then headed for the Academy.

Nime would go alone first. This concerned the safety of the people she loved, and she couldn't take them into a place she hadn't at least checked. She would hop in, make sure this "dome settlement" was safe, and then come back to get her friends. Overnight, she'd skimmed the Architects' plans for the settlement to get a general idea of where she might want to explore first.

"Nime," Chi said from somewhere behind her. Nime spun to see Chi standing by the water, body facing the rising sun. She looked over her shoulder at Nime and frowned. "You weren't planning on going alone were you?" Nime laughed a little. Chi knew her so well. If it weren't just as dangerous in Haven as it possibly was on the other side of the transporter, she would be going alone, or at least with people she cared less about. She shook her head and grit her teeth against a wave of pain that throbbed behind her eyes. Just one more day, all she had to do was make it through one more day. "Good because I'm excited." Chi smiled and sighed.

Nime stood next to her and looked out at the water. Pale gold light from the rising sun reflected off the Endless Sea. It was peaceful, though the rapid beating of her heart made it hard to appreciate.

The peace only lasted so long before Chi's constant peeking at Nime out of the corner of her eye got on Nime's frayed nerves.

"What?" she asked, without looking over. Not as sharp as she felt, but sharper than she wanted it to be.

"Is something wrong?" Chi asked. Nime opened her mouth to say, no, of course not, why would you even think that, but Chi kept going. "I know you don't want to talk about it in front of everyone. You might not even want to talk about it with me. But whatever it is—stress about your apprenticeship, assessments and match-making coming up, whatever—I'm willing to listen if you do." She stopped, and they stood quietly for a minute. "Anyway, you don't always have to do things on your own. You help us all the time, but we almost never get the chance to return the favor. But we'd like to. So if you do want to talk about it, or if you need help with anything, you can just say so. Just ask." She was quiet for a moment before continuing. "You're allowed to ask for help."

Nime didn't respond at first. What could she say? *Chi, I'm sorry I didn't tell you, but the generator is leaking Potential that might kill us all, and I'm feeling pretty stressed because of that?* No. That wouldn't help anything. And honestly, Nime had been mostly fine before the leak, before the transporter. A week ago, the heaviness of life had been bearable. But the knowledge of impending death weighed on her. The day before, with Ira, Nime had been close to touching the thought, the looming mass behind every second of her days. The size of it terrified her. She couldn't look at it head on, couldn't spend more than a moment thinking about it. Because if she thought about it, if she thought about how this might not work, how everyone she loved could be dead in a matter of days, how this could be it, the final, dying breath of humanity, if she thought about these things, she was afraid she would drown in it.

To pass that weight on to someone else would be cruel. Selfish.

"I am a little stressed," she said, and Chi touched her elbow. "But it's not anything I can't handle."

Nime felt Chi looking at her, so she stared at the sea, blinking until she was sure there was no chance of tears. And then Nime smiled at

Chi. After swallowing, her voice didn't even waver when she said, "Thanks." Chi nodded and bit her lip. She looked back out over the sea. The bottom of the sun passed the horizon.

Chi took a step back from the edge. "Anyway, let's go get our stubborn boys for an adventure."

"'Our stubborn boys?'" Nime said with a short laugh that only started fake. "Call Rem that in person and he probably wouldn't speak to you for a week."

Chi laughed, too. "Yeah, well, it's even more true for him."

Minutes later, the five of them stood outside the Academy in the soft new light of Nytherial's Day. Nime led them all inside, and she listened to Chi chattering to Sess about all the new information they would find. He sounded excited, his voice faster and louder than normal. Miel was silent until Rem gave him a scrap of gossip from the clinic, and then Miel begged him for more information.

They all piled into the elevator, and for a second it was all elbows and feet. When their movement made the elevator shift, Rem held tight onto the arm of the person next to him, Sess, who told him the statistical likelihood of an elevator accident. The sound of chatter and laughter filled the elevator. Nime smiled. Every time she thought it might be a good idea to tell them about the leak, she remembered that they wouldn't be like *this* if she had. It was worth keeping it a secret to keep them happy.

As they approached Ira's office, Miel's voice cut through Nime's haze of distraction. He was asking Rem if this was a good idea, if this was going to end with everyone dead in some kind of teleportation accident, and Nime grit her teeth, sliding open Ira's door. Miel was a skeptical person, she knew, but didn't he trust her? She would die before letting them get hurt. It was a dramatic thought, probably brought on by excessive amounts of stimulant and sleep deprivation, but it was still true. That was why she was going first.

She turned around once they were all inside and gestured to the transporter. Expressions ranged from gently curious—Sess—to bewildered—Miel. Rem looked a little surprised, but he shared the excitement that had Chi bouncing up and down on her toes and beaming like Navi in the sunlight.

"Sess," Nime said, handing her tablet to him, "can you find a connection while I make sure the power is functional?" He nodded, and Nime slid open the panel on the side that held the power extractor. She shined a focused light into the mass of wires and machinery, double-checking the connections. The one good thing about being stuck on a floating settlement in the Endless Sea with limited resources: technology hadn't changed much, so the power extractor on this 200-year-old machine was nearly identical to the ones Nime looked at every day. She pressed the power button. Nothing happened for a moment, and anticipation built in her stomach.

Then it powered on, and Nime breathed out. Sess nodded when she looked past the machine at him. She closed her eyes for a second. It worked. Then she opened them and took the tablet from Sess.

"There's only one linked transporter online," he said, and Chi crowded at Nime's elbow to see. Nime stared at the words on the screen, "Dome Transporter 1," highlighted with a green check mark.

"Wait," Rem said. "We should have a plan before we go." Nime held her breath for a moment, then released it slowly. She hadn't thought that far ahead. Bringing her friends with her had been the extent of her plan.

"I would love to get my hands on some primary historical sources, or at least pictures of sources," Chi said.

Nime nodded. "We need proof that this place exists, first of all. And pictures are probably a good idea." She paused. She also needed to be able to prove to Haven that it was safe.

"We already have a lot of the missing data from the memory chip," Sess said, "but if our metadata shows that we downloaded it from a different network, that would be proof."

"So we need to re-download maps, books, whatever we want, from the other side of the transporter." Nime crossed her arms. "I took a look at the building plans last night; there's some kind of archive or library inside a temple. I'm sure we could get plenty of data there."

"I'll try to run some flora scans while we're there," Miel added. "See if any of them show unusual properties or are species we thought were extinct."

And Nime could set her tablet to do periodic environmental scans. If the scans showed no danger, that had to be enough proof. She looked around at the group. They were all excited now.

"Great," Nime said, stepping onto the platform. "In case this doesn't work, I'm going first," she continued, and when Rem's mouth opened to argue, she added, "alone." And then she tapped the large, green "TRANSPORT" button before anyone else could protest. The machine vibrated beneath her feet. She had the space of a breath to worry before the world slipped away.

There was nothing for a long second until Nime could feel herself blink and hear her heart beat. She couldn't see anything, but as she looked down at her tablet, it became apparent that that was because it was dark, and not because the transporter had messed up her vision.

Nime gave it a few more seconds before she tapped again, and in another blink of nothingness, she was back on the platform in front of her friends. They yelled at her. Well, Rem yelled at her, but she ignored him.

"It works, and I didn't die, so you're safe to come along this time," she said, and Rem threw his hands up and stomped onto the platform. Sess was next, followed by Miel and Chi, who crowded everyone closer together. The platform was big, but not big enough to make this a comfortable fit. Nime called, "Ready?" and pressed the button after a chorus of "Yes."

The nothingness was less unsettling the second time around. It was over in less than a second, and all of a sudden Nime could feel Sess and Miel standing close and hot air on her face. She checked the time. It was still morning, still a half-hour after first light. Well, it was still a half-hour after first light in Haven. She had no idea what time it was wherever they were.

"Everyone hold still for a second," she said. She wished they could have brought lights with them, but the only portable lights were wisp-lamps, which were hardly brighter than tablet-light.

"No, I was going to walk off into the unknown," Rem said. He couldn't see the face Nime made at him, but she was sure he knew. She flipped her tablet around and turned the brightness to max, shining it around them. She could just about see walls at the edges of the light. She shined it at their feet. The ground was a floor of some type, made of wood, she realized after a moment of inspection. It wasn't visibly hazardous, so she stepped one foot off the platform, gradually adding more weight until she was sure it wasn't going to collapse underneath her. She fully stepped off, shining the light in a circle around her. The room they were in was similar to storage, with shelves that stretched from the floor to the high ceiling. Though, these were dusty in a way nothing in Haven ever was, thanks to the air filters. The transporter stood near a wall that looked like the retractable walls of the docks in Haven.

The only windows sat high on the walls, up near the ceiling. Nime could only tell that they were there by the fact that they were marginally brighter than the rest of the darkness, though whether that was from being covered in dust and dirt or from darkness outside, she wasn't sure. The space was silent beyond their collective breathing. It seemed completely abandoned.

"It seems safe in here, you can get down now," she said, shining the light back over to the ground next to the platform. Chi stepped down first, and the thump echoed. Sess pulled out his own tablet and followed, with Rem close behind. Miel was the last off. They began poking around the room, and Nime looked for a way out. She walked toward the nearest wall, where light outlined the edges of a rectangle.

Nime stopped short when she got closer to the wall and saw some sort of plant, though she'd never seen a plant like that before. Flat circles sat on top of stalks growing from the pitted and cracking wall. A sickly, yellow-white color, like the belly of a fish, they shone with slime. Nime got within an arm's length and then promptly backed away. They smelled like something rotting, with a sting at the back of her throat that made her gag. Nime lifted the collar of her sweater, which was quickly becoming stifling, to cover her nose and mouth. There, under a patch of the rotting plants, was what could be a door.

"This way," she called back over her shoulder. Chi came bounding over, though she stopped and grimaced when she got close enough to smell the plants. Rem gagged when he reached Nime, and she patted him on the back gently. "Cover your face with your sweater, it helps." Sess didn't seem to care about the smell, though as they got closer he started to look a little pained, and Nime realized he was holding his breath. Miel frowned and squinted at the plants.

Nime edged closer to the door, and even though she pressed the fabric of her sweater tight against her face, she still had to pause while she nearly retched. Up close the smell was so strong she started to feel dizzy. Reaching out for the handle, Nime's hand and arm brushed between a grouping of the plants. The slimy sliding and soft, mushy texture made her skin crawl. It stung after the first touch, like a mild burn.

All it took was a turn and a push, and the door fell off its hinges onto the ground outside. Nime rushed through the opening and gulped in air, trying to get the stench out of her nose. The others stepped through a moment later, breathing deeply.

Once Nime was no longer on the verge of vomiting, she looked around. They stood on a street made of stone in front of a large and crumbling building. The other buildings nearby were in a similar condition, with more of the plants growing on most of them. The light had a strangely dim quality to it that gave everything odd shadows and didn't look at all like sunlight, wisp-light, or the artificial lights of Haven.

And then Nime looked down and saw the bones. She froze.

That would explain why everything looked like it was falling apart. There may have been people there at some point, but now there were only off-white skeletons, broken and scattered about. One of them crumbled when Nime accidentally stepped on it.

"Are these bones?" Chi asked. She stared down at a partially crushed skull by her feet. Miel and Sess looked around silently.

Rem took a step back. "Maybe we should go," he said. "We don't know if it's safe to be here." Nime bit her lip to keep from responding immediately.

"These are old, though," Nime said after a second. "Whatever happened must have been ages ago."

"This is probably why they disassembled the transporter," Miel said. "I think we should stay, figure out the history of this place."

Rem looked at him and shook his head. "This isn't just history; people died." It was quiet for a moment, with no wind or waves to break the silence.

Nime didn't know what to say to keep him from leaving. The point of this was to keep them safe, to get them out of Haven. She couldn't let Rem go back.

"But if we can figure out what happened, we'll be recovering lost information and making life better for Haven," she said. "Let's look for a library or console and get what we came for." And then Nime would go get everyone else, and they could start making the place livable.

"Fine," Rem said. He shook his head again. "Just, give me a minute." He turned to face the building, and Nime saw his shoulders rise and fall with deep breaths. She pulled out her tablet and started the first environmental scan.

Miel walked closer to the plants than Nime would choose to, staring at one and poking it with a stick. He wandered back over to the group after a moment. "These look like some kind of fungus, though it's not one that I've ever studied," he said, tapping at his tablet. "I think they excrete an acidic substance, so best not to touch them." Nime grimaced. Too late for that warning. She hoped the fungus wasn't what killed everyone.

Chi and Sess stood still, looking up. Sess clutched his bag tightly, his lips pressed into a line. "What's wrong with the sky?" he asked, turning to look at Nime. Chi craned her neck and turned in a circle. Her lips parted slightly. Nime tipped her head back to see what they were talking about.

She frowned. The sky was so dark it looked like night without the stars. She turned in a slow circle, looking up at the sky, and she saw what could've been the sun, bright against the black sky, but that didn't make any sense. She squinted up at it, watched it flicker and go out for a second, and she sucked in a breath. For the moment the "sun" was out, she could see beyond the sky, could see that it was not the sky at all. A giant jellyfish drifted past, its frilly, luminescent tentacles trailing behind it. And then the light came back on and the name of the linked transporter made sense.

"I see now why it's called 'the Dome,'" Nime said.

Rem turned back around. "We're underwater," he said. He didn't look at Nime, but she nodded anyway. Of course. That was the only way for there to be land anywhere on Aht Carina. Sess looked down and cleared his throat.

"It's a bit unsettling," he said. Nime glanced at him, and he was the picture of uncomfortable, standing rigid and tense. Rem moved next to him, looking at Nime for assistance. The two of them gently touched his arms, and he gave them a shaky smile. "I just need to get used to it," he said, taking a deep breath.

"What's wrong with you?" Miel asked when he walked up. Sess pointed upward, and Miel leaned back to take it all in. "Huh, underwater dome. How deep do you think it is down here?" Nime didn't think he was doing it to be mean, but Sess closed his eyes anyway.

Nime checked the plans again. The temple and archive should've been in the center of the Dome. She didn't know what building they were standing in front of, but they could at least start by heading in the direction of the "sun." No one said anything more about the bones or the sky when they started walking down the street.

Everything they passed was covered in a thick layer of dust that looked like it had been undisturbed for years. It coated the buildings that lined the street in brown. And it coated the piles of bones that littered the ground, that lay in doorways, that were broken and scattered around like they'd been thrown.

When they reached what must have been the square, Chi stopped short in front of Nime with a gasp. Nime walked into her, looked at the square, and saw exactly why Chi had gasped. In the middle of the square, in front of a large, white and gold building, sat a heap of skeletons half as tall as Nime.

The pile was huge, wider than it was tall, and Nime wondered how many people had died to make it. A whole town-full of people, milling in the square around the temple on a warm spring day. One after another, they would have been thrown on the pile.

Nime looked down at herself, saw her hands dragging a headless corpse toward it, a knife dripping blood in one fist, saw her clothes soaked dark red, and she staggered.

Blinked.

And the pile became bones again, instead of bodies. Nime shook her head. She needed to sleep.

As awful as she felt, her friends had to be feeling worse. Even Miel, not the most sensitive of the group, stared at the pile with his shoulders up and a grimace on his face.

Looking away from the bones, Nime walked further into the square. The building straight ahead, the one with the golden roof, that had to be where they needed to go. But instead of walking to the temple, she stopped in front of a pair of mostly intact skeletons. Their bones were mixed together, and it took Nime a moment to realize that they were embracing, or they had been when they died. Nime stepped closer and bent down. Something that wasn't bone was stuck between the vertebrae of one of the skeletons and underneath the finger bones. It was a knife, rusty and stained. She reached out a finger and touched it. Chi stood next to her.

"What happened here? Some kind of disease?" Chi asked.

"Looks like these two were killed with this knife. I don't know about the rest." The sun flickered again, and Nime pulled her hand away.

"Come look at this," Miel shouted. He stood in the doorway of a tall building off to the left. As Nime approached, she could see a fist-sized hole straight through the door near the handle. The lock lay on the ground outside, trapped in the missing wood.

Inside, Nime's eyes adjusted quickly to the darkness. Dust and the light that managed to make its way through the dirty window blanketed the stained floor, and on the floor lay a skeleton's worth of bones. This one was alone, unlike the others, and was broken and splintered in several places.

Next to the skeleton, a tablet had been dropped on the floor. It was the first one they'd seen in the Dome. Nime bent down to pick it up as the others followed her in. The screen was cracked in one corner and covered in fingerprints of dried blood. When she powered up the tablet, the prints stood out brown against blue tablet-light. It opened into a message conversation with someone named Rena, the most recent of which sat at the bottom of the screen.

Please turn it back on, Rena, for me?

Nime scrolled up to the start of the conversation, goosebumps prickling on her skin.

Recent Messages

10:14 AM
You feel that up there?

Feel what?

The quake. I guess not.

Was there any damage to the dome?
Can't believe we didn't get even a ripple.

I don't think so?
I'm at the barn, so I don't know about anything else.

Then go find out?
Dad is going to flip. This is the third quake this month.
He's never going to let you keep living down there.

Yeah, yeah. It's just because of Nia-nin.
Once we find the third it'll be fine.
What in the Endless Sea?
All the animals are fighting

The alpacas are fighting?

Oh, Wardens
There's so much blood
Rena what do I do? No one is answering my calls

Hold on, hold on.
What is going on?

I don't know!
Why would the 'pacas kill each other?

You're the farmer, not me
    Just be careful, I'm gonna try to call somebody
    Go to the temple
    I'm sure that whatever is going on, somebody'll be there

Oh no

Ise?
    Tell me what's happening

There are bodies in the street. Dead people.
What is going on?

Was it the 'pacas?

I don't think so
I can't look
They're just torn apart

The Storehouse has a lock, right?
    Go hide there and lock the door behind you

Okay
I'm in and the door is locked
The temple steps are covered
Please come get me

I'm trying Everybody is panicking up here.
    Can you see out the window? Can you see anyone?

No
They're all dead
Wait
She just cut his head off
Emil
He had the day off

I said I'd take care of his shift today

What?
  She who?

Mouly.
She's out there with Nia-nin

When they're gone, go to the transporter
  you'll be safe up here

Turn off the transporter

No! We have to get you up here first!

Please turn it off!
Please! You have to, or they'll go up there too!

It's off
  It's off
  But what about you?

Stop messaging me
I don't want them to hear
They went into the warehouse. Thank the wardens you turned it off
Rena
They're checking to make sure everyone is dead
It's only a matter of time before they check here
You need to make sure they can't get to Haven
They killed everyone
Everyone
There is more blood than I ever thought
Our own Endless Sea
They were supposed to fix all of this why did they kill everyone instead?
Rena
They're heading this way. I think they saw me in the window.

Please please destroy the transporter so they can't get to you
Be safe. I love you, and Mom and Dad.

10:47 AM
Rena?
Are you still there?
They're gone, will you turn the transporter back on so I can come up?
Come on
It was a joke
I was playing a joke on you
It was funnier in my head, sorry.
But can you turn the transporter back on?
People need to use it
Seriously, turn it back on
Please turn it back on, Rena, for me?

Nime lowered the tablet and shivered.

"Moeth's salty abyss," Miel said. "I can't believe this is real."

"Wardens," Rem said, looking over the room. His voice wavered. Footsteps echoed on the wooden floor, followed by a thump against the outside of the building and a groan.

"I'll go check on him." Miel stepped back, and Chi took his place. She bent down to look at the pieces of bone on the floor.

"You know," she said, "last night after you sent us the files, I read up on this place. Their religion." Stretching one finger out toward a femur that ended in a splintered mess, she stopped just above it. "I found a passage about burial rites. And this is the worst way they could have been left: inside, where they can't return to Aht Carina." She stood up but didn't look at Nime.

Rem's voice drifted in from outside, a choked off "—torn apart!" that pulled on Nime's heart. She set the tablet down on the floor and turned around. Sess looked stricken. Nime gently pushed him outside, and when he stepped back into the light, he took a breath like he'd been underwater. Chi followed them out. If Navi were there, she'd almost certainly be crying. If Navi were there, she wouldn't be exposed to Potential, though.

Miel and Rem stood next to the building, and Rem pressed his hands to his eyes, murmuring something. Miel shifted closer, blocking Nime's view of Rem.

Nime scanned the square, and her vision sharpened for a moment. Even the dim "sun" brightened, and details came into focus. She could see the weave of Miel's sweater, and farther away, the pits and cracks in the white walls of the temple. Her ears picked up the sounds of breathing from her friends, Rem's sniffling suddenly, loudly, audible. Everything was clearer, even the smell of dust, the scratch of fabric on skin, and the taste of her mouth.

And then it wasn't anymore. Nime blinked and everything was normal, not the intense rush of sensation from a second before. What was that?

Closing her eyes, Nime took a breath. This place was messing with her head, or maybe it was the stimulants. She opened her eyes.

"Let's keep moving," she said, walking toward the white and gold building. Chi and Sess followed, but it took a moment before Rem returned to the group. Nime slowed to let him and Miel catch up.

"Where are you taking us?" Miel asked, and Nime pointed at what she'd assumed was the temple. It loomed over them as they approached. Despite the decay, Nime could see untouched portions of its circular walls and columns and stairs where the stone was white and smooth. With the golden, domed roof, it must have been a sight when it was maintained. She'd never seen gold like that before; in Haven, gold was as utilitarian as everything else, extracted from the sea for use in the labs and manufacturing.

As they walked to the building and up the stairs, Nime's head tilted back, her eyes focused on the golden roof until it was hidden from sight. The doorway, doorless now, was situated between two columns. Just inside, hinges and splinters of wood lay on the floor, and Nime found herself appalled at the thought of someone destroying *this*. The entry led to a hallway that wrapped around the building, and directly across from it was yet another empty doorway. Stepping up to the opening, Nime lingered, hesitant to enter without the others behind her. But they were taking forever, or maybe the seconds that she spent there stretched out too long. Either way, Nime stepped through long before the others.

The room inside stole the breath from her lungs in two startling, opposing ways. The first: if Nime thought the gold of the roof was beautiful, it was only because she hadn't seen this room yet. Empty of furniture except for a long, low bench at the opposite end, set in front of windows that let in light despite the grime covering them, the room was more striking for its emptiness. The floor, bright white with gold running through like the veins and capillaries in her wrist, was on full display, but even miniature rivers of bright reddish-yellow didn't hold a candle to the walls and ceiling.

Words overlaid the walls, a language Nime couldn't decipher written in gold ink on every inch of space. The letters flowed together in an unbroken line, looping again and again around the circumference of the room. She wanted to brush her fingers over the words, to see if they were engraved in the walls or painted on. Something about them felt fragile and old, like the skin and bones of a dying person, like the paper of a thousand-year-old manuscript, like the dreams she sometimes had of memories she couldn't remember that burned away in daylight. And if she just touched the words, she would remember them all, all the moments that felt oddly familiar, the flashes of *almost* knowing. These words had always been in this stone, would always be. They had been formed together with the planet and would die with it. If these walls were a book, it was the autobiography of the universe, and if Nime could just touch it she would understand.

Chi gasped when she reached the doorway. Nime blinked, and her fingers trembled a hairsbreadth from the wall. All at once, her breath caught in her throat, and she scrambled backward, stumbling over the second reason this room stunned her.

The skull she tripped over cracked and crumbled, but Nime refused to fall over. If she fell over onto this floor, all the cleanser in the world wouldn't make her feel clean again. The brownish stains beneath the scattered skeletons of what looked like nearly twenty people made her skin cold. Most of them were near the low bench, though some, like the owner of the now-crushed skull, were nearer to the door. It seemed especially awful in this room, with these walls looking down at them.

Nime looked away from the bodies, away from the words that still begged to be touched, and turned to her friends as they stepped inside gingerly. It was as much reverence as it was avoidance of the bones, Nime thought. The weight of eons pressing down on her lifted, and she felt less like an atom in the face of the universe and more like herself. She shook her head. Thinking of the last couple of minutes was like walking through water and fog, so she stopped trying.

Chi took pictures of everything she could, focusing on the details of the walls and the stone bench at the front. The others explored the space as well, with mixed reactions toward the bones and the beauty. Sess seemed better now that the expanse of water over them wasn't so visibly present. Nime tried not to think about the walls, tried to listen to her footsteps sound against the floor and not the whispers that made her turn her head when no one was speaking to her.

"This was a temple of The Mothers," Chi said, and her voice seemed startlingly loud among the heavy, silent whispers of the walls, though Nime seemed to be the only one to feel that way. The whispers made her fuzzy and distant. She had to concentrate to block them out. Was this a symptom of too much stimulant? It didn't feel like any kind of confusion she'd had before. This felt like something different. A chill crawled down Nime's spine.

Rem was close to the walls, touching them like he didn't know they were living. He tilted his head and traced his fingers over one of the letters.

"I can't tell what this language is," he said, gesturing Chi over. She took a picture and then looked closer. "It's close to Old Zhumian in the characters and grammar. But the words and the syntax are almost completely different." Rem pointed to one section of writing; it flowed like water, like fire. "The location and length of this word suggest that it's a verb, but that's not a tense marker I'm familiar with."

"Let me see," Chi said, pausing to tap her lips. Her eyes were wide. "That tense is a rare form that was pretty much only used for poetry in the Sacred Valley of the Mothers. It's only ever mentioned in passing in the compendiums because it appears only a handful of times throughout the body of work."

"What tense is it, then?" Rem frowned curiously at her. How could he not tell, Nime wondered. Everything in this room *sang* it.

"Forever," Nime said. A whisper, but the two of them looked up at her like they'd forgotten she was there.

"Yeah, basically," Chi said, nodding. "It's sort of an eternal tense? I think the way the book described it was 'past, present, and future combined to form a sense of timelessness.' You only use it for truly important things, because it's associated with The Mothers, and you're basically comparing whatever it is with the universe. Always there, sort of separate from the dimension of time." Rem pursed his lips and nodded slowly. He opened his mouth to say something else, but Nime spoke first.

"We should move along," she said. The walls were getting to be too much for her. She needed to leave before they drew her in again, before the whispers became more insistent. The five of them avoided the bones that littered the floor with careful steps.

As Nime stepped through the doorway and turned down the hall, the pressure seemed to lift. The walls in the hall were nothing like the walls in the room, and Nime focused on the texture of them. Cool and smooth, and not alive. Farther down the hall, they reached a stairway and paused.

"Down," Nime said, though she couldn't have said why, and they followed her. The steps were worn away in the center from centuries of use. They ended in another hall, this one dark until the air was lit by five tablets. Art lined the walls: paintings that looked ancient and fragile, each of which focused on three people. They were different every time but always positioned similarly. The scenes looked familiar, oddly, and Nime's eyes kept focusing on details, ranging from the face of a person to the color of the trees, that she knew were wrong. The thoughts slipped into her mind from some deeper part she couldn't access if she tried. The nose was too flat, she was sure it had been longer than that, and the trees had just started to flower, not drop their leaves.

The dust their feet kicked up gathered in a cough in her throat that she swallowed back. The stimulants might have been a bad idea. How could Nime focus and be convincing if she was seeing things that weren't there? She stopped looking at the paintings. Her eyes kept trying to wander back to them whenever she wasn't paying attention, though.

She stopped at an open door, and Sess bumped into her from behind. This was what they were looking for. Books filled the shelves, and Nime wondered how they'd lasted so long unprotected. Maybe they were made of the same material the books in Haven were. Once Chi and Rem saw what was inside, they stepped around her to get a look. Lights came on along the ceiling as they walked in, diffused by hundreds of years of dust.

The five of them drifted through the room, looking at the books in awe. Nime took a moment to breathe and compose herself. She didn't need to be there long, just long enough to find something that would convince Nadra, the rest of the Board, and everyone else in Haven to come down to this previously unknown settlement filled with skeletons. Easy.

Then she checked the status of her scan. It was finished already, and showed low air quality and high potential allergen count, but no other warnings. She started another scan.

Nime looked around the room at her friends, caught up in the thrill of new information. Miel stood holding an encyclopedia, his eyes narrowed in concentration as he read. Sess sat at one of two consoles—thicker than a tablet, thinner than the side of Nime's hand—but he was examining the system, not the data. Chi knelt, wide-eyed, on the floor, pulling books off a low shelf. Most of them were old and thick, though some were smaller, probably printed not long before the Fall. She held her tablet on her lap, making notes as she read. Rem moved slowly around the room, reading every title, occasionally stopping to pull one out and take a peek inside. His mouth moved as he translated silently.

Nime almost reminded them that they were looking for specific proof, not exploring for the fun of it. She almost forgot that she wanted them there as long as possible, preferably until Haven was safe again. She didn't say anything.

She made her way over to a table in the middle, the one next to Sess. The chairs looked sturdy enough, so she sat on the edge of one and wiped away a streak of dust on the console's screen with the sleeve of her sweater. The sweat that had built up in the armpits brushed against her skin. She took it off. It was infinitely cooler even in her thermals, and she breathed a sigh she hadn't known was building.

Sess looked over at her. "Everything is so different here," he said.

"It's exciting, isn't it?" Chi said from her spot on the floor. "The bodies were a bit…alarming, but look at how much knowledge is here!" Miel turned his head slightly toward them and glanced up.

"I'll admit, this is going to make a great offering for Nytherial," he said. "I owe you one for convincing me to come down here, Ni. If there's any way I can repay you—" his voice, now low, trailed off, and he raised his eyebrows at her.

Rem, passing the shelves behind Miel, flicked the back of his head. "Idiot," Rem said. Chi erupted into laughter as Miel held the back of his head and glared at Rem. Nime snorted.

The console was different from her tablet, but the technology was somewhat similar. She tapped around on the screen for a moment trying to find a menu, and eventually sliding sideways brought one up. Icons stretched across the screen in a line: the symbol for memory, a book, and a multitool being the only ones Nime recognized. She tapped on the book, and it opened into the interface for the Dome's digital archive. She licked her lips and leaned in before moving further. The prospect of being the first person to set eyes on this information for hundreds of years set her heart racing. She tapped through the archive, skimming entries that caught her eye and moving onto new ones. She found an entire subsection that Chi would die for, another full of the Architects' plans for Haven and their other works. She stumbled upon a copy of one of the Architect's notes, including side by side, original plans for Haven and the Dome, detailed down to the location coordinates. She downloaded it to her tablet.

"I found a map," Sess said, and Nime closed the document. She leaned over into Sess' space and looked at his console.

An image filled the screen, a picture of the Dome from an isometric view. Grass and trees filled in the edges, climbing up the sides of mountains that ringed the area. Fields of crops and animals surrounded the settlement.

It didn't look like it was meant to be a map, more like a record, but when Sess tapped on the golden, domed roof of what could only be the building they were in, a side window opened with information about it.

"Temple of the Mother Creator," Nime read. "Capacity: 300, occupants: 15." Below that were the numbers of people per occupation, she guessed, followed by power, water, and food usage. Priestesses: 9. Custodians: 1. Historians: 3. Hand: 1. Unlif: 1.

Hand? Unlif? The others all made sense, but the last one wasn't even a word, was it? When Nime thought about it for more than a second, her head ached. She reached over Sess and tapped on 'Unlif.'

"I was wondering about that, too," he said. Another side window opened with an image of a young woman. She was dark-haired and very pale, and her empty eyes stared straight into the camera. Nime quickly tapped open her details to cover her face. Nia, female, aged twenty. It didn't say much else, and Nime straightened up with a frown. Shouldn't there have been more records than that about her? Maybe the records were restricted? Chi walked up, and Nime jumped.

"Do you know what 'Unlif' means?" Nime asked. The word felt familiar in her mouth. Chi narrowed her eyes and crossed her arms. She took a second to think and shook her head.

"I can't think of anything, no." Chi reached over and reopened the temple information. "Though if she's listed under the temple, then it has to be something religious," she continued.

"As wonderful as this treasure trove of information is," Miel said as he walked up with Rem, "we do need to get back if we want to present this for Nytherial's day. Also, the heat is kind of killing me, so maybe we should wait to come back until the temperature regulation is working again?" Sess nodded in support. Chi pouted, but she was sweating too. Nime looked at the screen and pressed her lips together, debating whether to tell them about the leak. With at least two completed environmental scans, Chi's pictures, and the map, she had what she needed. All she had to do was convince Haven, and everyone would be safe. And her friends didn't need to be exposed to any more Potential. She could go alone.

Nime told them. It didn't go as well as she'd hoped.

"We can't even use Potential anymore. There's no way Haven is powered by some magical death ray," Miel said after, shaking his head.

He frowned and crossed his arms. Nime didn't respond.

"Well, we do, though." Sess' words were quiet, and everyone turned to look at him. "Most of our systems are designed to run on it. We have sensors built into our tablets, but the software to run them was left out of the most recent OS update." He paused. "I have a partition with an older OS installed. A few days ago, I kept getting alerts about fluctuations in local Potential levels, but I assumed they were errors and didn't think it was important." Miel's face dropped, and for a moment, his fear was obvious before he masked it.

"You didn't think that was important?" Miel's voice was sarcastic.

"Don't be angry at him," Nime said, cutting him off, just as harsh. "Be angry at my mother and the Board."

"And why didn't *you* tell everyone?" Miel shifted his glare to her.

"You think anyone would have believed me over the Advisory Board? With my reputation? You don't even believe me." Nime glared right back but softened. "And I didn't want you all to have that hanging over you. I wanted to find a way to fix it before I told anyone." Miel turned and stalked a few steps away.

Chi looked between Miel and Nime, an uncharacteristic frown on her face. "I guess you succeeded, then, as long as there's nothing deadly down here anymore." She glanced away. "If I'd known, I would have brought my family."

"There's still time, Chi," Nime said. "We have a few more days, at least. And it'll be okay because I'll go back up and convince them to come down here. Everyone will be fine."

"And you're planning to do it by yourself again and leave us down here?" Rem said. "No, we all need to go back up and present what we've found." Nime wanted to protest, to tell him that they all needed to stay safe, but she was already in cold water with them. And, as much as she hated to admit it, having others to back her up would be helpful. Rem shook his head. "That explains all the illnesses. I think a few days might be an overestimation."

Nime was last in the group as they headed back up the stairs. This time when they passed the main room, no one went in. Nime's head turned toward it as they walked, and Chi caught her eye. She looked concerned. Nime blinked and gave her a small smile. Her discomfort was equal parts the constant, heavy whispers; the worry that sat in her stomach; and too little sleep. The stimulants might've been what was causing her hallucinations, but it was too late to stop now. She shook her head when Chi looked away and took another stimulant. Rem whipped his head around to look at her when she bit it, but only narrowed his eyes at her. Nime let out a breath.

9

Nime's not at home when I wake up, and neither is Mom. I sit at the table and rub my eyes. I haven't seen my whole family in one place for what feels like a long time. Dad leaves too, not long after I wake up. He comes rushing out of his room.

"Good morning," I say as he slides on his shoes. He stops for a second and comes over to kiss the top of my head before going back to the door.

"Sunshine," he says. "I'm sorry to leave you all alone today, but I need to head over to Sanitation as soon as possible. Seia-nin is in the clinic with her son. Mos, you remember? He's in Foundations." I lift my head. He's just a toddler. Dad answers my question before I can ask it. "He's sick with something, they don't know what. I need to cover for her today."

My eyes widen. First the bees, now babies? I thought we'd have a little more time. Dad leaves, and the door slides shut behind him before I can say anything else.

And I'm alone. I pull my tablet closer and check the time. I need to be at the square before midday for the festival, but that still leaves a lot of time to worry and for the fish in my stomach to nibble at me. They don't seem to like my decision to tell the big secret.

I press my forehead into the table and close my eyes. I wonder where Nime went; I don't want to be alone with myself and these fish. I stand up and slide on my shoes. This restlessness won't go away just sitting here.

Outside, wispy clouds cast their shadows on the walkways. Between them, bright sky peeks through. Prime sits half over the horizon. I pass several people standing close and sharing their secrets with each other on my walk. And as nervous as I am about what I have to do, it's a relief to be bringing the truth to light on Nytherial's day. It feels right.

The Clinic seems oddly busy when I get close to it. As someone leaves and the door slides open, I see into the waiting room. Dozens of people sit on the couches and chairs, about half of them pale and miserable looking. I swallow, and it sticks in the back of my throat. This needs to be fixed as quickly as possible.

And what if it's not possible?

I don't think I can handle talking to another person now, so I keep well away from the square, circling around to the back of Botanics. The entrance here is much less used than the one that opens into the square, and I can slip in unnoticed. My feet start toward the apiary before I remember. I squeeze my eyes shut for a second. They water anyway.

Sticking to the back areas, I find a space hidden by tall hydroponic tanks full of bean plants and sit down with my back to one. My tablet beeps at me. Half an hour until I need to be at the square. The tank I'm leaning against is hard, but I lay my head back and look up to the glass ceiling. The lights are on, blue and red making a purple glow above the plants. A leaf sticks out above my face. I touch it gently with one finger. It's an older leaf, dark green and strong. Everything seems still around me, like I'm in a bubble, just me and the leaf and the memory of dead bees.

It feels like my head is underwater. Suddenly, the truth of what is relying on *me* climbs up out of my stomach and sticks in my throat. If I don't say it right, if no one believes me or I can't get it out, they won't know. They won't know that we could all die. Every person in the clinic right now could die. Even if Nime, or someone else, is trying to solve this problem, there's a too-real possibility that they can't. That there's too little time left, that there truly is no solution. I don't know what to do about that, but I do know that people need to know, that the more people know about it, the more chances we have.

And it's up to me to tell them, to tell Haven about what's happening. No one else is going to do it. Not Nime, not Mom. No one.

I name every color I can think of, holding them in my mind. I take deep breaths. After a few minutes that feel like hours, I lift my head and stand up. I sniff until my nose is clear enough to breathe, and I wipe my face. I can do this. I have to do this.

It feels like everyone is looking at me as I walk to the square. It's full of people, happy and unaware. That light pink feeling from yesterday is still floating around on the air, but I can't catch it anymore. The paths are lined with tents and old booths that are starting to get a little worn at the edges and seams. I see a few people setting up a machine in one of them, something about the size of my head. I wonder if the exhibition will go on after I tell them. I chew on my lip. It seems unfair. They probably worked hard on their offering, and it might not ever be useful. I keep walking.

Midra-nin is preparing in our class tent, and she nods at me. I slip into the tent where I'm supposed to change. Now that I'm not walking, the restlessness returns. I pace, three steps back and forth, until Ibbi-nin comes to help me dress.

"You'll be fine, Navi," she says before leaving. I barely hear it. All I can pay attention to is my heart in my throat and the ever-closer sound of the bell. There're only a few minutes left before I step out there, and the festival truly begins.

I hug myself and my nails press into my bare arms. What if I say it all wrong and everyone thinks I'm just some stupid kid trying to play a prank? Or—

What if I tell them and it doesn't help? What if no one wants to know? I breathe in sharply. That's not something I thought about. Would I want to know? If I had a choice? The mask clings to the skin of my face, and I can't breathe. I shake my head. I don't know. I don't know.

Breathe in and out. Like normal. My breath comes out in audible puffs, but I breathe. It doesn't matter if I would want to know or not. I think I probably wouldn't. But I can't make that decision for Haven. It's wrong to keep knowledge from others, no matter how sad that knowledge is. It's always better to have more information, isn't it?

This is going to ruin the festival. Maybe it shouldn't matter, but it does to everyone in Haven. If we're going to die anyway, I don't want to ruin the last Nytherial's day we'll have.

But I have to do this. It's the right thing to do.

The bell rings.

"Navi, are you ready?" Midra-nin asks. "It's time." I blink. Okay. I can do this. I have to. I leave my little dressing room and stand on the platform. Most of Haven is standing in front of me, waiting for the blessing, and all I can hear is a whooshing like the sea. I'm not ready for this.

The bell fades. I have to do it now. Right now, when everyone I've ever known is looking at me and paying attention to me and I'm still Nytherial. But I open my mouth and nothing comes out. I swallow. My head feels floaty and cold. For a few seconds, I stand there. Everything is silent except a ringing in my ears.

I see movement out of the corner of my eye. Midra-nin motions with her hands and mouths my lines. I stutter a few times before saying them. My voice is shaky, though I can barely hear it. There's a pause where I'm supposed to move to a new spot. I can't remember where it was though, and I can't see anything but the crowd. Habit carries me, keeps me speaking even though I feel like I can't breathe.

Say it, say it, say it. I bite down on the inside of my cheek and remind myself of why I need to do this. But my next line is coming up, and it comes out of my mouth instead. It feels like someone else is speaking, like I'm dreaming. I squeeze my hands into fists and let my nails dig into my palms. Why am I not saying it? There's not much time left; this line is my last one. Come on, Navi, just say it!

"Today there will be no secret left hidden, no lie undiscovered, and no truth left unsaid," I say.

That's it. That's all I say. And then I stand before the crowd for another moment, trying to make the words come out. But all I do is open and close my mouth in silence, while all of Haven watches, until the musicians start playing and everyone turns their attention to them and each other. My mouth is dry. I shut it. A tear slides down my face, trapped by the mask. Midra-nin pats me on the shoulder.

"You did fine, Navi, don't worry," she says. I don't say anything back. Fine? I did fine? No, I didn't. I failed. That was my chance to tell everyone, and have them maybe believe me, and I ruined it. I just stood there like an idiot. More tears. I wipe my chin where they collect. Why couldn't I do it?

"Can I just—" I walk toward my changing tent and trail off. Midra-nin nods and waits nearby. I should change back into my own clothes. I don't deserve to be dressed as Nytherial. Not when I can't tell as important a truth as this. Inside, I sit on the little chair, cross my arms, and lean forward. I stare at the ground, but I don't see the lite-crete blocks. I just see myself all over again, right at the moment when I should have spoken, the moment when I didn't. What is wrong with me?

I close my eyes and cover my face with my hands. The mask slips off and lands on the ground next to the lantern. I already know what's wrong with me. I'm too scared.

"Navi?" Midra-nin's voice makes me lift my head. I wipe my eyes, but I know I look like I've been crying. She doesn't come in, though. "Are you alright? You only need to act as Nytherial for another hour or so, and then you can enjoy the festival." I lower my head back down to my knees.

There's no way I can go out there and talk to the people I'm lying to. The people I just let down. They might not know I let them down, but that makes it worse. I clear my throat. Midra-nin must take that as an answer because I hear her take a step away. I can't face them. I'm still too scared. I'm always scared.

I stand up and peek out. Midra-nin's standing with her back to my tent, several feet away. If I go out there, she's going to make me talk to people, and I'm not going to be able to say no because I'm a weak, scared, spineless person.

Nime could say no. Nime could have told the truth. She's brave enough. I sit down again.

I wish I were more like Nime. Then I wouldn't *still* be waiting for someone else to save me. I would do it myself. Or at least, that's what normal Nime would do. It's hard for me to believe what I heard yesterday. And Nime hasn't exactly told anyone either, as far as I can tell. I sigh. My feet tap. I can't take this waiting around anymore. My stomach is in knots, and my head hurts, and all I want is for this whole thing to be over. I want to wake up to a world where there is no

Potential leak, no giant important secrets, and no ocean's worth of pressure weighing on me.

But that's not going to happen. If I want this to stop, *I* need to do something about it. My skin tingles. Thinking about that makes the world spin a little. I lift the back wall of my tent and look out. It faces away from the rest of the festival, and no one is in sight. I chew my lip. If I sneak away, I won't have to talk to anyone. The festival is between me and home, but I could hide in the library for a while. I crawl out the back of my tent and start moving toward the Academy. I glance back over my shoulder. No one seems to have noticed. I rub my arms and keep walking.

I was so close out there. I was so close to truly doing something about it, but I didn't. All I needed was to be braver. Me being too scared to do something isn't a new feeling, but for the first time, I want to change. Because as I am now, I'll never be able to do anything or help anyone. And I don't know if that's just a flaw in the way I am, if it's something that can't be changed. I don't think it is. So many people around me are strong and brave. Mom, Dad, Nime. Is it something in their DNA? Or something they became over time? I can't remember a time when Nime wasn't brave.

If bravery is something I can learn, then maybe I could do something. I wasn't strong enough to tell everyone about the leak, but maybe next time I get the opportunity, I will be. I shiver. My thermals are with the rest of my clothes in the tent. No going back now. I'll just have to be cold until I can handle being around other people.

Maybe someday I can even become strong enough to not be selfish anymore.

* * *

I open the door to the Academy, silent and empty, and take the stairs down to B1. The reading room just off the stairwell is dark when I walk in, and I leave it that way. I pick a plush chair, the white fabric thinning on the seat, and sit. I pull my knees up to my chest and hug them. My shoes stay on the floor, and I curl my toes under.

What do brave people do? I picture Nime.

Brave people help the ones they love even if they'll get in trouble for it. Brave people don't second guess themselves; they act. Brave people do the things that other people are too scared to do.

I'm not brave or strong. But I think I could be someday. Loving people means you have to do hard things for them, even when you're too scared to move. I press my forehead into my knees. I love everyone in Haven. I do. And because I do, I want to save them. So I have to be brave enough. It's settled. I lift my head and let my feet fall back to the floor.

The next time I can be brave for the people I love, I will. I can't run out into the middle of the festival and say it, but I will find a way to tell them. I breathe out all at once through my nose and stand up. No more hiding. I cry a little again, but in a good way this time. I can do it. Maybe I'll go to the clinic and talk to Remy, or one of the physicians. They already know that people are getting sick, and Haven will believe them more than me.

I head for the stairs, looking down at my feet. I only see a pair of shoes right before I run into whoever they belong to.

"I'm so sorry," I say. I wipe my eyes and look up. And forget to breathe. I bumped into Ira-nin. Celestial Wardens, I'm crying and dressed as Nytherial and barefoot, and I bumped into Ira-nin. What is he even doing here? He frowns, and I barely have a chance to apologize again before he stops and starts to smile. Or maybe he doesn't? His hand comes up to straighten his glasses and when it comes back down he just looks concerned. But I could swear that his lips twitched a little. I probably do look ridiculous right now. At least he's being nice about it.

"Are you alright, Navi?" he asks. He rests a hand on my shoulder as he tilts his head down. I blink. His hand is truly cold, even against my already cold skin. My heart beats faster anyway.

"Me?" Right, I was just crying. I sniff. "I'm fine. Sorry for running into you." Good. That was normal enough. Ira-nin just smiles that wonderful smile, and I feel like I'm melting. My eyes are stretched wide.

"Were you worrying about the Potential leak?" he asks, and for a second, I don't know what to say.

"How did you know?" I ask.

"Nime has been working on something that I think you should see." He turns around and starts down the stairs. "Follow me." I follow. If

Nime has a solution, maybe, despite my failure earlier, things will be fine. Ira-nin looks at me over his shoulder. "Your blessing today was well done." I almost miss a step, but the railing saves me from an early and embarrassing death. I clear my throat.

"Um," is all I can think to say for a minute. I concentrate on not knocking both of us down the stairs. "Thank you, but it was the same as always." I scrunch my face up and my eyes closed. Stupid. It's a good thing he can't see me. I relax my face as he turns his head again.

"But you're not always Nytherial," he says. "How can it be the same?" My entire head might be on fire. I think this is the first actual, non-math conversation I've ever had with him, and I know this is the first time he's ever truly paid attention to me. Don't be weird, Navi.

"I guess," I say. We both stop talking after that, and I bite the inside of my cheek. What happened to not being weird? The sound of two pairs of footsteps echo. That's how I can tell we're almost to B4. It's so lonely down here.

At the bottom of the stairs, Ira-nin stops and tilts his head down the hallway. It's wide enough that we can walk next to each other. I try to keep up with his much longer legs. What a time to have shaky knees. I sneak a look at him out of the corner of my eye, but I only get a glimpse of the side of his head—his hair covers his ears, and it's a shiny, deep brown. If I were painting it, I'd go pretty heavy on the red. And it's not exactly curly but more tousled—before he turns to look at me, and I look forward again. I blink a few times and act natural. If only natural Navi weren't so uncomfortable all the time. My stomach is twisting into itself.

"Come in," Ira-nin says as he walks into his office. The last time I came down here, it seemed like he was telling Nime it wasn't worth trying to fix the leak. I frown. Maybe I misunderstood. He seems to care about it now. He holds the door open for me, and I step in. I look around. It's a mess. There's a broken lamp in a corner, and a shelf of books, but the spines all look bent and cracked. Some are even missing. My eyes widen, and I can't help grimacing. That's a horrible way to treat books. And then there's the huge machine in the middle of the room with grease around it. The door slides closed, and I stop short. My heart gets caught in my throat. I swallow.

"What—" I say. Ira-nin steps around me and stands next to me. He's so close my elbow brushes his arm, and I pull it in close to myself, across my stomach. I can feel cold radiating from him, like the opposite of body heat. I shiver.

I clear my throat and try again. "What is that?" I glance over at him and then nod toward the machine. Ira pushes up his glasses and doesn't smile. He's going to, I'm sure this time, but then he doesn't.

"That is what I wanted to show you," he says. "You're worried about the leak, right?" I nod slowly, but he doesn't wait to continue. "Nime has been working on fixing this old transporter."

"Where does it go?" I ask. A transporter? But there's nothing else on the Endless Sea, that's why it's called the Endless Sea.

"It goes to a settlement on land." Ira-nin lets the smile out this time, but it's sort of sharp, like a shark's smile. I look down at my feet to get away from his eyes. Land. Is that possible? Land means dirt. Plants. Animals. Space to spread out and live. "I went there, to see if it was safe," he continues. I look back up. He looks normal again, and I'm not sure if the look on his face was real or if I'm seeing things. It wouldn't surprise me if I was.

"Is it?" Land means someplace we can go without worrying about being poisoned. Ira-nin rubs the back of his neck and looks away. He presses his lips together.

"Yes," he says, glancing at me and then away. Is this supposed to be a secret too? I don't think I can handle any more. "It is safe, but the trouble is getting people to believe it. It's improbable; of course everyone will be skeptical." He shakes his head and frowns. "It's too bad. More and more people will continue to get sick as they wait for confirmation. We just need to convince everyone that it's safe there, and quickly." He flops down onto his couch and rests his head in his hands, his arms on his knees. He looks so sad. My heart squeezes. And he's right, every hour we spend here is hurting everyone. I stand there with my arms around my stomach. This is an opportunity to help everyone, to make up for my earlier selfishness. I chew my lip and think.

"If more people went there, that would help, right? The more people who can say they've seen it the better?" I say. Ira-nin lifts his head and nods.

"The problem is finding people who are willing to go to an unknown place to prove it's safe." He sighs. "And who would be willing to do that?"

"Um, well, your students," I say. My hands press tight into my sides. "Remy, uh, Nyrem would, and Chiri and Miel and Sess." I pause and take a deep breath. "And me." At that, Ira-nin looks at me again. He's frowning. I shrink a little.

"You? I suppose that would help. You are Haven's darling, after all," he says, and there's almost something hard about the way he says it, like the frame of a bed underneath the padding. Me? I'm not anything special.

Ira-nin stands up, and I take a step back so I can see him properly. "But this is something you should leave to adults, Navi." I look down and nod, even though I don't agree. If it's safe, there's no reason I couldn't go there. And if it would help, I'd be willing. I chew my lip. Ira-nin walks over to the door and opens it. "Don't worry too much about it. I'm sure in the next few days everyone will be convinced, and we'll all move down there before too many people die."

Ira-nin nods toward the door, and I guess that means I have to leave. I look back at the transporter before heading out. Even one person dying is too many. We walk in silence back to the stairwell. If I could get back into his office and use it, I could be brave for once. And this is something that Nime would do, something that would help. At the stairwell, Ira-nin puts his hand on my shoulder again, and it feels heavier this time. Or maybe it's just me feeling weak and faint again.

"Head back up," he says. His voice is soft, and I nod. "Enjoy the festival, and don't worry so much. It'll be fine." He smiles at me, and I feel my face heat. I nod again and start up the stairs. After a second, I look back. He's not heading back to his office; he's going down the short side hallway to the bathroom. I hold my breath for a second. Will I have a chance like this again? I look between the bathroom and his office. I chew my lip. And then I stop thinking and hurry back down the hallway. I glance behind me as I walk, and then look at the nameplates next to each door. I stop in front of his door and touch the handle. He wouldn't have locked it, would he?

It slides open, and I slip inside and close it behind me. I pause for a second. Now that I'm here, I realize that I didn't think about what comes next. Does Nime normally think about what comes next? How do I even use this thing? I step close to the transporter and look all over it. It'll use a tablet as the interface, like everything else, right? I pull mine out and wake it up. It connects right away, already set to transport to someplace called "Dome Transporter 1." Well. That was easy.

I chew my lip for a second before holding my breath and stepping up onto the platform. I have to be brave like Nime. I can't let the sick feeling in my stomach or the fear holding tight to my heart keep me from helping the people I love. I can't, not anymore. I press the big button labeled "Transport," and close my eyes.

It's dizzy and spinning, and I feel lost in the void until the world reforms around me. I squeeze my eyes shut for a second until I stop feeling like I'm going to be sick. When I open them, I can't see anything, and for a second all my worst fears have come true: I got stuck in some in-between space where it's just me and nothingness, alone forever and ever. But there is light in here, and I notice it when I stop panicking.

I walk toward it, the rectangle of brightness, and then stop when I get close enough to smell. I press my hand to my nose and mouth. My eyes water. I need to get out into air and light, away from this awful, dead smell. I pretend I'm Nime. She would run through to get what she wants. I harden myself.

Pressing my hand harder to my face, I run through. I try not to look but I can see as I get close that the wall is covered in some kind of fungus, and that's what's making the smell. It coats me like mist as I pass through and out into the world. When I'm far enough away I bend over and throw up. I try not to look at that, either. A wave of dizziness washes over me. I wipe my eyes and my mouth and look around.

Everything is gray, like Haven. My heart sinks. This place is even worse. At least in Haven, we have the constantly-changing Endless Sea and plants and people. It feels so empty here, so lifeless. But it's land. I touch some of the dry dirt by my feet as I wander down the street. It's supposed to be full of life. This is just dust. It sticks in the air. At least it doesn't smell like dead things out here. There's no breeze, so every time I breathe, it's still and stagnant. The light gives an orange tint to everything: the building I came out of, the dead bushes along the street, the stones that stick out of it. The bones.

I freeze. Tears build up in my eyes until I can't see properly. Bones? All I can hear is myself breathing, and it sounds loud and harsh and fast. I blink. All of those beige, brittle things all over the ground are bones.

I don't want to be here anymore.

I tilt my head up to keep the tears from falling. The sky above me is black except for what looks like the sun, right in the middle. This place feels so wrong. It shouldn't be like this.

The last time I was here it wasn't under a dome. The valley was green and living then; it's against its nature to be brown and dead and dried up like this.

I stop. Where did that thought come from? I didn't know this place existed until about five minutes ago.

Or maybe I have been here, or at least, another me has. That's when it was green, and Aht Carina not covered by the Endless Sea. Yes, I'm sure of it, the Navi from the tower in the city came here with my cyborg and—

I came and—

I turn around and look for the building I came out of. I can't live down here, I can't. I know death waits above but it doesn't *feel* like it. Not the way the very air does down here. What was I even thinking, coming here? How is that going to prove it's safe? I don't realize I'm running until I skid to a stop in front of Ira-nin.

10

By the time Nime and the others made it back to the transporter building, all of them were sweating and layered with a thin coating of dust. Nime carried a bundle of sweaters, and the five of them looked like a matched set in their gray thermals. All of those warm-weather clothes in storage were going to make a comeback, Nime thought. Even without the other layers, she was still warm, and Miel fanned his flushed face with his hands.

"I'm ready to go back into real sunlight," Chi said, stretching and grabbing her sweater from the pile in Nime's arms.

Rem snorted. "You mean real lack-of-sunlight?" he said.

"It's better than this broken thing." Chi gestured vaguely at the artificial sun. It flickered again, as if to prove her point. "I would not have wanted to live down here instead of Haven." Nime looked away.

"I agree," Sess said with his face safely angled down. Nime looked further away.

"But it's land," Nime said. It came out quiet. "And, more importantly, it's safe."

Chi tilted her head to one side. "This will still be here, now that we have the transporter. If I want to stand on solid ground, I can, and people who like it better down here can live down here."

Nime nodded and stepped over the fallen door and into the darkness. She held her breath against the smell. Without the pressure of imminent death over their heads, the engineers could work on repairing the seal. It might take a while, but now they had time. The others followed her, gagging as they passed through the doorway. The stench faded as they got closer to the transporter.

Stepping onto the platform, Nime connected her tablet and waited for Haven to show up as an available location. It was taking a little longer than normal to connect. Even after all of them stepped onto the platform, it was still attempting. Nime's fingers tightened on the tablet. It had to work. Navi was still up there; it had to work.

"Come on, Ni, it's a bit tight," Rem said, and someone poked her in the arm.

"Hold on, it's connecting," Nime said. She scowled down at her tablet. "Work already." Shaking the tablet a bit, she refreshed the connection. Sess pulled out his tablet and attempted to connect. "Okay, mine's not working," Nime said and shoved hers back into her bag. The other three tried their own tablets.

Sess frowned and tapped around on his screen. Nime peeped over Rem's shoulder. His was still trying to connect as well. The loading symbol spun endlessly on screen.

"Anyone get a connection?" Miel asked, shutting off his screen. "I can't." Everyone shook their head. Nime's stomach sank. Sess was still frowning and tapping at his tablet.

Sess was always quiet, but the quiet that came from him now felt loaded instead of peaceful. He stopped tapping and lowered his tablet. His eyes darted between the others. Nime straightened.

"There, uh, there aren't any other transporters online right now." His voice was quiet, as was the moment of silence after he spoke, but then a cacophony of voices erupted.

"What do you mean there aren't any other transporters online?" Rem asked, his arms crossed over his chest.

"Just try again! Maybe there was a power outage." Chi sounded the most hopeful of the three, but her voice had an edge to it.

"Warden of Death, take me now. We're going to be stuck here forever." Miel was as dramatic as always, but at least this time it seemed justified. The noise and panic made Nime clench her fists, but she pressed her lips together to keep from saying anything. She stepped off the platform and faced the others.

"Calm down," she said, loudly enough that all heads turned in her direction, and the noise lulled for a moment.

Rem glared at her. "Calm down?" he said, his tone sharp. "We have no idea what's going on up there. Was there a storm? Did the transporter break somehow? Is everyone dead from a sudden spike in the Potential you didn't tell us about? We don't know. I think we have a right to not be calm." By the end of his speech, his voice was less sharp and more watery. He clenched his jaw and stalked off of the platform to stand a little ways away.

"Most of those are unlikely, which you would realize if you *calmed down*," she said to his back. Nime couldn't keep her annoyance out of her tone. "The transporter is old. The power's probably a little faulty. I'm sure we can just message Ira and have him turn it back on."

A throat cleared from near the doorway. They turned and looked at the source of the noise, and several sets of shoulders slumped.

"That's unfortunately not possible at this point," Ira called, rubbing the back of his neck. He stood a few feet outside the doorway, a little close to the plants for Nime's taste. As she led the others back out of the building, a coppery head peeked out from behind Ira, and Nime felt like a weight had been removed.

"Hi, Ni," Navi said.

* * *

Nime doesn't look as upset as I thought she'd be when everyone gets far enough away from the fungus to breathe. She looks between me and Ira-nin.

"What are you two doing here?" she asks. I hold onto her arm. The dizziness is gone now that she's here, but this place is still wrong. She helps with that, too.

"I wanted—" I start to say, but Ira-nin interrupts.

"Navi came down, and I followed to try to bring her back." He's calm when everyone else is panicking. Remy scowls and starts pacing. I clutch Nime's arm tighter. "So I'm afraid I won't be able to help with the transporter," Ira continues.

"Who else knows about it?" Remy asks.

"No one," Nime says. My stomach drops.

"So we're stuck down here," Miel says.

"It certainly seems so," Ira-nin says. Nime glances at him and then away. His mouth twitches with a hint of a laugh. He has a *weird* sense of humor.

***

Nime wanted to pace, but Navi clung tightly to her arm, so instead she squeezed and un-squeezed her fist. Navi seemed unsettled down there, in a different way than Sess. Her skin was pale, and she was clingy in the way she normally was when she was sick or anxious.

"The problem is that Haven's network doesn't extend this far," she said. "Even if Ira was up there, we wouldn't have been able to reach him. But if people were previously able to send messages between the Dome and Haven, we know that the networks used to connect."

"It's possible that without any maintenance for 200 years, the network base station here may have gotten disconnected from the power," Sess said. "Or the transceiver may need maintenance, or—" he shrugged. "Any number of things could be preventing us from getting a signal to Haven. But if we can get the base station up and running again, we should be able to send a message to someone," Sess said, and his quiet calm did what Nime couldn't: settled everyone down.

Chi looked between him and Nime. "Can you two fix it?" she asked.

"Nime can fix anything," Navi said from her place clinging to Nime's arm. "And Sess, too, of course," she continued, sheepish. Sess just smiled at her.

"I'll certainly do my best," he said. "If the tech is the same here as it is in Haven, the base station is designed to be durable and fool-proof."

"Don't worry, it'll be easy," Nime said, patting Navi on the back. "And we'll be home in no time."

***

I follow Nime and the others to a temple to look at a map. As we walk, I remember these streets. I grew up here. When I blink, I can almost see the way it was, stone roads lined with people, flowers in the air and their hair, cheering for me.

And then reality returns, and my stomach twists. I don't want to be stuck down here. The sick feeling I had earlier is mostly gone now, but I still hold on tight to Nime. She's like a raft in the middle of the Endless Sea. I try not to look around too much as we walk; I don't want to see the skeletons.

As we draw closer to the temple, I can't avoid looking anymore. It's huge, and it's all I can see. I look up. And up. It's tall and dilapidated and dirty, but I can tell it was a temple. It feels sacred, so much so that I slow my steps. It's beautiful, the most beautiful building I've ever seen. Not that it had much competition; the gray on gray on gray color scheme of Haven may be home, but I can't help but want to paint everything over. This, though, is perfect.

I take a step onto the stairs and press a hand to my chest. All of my breath rushes out at once. I know this place better than anything. I know this place better than myself. My heart beats so fast I'm afraid it might jump out. I've been here before.

Remy stops a few steps ahead of us. "If you think this is beautiful, wait until you get inside," he says, and he smiles at me. I smile back, and it doesn't feel like a lie. My stomach doesn't hurt anymore. I skip up the last few steps. This is home.

The door is broken, and I frown. Who would destroy the temple? Across a hall, I see the inside that Remy was talking about, full of light and sound, like whispers. I want to hear what they have to say. I walk toward it, but Nime guides me past it with her arm around my shoulders. I look back, and Remy and Chi are both glancing between Nime and the room. Ira-nin is already going down a set of stairs, and Sess and Miel are a few steps behind. Nime stops and turns halfway to face them. I lean over to peek into the room. It pulls my gaze like a magnet.

"Let's go, there's nothing useful in there," Nime says and walks on. I follow. I don't want to be left behind. She leads the way to a room full of books, and I stop just inside the doorway. I've never seen so many manuscripts in my life. I know they exist in the archive, but I'm not allowed in the manuscript storage. Only those people trained in the proper way to handle such delicate materials are. All the other books in Haven are made of treated paper, sturdier than the pre-Fall material.

Nime, Sess, and Ira start searching the consoles for information about a network base station. I wander over to one of the shelves and run my fingers over the books. They come away dusty. There's a dreamlike quality to the thick, still air. My feet take me to another shelf. These books have uniform red spines with black lettering, but there's one thin book among them that draws my eye. I touch it gently. I want to open it, but who knows how old these are? I don't know what to do with something so fragile. I look around. The others are handling them carefully. I look back at the book's spot on the shelf, but there's only an empty space.

The book is in my hands when I look down. Opening it is familiar. My hands remember holding this tightly to my chest, pulling it out from beneath my pillow and taking a pen to clean pages.

I open it to a page near the front. And I blink. It's an astronomical diagram, sketched without tools. My pen wobbled when I drew it, my hands shaking. Our Mothers, the moons, in opposition after a century. I run my fingers over it. The paper is soft. There are words below the diagram, and even though I can see my hand—not this one I have now; then they were as pale as Miel and thin—writing them, I can't remember what they say. But it's my birthday. At least it was. One of the Mothers is in pieces now.

That thought breaks through whatever focus I had, and I close the book. These thoughts are truly out of hand. I didn't draw that, and I wasn't born under the Opposing Mothers, because we have three moons, not two, and we don't call them that. I take deep breaths as I look around. Chi and Remy are standing close to each other, reading from the same book and arguing, while Miel leans against a shelf behind them. Nime and Sess are still at a console, and Ira-nin is—I turn my head and stretch my neck to see around the corner of the aisle. He's somewhere around here, probably. I chew my lip and open the book again. The diagram and its caption are the only things on the page, but when I turn it, there are unfamiliar words on the opposite side. I'm still learning the old languages, and this is one I don't know yet. I breathe out through my nose.

Remy should know how to read it. I tuck the book under my arm, next to my side. Neither he nor Chi looks up when I walk up to them.

"Remy?" I whisper. He lifts his head and so does Chi. Miel looks at me but doesn't move. I swallow and look between them. With the right page open, I stick out the book in Remy's direction. "Can you tell me what this says?" Remy passes his book, filled with what look like topographical maps, off to Chi, who closes it and sets it on a shelf.

They both huddle over my book as they did with the last one. I wait.

"'The priestesses watch for the Mothers,'" Rem reads. His eyes go back and forth over each word and sentence. "'To align in opposition and choose the Lif.'" He pauses and looks up at me. "That's a title, I think. I don't know a direct translation for it, sorry." He continues, "'Any child born under this could be part of the cycle, so when I was born under the full Creator and the new Destroyer, my parents took me straight to them and went home without me. Becoming the Lif, being filled with—' I don't recognize this," he says, tapping the page.

"'Creation'," Chi says after a moment. "It's a version of the word you don't see much outside of religious texts."

"'—Creation was supposed to make my voice stronger, to make it an instrument of the Creator. But all it has ever done is silence me underneath its weight." Remy frowns and stops reading. He flips the page over and looks at the diagram. "2485, the Mothers in Opposition," he says. Chi lifts the page and reads the other side while Remy looks between me and the diagram. He narrows his eyes, and I cross my arms over my chest. I look away.

"Wasn't that word, Lif, repeated a bunch upstairs?" Chi asks. "I think I saw it in some of the texts I read last night, too." She looks between me and the diagram as well. "What about this caught your eye?"

Miel takes a step closer and tilts his head. "The moons before the Fall," he says. I'm glad. I don't know the answer to Chi's question. "Back when astronomical events were more predictable. We still celebrate this." He taps the diagram. "Though Sec and Tersh don't exactly line up perfectly anymore. It's the New Century. The last one was 15, 20 years ago or so." Shrugging, he continues. "It takes like 10 years for them to completely cross, so technically everyone in this room was born under it."

"Which one is Prime?" Remy asks. "'Creator' or 'Destroyer'?"

"Destroyer. Creator was hit by a meteor in 4800-something, splitting in two, and, incidentally, ending the Fall in a final, fiery cataclysm." Miel raises his eyebrows and makes a face. "Personally, I like three moons more than two." A surprised half-laugh bubbles out of me.

"What *did* make you pick this up Navi?" Remy asks. Miel frowns at being ignored.

Chi nods quickly. "And also, can you show us where you found it?" she says.

I don't know what to say. "I—" I look at my feet, which are dusty and brown from walking barefoot. "I just picked it up. It was over here," I say. They follow me over, but when we get to the spot where I found it, there's another book in its place.

"Here?" Chi asks. She starts pulling the books out and checking them, one by one. "Aw, it's just a bunch of legal texts."

Something about the way she's searching the books reminds me: "Oh, I hid it inside this one," I say. And then I stop. No, I didn't. Remy and Chi look at each other, eyebrows high.

"You hid it inside a book?" Remy asks. "When?" I shake my head. I think I might be going crazy. I tell Remy that. He just raises his eyebrows some more.

"I keep seeing things, things that I'm sure are real, except they aren't." I shuffle my feet. "I saw myself writing that, and I remember hiding it inside *this* book," I touch one thick, dark red book. Chi takes it off the shelf and opens it. "And I've always daydreamed a lot, but the past couple of days it's like I can't stop." I press my hands to my eyes because I can already feel the sting of tears. "I even remember being here, in this temple. Is there something wrong with me?"

"Hand me that book," Chi says. And then the three of them are quiet for a moment. I take my hands away. They're all staring at the book in Chi's hands, but when I move they look at me.

"What?" I say. Chi tips the book forward, showing me the indented spot in the pages where my book fits perfectly. Pressed tight between the other books, no one would have seen it. Remy looks up at me and his mouth flattens into a line. Miel looks interested.

And Chi's eyes are as wide as the moon. She closes the book and clutches it to her chest. "You remember hiding it here? Truly remember?" she asks. When I nod slowly, she blinks. "Reincarnation was a well-known belief of the Children," she mumbles, and then she nods. "My theory is that you're the Lif," she says. The word is as familiar as my name. When she says it, I shiver. I'm not sure I want that.

"Okay, what? How would that even be possible? And also, what does that even mean?" Miel says. He looks at me. "Listen, I'll admit that the book thing is weird, but maybe you were looking through the books, found this journal hidden here, and—" he shrugs. "Maybe you thought it would be a good prank. Truly, I'll give you credit for it; it's clever."

"Miel," Remy says. I don't want them to think I'm a liar, but I wouldn't mind it if they forgot all about this. *I'd* like to forget all about this. "Navi's not the type. At the very least we should consider it."

"Consider what?" Miel keeps his voice low, but I glance back at Nime and Sess. "That Navi is the reincarnation of some kind of avatar of a deity? That this dead religion was the right one, and that these 'Mothers' have just kept on doing their thing for centuries, and now that *we've* come down here, this cycle, or whatever, is going to pick back up again?" He crosses his arms. "Even if Navi isn't messing with us, it's still more likely that there is something wrong with her."

Chi frowns. "Yes. Consider all of that. The Mothers of Aht Carina is a religion that existed for at least four *thousand* years before the Fall. This library is all the proof you should need."

"I just scanned her a couple of days ago. There was nothing wrong with her," Remy says. That's relieving to hear, and, at the same time, isn't at all.

"I think we should do some tests, of course," Chi continues. "But if she is the Lif, that's incredible! I don't know exactly what the Lif *is* beyond being related to the Mother Creator, but I'm sure we can find out." Again, 'Lif' sticks in my mind, and I can almost remember what that means.

I look down. The person—the memory-me—who wrote the book didn't seem as happy about it as Chi is. In fact, they seemed pretty upset.

"Can we just pretend this didn't happen?" I ask. I give my best pleading face. "I'm sorry."

"But—" Chi says.

Remy nods. "We can wait to talk about this more later. Maybe after things settle down." He looks at me, worried. Chi pouts but nods. I let out my breath. And even when I step away, I can feel the three of them staring at me.

* * *

Ira beckoned Nime over into the corner, away from Sess and the console.

"You need to be careful," he said, his face serious. Nime blinked and opened her mouth. Ira continued before she had a chance to ask why. "I saw some creatures outside. They look dangerous," he said, widening his eyes and then laughing a little. He coughed. Nime frowned. "They're going to try to attack us if we get close. Take this." He handed her a rusted knife, and she took it. Chills ran down her neck. And then she tucked it in the side pocket of her thermals. Ira smiled. "You'll have to use it to keep us safe from them. You will keep us safe, right?" He tilted his head, and his gaze felt like it was reaching into Nime's soul.

"Always," said Nime.

* * *

"Everything okay?" Nime asks from behind me. I nod and clear my throat. She pats me on the back. "We found a comms building that's likely to have a network node, so we should probably get moving."

I don't want to leave my temple. I want to go back to the sanctuary, the room Nime wouldn't let me go into, not back out into the dusty, dead Dome. But Nime starts for the door, and I follow out of habit.

Ira-nin leans against the door frame. His eyes are narrowed and hard, and I look away, right at the middle of Nime's back as she leads the way out. I don't understand him at all. One minute he's laughing, the next minute he's upset. Beautiful or not, it's a bit much for me. I don't look at him, and Nime leads all of us back up the stairs, past the sanctuary, and outside.

The Lif. The Mothers. Nime loops her arm through mine as we go back down the front steps. For some reason, I think of the old woman with gold in her mouth, and I stop for half a second before the slight pressure from Nime makes me move.

Lif. My city, my tower, my priestesses. All my other daydreams. I was the Lif in all of them. I was the Lif. The Lif is me. But, Miel is right, that doesn't make any sense; my daydreams have never made sense. Even if Chi thinks it's true, it's probably just a case of me being easily suggestible.

I watch my feet while I think. The dirt is fine and soft beneath them. As weird as this all is, being the Lif sounds like it could be pretty nice. I don't think I'd mind at all if I could use creative Potential, like imaginary-Navi. I press my hand to my chest, just left of center.

It feels like there's energy coming from every beat of my heart. If I did have the power to create, then this whole place would just be asleep, waiting for me to make it new. My fingers tingle like they do when I'm staring at a blank space, itching to fill it up. Right now, the Dome is a blank space. Everything is so bare and empty and still.

It's the colors. There are so few colors down here, just shades of brown and gray and gross yellow. Sometimes brown is nice. The brown of dirt is nice. The brown of trees is nice. The browns of my family's eyes are nice. But dust brown is getting old without anything to keep it company. If this were a painting, I would add water and turn the dust into mud. A light rain, maybe, just a soft tap tap tap on the ground, so it could soak in slowly. And then pale green, for baby plants. Maybe they would grow all over the lifeless buildings and turn them into hills. They would grow flowers, like in Botanics, and cover everything in vivid pinks and bright yellows. The smell of dirt and bones would become the smell of growth and fresh air. It would look like it used to, before the Fall, and before people came here. I remember the animals that used to live in this valley, before the people.

Nime jerks to a stop beside me, and she steps in front of me while I blink and look around. We're at the edge of the village, a vast expanse of open field before us. And I gasp. I can't help it, there's an *animal* only a little ways away. Almost like I summoned it with my thoughts. It looks like the alpacas that used to graze the mountainside almost. But this is not an alpaca as I knew them. This one is incorrect somehow. Like if someone had shifted the desk in my room an inch to the right. It's about as tall as me, including the long neck, and kind of gooey-looking. There's something stuck to its side, or maybe stuck in its side. Its eyes are yellow and wide open. It's probably never seen a person before, no wonder it's staring at us. Or is it just staring at me? I can feel its eyes on me. It takes a step toward us, and I try to walk around Nime to get closer.

"It could be dangerous," Nime says, holding out her arm to keep me back. I look from her to the gooey-alpaca. It's not doing anything, why would it be dangerous? Plus, it looks nice. It's kind of a pinky-beige color, with four legs and ears that hang off the side of its head. I smile at it, and now it's definitely staring at me.

"It doesn't seem scary," I say. My eyes catch on the stick in its side. "We should help it; it's got something stuck in it." It needs me to fix it. I take a slow step toward it, around Nime's arm. It follows me with its eyes and comes forward to meet me. I take a deep breath and reach out for it.

Nime darts in front of me and does something I can't see, and the animal drips red mixed with whatever gooey stuff covers it. I step back, and it falls over. For a moment none of this seems real. I look at Nime, and she's holding a knife, but why would she have a kitchen knife down here? I look back at the animal. It breathes and moves its feet, and Nime stabs it in the neck. I gasp again. It stops moving.

I back up into someone. They turn me around. It's Chi, and she hugs me to her chest. I don't understand.

"Why did you do that?" Remy shouts. I turn my head to see him. He's looking down at the animal, and his whole face is scrunched up. "Where did you even get a knife from?" He looks away and swipes at his eyes.

"It was dangerous," Nime says. Her voice is calm. "It was going to hurt Navi; you all saw it. I'm not going to let that happen."

"You didn't have to kill it." That's Remy again, not yelling anymore. He sniffs. "It wasn't doing anything. The first animal we see here, and you killed it."

"It was going to attack Navi." Nime's voice is quiet, and she hesitates before speaking again. "I won't let anything hurt any of you, I promise."

I pull away from Chi's arms. A sharp and bitter scent fills the air. I feel sick again. Sess, standing just behind Chi, looks like he feels the same. Chi grimaces at something behind me, and I know I don't want to look.

"Let's keep going," Nime says. I close my eyes and reach out, and I think Sess catches my arm and leads me. We walk for a little ways.

"It's okay now," he says, farther down the road, and I open my eyes.

He pats my arm and lets go. I don't look behind us. Nime is leading again, walking with Ira-nin. She's scrubbing at her arm, wiping it off with the hem of her shirt. It's a little red.

I breathe through my nose and try not to think about the animal. I try to get back into that place, where I can imagine things and make them real, but it won't come. I squeeze my eyes shut for a second. Come on, just imagine it. But when I open them, the world is still dull and empty. My shoulders slump.

It was a stupid thought anyway.

Nime walks at the front of the group and looks straight ahead, and Ira-nin is talking to her. Maybe about the animal. I don't want to think about it. But maybe she was right? I didn't think it was dangerous, but she did. And, I guess something had to have caused all of this death.

I swallow, but my throat is dry. I look around. The fields we walk through were once the most productive in the world, I remember. Now they're little more than empty, bare ground. In the distance, I can see something else, a wall maybe. There are a few more of the gooey-alpacas lying on the ground. The closest one lifts its head to look at us. Stay over there, I think at it. Nime has the knife out again; she holds it in her hand like a weapon. There aren't any weapons in Haven, so I'm not sure how she knows how to use one. "Stay close to me," she says, and she looks back at me. Remy huffs.

"Is that necessary?" Chi asks, gesturing out at the gooey-alpaca. "They're not even moving."

Nime scans the field, eyes narrowed. "I'm just being prepared. We don't know what these things are capable of, and I don't want anything to happen to you." Her fist does loosen a little around the knife handle.

"I know, we know. But there's no need for violence. They're innocent creatures," Chi says gently. Nime scowls and glares at the nearest one.

"They are not innocent. They're dangerous." Nime practically spits out the words, and Chi winces a little. I understand. It's not fun when Nime's mad, even if you're not the target. It's always scared me a little when she gets like this, and it makes me feel guilty. Here I am, scared of my own sister when all she wants to do is protect me. And then when she does protect me, it's usually unpleasant for the other people involved. I could barely eat for a few days after she broke Erden's arm.

All he did was push me and say some mean things—I can't even remember now what he said—and she broke his arm when he wouldn't apologize. I cried, and Nime never did anything like that in front of me again. I know she's done it without me knowing since then. I can always tell because when something like that happens, Nime gets a summons to the Advisory Board, and I get a whole lot of space for the next few weeks.

After Erden, no one would talk to me in class. That was when I started spending time in Botanics, with the bees. Bees don't mind when people cry in front of them.

"How much farther is it?" Miel asks from behind me. He's sweaty and a bit red in the face. Remy hands him a bottle from his bag. He takes a drink of water while Nime checks the map on her tablet.

"Only a little longer," she says. "Then you can rest." She starts walking again like she doesn't need to rest. Maybe she doesn't. But she's sweaty and dusty, and her knuckles are white from gripping the knife. Miel groans but follows. It is hot down here, hotter than I've ever felt, and I'm glad I'm wearing the Nytherial costume. There's not much trapping the heat to my skin, nothing compared to thermals. But the dusty air is still a problem. It sticks to my sweat and coats my throat, and I realize I am so, so thirsty. I look back at Remy, with his bottle of water. I swallow again. Everyone else is thirsty too; I can't be selfish. That was the whole point of coming down here. Nime sees me looking and nods at me. "You have some water too, Navi. I'm sure Rem has enough for everyone." She looks at Remy over her shoulder.

"Don't let yourself get dehydrated," he says as he passes the bottle to me. "I can't believe I'm the only one with a water bottle. Don't any of you care about hydration?" Chi laughs, and Miel says something I don't quite hear. Sess' back loosens a little, and now that it's gone, I can feel the memory of the tension like a blanket in this heat, smothering. I look inside the bottle. There's not a ton. I shouldn't.

"We can get more from one of the houses. The life-support systems all seem to be functioning still," Nime says without looking back. It's like she can read my mind. My throat *is* dry. I take a drink. I've never tasted water so good. I take another. It's cool down my throat. I sigh. Remy nods when I hand it back to him. He doesn't drink anything.

The water sits heavy in my stomach.

11

They saw the first creature sooner than Nime had expected. Right at the edge of town, it walked out onto the path ahead of them, and she stopped. Her whole body tensed. Her hand touched the knife. The thing was horrible, like Ira had said, pink like raw skin and covered in slime. Its beady eyes radiated malice. Nime kept Navi behind her.

"It could be dangerous," she said when Navi tried to get closer. She was too sweet. She'd never met something that truly wanted to hurt her, and here she was trying to make friends with it. The thing looked at Navi with those eyes, and Nime grabbed the handle of the knife. She would keep Navi safe, no matter what.

"It doesn't seem scary," Navi said. Nime grit her teeth. Of course it wouldn't seem dangerous to Navi. She didn't think anything was bad. "We should help it; it's got something stuck in it." Navi stepped forward and reached her hand out. The animal reared back, bared its teeth, and Nime saw red. She pulled out the knife. Navi didn't seem to notice the thing about to attack her, just kept reaching for it like she was going to pet it. There was no other option now, when the thing braced for a kick, aiming right for Navi.

Nime lunged between them and flipped the knife in her hand so that it pointed down at the creature. It cut through the slime and into the neck, and she pulled back. Her pulse was a rush in her veins, and when the creature fell, she went back in for another stab. This one killed it. Breathing heavily through her nose, Nime stepped back and turned to check on Navi. But Navi was pressing her face into Chi's shoulder, and everyone else was staring at Nime.

"Why did you do that?" Rem yelled. He stomped over to her, and Nime wasn't sure whether to be angry back or confused. "Where did you even get a knife from?" And Nime understood why he was so upset; there weren't any weapons in Haven, just like there weren't any blood-thirsty animals. Rem was overwhelmed.

"It was dangerous," Nime said. She kept her voice steady and calm. "It was going to hurt Navi; you all saw it. I'm not going to let that happen." She breathed out. It was supposed to have been safe down here. She would never have brought anyone if she had known.

Nime glanced around at the group. She frowned a little. No one looked relieved or grateful. Not that she expected them to be falling all over her, but still it seemed odd for everyone to be so upset. Navi hid her face against Chi, Chi stared at Nime with wide eyes, Sess looked like he was going to be sick, and Rem glared at her. Miel at least didn't seem mad at her, just scared and a little pale. Ira alone looked glad about the whole thing. He looked at Nime out of the corner of his eye and smiled slightly.

"You didn't have to kill it." Rem was calmer now, though he stopped to sniff. "It wasn't doing anything. The first animal we see here, and you killed it." Nime's chest hurt a little. She shouldn't have killed it in front of everyone. She should have expected this. She should have dealt with the creature before her friends got outside.

"It was going to attack Navi," she said. She paused. Her stomach clenched at the thought that they didn't feel safe anymore. "I won't let anything hurt any of you, I promise." Nime turned back to the path ahead and held her breath for a second. When she spoke again, she was fine. "Let's keep going."

As they walked, the sticky slime on her arm began to heat up and sting her skin. She wiped it off with the hem of her shirt.

"You did well," Ira said quietly from beside her. The compliment swelled in Nime's chest. "It would've killed Navi if you hadn't stopped it." Nime clenched her fists and narrowed her eyes. Never.

As they pass through more empty fields, Nime tensed at the sight of those creatures again, more of them. Most seemed to be asleep, but a few lifted their heads and growled as the group passed. Nime pulled out the knife and turned back to the group.

"Stay close to me," she said, looking at Navi in particular. Navi nodded, but she looked at the knife warily. Rem sighed.

"Is that necessary?" Chi asked. "They're not even moving." Nime scanned the field. Pretending to sleep would be the perfect disguise for an ambush. But she didn't say that. She wanted to keep them safe, not scare them.

"I'm just being prepared. We don't know what these things are capable of, and I don't want anything to happen to you." Nime relaxed her hand a little around the knife.

"I know, we know," Chi said softly, like Nime needed to be consoled. "But there's no need for violence. They're innocent creatures." Nime scowled at the nearest one.

"They are not innocent. They're dangerous." Nime's voice was hard, and she knew she sounded angry. She didn't like to sound angry at her friends, but she was angry. Angry that these things would dare try to hurt the people she loved most in the world.

Nime started walking again, gripping the knife and not looking back at her friends and Navi. She took a deep breath. They walked for a while. Sweat dripped down her spine. She could hear everyone breathing hard behind her. All this heat and dust, no one had trained for this. Part of her worried about overexertion and dehydration. Maybe she should give them a break. But the rest of her wanted to get them out of this place as fast as possible now that she knew it wasn't safe.

"How much further is it?" Miel asked. Nime wasn't surprised; it would have been him or Navi that needed a rest first. Ira was holding up surprisingly well, which Nime was glad about. She looked over the group. They were sweaty, yes, but Rem handed Miel his water bottle, and no one looked like they were in real danger of collapsing. She checked the map.

"Only a little longer," she said. "Then you can rest." They need to keep moving. The sooner she could get the network up and running, the sooner they could contact someone and get the transporter working. The people who needed protecting would go wait up in Haven while the people who protected made the Dome livable. Then everyone would be safe.

Navi coughed a little, and Nime looked back at her. Navi eyed at Rem's bottle of water but said nothing.

"You should have some water too, Navi. I'm sure Rem has enough for everyone." Nime looked back at Rem, whose cold eyes softened for Navi. He passed her the bottle. Nime turned back around as Navi drank.

* * *

One of the gooey-alpacas stands close to the path, and as we pass it, Nime's hand with the knife comes up. Ira-nin trips, and Nime catches him, moves him behind her.

"It attacked me," he says loudly, his voice shaking. His eyes widen. I frown, confused. Nime rushes forward with the knife, and the gooey-alpaca hasn't moved at all. I close my eyes, but I still hear the sound—a squishy, sloshy sound—and an awful sort of cry. I feel dizzy. I press my hands to my stomach.

"Stop!" Remy shouts. He stomps over to Nime. "It didn't even move; you can't have seriously thought it was a threat." Nime frowns and looks down at the body, and then up at Ira-nin.

"It attacked Ira," she says. "I already told you that I'm not going to let anything happen to you. If that means I have to kill some wild animals to keep everyone safe, then I will." Remy shakes his head and looks up and away. He breathes in slowly and then looks back at Nime.

"I don't want that. Don't kill things for my sake, especially when they're not doing anything," he says, and then he turns around and walks back to the rest of us. Nime's eyes are wide and hurt. She looks away and clears her throat. Ira rubs the back of his neck and smiles sheepishly.

"Sorry, I thought it was attacking me," he says, and Remy turns to glare at him instead. I don't think I've ever seen him this angry.

"Well, it wasn't." Remy crosses his arms. Nime stops looking hurt and starts looking angry.

"Yes, it was," she says. "I saw it."

"I didn't see it do anything," Sess says, hesitating. Nime turns her glare on him, and he shrinks a little. How does Nime always seem so much bigger than people twice her size?

"It happened," she says. "I wouldn't have killed it otherwise." She turns to the path and starts walking, not looking back to see if we follow. I do. Chi sighs and goes over to Remy. Miel starts following Nime, and Sess does too, after a second. Eventually, Chi and Remy catch up with us. Remy's eyes are red.

Ira-nin walks next to Nime up front. After a moment, he looks back over his shoulder at me and winks. I stop walking. He turns his head back around so quickly I'm not entirely sure it happened at all. What was that? I look around at the others to see if they saw it, too. Miel meets my eyes and nods, his face grim. After a second, he returns to the vaguely disinterested look he's been wearing most of the time we've been down here. I slow down, let Sess and Miel come between me and the front.

"We need to get Nime back up to Haven quickly," Remy whispers to Chi, at the edge of my hearing.

"Yeah, but we can't truly do anything about that until the transporter is back online," Chi says.

"I know," Remy pauses, and there's silence between them for a few seconds. "Something's wrong. When we do get back, we need to convince her to see one of the counselors." He sighs.

"Good luck with that," Chi says. They stop talking, and I chew my lip. He's right. Nime is different than usual. A soft gasp from Chi grabs my attention. "Rem," she says. She makes an effort to sound calm. "Do you think it maybe has something to do with Ira?"

"What do you mean?" Remy asks. "Are you talking about—"

"I'm talking about what we read. In the temple," Chi says. Remy goes quiet. "Lif and Unlif."

"We need to go back there," Remy says after a moment, "we need to figure out what's going on." And then both of them stop talking. What could this have to do with the Mothers? In the back of my mind, I almost remember something. A feeling? A person? Someone like Nime. An empty, sucking sensation. The sun flickers again, and I blink.

"Here we are," Nime says. A gray building stands low and wide near the edge of the Dome. Finally, a building I don't remember. It doesn't fit the style of the rest of the Dome—that ancient, mythic aesthetic with all the wood and stone. This building is practical and boring. It must have been a popular style just before the Fall, since Haven's buildings are the same.

Nime turns around. "Sess and I will go see what we can do to get the network working again. The rest of you should take a break, or explore the building if you want," she says. Then she gestures to Sess, and he follows her inside.

I look around. We're near the edge of the forest that once painted these mountainsides white and pink in the spring. All the trees are leafless and dry, now.

I walk up to one and touch it. Poor tree. It's rough and warm under my hand. Miel looks at one nearby and scans it with his tablet. After a second his eyebrows rise, and he looks at me.

"Surprisingly, the trees aren't dead," he says, and I straighten up. Truly? "This one at least is just dormant." I frown and tilt my head, looking at the tree again. The only tree I've ever seen is the giant one in Botanics. But this one is different, I think. Different bark. Different feeling when I look at it. Crabapple, I remember.

"Do you know how long they'll be dormant?" I ask, but Miel is gone. Probably inside, away from the sun. Now that I look at it, the fake sun seems dimmer than it was earlier. It doesn't move, but I think it's already late afternoon. I hope Nime and Sess can fix the network soon. The idea of spending the night down here is not appealing.

I look around for everyone else, but I'm alone outside. At least, I think so. Around the corner of the building, behind the trees, I think I see movement, something tall. But when I look again, there's nothing, so I turn back to the tree. I look around one more time, and then I step closer and wrap my arms around its trunk. I press the side of my face into it, and for a second I hold it tightly.

A yawn stretches my mouth, and I blink away stray tears. Now that we've stopped moving, my whole everything feels tired. Body and mind. I sit down with my back against the tree and let the fake sunlight soak into my skin. My eyes fall closed, and I nap in the sun.

* * *

When I open my eyes, I'm not in the city, thank the Wardens; instead, I'm in the Dome, in the valley. It's the way I remember it, cool and green. I sit on a sun-warmed rock in the grass.

I blink.

The trees grow a little taller.

I keep blinking.

And there are more trees yet. The animals I can see change, too. A baby tortoise grows bigger every blink until it's gone, and more are in its place. Some animals disappear while my eyes are closed, like the little mice hiding in the grass. Some change, like the dragonflies as long as my arm. They get smaller every time I see them. Some are only there once, and I never see them again: a sloth the size of my bedroom, a brightly glowing boar.

The valley keeps changing. The plants change, too, though they aren't as noticeable. Mostly they get smaller, and the trees get bigger. They begin to grow flowers. Humans come to live in the valley. They build homes and keep me company, and they change, too. Of all the creatures that live and grow around me, humans are my favorite. They remind me so much of my Mothers.

I sit there, and the world changes around me. And at first, I don't notice, because the rest of it holds all my attention, but I'm changing, too. Every blink I'm different. All the different Navis there ever were. We all love this valley. We love the whole planet, but this valley is home.

But then one of us stands up, and the world between blinks changes again. We aren't in the valley anymore, we're outside, and it's hotter. It's gotten too hot, too fast. The humans can't live in this environment for long; almost nothing can. My heart starts to race. Another blink, and there aren't many more humans. There are mass graves in battlefields and wastelands. There are oceans where there used to be continents and nothing where there used to be ice caps. My moon is being broken in two, and the debris from the explosion comes falling straight onto Aht Carina. My heart is in my throat. They can't survive this.

I'm afraid to blink, but eventually I can't resist. And the world is water. I don't see any humans, but I do see fish and plankton and seaweed. I don't recognize most of them, except jellies that were around when I first sat on that rock. And the humans are almost gone. Nearly extinct, like the lizards and the elephants and the beetles are extinct. There are only a couple thousand of them left.

Tears sting in my eyes. This is all my fault.

12

Nime was parched and shaking by the time she and Sess finished cleaning and rebooting the network base station. Sess had been right, the system was in decent condition despite its age, and the main thing she'd needed to do was clear out 200 years of dust from the components while Sess had rewired the power supply. Nime took another stimulant when he wasn't looking; she needed to be alert to keep everyone safe down there. If they'd fixed things correctly, and they had, then all it would take was a call to someone in Haven, and they could go home. Hope lodged itself in Nime's chest.

Slightly fresher air greeted them as they stepped outside. Rem hurried over as Sess opened up a call. Ira sauntered around the corner of the building and leaned on the wall behind Nime. They waited, only the sounds of Chi and Miel talking breaking the silence.

"Sess," Nime said, after enough time had passed that he should have been able to reach someone. Sess looked at her for a split second before looking back down at his tablet. He shook his head. "Try again." She glared at the tablet as if she could intimidate it into working. Sess pressed his lips together and tried again.

"I still can't even get a signal to anyone here," he said.

Nime grit her teeth. "Give it to me." She grabbed it out of Sess' hands, and he took a step back. His eyes widened, and Nime hated herself. Why was she acting like this?

She tapped aggressively on the tablet, and yelled when the call still wouldn't connect. The wave of frustration that washed through her felt uncontrollable, like the anger she'd felt the day before. The fear of the animals, the desire to keep everyone safe, anger at herself for hurting her friends, all of it combined into a hard knot of fury. Sess pulled the tablet from her hands and stepped away, and Nime snapped. She spun and lashed out at a nearby tree, about the width of her arm. Her fist connected with a crack as satisfying as it was painful. Her breath rushed in and out in hard pants. The tree splintered where she'd hit it.

With her back to the group, Nime looked at her knuckles, red and bleeding for the second time in two days, her toughened bones aching. Before all of this started, she'd never not been in control of herself, and that? That was not control. And she was a good fighter, but not *that* good. She knew exactly how strong she was, from countless hours of PT, and it was not enough to crack a tree.

Something was different lately. From the anger and the sudden bursts of violence, to the walls of the temple whispering to her, to the strange moments of sharpened senses, something was wrong with Nime. On top of that, she was having trouble remembering things. Had the creatures attacked Ira, or had he tripped? What did they look like? In her mind, she could see two images overlapping. One a monstrous thing with bared teeth, the other a harmless looking animal. And when had she gotten the knife in her pocket? When had questionably monstrous animals become more threatening than the Potential leak? That morning, Nime would have given anything to keep her friends and Navi and Ira down in the Dome. But now—

She felt over-sensitive again, every sound and movement noticeable, no matter how small. She closed her eyes and swallowed. Was it the stimulants? Hypersensitivity wasn't a side effect that she knew of, nor was increased strength. When this was all over, she would have to stop taking stimulants for good. For now, though, she might just collapse if she ran out.

After a second, Nime composed herself and turned around. Navi was turned slightly away, head in her hands, and everyone else stared at Nime.

"What is wrong with you?" Chi asked. Nime blinked. She clenched her jaw to keep her face straight.

"Nothing," she said. She looked at the group and blinked a little faster. She couldn't stand this feeling, out of control and confused. It made it hard for her to breathe. This was not who Nime was.

* * *

Something touches my shoulder, and I take a huge breath and open my eyes to dusk. I blink a few times, and any tears that may have come are gone. Chi crouches in front of me, waking me up. This is all my fault.

Nime talks with Sess and Remy near the door to the building, and Ira-nin stands behind them, looking over Nime's head. Miel is staring at me. Or rather, he's staring at the tree I was leaning against. Chi looks behind me too, and her eyes widen. I turn to look, and for a second I don't see it. My head tilts to the side, and I look closer. There's something green on the tree.

I breathe out and lean in. There, on the tips of the little twigs, are teeny tiny spots of light, baby green. I take a step back and look at my feet. Chi says something, but all I can hear is my heart in my ears because there's even green on the ground. Just a little bit, mostly under where I was sitting. I have to squint to make sure it's truly there, it's so faint. I cover my face with my hands.

"Try again," Nime says. I peek out. Everyone turns toward her. She's clenching her fists and glaring at Sess. At his tablet? He taps at it a few times and presses his lips together.

"I can't get a signal at all, not even to anyone here," he says after a moment. My heart sinks. That's not good. Nime grits her teeth. Her jaw is tight when she talks again.

"Give it to me." She grabs it out of Sess' hands, and he takes a step back. He frowns and hugs one arm to his side. Nime taps with more force than necessary, and then she shouts. My shoulders come up to my ears. Sess slides the tablet from her hands and hunches over it, tapping quickly. Nime turns around. And then her arm swings, and her fist hits the tree closest to her. There's a loud cracking sound, and the tree splinters. I swallow. Nime breathes hard and stands with her back to us.

No one says anything. After a bit, Nime turns around and looks back. For the first time I can remember, I can't read her face.

"What is wrong with you?" Chi asks. Her voice is quiet, but it carries in the silence.

Nime blinks. "Nothing," she says. She looks around at everyone, and it's like she gets a little bit sadder, a little more confused at each of us.

When she gets to me, I can see her blink faster. She looks away. After another second of silence, Nime turns her head toward Sess but doesn't look up. "Sorry." Sess doesn't answer. His neck is tense. There are shadows on the tendons there. Nime looks up, and she looks almost normal now. That same confident expression she always has. "I want to get us back to Haven as soon as possible, and it's frustrating that the network still isn't working."

"We're all tired," Ira-nin says. He steps up next to Nime and rests a hand on her shoulder. "We should head back into town and rest in one of the houses. I know I could use some water." He laughs a little, and Nime looks up at him. She straightens and nods.

"Let's go, then." She starts walking back the way we came, and as she passes me, I can see that she's still clenching her jaw, and her shoulders are tight. She looks miserable. I sniff and try to blink away the tears that fill my eyes. Remy comes up beside me, and his arm presses against mine. The five of us trail after Nime and Ira-nin, and the silence gets in under my skin and smothers me.

* * *

It's fully dark by the time we get back into the village. Nime lights the way with her tablet, but the rest of us are so far behind we're not in the circle of light it makes. No one seems to want to get close to Nime, and she knows. It floats around her like a storm cloud, all dark gray and looming. It closes up my throat. I know how that feels, but I have no idea how to fix it. It's like this darkness, down here where Prime can't reach. I look down at my feet. What do I do?

I trip over things I'm glad I can't see, but once we're back among the houses there's light again. I can't tell where it's coming from—it's not casting shadows the way it should—but it's comforting all the same. I hold onto Chi's arm as I walk. My eyes and legs are so heavy. Everything is so heavy.

We walk forever before Nime stops in front of a house, breaks a window with her elbow, and opens the door from the inside. I barely even see it as we file in, I just follow along and trust Chi. She's probably exhausted, too, but I've just decided that she's going to guide me. I straighten up and pull my arm away.

"We'll rest here for a while," Nime says. She searches the kitchen area, pulling out several cups. She messes with a handle of some kind until water comes out and fills the cups up. I blink and look around. It's not a huge room, but there's space for all of us. One half of the room is lined with counters; in the other, a square, wooden table sits surrounded by cushioned chairs. I almost sit on one, but I pause. There are seven of us and four chairs. I sit on the floor instead. Remy disappears into a doorway opposite the door we came in. Chi pulls a chair up behind me and braids my hair. I close my eyes and let my shoulders fall.

I can hear cups being set down, and the sound of drinking. Someone is typing rapidly. Sess, I guess. Chairs get moved around. There's a sweeping sound and a tinkly clinking that goes along with it. The door opens, and I open my eyes. They almost close again before I catch them. Nime comes back into the house and brushes off her hands. Remy sticks his head through the doorway.

"There are a few bedrooms down this hallway. Not enough for all of us, so we'll have to figure that out," he says. Nime hands him a cup, and he stares at her for a second before taking it and drinking. "Thanks."

Nime nods and looks away. "We're not sleeping here," she says. I lean my head back against Chi's knees. Her hands stop moving in my hair.

"What do you mean? It's late, it's impossible to see outside," Miel says. He sounds as tired as I feel. He's sitting in one of the chairs. Nime hops up onto the counter.

"I meant what I said. I don't want us staying down here any longer than necessary. We'll rest for a bit, but I'm going to figure out what's blocking us from connecting to the network, fix it, and then we're going home." Sess stops typing and clears his throat. Nime focuses on him.

"Uh, I may have figured it out," he says. Nime hops down and walks up next to him. She nods at him to continue. "So, normally this kind of block is caused by signal interference. I did a sweep of all signals being sent to this base station and found tons of packets coming from one address, which prevents any other signals from getting through. It's significantly more likely to be some kind of jammer than anything else."

"Sess." Nime crosses her arms.

Sess stops and looks up at her. "Yeah?"

"Get to the point."

I chew my lip. Sess looks down at his tablet and nods. Nime's never this mean. Chi's hands tighten in my hair and then go back to braiding.

"Oh. Well, we just need to find whatever is jamming the signal, and then we can disable it and connect to the network."

"Great," Remy says. He sets his cup down on the table. "Then we can do that in the morning. We'll sleep here tonight." Nime's face hardens.

"This isn't up for debate. It's not safe to be here any longer than we have to." She pushes her hair back from her face. "We need to keep going."

"We're all really tired, Ni," Chi says. Nime looks down at the two of us. But instead of giving in like she normally does, that moment where I can always tell she's doing something for my sake, she frowns more.

"That doesn't make it any safer here," Nime says. "Look, I get it, it's late, it's dark, you're hungry and sweaty and want to rest. That's why I'm giving you a rest. But staying the night is not an option. I won't spend any longer down here than I have to." I close my eyes again while she talks. If we're only going to be here for a bit, I need to sleep. At least a little bit.

"Lack of sleep can cause a decrease in cognitive performance, inversely proportional to levels of deprivation." Sess' voice is quiet. "For you, us, to be at our best, it's probably a good idea to get a full night's sleep." I open my eyes. I don't know how to describe the feeling in my chest. Sess makes me think of myself in five years. But no matter how hard I try to be brave, I don't think I'll ever be as brave as him. It's not that I never argue with Nime, it's that I wouldn't be able to find any words at all if she were glaring at me like she's glaring at him, if she had yelled at me earlier like she yelled at him. It's that it's easier to follow her than to suggest my own way.

"No." Nime turns around and stalks back to the door. She steps outside and takes a breath. Chi ties off my braid and pats my shoulder. Sess just sits where he is. He swallows. Ira-nin stands up, and it makes me jump. He was so quiet before. Now, he walks toward the door.

"Nime, come back inside," he says. He must be tired, too, though he doesn't look it. In fact, he looks more energetic than I think I've ever seen him. Nime comes back in. She closes the door behind her. He smiles and straightens his glasses. "We'll sleep here tonight and continue in the morning." Ira-nin may be their tutor, but I don't think I've ever seen any of them treat him like one. They don't even use an honorific when they talk to him. It's more like he's an older friend or student than someone with authority. It doesn't help that Nime so often takes charge of things. I brace myself for an awkward stand-off between him and Nime, but it never comes. Nime just stops for a second, and then she nods. I blink.

"Truly?" Remy says. He stares at Nime and shakes his head. "I don't know why you're acting like this, but I'm done." He crosses his arms and looks toward the rest of us. "I'm taking one of the beds. They're big enough to share, so, feel free. Goodnight." He doesn't look back as he stomps down the hallway. A door slams, and Nime stares at the place where he used to be. Her face is blank on the surface, but she blinks too quickly, and then I can't help it, I start crying again. I lower my head and pull my knees up to my chest.

"Navi," Nime says. I don't lift my head. I know she already feels bad, I know she's already upset. And I know that if she sees me crying, it'll only make it worse. I'm such a crybaby. I try to keep my breathing even, so I don't shake. I can't tell if it works, but Chi pats me on the shoulder again and stands up.

"I'm going to find someplace to sleep," Chi says. Footsteps move out of the room, and then a door opens and closes. Nime takes the spot Chi was in before. Her fingers lightly trace my braid. Misery rolls off of her in waves.

"Well," Miel says. A chair shifts. "I'm going to claim a spot before all that's left is the floor." He leaves. Another set of footsteps leave, big, loud ones. It's quiet for a minute, and Nime just sits there behind me. The last other person clears their throat. That's Sess, then.

"You," he says and clears his throat again. "You two should get some sleep as well." Nime takes a breath and then lets it out as Sess leaves. I don't look up. Nime slides out of her seat and kneels next to me. She hugs me, and I lean against her.

"Sunshine, I'm sorry," she says. I try to sniffle without sounding like I'm sniffling.

"S'okay," I say, rubbing my eyes against my knees. Nime pets my hair. "Are you alright?" I ask.

Nime breathes out a laugh. "You're worried about me? I'm not the one who's been miserable the whole time we've been down here." Her voice is tired, but she tries for a light tone. I lift my head. That wasn't an answer to my question. "I wish you hadn't come. It's dangerous down here," she continues.

"Are you sure?" I ask. Nime frowns a little, and she gets this look in her eyes, like she's remembering something. But she doesn't respond. I tilt my head. "Ni?" I whisper. She looks at me, and my skin prickles. Her eyes are empty, like she's not seeing at me, or anything else. I've seen that look somewhere before. And then she blinks and truly looks at me. She takes a deep breath and opens her mouth. Hesitates. Closes it again and looks away. I slump down a little. She was so close I could feel it. Nime is always so willing to listen to me and help me with my problems, but she's never even told me about hers.

"I—" I start. This is the worst. I have no idea what to say to let her know that I want to help. That it's the least I could do. "Is something wrong?" For a second, Nime doesn't say anything. She looks off to the side. When she speaks, her voice is barely there.

"I keep having this feeling," she says, and then she stops. She grits her teeth, pulling back a little, and I reach after her. "Never mind. It's not important. I'll take care of it." She stands up and picks up her sweater from the pile in the corner. She folds it over a couple of times and drops it on the floor. "Why don't you find a spot to sleep? You could ask Rem or Chi to share."

I rub my eyes and unfold my legs. "What about you?"

"I'll sleep out here," she says, nodding down at the folded-up sweater. "I need to make sure nothing happens overnight."

"Okay," I say after a second. I chew my lip and head for the hallway. Nime shoos me on when I stop to look back at her. Outside the bedrooms, I look down. Okay? That's all I can say when she's going to sleep on the floor to make sure nothing bad happens? It's not okay. Not at all. What if something bad did happen, and Nime was all alone out there? But I can't even get myself to say I don't like it. This trying-to-be-brave thing was a waste of time. I've only been as scared as I always am.

And I'm pretty sure I've made things worse. I just had to come down here, making Ira come down after me, and now no one knows where we are or how to get here. It's all my fault.

I shake my head and squeeze my eyes shut. I don't want to cry again in front of everyone. So I blink and breathe until I'm okay and peek inside the one open door. It's dark except for the glow of four tablets. I look over at the other door. I guess Ira-nin's in that one. I tap on the open door and their heads pop up.

"Can I sleep in here?" I ask, looking around the room. There are only two dusty beds, but plenty of faded blankets folded in a stack on the floor. A tall wardrobe takes up the space between the beds.

"Of course," Remy says. "Want a bed or the floor?" He lies on his stomach on one of the beds, his head at the foot, with Miel doing the same next to him. "You could share with me if you want."

Miel turns his head toward Remy and pouts at him. "Hey, this was my spot first," Miel says. Remy sighs and rolls his eyes. "You just don't want to share with me because you know I'll find out about your weird sleep habits, but Navi probably already knows." Miel says it like that's the only possible explanation, and Chi laughs from her spot on the other bed. Sess sits cross-legged on the floor, leaning against the wall. He half laughs through his nose and smiles a little.

Remy opens his mouth and squints at Miel. "What are you even talking about?" he asks.

"Come on," Miel says. "You definitely drool or sleep-talk or something. And you're worried that I'll find out, so you're trying to come up with an excuse to not share with me. It's fine, I get it." Remy leans onto one arm and uses the other to shove Miel over.

"You're so dumb. Fine, maybe Chi will let you share with her." He looks back at me and smiles.

"Yeah," Chi said. "There's plenty of room."

"Thanks, but I'll just sleep on the floor," I say. After today, even that sounds comfortable. Remy nods and leans forward off the bed to grab me a blanket from the stack.

"At least these are all still in decent condition," he says as he hands it to me.

"I wouldn't test the tensile strength of at least 200-year-old fabric, though" Sess says from the corner. He has the tiniest hint of a laugh around his mouth. Then he turns back to whatever he's been working on all night. Remy ignores Miel, who's still asking about weird sleep habits. I start to unfold my blanket, and I smile behind it when Remy reminds him that they've slept in the same room before, so Miel knows he doesn't do any of those things.

Chi reads something on her tablet, and she looks up when I take a step into the room.

"Can you close the door, actually?" she asks. I nod, and go back to close it. It's dark down the hall. Nime must have gone to sleep already. I look back at the room. Sess is in one corner with a bunch of blankets in a nest around him. The space between the wall and Chi's bed looks good, so I make my way over to it. I have to step over Sess' blanket nest to get there. Chi scoots over and gestures to the empty part of her bed with a questioning look. I shake my head. She shrugs and goes back to reading.

I shake out the blanket and wrap it around myself. It's like a seaweed roll, and I'm the fish inside. My arms make a pretty good pillow when I roll onto my stomach, face toward the wall. I touch the blanket. It's soft in a way I've never felt before. It's closer in texture to hair than to the stiff fabrics we can make in Haven. And the pattern must have been cute when it was new, too. The grayish blue fabric is covered in a faded, repeating floral design.

For the first time all day, I relax. My eyes close. The sound of my breathing is the only thing I hear, and I'm so close to falling asleep that time and sound and everything outside my head seems fake and dreamlike.

A creak. A shuffling. Whispers. I sigh and crack open my eyes.

"We need to talk about Nime," someone says. The whisper of it makes it hard to tell who. I consider covering my head with the blanket so I can't hear. I was trying my best to not think about Nime. But I breathe evenly and listen.

"What we need to do is get her away from Ira."

"You're sure he's the problem?"

"I mean, I haven't tested my hypothesis, if that's what you're asking, but yeah, I'm sure."

"I was just reading a book I downloaded from the temple, about the Cycle of Rebirth. About each of the three aspects. Navi is obviously the Lif, who should be able to use creative Potential."

"Sure, let's assume that's true. And?"

"Well, aside from the whole creation part, there's also the destruction part, a person who has the same tendency toward breaking things that Navi has toward making things, who I guess they called the 'Unlif.' It's the duality of the Mothers."

"And then the final part is humanity."

"Right, the third part is the balance, the human aspect. So, you have these opposing forces of creation and destruction, sort of embodied by the Lif and the Unlif, and then in the middle, you have the Hand, who acts as, I guess, a servant of the other two?"

"From what I read, it was more like the Hand is a tool of the others. Essentially, these two opposing forces could control the neutral human force, who is drawn toward both of them. Like a fish to a deep-lantern."

"That's pretty interesting theology."

"Sess."

"Um, but from a more practical perspective, it's also alarming. When you say control, do you mean—"

"I'm talking mind-control, human-puppet stuff here. I didn't have a ton of time, but there was an entire book of reasons why it's best to keep the Hand away from the Unlif, of what the Unlif can *do* with the Hand. Now, this is from a temple dedicated specifically to the creation half of this duality, but the disasters that were in that book...the massacres..."

"Oh."

"Yeah."

"Okay, so Navi is the Lif. One guess who the Hand is."

"I want to double-check to be sure, but it's pretty clear that Nime is the Hand in this iteration of the cycle."

"I know we found a whole lost settlement, and it's got a fancy temple and tons of new information, but how do you know Navi is this Lif? How do you know this is real, and why is it happening now?"

"I know you were skeptical before, but you saw the trees. They started growing after Navi was near them. What other explanation is there? Obviously, there's a lot we don't know, but that much is undeniable."

"Great."

"We're sure the Hand is Nime? Not someone who is conveniently up in Haven?"

"The Hand is supposed to become incredibly powerful under the divine influence of the other two. Powerful beyond normal human capacity. She can't normally punch trees apart, right? Also, who else do you know who would do anything for Navi?"

"Poor Navi. She'll feel so bad."

"Navi is not who I'm worried about now."

"Ira."

"Yeah."

"Where does Ira come into it?"

"He's obviously the Unlif. Think about it."

"Okay, he's been acting weird all day. And yeah, Nime does always listen to him, but you really think *Ira's* this destructive force?"

"He does break things pretty often."

"Yeah, because he's clumsy. I sometimes get lucky with the random number generator in a game; that doesn't make me Cera, the Warden of Luck or anything."

"Just listen. Stop thinking about Haven-Ira. Think about everything that's happened while we've been down here. Nime was normal until Ira showed up, and then she got violent. I know she's a little aggressive, but she doesn't go off like that unless Navi or Ira are involved. And do you think Nime is lying about believing those animals were dangerous?"

"Yes? They were clearly not moving."

"Did it seem like *Nime* was lying about seeing them attack?"

"What are you even saying?"

"She's saying that Nime truly believed the animals were attacking, that she truly thinks they're a danger to us."

"Yes. When has Nime ever not had our backs? She's always been the one to get us out of trouble or take the punishment herself. And she's not normally a liar, not to us."

"You think Nime is, what, seeing things?"

"I think it's weird that she would pretend there was danger just so she could kill some animals."

"You did say, uh, mind-control, human-puppet, right?"

"That's the problem."

"If Ira is this Unlif, how would we know? What could we even do?"

"I don't know, but look at how much time the two of them are spending together. Look at how he's been acting. I'm worried he's going to take it too far and hurt Nime."

"Too far? If Ira's making Nime do anything, he's already taken it too far."

"I don't want to see what might happen if we leave them alone anymore. We can't, someone has to be with them at all times from now on, at least until we can get back to Haven."

"Anybody have a rope handy?"

"Miel."

"What? Don't act like I'm being unreasonable. If we tie them up— separately, of course—then this whole problem is solved. Easy."

There's a pause.

"He's not wrong, and this is kind of an unknown situation. I don't think it would be the worst thing in the world to be prepared to restrain them. If Ira can use destructive Potential, this could get much worse."

"That's Nime and our tutor you're talking about, you know?"

"We don't have a rope, anyway."

"Not the point. We can't tie them up."

"Why don't we think about it for now and talk about it later. In the meantime: Navi."

"What about her?"

"Can she human-puppet Nime too?"

"In theory."

"So couldn't she just say, 'hey, Nime, don't listen to Ira anymore, just calm down and stop killing stuff?'"

"Probably."

"Navi is not going to want to mind-control her own sister."

"How about we try to not let Nime be a tool? Why don't we try for her not being controlled by anyone?"

"You didn't want to tie them up. I know it sounds bad, but I truly think that that's the best option. If what you're saying is true, who's to say Ira isn't planning on doing something worse? What can we do? Nime's a handful, and I know I couldn't stop her myself. If we're not going to tie her up, then Navi is our best bet."

"You really think she could do something like that? Knowingly?"

"Let's just focus on getting back to Haven, first. Once we're up there and we have a little more back-up, we can keep them separated while everyone else deals with the Potential problem."

"Fine. But think about it. If it gets worse, I'm not going to let myself get hurt because you all don't want to do anything about it."

"Stop it, Miel. I won't let you guilt Navi into doing that."

"Let's all go to sleep and talk about it in the morning. It's bad enough with Nime, we shouldn't start yelling at each other."

"Yeah."

"But—"

"Go to sleep."

Silence falls. I open my eyes. The wall in front of my face is rough, and I can see the swirling texture of it.

Nime can't be controlled by another person. It's the most Nime thing about her, that she does what she wants, what she thinks is right, no matter what the rules are, or what people will think. And that's a good thing, most of the time. Nime's not a bad person. She would never do bad things for the sake of it. She's trying to protect us.

The others can't be right. I can't control Nime like that. No one can. It's not possible. It can't be, because even allowing that idea to creep into the edges of my mind is the scariest thing I've ever thought. If I can control Nime, what does that mean about us? What does that mean about our relationship?

I squeeze my eyes shut and pull the blanket tighter around myself.

* * *

Nime laid down on her side with the folded up sweater under her head and cried silently when Navi left. Everyone hated her. Even Navi didn't want to be near her. The only exception was Ira, but Nime couldn't remember half of the things he'd said to her while they had been there. The moments she'd been with him were fuzzy and clouded, and they felt like the memories of someone else. She remembered him giving her a knife, but where was it now? She'd done something with it, something to make everyone hate her, but the rest was unclear. Dread hovered over all of it, this nameless danger that set her heart racing.

Nime never cried. At least, she hadn't before. Fixing the problem was a better solution than crying. But she didn't know how to fix whatever this was. Sure, her friends, Navi, and Ira were safe, but what would they think about her now? Nime was nothing without them.

Her eyes stung, and she scrubbed at her face. She was nothing without them, so keeping them safe was worth whatever it cost her. Whatever it took. She sniffed and breathed in, closing her eyes and composing herself.

Breaking down was not an option. If she could burn the weakness out of herself, like distilling water, she would. But since she couldn't, she'd just have to bury it deep enough that no one else could find it.

* * *

My dreams are not exactly nice. I can't remember them, but when something wakes me up in the dark, my skin is crawling. Whatever they were, they've left my stomach all knotted up and unsettled. I stand up. My mouth is dry. I rub my eyes and step over blankets to get to the hallway.

Dreams aren't prophetic. They're just one of the ways our minds deal with our waking life, and I know that whenever I go to bed with my stomach in a knot, I wake up with a bad feeling that lingers. Knowing that doesn't make the bad feeling go away any faster, and it doesn't make me any less anxious about the future.

I yawn as I walk, eyes closed. They're still too heavy to keep open for long, so I don't. But I pause at the end of the hallway, at the open door to the front room. Someone is talking, and I'm getting tired of overhearing conversations. I turn around. I can wait until morning for water. But the voice gets louder, so I turn back. Maybe Nime was talking to me?

But no. It's Ira-nin talking to Nime. He stands looking down at where she's kneeling. He's smiling, but it's the worst smile I've ever seen in my life. A chill crawls down the back of my neck. It's sharp and cruel. I don't know where to look, so I look at Nime. She kneels on the floor and looks up at Ira-nin. Her face is blank. Like earlier, when I asked if she was alright.

"Your friends don't seem like they're happy about your protection," he says. He was quieter before. Now he's speaking at a normal level. It sounds louder in the quiet of pre-dawn. "That's pretty ungrateful of them, don't you think?" Nime nods. I chew my lip. They're not ungrateful, they're worried. "It's too bad you can't convince them to listen to you more effectively."

"How could I do that?" Nime asks. Her voice is just like her face, empty. I wrap my arms around myself when I hear it. I have seen that face before; only before, it was on someone else. For a second, it's like my cyborg is overlaid on top of Nime, their faces lining up in a blank mask.

"Sometimes force is necessary to keep people in line." Ira-nin smiles a little wider, and I bite down on my lip to keep from making a noise. My eyes start to sting and water. Nime leans back at that. Her eyebrows pull together.

"But I want to keep them safe, not hurt them."

"Yes, yes, I know." Ira-nin clenches his fists. "But if they're resisting your attempts to do that, you shouldn't be afraid to make them listen to you."

"With force?" Nime's mouth turns down. She hesitates. I take a breath. Ira-nin looks up and meets my eyes. I hold my breath. I can't seem to look away. He smiles that awful smile at me.

"With force," he says. He doesn't look at Nime, just keeps his eyes locked on mine. I swallow. "I want you to hurt your friends if they challenge you again, do you understand?" Nime doesn't answer for a second, and Ira-nin's smile tightens around the edges. After a moment I see her nod in the corner of my eye. Ira-nin winks at me again. I turn around and run back to the bedroom. I get back into my roll of blankets like they'll keep this bad dream away from me, pulling them up and over my head.

I squeeze my eyes shut and try to breathe deeply, like Athis-nin told me to when I'm nervous or scared or absolutely, one-hundred percent panicking. That can't have been real. After a minute, my heart slows and so does my breathing, and I pull the blanket off of my head.

No, it obviously wasn't real. How could it be? Before I fell asleep, I overheard something scary, and it involved Ira-nin and Nime. It makes sense that I would have a realistic nightmare about it. Yes. It makes sense. It's the only thing that makes sense because what I just saw doesn't make any at all. Ira-nin is—well, he's not evil, of course. He's clumsy, and a little clueless, and generally a pretty nice person. He's a good tutor. Maybe not the perfect candidate for a teacher, but that's not because he's bad. I've heard the rumor that it's because he had a low score on his psych eval.

But more importantly, seeing Nime as my cyborg proves that this was all my imagination. My daydreams have been getting mixed up in my real life too much lately, that's all. That's why they seem so real, so close. That's why, down here, I can barely take a step without imagining some other life, some other Navi.

I breathe in.

I just woke up from a nightmare.

I breathe out.

But it wasn't real. Tomorrow, we will all wake up, get the network working, and go back to Haven. And no one will hurt anyone.

* * *

Nime only realized she'd been asleep when she woke up to a noise. She rolled to her knees in a second, eyes wide and ears straining. After a moment, she saw Ira standing in the doorway, and she relaxed. Blinked. It was dark, but she could see him clearly.

Ira moved, and it caught Nime's eye. "Good, you're awake," he said, standing in front of her. She started to stand, but he held up a hand. "Stay there." Nime stayed, even though the wooden floor pressed hard against her knees.

And then she squinted. It was awkward to be kneeling and looking up at him. Why didn't she just stand?

When she tried, her legs didn't move, and Nime glanced down at them. Something like dread took root in her stomach.

Ira looked down at her, and she looked up at him. As she did, part of her drifted away, like she was sleeping, like this was a dream. Like the memories that felt like someone else's, she was there but not.

"You did well earlier against those terrible creatures," he said finally, his voice a combination of pleased and mocking, and she remembered. That was why the skin of her hands and forearms felt a little raw; the monsters that she'd killed were caustic. But were they truly monsters?

"Your friends don't seem like they're happy about your protection. That's pretty ungrateful of them, don't you think?" He asked, tilting his head. Nime nodded. She's always worked so hard for them, but they've never thanked her. Far away, she rejected that. That thought did not belong to her. But Ira was right. "It's too bad you can't convince them to listen to you more effectively." His mouth turned down a little at the corners.

"How could I do that?" Nime asked, as if with someone else's mouth.

Ira smiled again, like he was glad she'd asked. "Sometimes force is necessary to keep people in line," he said. Nime came back to herself a little at that. She leaned away. Force? Against her friends? Goosebumps crawled up her arms.

"But I want to keep them safe, not hurt them," she said. Ira sighed.

"Yes, yes, I know," he said. "But if they're resisting your attempts to do that, you shouldn't be afraid to make them listen to you." Nime felt herself drifting far away again, but this time, she tried her best to come back. It was like struggling to stay awake when she was exhausted; all she could do was keep her head up.

"With force?" she asked, frowning. She didn't want to.

"With force." Ira's voice burrowed deeply into her head until it was all she could hear. "I want you to hurt your friends if they challenge you again, do you understand?"

Nime froze. She couldn't. But Ira wanted her to. She had to.

She nodded.

By the time morning came, Nime had bitten her fingers red and raw around the nails. She was on two stimulants at once to keep herself awake and moving, and she could feel it in every stuttering beat of her heart.

Rem woke before anyone else, and he took one look at Nime before sighing.

"Why do you do this to yourself?" he said, his voice weary. Nime swallowed down the shame she felt at worrying him.

"Do what to myself?" she asked. Even as she said it, she could tell Rem wouldn't buy it, not this time. She had to try anyway. He looked at her for a second before shaking his head and sitting down at the table with his tablet.

Nausea climbed up Nime's throat. She was going to lose them.

13

I must fall asleep again because one moment I close my heavy eyes and the next the odd light of the artificial sun fills the room. Soft sounds filter in from the other room. I sigh, and it stretches into a yawn. I sit up. Both beds are empty, but there's a long lump on the floor, with a bit of floofy dark brown hair sticking out the end of it. I stretch my arms up and overhead. The nightmares I had last night stick to my skin and leave a lingering fear in my stomach. I remember Ira-nin smiling at me like he was going to eat me.

This is not the first time I've woken up still scared from a nightmare. But this is one of the most rememberable nightmares I've ever had. I look out the dirty window next to me. The little green things are here, too, on the ground between this house and the next. And they're bigger this time. Less a dusting of pale color and more thick brushstrokes of a saturated moss green, something between Miel's eyes and Sess' darker ones. It looks soft. I want to stick my hands in it.

This only reinforces what Chi and Remy said, about me being the Lif. In Haven, I would've loved a little more spontaneous plant growth around me. And I like it now. Even though most of me is trying to avoid thinking about what it means, seeing these little green things fills up a part of my heart.

I look away. I can think about that later, preferably never. I stand up and head for the door, but I look back at Sess. I bend over and softly poke at where I think his shoulder is.

"Sess," I say, a little above a whisper. Nothing. I poke a little harder, and he moves. The blanket reveals a set of mostly closed eyes. "Um, I think everyone else is awake." He blinks a few times and nods. I stand back up and give him some space. After a few seconds, he slowly sits up, bringing an impressive pile of blankets with him. His eyes remain closed. "Are you awake?" I ask.

"Yeah," he says. I'm not sure I believe that, but Sess makes a valiant effort to open his eyes fully.

"Okay, I'm going to join the others, so, uh," I say, walking half-backward to the hallway. He nods again, and I turn around and leave. I'm pretty sure I hear the thump of a person falling back into a pile of soft things.

Murmurs travel from the front room, and I follow them. Everyone but me and Sess sits around the table, except Nime, who's sitting on the counter again. She looks like she didn't sleep at all, her eyes red and her shoulders slumped. And her face—it's not gray, not exactly, but if I were painting her, that's the color I would make it. She smiles at me when I come through the door. Remy stops talking and nods at me.

"You're awake," Nime says. Her voice is normal enough, at least. Maybe she had nightmares, too. She's not tired because of late-night conversations with Ira-nin, of course. I nod and rub my eyes. "Did you get enough sleep? You look tired," she continues.

"I just had some bad dreams." I try not to look at Ira-nin as I say it, but I do anyway. Maybe to show myself that he isn't some monster from a story. He looks normal right now. He smiles at me sympathetically and tilts his head.

"Oh?" Ira-nin asks. "What about?" Something about the way he says it makes my skin crawl. There's an edge to it, an undercurrent. I blink a few times. Stop, Navi. It was a dream. I shouldn't let it seep into real life any more than it already has.

"I forgot," I say. I didn't. But I'm certainly not going to give him the real answer. And the shivery feeling under my skin doesn't want to know what he'd do if I told him. I chew my lip and nod my head back toward the hallway. "I tried to wake Sess up, but I'm not sure it worked." Nime frowns. She straightens up and shakes her head.

"Of course." She hops down and starts pacing. She's skittery, like a water-walker, all moving parts and tension to stay afloat. "It's fine, we can start talking about the plan in the meantime." She stops and looks at Remy. "Wake him up, will you? We need to get home soon." Remy doesn't respond at first, and Nime doesn't seem to notice. She keeps pacing, and she chews on her nails. I start a little at the sight of them. Her nails are chewed down as far as they can be, and the skin around them is red. Even bleeding in some places. When she sees Remy again, she crosses her arms. "Rem. Can you wake Sess up?"

They glare at each other for what feels like full minutes. I can practically see the angry energy between them. Eventually, Remy scowls and stands up, letting the legs of his chair hit the floor. He stomps out into the hallway. Nime takes a deep breath and starts pacing again.

"As soon as Sess comes out, we'll be leaving." Nime doesn't look at anyone as she walks, just stares out, like she's thinking. "First, we find where the interference is coming from, then we eliminate it. We send a message to Haven. And then we go home and get some food." She stops at the far end of her path. "That's it, basically." She turns around to look at us. There's something lost in her eyes, behind the determination, behind everything. It takes my heart in its hand and squeezes. Nime should never look like that.

Remy comes back into the kitchen with Sess trailing behind him. Nime blinks a few times and doesn't look at Remy.

"I can track the jammer," Sess says, blinking his eyes open slightly. "I was working on it last night." Nime's eyes snap to him.

"Perfect. We can leave then. No reason to wait around," she says, nodding and moving toward the door. Sess holds his tablet to his chest as he follows. Ira-nin smiles at me as he stands and passes me. Chi and Miel groan and complain as they get up. I sympathize. Remy scowls and stands up with more strength than anyone. Anger gives some people energy; it only makes me feel drained.

Remy stomps out the door, where he turns around and waits for the rest of us. I end up being the last one out, and I close the door softly behind me. He takes a deep breath.

"I'm going to the temple," he says. He stares at Nime while he says it. "The rest of you should find the jammer and then let me know when the network is back up."

"No," Nime says.

"I'm not asking you for permission." Remy is as stubborn as Nime is, and it's making my stomach hurt all over again. "I have things to do, and I need to be at the temple to do them. So, I'm going to go, and we'll meet back up when you're done." He turns to head in the direction of the temple, the golden roof I can see above all the other buildings. Nime is next to him in a second, grabbing his arm to keep him from leaving.

"I can't keep you safe if you're not with us," she says. Remy turns his head and glares at her, and I think it's the coldest I've ever seen him. He tries to jerk his arm away, but Nime holds it tighter, so tight her knuckles go white.

"Let go," he says, and my heart is caught up in my throat. This is reminding me too much of that dream, that nightmare, and no one seems to know what to do. When I look over at Ira-nin, he's hiding a smile behind a hand on his mouth. He catches me looking and winks. My stomach drops. Nime is still holding onto Remy, but she looks threadbare. Like if I tug hard enough, she'll unravel. Remy pulls away, but Nime is stronger than him, everyone knows that. I'm close enough to see when her bitten nails start to twist his skin and to see the shock, the betrayal on his face.

"Don't go," Nime says. It's supposed to be an order, but it wavers. Her voice is desperate.

"You're hurting me, Ni," Remy says, not even trying to pull away anymore, just grabbing at her hand and trying to get it off of him. Nime's face goes from wide-eyed and desperate to wide-eyed and scared. Her eyes water and dart around like fish. She looks down at her hand and back up at Remy. I can't take it, I can't take this. I press my hands into the sides of my head.

"Stop." I don't realize I'm saying it until it's coming out of my mouth over and over again. "Stop stop stop." I'm looking down at the ground, so I don't see Nime let go, but suddenly she's right next to me, her hand hovering, trembling, near me. She swallows.

"Navi?" she says. I wrap my arms around my stomach.

"I want to go to the temple," I say. It comes out quieter than I meant it to, but Nime hears, and she nods. She swallows again and almost touches my shoulder, but her hand stops an inch away.

"Okay," she says. I close my eyes, and I hate myself. I do. I know why she said okay to me and not Remy. I hook my arm through Nime's, and I can feel her relax next to me. It's like I lifted a weight off of her, like I'm doing her a favor. When instead I'm using her. Just like Ira is.

It was so obvious, only someone as stupid as me could have convinced themselves it wasn't true. Only someone as selfish and cowardly as me. It wasn't a nightmare, and I knew it all along. I just made myself believe it was, so I wouldn't have to do anything about it. And all the stuff Remy and Chi were saying last night, about me being able to control Nime? It has to be true because I know Nime wouldn't have stopped for anyone but me. Anyone but me or Ira. I have to hold my breath and grit my teeth because I'm sure I'm about to throw up.

We walk, and everyone is silent at first. Slowly, slowly, like ice melting at first light, I hear voices behind us. Nime doesn't say anything, and I can't open my mouth. But Chi is talking, filling up the air in a way I wish I could do on command. Miel joins in, and it sounds like they're talking to Ira. Of course, keep him away from Nime.

Ira laughs behind us, and I don't think I've ever felt this kind of anger towards someone before, except right now, at myself. How could he do something so awful? How could I?

* * *

It was Rem again who fought Nime when they left the house to find the signal jammer. He announced he was going to the temple, and the fraying rope that was Nime snapped.

"No," she said. It wasn't a discussion. It wasn't safe for him to be alone down there. It was even more important than it had been the day before, but when Nime tried to think why, the memory distorted and twisted away from her. It didn't matter. What mattered was that she'd do whatever was necessary to keep him safe.

Rem turned to walk away, and Nime's arm shot out to grab his. She covered up her confusion with a glare. She hadn't told her arm to do that. She remembered fear, the night before: fear that reappeared now in the thudding of her heart.

"I can't keep you safe if you're not with us," she said. Please, she wanted to say, please don't fight me anymore. She didn't want to, but she would keep him here however she had to. Why did she have to?

"Let go," he said, pulling away. Nime tightened her grip. She was sweating already, even though the heat hadn't set in yet. Her fingers pressed into Rem's arm, nails making marks in his skin.

"Don't go," she said. But she was hurting him, and he pulled at her hand to get her to stop. She couldn't stop. Why couldn't she stop? She was hurting Rem, who might as well have been her brother. Why was she doing this? She looked down at her hand, shaking but still holding onto Rem, and back up at him. He pulled desperately at her fingers.

"Stop."

Nime stopped. She dropped Rem's arm before she even recognized Navi's voice. Nime stood next to her in a heartbeat.

"Navi?" Nime said.

"I want to go to the temple," Navi whispered. Nime heard her over the roar of her pulse and the whispers of her friends. Whispers about Nime. She reached out to comfort Navi, but at the last second pulled back. She wouldn't want comfort from the person who had made her upset.

"Okay." Nime relaxed without the weight of Ira's order. That was right, she remembered. He'd told her to hurt Rem. How could she have forgotten? More importantly, how could she do it? The fear did not leave.

* * *

I don't have to open my eyes to know when we reach the temple. I can feel it in my chest. Up at the top of the front steps, Ira wanders off down the hall. I glare at his back, filled with this angry, sick yellow feeling.

"Let's go over here for a bit," Chi says, gesturing with her head. She gives me a small smile as she herds Miel, Remy, and Sess down the hall in the opposite direction from Ira. They look back, confused, but Chi keeps going until they are out of sight. I can feel Nime looking at me. I don't look back. I can't, not after that. To take away a person's free will like that, I'm even worse than I thought.

I sniff and look up. We're standing in front of the room Nime wouldn't let me go into before. This time, nothing's stopping me. Nime follows close behind, but I almost forget she's there after I cross the threshold. I heard the walls whispering before, but now, in here, they speak loud and clear.

The universe is written on these walls. I can't read it, but I don't need to. They're telling it to me, right now, from the very beginning.

Creation. Life. The mingling of past and present and future. The walls pour their words into me; they sink into my skin, warm like the sun. And I know everything.

It's so much. Too much. At first, I can't concentrate on anything. The universe flies by in bursts of light and heat, in the slow and steady pull of gravity and time. And then I see Aht Carina. The walls tell me every living thing that used to be, every living thing that will be, everything that has ever existed. I know all their names, the shapes of them, each link in the great web of life, the intricate interconnectedness that makes the world work.

Web. That's new. Spiders make them to catch insects, to eat. And birds—all kinds of birds in so many colors that I could only have dreamed of before—they eat the spiders, some of them, and others eat seeds. Some of those seeds need to be eaten to grow; they grow into plants that produce fruit, that bear more seeds to be eaten. Eaten by other animals, like deer, who have millions and millions of living things in their stomachs, tiny bacteria like wisps, that help them break down the woody bits of trees. Trees! There are so many trees in my head, flowering, fruiting, pollen-spreading, thorny, dropping nuts and seeds, some to be buried and sprout into more, some to feed beetles and fungi.

And if land and sky are packed full, when I move on there are still the oceans, filled with more life than I can comprehend at first. When I take my time, they stand out. Fish, so many fish, and plankton, and jellies. Huge whales that can barely fit inside my head alongside billions of single-cell organisms. Before, there were creatures that lived on land and water, but those are either gone or have adapted. And that's another thing: adaptation. The ebb and flow of life. Some things live and some things die. The water-walkers, who came from pond skaters, the sea birds and ducks, who adapted as the water rose to no longer need land, to grow stretchy skin between their toes so they can float on the water the way they do on the air.

I remember to breathe. The planet below my feet is so full of life, and even though it's not alive, I can feel it, all of the movements and crashes. The rock and the magma and the atoms that make up every part of it. Water and dirt and the air surrounding me. They're not alive, but they're full of energy all the same.

The flood of creation slows. I blink. And now, without the distractions, I can *feel*. This place is so full of creative Potential, it makes my head swim. I want to run outside right now, stick my hands into the soil, and let it grow. The little green things that just couldn't help themselves and grew up around me earlier, that's grass. They were waiting for me, waiting to come to life. I can feel them, but it's almost like a sound. A new sense? Sight-sound-movement all in one.

I can feel Nime behind me. I don't need to turn around to see exactly where she is and, more importantly, how she is. She is dim around the edges and stretched out, like someone has been siphoning off bits of her. I can feel Remy, and Chi, and Sess, and Miel. They are less loud at the center of them than Nime, but whole. Distantly, I can sense the people in Haven.

I look for Ira, but all I can see is an emptiness, nothing concentrated in a point that sits just outside my temple. No, different than nothing. This is a vacuum, sucking in what's around it, taking the life from its surroundings. It will wilt my baby grass, pull the wrong-ish life from the gooey-alpacas, and it will chew at the edges of Nime like she is a very big leaf that a caterpillar has found. Except this is not like a caterpillar, who will go on to be a part of the web. This doesn't contribute to life, it only takes. The Unlif.

Many things make sense now that didn't before.

Nime touches me, a worried frown on her face. I smile at her. How could she be worried in this place?

"Your skin," she says. I look at my hand. There are traces of gold all over it, faint words from the walls, which whisper to me still. It's distracting, like they're singing a song I know well just outside of my hearing.

"It's alright," I say.

Nime doesn't look convinced. "You're not hurt, are you?"

Hurt? This was always going to happen; this is how it should have always been. I was meant to be covered in the words of Creation.

"No," I say. Nime sighs, and her shoulders relax. She looks better than she did earlier, not as gray. I feel better, too. This place is a sanctuary in every sense. The walls want people to be well here. My mind drifts into the place where everything is. "The walls were telling me about the beginning of time and how the universe began. They were born here, formed along with Aht Carina, and they've seen everything there is to see." I blink, and Nime is staring at me. "I'm—" the Lif, I almost say. But that means that Nime is my Hand, and I don't want her to know. I'm afraid if I tell her, she'll remember everything I've done to her in our pasts.

"They spoke to me too." Nime doesn't look happy about it.

I don't know what to say to that. Despite the certainty that I belong here, despite the wonderful things I know and feel now, I am scared. But I'm being selfish again, and I came here to fix that. Past-Navi, the one from the city, was selfish, too. I don't want to repeat my mistakes. And there is so much I want to talk about to someone who will understand when I say that my heart beats in time with the music of life, and everything waits for its turn to join in.

"Can you feel it, then? All around? This whole place is *filled* with Potential. It's just waiting for me. Look," I say. I skip over to a pile of bones. They made me feel awful before, just thinking about them being *here*, in my sanctuary, but now I can see that they're just a part of life, just one of the materials that I'll use to remake the world. Energy doesn't come from nothing, not since the beginning. I need to have something to start with. Take the bones, they're dry and brittle because it's been so long, and they haven't been able to go back into the world. When I add dust, full of dirt and cells and old pollen, fibers, even material from beyond this planet—this dust is ancient, as old as the walls; it just hasn't always been dust—I have everything I need to make something new, something amazing.

The last time people did this kind of magic, it was called shaping. I used to be good at it, but after several lifetimes with no practice, I can barely remember how it's done.

I scoot the bones into a pile and sprinkle a handful of dust over them. I already know what will come from this, a little thing that didn't exist until right now. With my creation fixed in my mind, I start to push and pull at the matter, and I let loose the Potential itching in my skin. It flows out and into the bones and dust, and I arrange the atoms, the particles into the correct shapes. It is clay now, coating my hands and fingers. I give it a body, I give it two wings and two legs and a head. I sculpt them into existence, and I smile when it starts to wiggle on its own. But it's not ready yet. It needs a face, and it needs something else, something I'm not sure how to make: a soul.

Face first. Faces have eyes, so I press two into the clay. Mouths are good, too. I carve a beak out of nothing. There. I smooth out the last rough edges of my thing, *mine*, that I made, and I set it down on the ground. I sit back on my feet. Now for the last piece.

"Navi, what—" Nime says, but I shush her. This needs to be perfect.

It lives now, but it lacks the spark that separates those that know from those that do not. The soul. I close my eyes.

If I can't make one, then I can find one. My mind stretches beyond the planet, beyond the physical universe. I've forgotten so much, but I know there's a place souls come from.

Out of darkness, I see a tiny glimmer. I reach for it, hold it in my hands. As it flickers, I feel something watching me. I am terribly, completely seen. Seen as if I am transparent, and the heart of me is on display. A voice murmurs something I can't understand.

I open my eyes, press my cupped hands to my creation. I'm not sure what that was. I'm not sure I should have been there.

And then it moves. It stretches out its wings and legs, it blinks its eyes and opens its beak. I look at it; it's like looking at a piece of art, and *I* made it. It tries to walk but falls against my knees. I hold it, and it looks up at me, and I've never been so happy. My creation is small, fitting in both of my hands. Its feathers, now that they're finished, are shiny white and prismatic like the walls of my temple. And its eyes are large and soft and dark.

"What should we call it, Nime?" I ask. I lower it to the ground and lead it around in a circle, its long, three-part tail trailing behind. It's shaky, but it learns quickly.

"What even is it? What did you just do?" Nime asks. I lead it toward her, and she leans down to touch it. She scrunches her eyebrows when it reaches for her with its wings.

"I created it," I say. And the fear I feel lessens. She doesn't remember. Guilt grows in its place. She doesn't remember who I am, or me leaving her. Chewing my lip, I decide to be honest. "I'm the Lif."

Nime looks at me, and her mouth opens slightly. For a long second, she seems frozen, and then she nods in understanding before looking down at my creation.

"What do you want to be called?" she asks. It looks up at her and doesn't answer. I sigh. It hugs my knees with its wings and oh, I love it. It may not be able to speak, but I made it intelligent and kind, and maybe someday it'll learn.

"I don't think it can talk yet," I say, and pat its little head. "Until it gets bigger, I think all it can do is waddle around and look cute."

"Well it does those two things well, at least," Nime says. She looks at me with a straight face, but laughter bubbles under the surface. It shows at the corners of her eyes and when her nostrils flare. When I look back at her, she cracks, and it falls out. I giggle, too, and my creation dances between us in circles, its tail sweeping along the floor in long arcs.

"Let's call it Anue," I say as I stand up. It lifts its wings, like a baby asking to be picked up, so I do.

My eyes catch on a glitter in the wall, and I move toward it. I blink. "There you are," I whisper by its head. Its name is curiously double-layered, almost shadowed. I trace the word with my fingers. They tingle.

Remy and everyone else is coming. I can hear-feel them from the hallway. I barely have a moment to worry about what they'll think before they're in the doorway, talking and breathing and living. Miel stops just inside the doorway and nudges Remy when he sees me. Remy opens his mouth and narrows his eyes but doesn't say anything. Sess blinks a few times, his eyes going straight to Anue.

"I was right!" Chi says, pushing past them. "You really are the Lif. This is so exciting." She beams at me and hurries into the room, slowing when she gets closer. "What's this?"

Nime steps in front of me protectively, a familiar gesture. My Hand always does that. "This is Anue," she says, nodding her head. Chi and Sess get over their hesitation first and come close to look at it. Remy and Miel aren't far behind, although they're still staring at me, not

Anue. Ira stares at me from just beyond the threshold, unnoticed by the others. My fingers curl around Anue; it's as disturbed as I am. Maybe it can sense the hungry emptiness of Ira, too. My sanctuary would be a feast for him if he stepped inside.

My eyes widen. But that's not true. Ira can't come in here. The void of him might not give back to the world what he takes, but *I*, this sanctuary, can make him give it back. I will eat at him like he eats at me, and he'll fall apart if he comes in here.

He stalks away.

"It's so cute!" Chi says, her voice high pitched, and she strokes a finger along the soft feathers of Anue's forehead. It presses up into her hand and she giggles. "But where did it come from?"

"Are we just going to ignore Navi's…uh," Remy trails off, gesturing at me. He frowns as he looks me over. "Is Chi right?" he asks.

I nod, and Remy presses his lips together. His eyes are sadder than I've ever seen them. I think I understand. If I'm truly the Lif, there's no question who my Hand is. I can feel the link like a physical string connecting us. But I don't want to think about that.

"I made it," I say to Chi.

"You made it?" Miel asks. His face is unreadable. "What do you mean you made it?"

"I created it from bones and dust," I say. How else would I have made it? "I can do it again if you want to see?" Shaping is fun. It's good. While every heartbeat pushes Potential outward, this is more purposeful. "Nime, can you get me some water, please?" I ask. I wince a little when she does it immediately. I tried to not make it an order, but using my Hand is instinctive. That doesn't mean I have to do it, though. I set Anue in Sess' hands; he starts cooing at it.

Nime hands me a water bottle, and that's all I need, so I begin. I kneel and sweep my arms out and in, pulling together a pile of dust. This dust has cells in it from plants that became dirt a very long time ago. The bottle clanks against the ground, and I pile the dust up and up and up until it's a mountain. Then I pat it down, dig my finger in until there's a hole at the top. Like a volcano, which I didn't know I knew about until the walls reminded me. Volcanoes are frightening, all fire and smoke that kill and destroy. But after they're done with all the destruction, they put down new soil and build land where there was none before. They're like the Mothers that way.

I never appreciated how amazing water is before now. The place all life on Aht Carina came from, and up until now I hated it. It locked us in, kept us from expanding and thriving, but humans aren't the only life in this world.

I pour the water slowly, so it doesn't overflow. It comes out shimmery and dazzling, like crystal in the sun, from the Potential I put into it. The water pools in the hole. I don't let it sink in, not yet, and I pour until it reaches the edge of the crater. I can see the molecules where they hold tension, keeping it from flowing over the edge.

Folding the water and the dust together, I take care that the water doesn't slip out. I press them together until there's no space between them, until they mix and come together and become dirt. It's cool and dark and soft, and smells almost sweet. My fingers know this dirt, even though I've never touched it before. Past-Navis have plenty of experience.

So, the dirt. And in the dirt, a seed. I spin DNA into strands, and I can see in my head the way it's going to come out. I'm getting the hang of this now, like painting with a new medium. Painting with genetics. Finally, I pat down the dirt into a little hill and sit back. It's going to be big. It just needs to wake up.

The top of the hill splits open, and light flows out. The seed sprouts and sends up a tiny little seedling, all pale and green and delicate. Its cotyledons uncurl. Anue hops over and watches my plant grow, too. Potential spills out of the dirt, and the plant keeps growing taller and taller, until it's a couple of feet tall and swaying like there's a breeze. More leaves, green and alive, open up along the stem.

Anue stretches out its wings and brushes the very tips across my plant, and another stem grows from the main one. More shoot off from the sides until it's covered in branches. Buds form along the branches, and they swell until they burst into flowers, golden and soft and so full of petals it would be impossible to count them. I wanted them to be pink and white, but gold is nice too. The trunk starts to droop a little under the weight of so many branches and leaves and flowers, but then it grows bark and straightens up, thick and sturdy. And the fruit?

Nothing happens for a while after the flowers bloom, and everyone stares at them like they can't look away. I'm not sure if that's a good sign or not. It's not a good sign that the fruit didn't grow, and I chew my lip as I look at the sapling. Where did I go wrong? I thought it was so easy to read the DNA. So much for getting better at this.

"So, there you go," I say. I hug myself and look down at my tree. Anue prances in a circle around it. "Do you like it?" No one responds for what feels like ages. And then Nime touches the top of my tree and her face softens.

"It's wonderful," she says. I brush my fingers against one of the flowers and hug my other arm tighter around my middle. I'm not looking at my hand, so I jump when I feel something pushing against my fingers. It's a fruit, small and pale yellow, but getting bigger every second. I let out a short laugh and touch all the other flowers I can reach, and all of a sudden little yellow fruits grow all over my tree.

"This is amazing. I can't believe this is real," Miel says, eyes wide. He steps up and looks all over my tree. He even scans it with his tablet, and he makes a face when it beeps. "This tree isn't in the database. How did you do that?"

"I shaped it," I say, "out of Potential." Miel just stares at me for a second, and then he grins and stands back as Chi comes up to the tree, and Remy does too. Sess goes around to the other side.

"Are these edible?" he asks. Someone's stomach grumbles. I nod. Nime picks one and sniffs it, then takes a small bite. For a second she just chews suspiciously, and then her eyes widen, and she swallows.

"It's good," she says, and she bites down into the fruit to hold it while she picks some more, passing them off to Remy and Miel, while Chi and Sess grab some for themselves.

I step back to give them a little more space. I'm not hungry even though I haven't eaten since breakfast yesterday. This is common, the walls say. The Lifs that came before me didn't eat either.

"What should I do with this?" Nime asks, holding up the pit, which is a lovely dark blue color. I didn't plan that, but I like it. They've never eaten fruit with a pit before, and neither have I. Except, once I walked through a grove of peach trees with my Hand, and we grew a crop in winter for the starving. I blink. These past-Navi memories are still making things confusing.

"Don't eat them, please," I say. Everyone looks at me. They all have pale yellow juice around their mouths. "Can you just throw them on the ground?" Nime drops hers immediately. Remy frowns while he chews.

"That seems a bit disrespectful," he says when he swallows. Miel wipes his mouth and picks another. I flinch a little.

"They're seeds," Miel says. Remy just looks at him.

"And?"

"It seems less disrespectful than what's already here, considering this is a temple dedicated to the Mother Creator," Sess says. He has to reach up to grab his next fruit, my tree has grown so tall.

"Um, it's all fine," I say. Everyone looks at me again, and I fight to keep my shoulders down and my fingers from fidgeting. "Death is just the transformation of one thing into Potential for another. Everything in here will be made into something else." Now everyone *looks* at me, and I chew my lip and rub my arm. "Never mind."

Remy raises an eyebrow at me but drops his pit on the ground anyway. Chi slides over toward Sess and elbows him a few times, and they look at each other with bright eyes. And then Chi turns to me, and she is smiling.

"When we get back to Haven, the three of us should have a conversation on the theology of The Mothers," she says. Sess nods. I nod back. Out of the corner of my eye, I catch Miel staring at me, and he doesn't look away when I do. In fact, he comes over to me and smiles. I look down at my feet and ignore the way my face and neck feel hot. And I don't even have my hair to hide it since it's still in the braid Chi did for me.

"So, Navi," he says. It's embarrassing: he's been friends with Nime for a few years, and with Remy for longer, but even now I can't think of what to say to him. I glance at him before I remember that that's probably not a good idea. It's like he turns up the volume on his smile when he senses weakness. "Do you think you could make anything?" he asks. In this place? Probably. I nod. "Could you make iron? Or—"

Nime narrows her eyes. "No, you are not using her as some kind of manufacturing plant," she says. I scoot a little closer to her. "You want something, make it yourself."

"Nime," Miel says. His voice gets even smoother, all honey and charm, and he lifts his palms. "I understand where you're coming from, and I get that you want to protect her, but if she could make endless wood, or metal, or dirt, we wouldn't have to worry about finding places to live, or about the leak, or anything. We could build new settlements, new ships. We could find out if the Endless Sea is still endless. If Navi can make something like hydrazine, we could settle Prime, never have to see this stupid ocean again." He loses the calm neutrality he normally has, and a little of his excitement spreads to me. He grabs Nime's shoulder. She doesn't react. "Think about what we could do with infinite resources." He pauses and then looks at me. "Navi, you could save us all," he says softly. And I blink. My heart lifts. Save everyone? That's what I wanted to do all along, wasn't it? I remember my priestesses telling me that I could save the world, and instead I destroyed it. I have to at least try in this life.

The biggest threat at the moment is the generator. The relic of an Unlif past, spilling destructive Potential still. Mom said that Potential had sealed the relic away, and only Potential could seal it again. I could save Haven. This time around I've only made things close to me, but I know I've shaped across long distances before, so I can do it now.

"No," Nime says, and she steps into Miel's space. I open my mouth, breathe in. I brace myself.

"I want to though," I say. I slip my arm through hers and she relaxes. She nods, and I try not to think about how weird it is that my sister is my Hand. About how it must have changed our relationship from the very beginning. I push that way, way back, save it for some other time, when I have more time to think. Maybe when fewer people are around to see me cry. "I think I can reseal the generator, just, um —" I trail off and look around.

"If you can, then please do it," Remy says. He looks serious. "We've spent too long down here, messing around when people are already getting sick." Suddenly everyone looks down, and the mood drops into guilt. He's right. I got so caught up in my own problems that I forgot about why we were here. Dad and Mom are still up there, and I've been so focused on myself.

"I can," I say, nodding. Step one of being less selfish: if I can help, I should. I wonder what relic it is, what object from which Unlif the Architects found and harnessed. In the end, it doesn't matter. As I concentrate, I can feel it in Haven above us, a void like Ira. The walls that surround it are functionally useless; it's the creative Potential that's been woven into them that truly keeps the energy in.

A crack stands out to me, a hole that's torn through both the wall and the seal. I clench my fists. Only destructive Potential could have done this. Only Ira.

It's hard to use the raw, unfocused energy, to smooth it over the hole and enclose the relic again. In this life, I've only channeled it into shaping, not worked with the Potential itself. I concentrate, imagining the Potential as a physical thing and pulling it over the crack. It resists, wanting to be made into something, and I pull harder. Finally, it gives in and allows me to weave the edges together into a barrier. My shoulders slump when the crack is sealed.

"I did it." I breathe deeply, exhausted. I'm nowhere near as good as past-Navis.

Chi sighs in relief. "Thank you." She beams at me, and I feel, finally, like I'm helping.

"I'm not sure if I fixed it permanently, but it should hold until we get home," I say. Everyone relaxes, even Nime. The last remnants of tension lift away.

"Could you do something else?" Miel asks. Nime's head whips around so she can give him a half-hearted glare, but I nod. If I can help, I have to. "Do you think you could fix the transporter?" he asks.

I stare for a second. Machinery is hard. Organic things, natural materials, those are easy. But any human-made thing requires more control. I'm not sure how to make something as complex as a transporter. After a moment, I nod. At the very least, I'll try.

The school of fish is back in my stomach. I close my eyes, picture Ira's office, the transporter standing inside. I try to feel it with my new sense, but something stops me. I frown.

Like a glass wall, something keeps me from getting close to the transporter. The sensation of it slips away from me. For a second, I can feel the copper atoms of the wires, and then it's gone. A drop of sweat rolls down my forehead, itching, but I ignore it. Why isn't it working?

I grit my teeth. If I can't do it the same way as before, I'll try a different way. I can make this work. My head hurts, but I can do this. If I just concentrate, I'll be able to get around whatever is blocking me and reach the transporter.

I stretch my senses out to it again, and this time I make progress. I can see the shape of the plastic and silicon, the pathways the electrons take through the machinery. It doesn't want to let me, but if I press hard enough, if I just *make* it, this will work. I try to tap into the Potential in the air, but something pops in my nose, and I taste metal in my mouth. There's something wrong with the transporter; something about it resists me. My heart pounds. I can't stop shaking. I can't keep still, can't hold onto the shape of it any longer.

I let go.

I open my eyes. I'm propped up by Nime and Remy, and I'm shivering. Nime rubs my back.

"Sorry," I say. My heart beats fast, like a rabbit's. "I couldn't fix it."

"Navi, what happened?" Remy asks. My stomach twists up again. He looks so worried; I can only imagine how Nime looks.

"I don't know," I whisper. "It felt wrong, and I couldn't get a sense of what was broken. It was like magnets repelling each other." Even a difficult shaping like the transporter shouldn't have felt that way. I wish I knew what I did wrong. Normally I have the help of past-Navis, but my memories are too faint and faded by time, and I'm not a good Lif on my own.

Remy looks over at Chi, frowning, and then back to me. "Well, your pulse is back to normal," he says. "Maybe we should take a break with the Lif stuff for now."

I look down, and I make a face. That attempt at shaping may not have worked, but the Potential that came out of me did produce something. At my feet there is a thing, a blobby, mushy…thing. It's an awful, slimy yellow, and it doesn't have a shape. It's hard to look at for long without getting dizzy. I couldn't give the Potential a destination, and now it has a shape that doesn't exist. I look away.

Miel stares at it, running a hand through his hair. He glances up at me and rubs the grimace off his face. And then he looks me over and seems to relax.

"I'm sorry, Navi," he says. "I shouldn't have asked."

I shake my head quickly, and my braid hits my shoulders. "No, no," I say. "It's okay, I'm fine now. And anyway, that was my fault. I just couldn't do it." I look down at the shapeless thing. I almost feel bad for it. "I wanted to help." My voice trails off.

"After all this is over, we'll have to come back down here and figure out what you can and can't do," Chi says.

"That would be a good idea. In the meantime, we'll just find the signal jammer like we planned," Remy says. He comes up from behind me and looks around at the group, and then frowns. "Where did Ira go?" Miel sighs and looks at Remy.

"Truly?" he says. His voice is flat and annoyed. I'm with Miel on this one. Why can't we just forget Ira exists? But Nime freezes and looks around the room quickly. Her breath catches, and my heart sinks. I squeeze my eyes shut. I wish she would forget about both of us.

"We need to go find him," Nime says. She pushes her hair back from her face and starts moving toward the door. Sess steps out in front of her and holds his hands up. She scowls at him but stops. Without Ira around, she's easier to reason with. Miel was right, last night. Under Ira's and my influence, Nime's going to be nearly unstoppable. I'm not going to control her like that, but if we can keep Ira from controlling her, too, then we won't need to stop Nime at all.

"Hold on," Sess says. "Let's think about this." She stares at him.

"Why do you need to find him?" Remy asks. He's back to being sharp. I think he hates Ira as much as I do.

"I'm not leaving him out there alone, potentially in danger," Nime says. Everyone is tense again, and I hate it.

"Nime," Chi says. "We all know there's not truly any danger. Did Ira tell you that? Did he tell you to kill those animals?" Chi asks.

"No, I—" Nime protests, but she has the same empty-eyed look from last night. "I thought—" She looks around the room. I don't say anything. I want to tell her that Ira was lying, that he was manipulating her and using her, that she should never listen to him again. But I can't turn off me being the Lif any more than I can her being the Hand. If I say those things to her, she'll believe them, but not because they're true, or because she wants to.

"You're being used, Nime," Miel says. Nime doesn't respond. "Did he tell you to hurt Rem, too?" At that she squeezes her eyes shut and tightens her hands into fists.

"I won't hurt him again," she says. "I won't hurt any of you. I'd rather die." Remy scowls, and the room is silent for a moment.

"Stop being an idiot, Ni," he says. "Not only are you being stupid, but you're treating us like we're stupid. You think we can't tell what's going on? You think we haven't already guessed your self-sacrificing plan?"

Nime swallows.

"Let me make a few things clear to you since you're being stubborn. First of all, I'm still not over how you didn't tell us about the leak. You just brought us down here and didn't let us tell our families. And now we're trapped until we figure out whatever is blocking the signal. Navi *just* fixed the leak. What if my parents are dead already? What if our grandparents are dead? What if it's too late, and Haven is dying right now, and we don't get to be with our families in the end? I know you were trying to keep us safe, but Wardens, Nime, you should give people a choice!"

I don't want to interrupt, but I also don't want them to worry about that anymore. "No one's dead up there, Remy," I say. I can feel everyone in Haven, and while some of their life-lights are weaker than others, they're all alive. I don't know how I could live with myself if they weren't.

Remy pauses, and for a second his scowl drops, and he blinks quickly. He nods and then turns back to Nime. The scowl returns.

"Second of all, if you thought I didn't know about your little stimulant habit, you're wrong, and it's an insult to my intelligence. Stop taking them, and when we get out of this mess, go to the damn clinic so I can be sure you're not destroying yourself. Third, I know how you are when you focus on a project and the physiological response to stimulants. When was the last time you ate? And this," he gestures to the tree, "doesn't count, because you had one and that was it. We know you, Nime. I know you. I know what you're doing, and it's stupid. Why wouldn't you just tell someone? Huh? Why would you look at this situation, where you're being mind-controlled by someone who has already made you kill animals, and decide to keep quiet about it? And then, after not telling anyone who could help you, you decide that the best course of action is to, what, starve yourself? Make yourself weak? Why don't you trust us?"

"I can't hurt you," Nime says. Her shoulders have been slowly creeping up, and now they're near her ears. "He's going to make me hurt you, and I can't stop it." Her voice lowers, and she looks down at the floor. "Don't you get the danger you're in?" She looks up. Her eyes dart around, never landing on anyone for more than a moment. "Those messages, the massacre that happened down here—that was me. I did that. This whole place, I killed everyone. And I liked it. I remember I liked it."

I move closer to her and slip my arm around hers. She closes her eyes. The memories of past lives are hard to accept, especially ones like that.

"You'd all be better off without me. I can't—I can't hurt you, but as long as I'm around I'm going to anyway. I'm trying to keep you safe." Nime opens her eyes, and tears stream down her cheeks.

"You don't need to sacrifice yourself to keep us safe, Nime," Sess says. He looks at Nime with mournful eyes. One hand touches her lightly on the arm. "Do you think we want you to be hurt instead of us? We don't. Like Rem said, give us a choice, please. Let us help you, and it doesn't have to be a question of whether you get hurt or we do. You're always so eager to protect us, why won't you let us protect you?" For a second, Nime doesn't say anything. And then, like the first raindrops of a starting storm, more tears gather at her eyes. Her mouth trembles, and she buries her face in her hands as the storm breaks. The others move in, and I take a step back to give them space. Sess wraps his arms around her and presses her close. After a second, her own come out to return the hug. Her hands make fists in his shirt.

Chi strokes her hand over Nime's hair, petting her like a cat. After a moment, Nime lets go of Sess and squeezes Chi instead.

"You mean as much to us as we do to you," Chi says in a murmur, still petting Nime's hair. Nime rubs her face into Chi's shoulder.

Miel stands close by Chi, and when Nime lifts her head, he doesn't say anything. He uses his sleeve to wipe at the tears on her cheeks. He looks Nime in the eyes until she looks away. Maybe that says more than his words could. He steps aside when Remy comes over, arms crossed.

"Stop being stupid," Remy says. "You might not have realized, but you matter to us." Nime moves from Chi to him, and when he hugs her, I hear her faintly say, "Sorry." Her voice breaks on it.

I blink away my own tears. Over Nime's head, Chi looks at Miel, and then they both look at me. Chi mouths the word "rope," and Miel mimes tying a knot. I stare at them for a moment. Isn't this enough?

I already know it's not. All it would take is for Nime to think that Ira's in danger, or for him to come here and command her, and she'd be lost again. And we're so close to getting home.

So I make a rope, and I can't tell if I feel guilty or not. Each shaping is easier than the last, and the fibers come easily: I know flax and its makeup intimately now, well enough to form strands in my hands. Each heartbeat they grow, until I convince them to twist and braid together, and when I pull my hands apart a length of rope stretches between them. I drop it and pull more until I have a pile of rope the color of Miel's hair.

Miel takes the rope from my hands and nods. Remy lets go of Nime, and while she blinks and sniffs, Miel and Chi close in behind her. Chi holds her arms down while Miel wraps the first couple of loops around her, trapping her arms to her waist. Nime tries to wriggle away, but not with the same ferocity she normally would.

"What are you doing?" Nime asks. Her voice is frantic. "Stop!"

"This is for your own good," Miel says. Remy frowns and looks away. Nime tries to pull her arms out, but the rope is tight against her elbows, and she can't move much more than her forearms. "And, for ours, too. Didn't you just say you were going to hurt us?"

Nime stops struggling for a second to look up at him. "This isn't enough," she says.

"Sorry," Chi says. "None of us want to do this, but we don't have a ton of other options."

"You don't understand, this isn't enough!" Nime struggles as Miel ties a knot at the back. "I can get out of this; this isn't going to be enough to stop me."

"I figured, but that's why we're also putting you someplace secret, so Ira can't find you." Miel comes around to Nime's front. "We'll come get you when Ira is no longer a threat." He's careful about how he says it, but Nime still lunges toward the door anyway.

"You can't hurt him," she says.

"The only person hurting anyone here is him," Remy says. "Don't worry." Nime looks at him and then down at his arm, and she sags.

"Come on, let's find you someplace comfortable," Chi says, pressing one hand to her back. Nime shakes it off and walks on her own. Sess follows Chi and Nime, and the three of them turn out into the hallway.

I sigh and close my eyes. As awful as tying Nime up is, it's better than me controlling her thoughts and actions. After a few minutes, Chi and Sess come back, without Nime.

"There are a few bedrooms back there," Chi gestures to her left, "so we tied Nime to a bedpost in one of them."

Miel nods. "Great. Now we can figure out the whole network interference thing without having to worry about Ira."

"I already have a general location for the jammer, and once we find it, it should be a simple matter of disabling whatever device or program is causing the interference," Sess says.

"Someone should stay here to make sure Nime doesn't escape and to make sure Ira doesn't come looking for her," Miel says.

"I will," I say. I chew on my lip. "I'll keep her company." I'm afraid to even speak to her, but I don't want her to be alone. Remy comes over to me and puts his arm over my shoulder.

"I'd like to as well. I think it would be good for Chi and me to stay here and see if we can figure out a way to deal with Ira; you and Sess can go find the jammer and take care of it."

"We could take Ira in a fight if we found him, don't you think?" Miel elbows Sess in the side.

Sess looks alarmed. "Uh, well, maybe? I'm used to sparring with Nime, and I'm not sure how much PT he normally does. If he even does the recommended amount."

"You're not going to need to fight him," Remy says. "I just got done lecturing Nime about being stupid, don't make me give you one, too." He glares at Miel, who holds up his hands and widens his eyes.

"Navi, you have any more of that rope?" Miel asks. Now my eyes widen. I would feel a lot less bad about tying up Ira than Nime. I start shaping more flax fibers.

"No, you're not going to tie him up, or fight him, or any other idiot idea you have in your stupid head." Remy crosses his arms. I keep making the rope behind my back. "We currently have no idea what he's capable of. What we do know is that he's probably the divine avatar of a destruction goddess, with potentially the same scale of ability as Navi, who, let me remind you, just created a literal bird and tree. Out of nothing. We also know that he's more than willing to hurt any of us. So," Remy steps close to Miel and pokes his finger into Miel's chest, "if you see Ira out there, don't be a dumbass. Stay away from him."

Miel, eyebrows raised, blinks and opens his mouth. The look Remy gives him makes him close it again and nod. "I won't be a dumbass," he says.

"Good." Remy comes back over to me. "Don't worry, Sunshine. This is almost over with. We should be back home by midday." He smiles at me, and I can genuinely smile back for the first time in days. The hardest part is over.

Sess and Miel head for the door, and Chi calls Remy over to the wall to talk about something. When Miel passes me, I slip the rope coiled in my hands to him.

One corner of his mouth quirks up. "Good work," he says under his breath. And then they're gone.

14

The blob sits there. Menacingly. Chi and Remy argue about something over by the wall.

I should go sit with Nime, but I'm afraid. If I weren't the Lif, would she love me still? Without the bonds of fate and reincarnation, would she even care? At some point, she'll remember all that I've done to her. I don't even remember most of it, and it still makes me feel sick.

I breathe out. Close my eyes and open them again. Looking at the blob makes me want to stop, but I want to know why this one came out as an abstract, shapeless thing, instead of thinking about Nime and the past.

I stick out one finger and poke the blob.

And it dissolves. It explodes into glowing mist and fills up the room. Chi and Remy look up and over at me.

"Um," is as far as I get before the mist settles into the room and the floor shakes a little. And then the floor is dirt, and tiny sprouts poke up out of it, very quickly growing larger, and I have to stand up because something is trying to grow underneath me.

"Navi, what did you do?" Chi asks. I look over. She and Remy stand in thick grass, eyes wide, mouths open. Vining flowers grow up them, using them as support. I clap my hand over the laugh that bursts out of me. My tree is much taller than me now, and one of its branches brushes the top of my head. I squeak and jump, and Chi starts laughing too. After a moment, Remy joins in. The plants bend and turn as they grow. Other trees sprout, and the floor is all soft grass and flowers and moss.

By the time I catch my breath and look around properly, everything has slowed down. My tree is surrounded by others just like it, and they're beautiful. All the colors I could have asked for. They are dark and silvery, with delicate green leaves. They have buds on them; some of the flowers are already peeking out, ruffled pink and white. This was how they were meant to look.

I've never seen so much green in this life. The grass, dotted with little yellow flowers, comes up to my knees. I crouch and look at them more closely. Remy does the same, examining some lichen that's growing on another tree, and Chi sits down. I can see the top of her head above the grass. Her curly hair is tangled up in some of the longer blades of grass. I remember similar groves, dotted with trees and flowers and a different kind of grass, where the sun filtered through the leaves and warmed my skin.

I stand and walk over to Remy. The grass springs up after I step on it. He looks at me. There's still a bit of vine and a flower in his hair.

"Did you do this on purpose?" he asks. He pulls up a bit of grass near his hand, and I flinch again. It startles me, like the fruits. "Sorry," he says. He gently places the grass on the ground. "I guess we shouldn't pick anything in here, then." Chi leans back into the grass and looks at us upside down.

"No," I say. "I mean, I didn't do it on purpose. You can pick them if you want." Anue perches on a branch in one of my trees.

"Can you read the walls?" Chi asks. I blink. "If you can translate them, we might be able to figure out why you can control this well enough to create a single tree, but also accidentally grow a forest." I look down and chew my lip.

"I can't *read* them," I say. I look back at her, and then at Remy. "But I know what they say. It's in me." I hold out my arm and tap the skin. Chi hums and sits up, turning around to face me again.

"For now, let's go keep Nime company. This is something we can figure out when we have time to truly get into the manuscripts here." Chi stands up and loops her arms through mine and Rem's. When we go out into the hallway, my elbow brushes against the wall, and I turn my head to look. The walls are dirty out here, and it's dark in the hallway, but the shadows around that bit of wall fall differently than everywhere else. I frown and lean closer. Remy and Chi turn to look when I stop moving.

"Um, just give me a minute," I say. Remy narrows his eyes, but he and Chi move on down the hall. This isn't about me avoiding Nime, although I think Remy thinks so. This is about what's behind that section of wall. I run my hand over it. My fingers find edges in the shape of a door. I stick my nails into one edge and try to pull. It doesn't move. I step back. Something hangs in the back of my mind, like a word I can't remember. Past-Navi remembers, maybe? I chew my lip and close my eyes. Even after the walls told me everything, the memories from my past selves are still fleeting and strange, and I can't seem to choose which ones to relive. If I could, I would go through them all to figure out a way to deal with Ira. I squint and tilt my head. Maybe I need to look at it from the right angle. I don't remember anything in particular about this door.

"Please open," I whisper. Nothing happens. I ball my hands into fists in frustration. That doesn't help me remember either. I close my eyes again. I lean against the wall on one hand. Something beeps.

I open my eyes to see the door scanning my hand with blue light. I blink. The door slides into the wall beside it. I glance over to where Remy and Chi disappeared around the corner. They shouldn't see this. I'm not sure why, but this room is only for me. My sanctuary, the rest of this temple, I want to share. But no one else should see this room. Which is probably why it's locked behind a handprint scanner.

The little room is intact, untouched, unlike the rest of everything down here. It's not even dusty. This is what the temple should look like. The marble is the same prismatic white I remember: plain when viewed in low light and bad angles, but a dazzling rainbow in the sun. Gold runs through it all, vines spreading up walls like the flowering kind that used to grow on the temple. I sigh. Past-Navi has some wonderful memories.

I step inside, and the door slides shut behind me. There's not much in here, just the lights in the wall and a box on a pedestal. I walk up to it. My stomach turns. The box is gold and covered in gems. A devoted Child, the king of some empire or another, gave this to me many lives ago. He'd had it made from the things he treasured most, which was sweet. I, the now-Navi, don't get what's so special about them. They're just stones; I could make more without much trouble. My finger brushes a dark blue stone the size of my thumb. It's smooth as glass. I touch the edge of the lid. It feels heavy, but maybe that's just because I don't want to open it. I open it anyway.

Images crowd my mind so that I can barely see what's inside, but I catch an edge of glass, a golden handle.

Oh. Now I remember what this room is for. I let the lid fall closed again. Not all of Past-Navi's memories are good ones. Some are sad, and some are hard to look at for long. Someone like Nime holds the thing in the box, and I have to tell them to use it because they won't on their own. Nime wouldn't either. Because she's my Hand. My sister. And she can't. She would never.

Nime would never do that. Not even if I asked her to.

She would. Past-Navi knows it, or do I? I leave the room and the memories and go back into my sanctuary. But the thought doesn't go away. I sit down in the fake sunlight, in a bed of grass and flowers. And I see myself arriving at this valley with my cyborg in tow. The priestesses have hidden this from me, but I know what waits for me here. Still, I came with them willingly enough. I like the valley. It's my home more than the tower ever has been.

I find the room. I open the box. The priestesses tried to keep me out, to keep me ignorant until the last minute, but I know this place better than they ever could.

I open the box, and I run.

In the real world, I shake my head. The memory of me, before, controlling other Nimes, it won't leave me alone. It doesn't matter what I remember, because *I* would never ask that of Nime. I don't want to control her, and I don't want to do *that*. I don't need to, it's only for emergencies. A tiny snake, black and brown, slithers across my fingers and up my wrist. How could they do that? Take away someone's free will? It's wrong.

But Aht Carina will continue to become more and more hostile to life unless something changes. Unless I renew the Potential of the world. It may not be now, it may not be for a long time, but it will happen unless I do something. The walls tell me how to restore balance in one quick moment. I press my hands over my ears. I know already. I know what I would have to do. I swallow. I don't want to think about this anymore. I blink back tears. Anue glides down from the tree to me. It softly taps my knee with its beak. I try to smile.

And then I take a deep breath and stand. Poor Nime is tied up, and I'm sitting here feeling sorry for myself. The wisdom and experience of hundreds of lifetimes, and I'm still the same Navi I've always been. It's time for me to do what I've been saying I'll do and be brave.

If Nime doesn't want to be around me anymore, well, then, I'm not going to keep hurting her like I've done in the past.

She's in one of my old bedrooms, from back when I lived in the temple. I remember sleeping and dreaming in this room. Nime looks up at me; she's tied to one of the wooden posts, and Remy and Chi are sitting on either side of her. They're chatting to her, glancing for a second at me when I walk in. It's good. They help her, ground her in humanity. I'm happy; too many Hands have been consumed by us, and I want her to exist apart from us.

Nime relaxes against the post when I step into the room. We sit for a while, listening to Remy and Chi.

Remy stands up after a few minutes. "I'm going to keep an eye out for the others at the door," he says. Nime shifts a little under her ropes but doesn't try to get out of them.

* * *

Nime could hear Sess and Chi walking behind her, but she didn't look back. It was too much. The ropes, the lecture from Rem, being hidden away—it was too much. She looked at the floor as she walked, and her face burned. At least they'd left her legs free. It would be even worse if she had to be carried off. At least she'd been spared that indignity.

Powerlessness was not something Nime was used to feeling; she took care that it wasn't, that there was always something she could do. Even now she had choices: walk on her own, don't walk, accept the ropes, keep fighting against them. They might not have been good choices, but they existed. That was more than she could say about the situation with Ira.

Nime walked further down the hall, the steps familiar. Doors lined the inner wall, and she stopped in front of one at random. Chi touched her shoulder, and Sess hovered behind her.

"It'll be okay, Ni," Chi said, opening the door, "better than tearing yourself apart." Nime led the way into a bedroom, dusty and threadbare, that must have been comfortable when it was new. Chi was probably right. It would be better to keep Nime out of the way and unable to hurt anyone. The only problem was that she already knew these ropes were not enough to do that. Sess lingered at the door, looking at her with his head lowered. She wanted to reassure him, to tell him it was fine. But it wasn't fine.

Nime knelt and then sat against one corner of the bed frame. Chi knelt beside her and leaned forward, arms reaching around to the knot at Nime's back. The rope shifted against itself, and the constriction loosened slightly.

Choices: Nime could break free now. Chi was untying the knot to retie it to the bed frame. And Sess wouldn't restrain her like Miel would.

Or, Nime could sit still and allow Chi to tie as tight a knot as she was able. She could let her friends put the knife at their necks into a drawer and keep themselves safe. Or try to, at least.

Before she could decide either way, Chi tightened the knot and leaned back.

Doing nothing was a choice, too.

Chi stood up and sighed. Nime didn't look at her or Sess.

"We'll be back in a bit," Chi said. They left, and closed the door behind them.

Nime gave herself one minute of panic. No tears, not when they could come back at any moment, but she took a ragged breath and allowed the fear that had been building to come to the surface. Tears happened anyway.

For a while, Nime couldn't breathe.

Rem and Chi walked back in some time later, followed after a few minutes by Navi. By then, Nime had blinked away any tell-tale moisture in her eyes, and if they were a little red around the edges, none of the others mentioned it. Navi looked at her like Nime was a sad memory and said nothing. She sat with her shoulders curled forward, her head down. If Nime knew Navi, it was because Navi felt bad about something. More specifically, about what she, as the Lif, could do to Nime.

Nime leaned her head back against the bed and closed her eyes. She wasn't crazy, she hated it too. The memory of mindless obedience, of her body moving without her permission, of her fingers bruising Rem's arm even when she'd wanted to stop. But that was Ira. And she loved him—she couldn't *not*, she'd been born to love both of them—but his influence was a lot different than Navi's would be. Navi's reluctance to say anything proved that.

"Ni," Chi said. Nime blinked, and opening her eyes again took almost more effort than it was worth. They stung, and for half a second, she considered leaving them closed. She opened them. Chi leaned her elbows on her knees. "How are you?" Nime closed her eyes again. That was not a question she wanted to answer. Chi sighed. "I see."

Navi cleared her throat and started talking. The words blended together and left Nime's mind as soon as they arrived. It was easier to not think about anything, to let it all wash over her. Chi joined in, and their voices were calming enough that Nime almost slept.

And then their words faded out beneath white noise as Nime's head snapped up and chills crawled down the back of her neck. She breathed in deeply and scanned the room. The hypersensitivity was back, and she noticed all the things that her brain normally filtered out. Smells in the still air: Chi and Navi, sweaty and dirty but still essentially themselves; bones and the mushrooms that smelled like death; dust; beneath it all, an oily, metallic smell, like a machine that was broken and overheating, leaving a puddle of lubricant and missing pieces behind. It stunk of death, too. Now that she'd caught it, it was the only thing she could smell.

Dust motes stood out clearly in the air. The separate strands of rope scratched Nime's skin. Navi and Chi's voices were loud, but beyond them, she could hear other voices and the sound of Rem running. Nime's pulse raced.

Rem stepped into the room, his chest heaving. "Chi, come here for a second." He glanced at Nime.

Chi unfolded and stood quickly, Navi right behind her. Navi looked over her shoulder at Nime as she left.

Once they were gone, Nime pushed her arms out against the rope. It shifted just enough for her arm to slip a little further back. Wiggling her fingers, she searched for the bedpost she was tied to. The tip of her middle finger brushed it, and Nime grit her teeth and tried again.

* * *

Remy starts jogging when we leave Nime.

"What's wrong?" I ask. He shakes his head. His lips are pressed into a line. At the entrance to the temple, Miel and Sess are waiting, breathing heavily. Miel leans against the wall. Sess' eyes are wide.

"Quick run-down," Miel says between breaths. "Real monster. Coming here. Ira." I make a face.

"There's a—" Sess says. He's less out of breath than Miel. "Thing. I don't know what to call it. A corpse?"

"Sorry, what? A corpse? Coming here?" Remy asks. He narrows his eyes.

"Dead body walking." Miel coughs for a few seconds, and Chi pats him on the back. He shakes his head. "It was with Ira. It's following us."

"It's the source of the interference," Sess says. "I think he's using it somehow."

"How is that possible?" Remy asks. Sess shrugs.

Chi takes a deep breath. "Okay, so can't you disable it or something? If that's the jammer, then that's good, right? We know where it is, and you already know how to stop it."

"Theoretically I know how to disable the jammer, but I don't know if there's security I'll need to bypass, or how this thing is jamming the signal in the first place." Sess looks down. "Also, um, this thing punched through a door. It's slow, but I can't work if it's trying to kill me." He rubs his sternum with one hand, and I can see that his hand is shaking when he lowers it. I can't sense any life like the one they're describing; only the vacuum that is Ira.

"You outran it though," Chi says.

"So you want to outrun this undead thing until Sess fixes the network, and then keep outrunning it until someone gets the transporter working again? How long will that take?" Miel asks. He frowns and shakes his head again. "That's not a good plan."

"What else do you propose?" Chi asks.

A breeze brushes against me, and I turn in time to see Nime running past the five of us.

"Sorry!" she calls as she sprints out the door. She still has the rope binding her arms to her sides, but as she runs down the stairs, it loosens and drops. She jumps over it. I turn to look at the others. They stare with open mouths at Nime's back, and then Remy takes off after her, Chi and Sess only a step behind him.

"Nime!" Remy shouts. She doesn't turn around. Miel groans and leans forward with his hands on his knees. I pick up the skirt of my costume and follow the others. Miel follows, too, wheezing somewhere behind me. We were so *close*.

* * *

Nime could hear the conversation as well as if they were having it in front of her. At "it's following us," she missed the post and grabbed air. If the sudden anxiety and hypersensitivity weren't enough to concern her, that would've done it.

She pushed out and reached for the post again. With a little maneuvering, she managed to get both hands on it. The wood grain stood out in ridges against her fingers. Breathing in and pushing her elbows out, Nime wrenched the post to the side. A crack sounded as the wood splintered. She breathed out through her teeth at the sharp pain in one of her shoulders and repositioned. This time Nime pulled forward with her body weight, and the bed creaked and snapped. She lurched forward as the bottom of the post ripped off, and she and the bed hit the floor with a thud.

Getting her feet under her, Nime stood and worked at the knot still tied to the chunk of wood in her hands. Now that she could pull it down within reach, she loosened the knot as she ran down the hall. The others stood near the door, Sess and Miel out of breath. Nime sprinted past them and out of the building, shouting a "sorry" over her shoulder. She dropped the ropes on the stairs and kept running.

Layers of sound separated as she ran. Footsteps from behind her, lungs breathing and hearts beating, the swish of fabric. Softer than the others, a sound turned her head. It sounded like creaking, rusted metal, like the groaning of the walls she sometimes heard in the deepest parts of Haven. A screech of metal on metal that even the others must have heard. And then, more quietly, two rhythmic beats. It was hard to distinguish them, but Nime stopped completely and held her breath. One of them was heavy, thudding footsteps. The screeching cacophony grated on her ears.

Ira was nearby, too. His heart beat fast, but not from fear, like her own. His raced from excitement.

The thing was much closer now, and a thrill of fear ran through Nime. She ignored it. This could be the way to make herself unusable as a weapon. If this dead-body-walking was violent, Nime would fight it. And if the thing managed to land a few hits on Nime, all the better. If the others decided to tie her up again, it would be easier after. They would be safer.

Nime could tell when the others began to hear and smell the thing because at least one person gagged and stopped running behind her. It was putrid, rotting fish and flesh and bone, mixed in with an acrid, oily tang that only intensified the scent. It was the worst thing Nime had ever smelled in her life. She slowed down and scanned the area. It was close.

And then, from behind a house about twenty yards away, Nime saw it. A figure walking at a moderate pace toward her. Details clarified as it approached, but Nime wished they wouldn't. The thing *had* been human. Now it was a rotting, gray corpse with dull metal showing through its skin and muscles. It stood about as tall as Sess, with long, black hair that was startlingly healthy-looking, for a dead person. It had been a woman, judging by the body and face, with robotic eyes that moved fluidly. Those unnerving eyes moved and presumably saw without any kind of life behind them. It came to a halt about midway, turning its head side to side. When it spotted Nime it moved again, more quickly than a decaying body had any right to. It ran down the street between the houses, its steps loud and pounding, distinct from another percussive sound Nime could still hear.

The others stopped just behind her, and Nime turned to look at them. "Go hide somewhere," she said. She glanced back at the robot-corpse as she gently pushed Miel and Navi toward a house. Sess pulled his tablet out with shaking hands.

"That's a bad plan," Rem said.

"Rem." Nime spared half a second to look at him. He looked at the thing, eyes wide and one hand over his nose and mouth. "I just need to distract it long enough for Sess to shut it down." As it got closer, Nime ushered him and the others toward the house. She needed them to stay out of harm's way. "I can do that more easily if you're not in the way."

Navi and Chi took up spots near the window inside the house, followed by Sess.

Rem shook his head. "Fine, but if you get into any trouble, I'm going to help you whether you like it or not." Then he slipped inside.

Nime shut the door after him and moved back into the street. The thing was close now, and Nime bounced on her toes. But instead of coming straight for her, like she'd assumed it would, it veered left toward the house. It scanned the house with a red light before reaching for the doorknob.

"Hey!" Nime shouted, waving her arms, almost dizzy with fear that this thing was specifically looking for one of the group inside. She wasn't going to wait to find out who. The robot paused and looked over, assessing her with that red light, and went back to opening the door. Nime frowned and leaned down.

If it wouldn't pay attention to her, then Nime would make it. She grabbed a rock from the ground and hurled it at the thing, listening for the clunk of rock against metal. It didn't come the way she expected it to. The robot, fast as light, turned and caught the rock in its hand, metal fingers crunching around it. It stepped back from the door and turned to fully face Nime, whose eyes widened. She barely had time to wonder if this might not go according to plan before it lunged at her, stink and sound and movement all in one. Nime picked it all apart, ignored the distraction of the stink and the sound, and focused on the movement, on where the robot would land, where the swing of its arms might hit her. She darted to the side, trying to circle around and get behind the robot, to pull it away from the house.

It was a delicate balance of allowing herself to get hurt while remaining able to protect the five of them. Six, now. Ira leaned against a nearby house nonchalantly, ropes wrapped around him like they had been around her. Sess opened the door and held his tablet in both hands, mouth pressed into a thin line as he worked.

The robot spun, its back to the house. Nime kept moving, scanning the ground for more rocks or anything she could use to keep its attention away from the door, which Miel was now peeking around. He paled at the sight of the robot. Nime lingered long enough to tempt it into another lunge before scrambling backward. Her foot caught on a brick sticking out of the road, and she stumbled, grabbing it as she steadied herself.

Nime righted herself in time to see a metal hand coming at her like a tidal wave, inexorable and huge. The robot hit her hard, and she landed on her back and slid a little. The hit knocked the air from Nime's lungs, and she couldn't seem to move. But the robot turned and focused on Sess in the open door, and her breath came back in a gasp. Her hand didn't wait, however, and she chucked the brick she'd picked up as hard as she could. The angle was bad, and she couldn't get a great throw in, but it hit the side of the robot's chest anyway. The bits of its face that were still fleshy grimaced, and it turned back to Nime. She wrapped one arm around her chest. It hurt every time she breathed, so at least one of her ribs had probably fractured. Good.

Nime's fingers and feet scrabbled against the ground in her haste to get up. She let another hit land on the side of her head, and the impact left her dizzy.

Chi ran out the door and stared at the robot for a moment before taking a deep breath. "Hey, look at me," she called. It turned toward her, leaving Nime blinking and reeling.

"No, Chi," she said. Chi swallowed and moved away from the house, and the robot turned to watch her. The skin and muscle over its chest were gone where the brick hit. There was metal underneath, artificial ribs and sternum, and something like a cage behind that: the source of the persistent thumping. It was plastic, unlike the rest of the robot, pliable, beating like a heart.

Nime kicked, and it connected with one of the robot's knees. A sharp pain spiked in her foot. Instead of paying attention to her, the robot turned its head toward Sess, whose fingers moved frantically across the tablet balanced on his knees. He glanced up and redoubled his efforts, biting his lip when he had to think for a moment. Nime lurched forward, stepping heavily and gritting her teeth through the pain. She punched the robot's exposed heart. It staggered before spinning around with its hand outstretched, catching Nime by the neck. Heat burned against her skin.

Nime gasped and gripped the robot's wrist, struggling against its hold. Rem yelled at it from the door. Nime couldn't hear what he said through the ringing in her ears. This was what she wanted, what needed to happen. But still she squirmed, kicked, scratched, and the robot held her neck. It ignored Rem, still yelling, and Chi, who had an armful of rocks and threw them at it one by one. And then the robot slowly tightened its fist and lifted Nime. Panic surged through her. She wanted to be injured, not dead. She grabbed at the metal fingers around her throat, trying to worm her own underneath them. They heated under her hands.

Sess glanced between his tablet and Nime. She shoved her fingers between the metal and her skin, ignoring the painful pressure against them and pulling with all the desperate strength of adrenaline. She breathed shallowly, dizzy. The world swirled black around the edges of her vision.

And then the robot stopped. The red light in its eyes faded and died out, and it froze in place. Nime's fingers tightened over the metal and pulled again, and when Sess and Rem ran over and added their strength to the effort, she slipped out of its grip and tumbled to the dusty ground. Nime breathed against the pain in her chest, blinking slowly as the world came back into focus. Each breath scraped against her throat, raspy and ragged. She winced as she gingerly touched her neck, gliding over the places the robot pressed, scratches from her nails, and the burned imprints of fingers. Rem knelt next to her, hovering and comforting. Ira, who had been leaning against a wall, straightened and inspected the robot's still form.

Was this enough? Nime thought as Rem scanned her with his medtab. Would this be enough to stop her? She hurt, sure, but fractured ribs and abrasions on her neck weren't incapacitating. The possible concussion though—she lifted a hand to the side of her head, and her fingers came away bloody. That should slow her down. The world was already unsteady. It would only be more so when she started moving.

Navi and Miel emerged from the house, and Nime looked Navi over. Navi stared at the robot with wide, teary eyes. Sess tapped out a message on his tablet, and then he dug through his bag.

"I don't have any medicine," he said.

"It's okay, I have my salve that I was going to present yesterday," Rem said. Nime waved them off, even though her palms hurt at the movement.

"Medicine?" Ira said. The others jumped a little, finally noticing him. "Nime's not that badly injured, right Nime?" He smiled as he asked. Nime nodded, the skin of her neck pulling painfully. She was glad he wasn't ordering her to be healed, though she didn't know why.

But it made sense when she listened to the side of herself that had enjoyed every fight she'd ever been in. If Navi was creation, then Ira was destruction, and there was something fascinating about seeing how much she could bend before she was broken.

✳ ✳ ✳

The only thing I can see is the dead cyborg. My cyborg. My Hand. This is what's left of her, after me. The Unlif helped, but the only person to blame for her current state is past-Navi. I was the one that left her.

Nime sits on the dusty ground next to my cyborg. Red marks cover her neck, and she breathes shallowly, holding her hands so they won't touch anything. Blood drips down the side of her face. Here, in front of me, are two people I've betrayed and taken advantage of. I never deserved them.

"I'm not that badly injured," she says, her voice rough. The words are short, like they're hard to get out.

Remy pulls a jar out of his bag and reaches for her, but she shifts away. She clenches her jaw when it jostles her ribs. I wince for her, since she won't. I step a little closer, and she doesn't move away from me. Remy glares at her.

"I'm going to treat your injuries, don't be stubborn," he says. Nime shakes her head, and this close, I can see that it must hurt so much. A ring of red bruises circles her neck. And above it, lines of a darker, bleeding red. Scratch marks. I kneel next to her and gently pick up one of her hands. She lets me, but I can hear the sound she makes, a hushed whimper locked behind her teeth. Her palm is even redder and hot to the touch. Her nails are bloody.

Remy scoots closer, and Nime tenses but doesn't move. When he tries to touch her, she pushes away hard with her right foot. She clenches her jaw, but another small sound escapes. Remy's eyes widen.

"We talked about this. Let me help you," he says. When she doesn't respond he looks at Ira, and his face goes dark.

"Navi," Chi whispers, closer than I realized. When I meet her eyes, she looks sad. "She'll listen to you." I shake my head quickly. I've already done enough to her, in this life and the past. I don't want to do that. Chi nods and says, "I know, it's horrible, but think about it. She needs help. You can help her." She pauses. "It would be for the best." What would Nime want? I know my sister. She wouldn't want this. But now she's hurt, and I can help her. Is it selfish to refuse?

"Nime," I say, and her head snaps toward me. I wince. That's got to hurt. I breathe in. This is for her, not me. It's for the best. That doesn't lessen the guilt I feel.

"Please don't," she says. I almost can't hear her, she's so quiet. I swallow. She closes her eyes, and it's quiet for a moment.

I look at my cyborg. I can't understand what happened here. What part of her programming made her attack? Because programs and cybernetics are all that's left of her; no hint of the person I once knew remains. My eyes water. I loved her, centuries ago. It's my fault she's like this, this still-walking body with no soul. Supported by the metal and wires that made her a tool for my priestesses in life. And now, a tool for Ira after death. Where did he find her? How did she remain for so many hundreds of years?

"We should destroy this thing," Ira says. Right. That's why. He must have sent her after Sess and Miel after they tied him up. He stares at the cyborg, but when no one responds, he looks at Nime.

Sess clears his throat. "There's no need for that," he says. "I crashed the system, so it can't do anything anymore."

Ira looks over at him and flashes a cold smile. Then he turns toward

Nime and me.

"Nime, I need you," Ira says. She stands up immediately and limps over to him. Remy tries to stop her, but she pulls out of his grip. Ira smiles, and it's the cruel one again, the one that makes my skin go cold. "Good girl." Ira doesn't look at anyone other than Nime. "Go on, destroy it." He nods at my cyborg.

Nime presses her lips together, grabs a brick from the street, and begins. I close my eyes and turn away. Remy yells at Nime. Someone comes close to me. I open my eyes. It's Miel, and the look in his eyes is intense.

"Navi, I know this is a hard thing to think about, but you're the only person who can help Nime right now," he says. I shake my head. There's a loud sound behind me: the smack of something hard against metal. "We need to separate them, so Nime can be free. You have to tell her to stop listening to him, to come back to the temple." He's whispering, but his voice gets louder as the sounds behind me slow down. I take a step back. I'm not going to do that ever again. It's wrong. I turn around. Nime drops the brick and stands next to Ira. Her face is empty. And Ira watches us, a bored look on his face. It's like he doesn't even notice the ropes tied around him. Miel grabs my shoulder and half turns me toward him. "Tell her to go back to the temple," he says.

"No," I say. I glance back at Nime out of habit, the come-save-me look. She stares at us like she wants to say something, but she doesn't move at all. She's as still as I've ever seen her. "I can't do that."

Miel grips both of my shoulders tightly. "You *need* to, Navi." I try to pull away from him. "Tell her not to listen to anything Ira says!" I pull hard enough to slip free, and end up stumbling back into the source of the black hole in my senses. The destructive Potential that radiates from the Unlif. Miel looks behind me, hiding all of the desperation from a second ago behind a mask of caution. I scramble away from Ira. He laughs. I end up next to Sess, who steps partially in front of me. Miel backs away.

"Oh, come on Navi, I know you want to," Ira says. He rolls his eyes. "Don't act like you've never done it before. Look, I'll show you how. Nime, slap Miel across the face." His voice goes from playful to sharp in a split second, and before anyone has the time to process what he says, Nime is in front of Miel, hitting him hard with the palm of her hand. He barely has time to flinch before the loud smack. And then he just stands there, hand over the red mark on his cheek, staring at her. Her face isn't blank anymore. She looks like she's going to throw up, face pale, mouth open. Her eyes water. Remy starts yelling, and Miel locks eyes with Ira. It's chaotic and loud and quick, and in the midst of it, Sess leans close and whispers to me.

"I sent a message to everyone in Haven," he says. I've never heard him speak so fast, and he's never made eye contact with me. But now he does. "Go back to the transporter and try to fix it again. If you can, we might be able to get some help." I open my mouth, but I have no idea what to say. It feels like running away if I leave. It feels like he's giving me an escape. "Navi, go now, while Ira's distracted." Sess steps completely in front of me, so I can't see anything but his back, and he points behind himself at the alley we're standing in front of. I stare at him. He turns his head slightly toward me. "Go, please. We'll be fine."

I almost do. I almost leave them and run away.

But I can't.

I don't go. I can't go, not when I could do something. Ira watches me, head slightly tilted, and in the middle of the chaos, he looks satisfied. I can't leave them with him, leave Nime to be controlled and the others to be hurt.

As much as I don't want to believe it, Miel is right. I'm the only one who can help Nime. And so far I've been afraid of controlling her, afraid that if I do, that means she never truly loved me, she was never truly my sister, just my Hand. And because of that, I've watched as Ira controls her and she tears herself apart. I could have stopped this from the moment I remembered. But I didn't, because despite all my resolve to be brave and unselfish, I never stopped being afraid.

I can't keep letting this happen. I've let Nime get hurt, I've let her hurt Remy and Miel, I've let Ira control her. And for what? So I don't have to do something hard? Controlling Nime isn't right, but neither is letting *him*.

"Nime, stop," I say. Nime freezes where she is and looks gratefully at me. How could I justify not stopping her when it's clearly what she wants? "Come here." She comes. Ira stands silently, staring at me. I stare back.

"Let's go back to the temple," Remy says. Miel nods next to him. "Leave Ira here and let someone else take care of this." I nod, too.

"Come back with us," I tell Nime. I'm not sure it's necessary—she's already with me—but I want to make sure she doesn't stay with Ira. Nime nods and sticks close to me as we turn and start toward the temple. Her breaths are labored and shallow, and she limps. It hurts to see her like this, but I need to get her as far away from Ira as possible, as soon as possible. Once I get her away from him, I won't need to order her to do anything ever again. This is the last time I'll use this.

15

As we walk away from Ira, I hear a soft thump, and hands wrap almost tenderly around my mouth and waist. The body behind me is freezing cold and an empty pit in my life-sense. Ira. I jump and try to pull away. What happened to the rope he'd been bound with?

"Mmm, I don't think I want you to do that, actually," Ira says. He is much stronger than me. I should have put more effort into PT. I should have known he wouldn't just let us leave.

"Run back to the temple," I say. Or rather, I try to, but Ira's hand over my mouth presses hard at the first sound. Only a squeak comes out.

"What was that?" he asks. I can see Chi in the corner of my eye, frozen. "Nime, don't let anyone come near us." Nime stands stiffly, looking at the two of us. Miel whispers to Sess as Chi steps forward. Her face is angry, mouth twisted down in a way I've never seen on her before.

"Let her go," she says. Nime holds her arm out when Chi tries to take another step. In a move I barely see, Sess comes up behind Nime and pulls both of her arms behind her back. He says something quietly in her ear. Nime staggers back against him. She struggles when Chi keeps walking towards me, but Sess holds firm.

Ira's arm around my waist leaves for a second, and I try to twist away. But then it comes back, knife in hand, and he presses the blade just below my chest. He pulls me closer, ignoring my attempts to pry his hand off of my mouth.

"If any of you come closer," he says, "I will kill Navi."

217

Chi stops. I stop.

"Chiri, take a step back," Ira says. She hesitates for half a second until he presses the tip of the knife in a little, and I cry out.

Chi steps back, and Ira laughs.

"It's almost like I can control all of you, instead of just Nime," he says. Nime stares at the knife for a second before looking up at me and then Ira. Horror grows on her face. I wish I had been brave sooner.

I look at Remy until he meets my eyes. The plan hasn't changed; we still need to get back up to Haven and get help. Only now, I can't go with them. I try to tell him that with my eyes. He nods slightly and leans closer to Miel, speaking quietly. He edges in the direction of the temple.

"If you want to try leaving, you certainly can," Ira says. "But, are you sure someone will be coming to help you? I put a lot of effort into making sure no one else would be able to get near the transporter." He takes a step back, pulling me along. The others seem to come to a decision, and Miel, Remy, and Chi take off running toward the center of the Dome. I'm glad. Them being here only adds to the number of people who might get hurt. I'm not worried about me; Nime can't hurt me unless I tell her to, not even if Ira does.

Ira leans down a little. "Don't worry, Navi, they won't be left out of our fun." I shudder. I should have spoken up sooner.

For a moment after they leave, it's quiet. Nime's breathing is audible in the stand-off, ragged and pained. Sess keeps a tight hold on her, even though he looks like he's about to cry. And then Ira taps his foot and sighs.

"Well, I'm bored, so let's move this along," he says. "Nime, come here."

Nime struggles. Each step must be painful on her foot and in her ribs, but she ignores any pain and wriggles and pulls. Sess makes a noise but doesn't let go. My heart is in my throat. Please hold on, Sess. Nime kicks back at his legs and wrenches herself away from him. She gets one arm free and uses it to pull at his hand. Behind me, Ira cheers her on.

Even now, I can see that she doesn't want to hurt him, using her fingers instead of her nails and being careful with her kicks. Eventually,

Nime pulls herself away, and my shoulders slump. Sess staggers backward from the force of it. His feet catch against one of the loose stones in the road. His arms flail as he falls. I breathe in sharply, and my eyes widen. Sess lands on the ground with a thud and a crack.

When I see blood pooling under his head, I struggle again, the world blurring through tears. Nime winces but walks toward us. When she reaches Ira's side, she turns and lets out a choked sob.

Sess is still alive, I can feel it, and he breathes in short, sharp gasps. Nime reaches out a hand, but she can't go over to him. Her outstretched hand shakes.

"No," she breathes out.

"Oops," Ira says. "I might have helped out a little. Go ahead and finish him off. Smash his head against the rock again."

Nime's hands are still shaking as she moves back to Sess. I yell against Ira's hand, but I can't get out any real words.

Time seems to slow as Nime kneels and takes Sess' head gently in her hands.

She hesitates, thumb brushing over his temple.

I bite Ira's hand, hard.

Nime lifts Sess' head.

Ira taps the blade of the knife against my neck.

She takes a breath.

"Little Lif," Ira says.

Nime clenches her jaw and brings Sess' head down with force. There's a crunch this time.

"Don't you remember?"

Nime lets go and sits on her feet. Her shoulders shake.

"You can't hurt me."

Nime's whole body is shaking now, and she holds up one red-tipped hand.

"I *am* destruction," Ira says. I bite him again. He sighs. "You know, you deserve this, Navi. Bring me that rope."

Nime immediately stands up and steps behind Ira, grabbing the rope. She's crying as she carries it to us. It's rotted away in several places where Ira's destructive Potential has eaten away at it. I should've known.

Ira takes one end of the rope and brings it up to my face. "Go—" I get out, when he replaces his hand with the rope. Nime perks up, but Ira pulls the rope into my mouth, and I can't speak. Some of my hair gets caught up in the knot he ties at the back of my head, pulling against my scalp. I wince. There's a sawing sound as he cuts the extra rope off and hands it to Nime.

"No, stay," he says. "And tie her hands together." He spins me around and pulls my arms out behind me, pressing his arms against me and tightening his grip on my wrists until it hurts. I glare up at him. He smiles at me. After a moment, I feel Nime's hands gently wrap the rope around mine, tying a loose knot. Ira rolls his eyes and reaches down to tighten it until my wrist bones press painfully together. I shift my arms, and the rope scrapes against my skin. "Perfect." Ira spins me back around and holds the knife to my chest. "Now, let's go find those friends of yours, hmm? And when you find them I want you to hold them and wait for us."

Nime runs toward the temple. Ira pushes me along behind her, his hand gripping my arm tightly. I hear Remy's voice after a few minutes of walking, and my heart drops.

We step out of an alley and see them, Remy and Nime wrestling on the ground. Nime pins Remy quickly. I stumble along with Ira as he moves closer to them. Nime looks up at him, tears streaming down her cheeks, jaw clenched.

Ira passes the knife down to her and then pulls me a few feet away. "Go ahead," he says. "Kill him."

I twist and pull, trying to shout around the rope in my mouth, but I can't get away. I can't stop Nime when she takes the knife, holds Remy down, and drags it across his neck.

He gasps. Nime moves to his side. She leans over him, and I can't hear what she's saying, but she speaks to him as he grips her shirt with white knuckles. After a few seconds, his hands loosen and fall. Nime looks at her blood-covered hands. So do I, until I can't anymore. I close my eyes.

"Nime," Ira says, dragging out the 'i' in a whine. "It's not much of a show if it's over that quickly."

I shake my head. Remy is dead. My cousin is dead, and Ira is complaining that it was over too quickly. He cannot be human. I can't believe that a fellow human could *be* this way.

And I know, even as I think it, that he is; he is as much a human as I am. And that's the problem. Destruction is something that all creatures do, every day. So is creation. It's part of human nature to destroy, and even though I don't like it, I know it's necessary. But this, this isn't necessary. The world is a complex web of living and dying, all things in their time. Remy would have died eventually, but this is not his time. Everything is off-balance.

Tears leak out from my closed eyes. I don't know what to do to put things back to rights. Something like this has to have happened before; I've lived hundreds of lives, surely there's something I remember. But it's been a long time, and my memories seem to only come in bursts. Think, Navi. Remember. I open my eyes and look around, hoping for something to jog my memory.

Chi cries out when she runs around the corner and sees Remy and Nime. She shakes her head, and Nime does too, sobs making her back and shoulders shift.

"You all are making this too easy," Ira says. "You're supposed to run away." Nime advances toward Chi.

Chi looks past her to Ira. "Monster," she shouts at him, before turning and running. She doesn't make it around the corner before Nime is on her, pinning her to the wall of a house.

"This time I want you to take it slower. Give little Navi a show," Ira says. He looks down at me, and I don't understand. Why? What could make him want to do something like this, to give me a show?

"Let's go with…" Ira tilts his head. "A stabbing."

Nime shakes her head. Her hand brings the knife up and down. Chi holds her hands in front of her, but they don't offer much protection. Nime's knife cuts into her palms, and Chi screams. Nime doesn't stop.

I have to look away, so I look up at Ira through my tears. He's watching Nime, but after a moment he looks down at me. I glare as hard as I can. He frowns.

"Don't look so sad, Sunshine," he says, grabbing the top of my head and turning me back to look at Nime and Chi. Nime's hands and arms are covered in blood. I see Chi's face over her shoulder, a stunned, pained expression on her face. Her lips are moving, pausing every time Nime stabs her. Again and again. Nime's other arm presses Chi against the wall. "Remember the last life the three of us spent together, Lif? On the island? That was fun, wasn't it? We had a good time." He looks down at me with something like fondness. I remember. I don't want to, but I do. And then the look on his face grows hard again. "And then you left us. She still loves you, even after you betrayed us. She loves you more than me." Ira's hand holding my arm tightens. "Just like everyone else."

I try to look at him again, but he holds my head where it is. What does Nime, or anyone else, loving me more have to do with anything? Why would he make Nime kill her friends over that? I don't understand. If Ira wants Nime to love him more than me, then is he punishing her? Is he punishing me? I suck in a breath around the rope.

Ira pulls my head back so he can look at my face. He's smiling like he's satisfied. "Does it make it worse to know that this is your fault, too?"

I can't see through the blur of tears, and my legs wobble beneath me. Ira pushes my head back down. Nime is still stabbing Chi, but Chi isn't moving at all anymore. Her body is limp.

He's punishing me. He's doing this to hurt me, destroying Nime to destroy me. It was bad enough before, but he's right: it's worse to know that it's because of me. And there's nothing I can do to stop it. I failed and missed my chance.

Nime's hand slips on the knife, and it falls to the ground. She looks back at us, her face and neck speckled in red droplets. I close my eyes and breathe, but I can smell blood in the air.

"Perfect, Nime, you are perfect. Now go find Miel." Ira tugs on my arm and raises an eyebrow at me when I don't walk. "I can always make it worse for her," he says.

I walk. Nime disappears between buildings, heading for the center of the Dome. I don't know what could be worse than this for her, what could hurt her more than this, but I don't want to find out.

Nime stops near the steps of my temple, and even though I can't see it yet, I know Miel is there, too. I can feel the life of him there. I hope he runs. I hope he makes it into my sanctuary because at least there

Ira's influence will be all but gone. Nime calls out, and Ira pushes me to a jog to keep up with his long steps.

Nime is pulling Miel down from the temple steps and into the square when I get close enough to see them. She has him by the legs, and he kicks and claws at the ground.

"Nime, please, you don't have to do this. Please," he says. But Nime shakes her head and presses him into the ground by his throat.

"Good idea," Ira says. Nime turns to look at him, and her face is empty of expression, except for her eyes. Her eyes are wide and scared. "Keep going until I tell you to stop."

Nime's chest heaves, but she presses her other hand to Miel's throat. This time I struggle harder, kicking backward like Nime did, and trying to yell around the rope in my mouth. Ira shoves his knee into the backs of mine, until I fall to my knees. He pats my head.

Miel claws at Nime's hands, scratching bleeding lines into them, but Nime never lets up. It's not long before his hands fall to the ground. He's not dead yet, but it won't be long now.

Ira tells Nime to keep going. Nime cries.

I can't look anymore. I can't watch another person die. It's too awful. Instead I look down at the ground under my knees. Tiny purple flowers are already growing up between the cracks in the road. Despite everything, life will go on. Maybe in a few millennia, Aht Carina will be a completely different place, with different life, with no Lif or Unlif to interfere. I close my eyes. That doesn't make me any less afraid now, though.

"How are you feeling?" Ira asks me. He reaches down to touch my face. I jerk away. "Don't be like that. I told you, you deserve this. You always get what you want: all the praise, all the love. Humans always pick you over me, and you think you're better than me because of it. But you don't deserve their love anymore than I do."

I don't look at him, but a few more tears drop into dark circles in the dust. Everything happened so fast; I should have spoken up sooner, but I didn't, and now Nime's being tortured for my mistakes. Ira's hand squeezes the back of my neck, just tight enough to hurt.

"But I'm going to end this pointless cycle. I'm sick of coming back to be hated. So, after Miel, it's Nime's turn. And then I'll kill you," he says. I close my eyes. "I haven't decided how, though. If you have suggestions, feel free to share." He lets go of my neck, and I breathe in through my nose.

He's going to kill me, here in my valley, just like—

I open my eyes again. I remember the gold-throated old woman in the rooftop garden, warning me of what my priestesses were going to do. They were going to kill me, here, in my temple, with my Hand. My eyes widen. Why? Why were they going to kill me? What happens if the Hand takes the blade from my secret room and sacrifices me in my temple?

I swallow.

I know how I can fix this.

16

Sess, sweet Sess, held Nime's arms behind her back, and she wanted to scream. She wanted to cry. She wanted to wake up and find that this had all been a terrible dream, a nightmare of the worst thing that could ever happen.

"I'm sorry, I'm trying to help," he whispered. Nime knew; of course he was trying to help. She sagged against him. She was exhausted, but she couldn't sleep or stop or relax.

Because Ira held a knife to Navi's chest. When Chi got too close, he pressed it in, and Nime regretted everything. She would have taken back every decision that led to this point if she could have. She would have told Haven about the leak, she would have died of exposure to Potential, if it meant that *this* would have never happened.

Nime's mind felt sluggish as she stared at Navi and Ira. She could hear Rem and Miel whispering, she knew when they and Chi left, but everything outside of Navi and Ira was meaningless. Sess' hands felt like the only things keeping her from washing away.

That feeling lasted until Ira told her to come to him again. Pain sparked all over her body, from overused muscles and fractured ribs, and a sickening dizziness filled her head. But she did her best to get away from Sess. Tears burned in her eyes.

Sess was too sweet, even now. He wasn't using his full strength to hold her, *now*, when it mattered most.

She could tell the moment he lost balance. It was what finally freed her. And she could hear the impact of his head on the ground. And she could tell, when she reached Ira and turned around, that this was the end. She would have rather died than obeyed Ira, she would have rather died a thousand deaths than do this. This would kill her.

"No," she said. She barely heard Ira's words over the ringing in her ears, but her body moved to where Sess lay, eyes open and blood pooling, on the ground. She tried to slow, tried to stop her feet, but the force of Ira was on her heels, and she had to keep going. Her eyes stung, but closing them offered no relief.

She took Sess' head in her hands. He didn't deserve this.

His head hit the sharp rock again with a crack. The ground turned dark red beneath his head. Her fingers lingered in his thick hair, on his warm scalp. Her hands were coated in blood, sticky and burning hot on her skin.

She couldn't breathe. Her hands shook, dripping with each tremor. Her mind was blank, empty like Sess' eyes. No, she thought.

Ira made her tie Navi's hands together, and Nime did her best to keep the blood off of Navi's skin. She would keep death as far away from Navi as she could. Hands like hers had no business touching anything good.

And then she was off again, following the sound of the others. How could she hear them, when everything was so out of focus? Nime-the-body moved automatically, instinct moving her while Nime-the-mind floated in an ocean of emptiness. Her body didn't need her mind anyway, not for this. Buildings passed in a blur around her. The only thing she could feel was Ira behind her, following. Always behind her.

For a few moments, Nime ran, ignoring the blood on her hands and the pain in her body. She slowed at the entrance to the street Rem ran along. Poor Rem. He'd never liked running or any other part of PT. He looked back and clenched his jaw. There were tears in his eyes. He stooped to pick up a stick, holding it in front of him like a weapon. Nime's eyes blurred again. Rem had never liked violence, either.

When she came at him, he held his ground, swinging the stick at her in defiance. He moved so slowly she hardly had to dodge to tackle him. Once she did, he wasn't strong enough to push her off of him. She pinned him to the ground and closed her eyes.

Ira handed her a knife.

A single swipe under his jaw with the knife stopped Rem's struggling, as red stained his neck and the collar of his thermals. His eyes were so wide and dark, Nime could almost see herself in them. She leaned forward.

"I'm sorry, I'm sorry, I'm sorry," she repeated over and over. He gripped her shirt hard, knuckles white, as blood flowed freely from his neck. He gasped and coughed, splattering blood on Nime. She held him until his hands fell free and his body stopped moving.

Nime gently pressed him down, her hands leaving red prints on his shoulders. She stood and looked at her hands. They were stained red and shaking, nearly dropping the knife. But Ira was still there, audible even through the muffling ocean in her mind, telling her to keep going. She swiped at her eyes to brush the tears away, but that made it worse, smearing heat across her face. She had no choice but to keep going, though her heart and head ached, a deep pain that pushed her further into the empty ocean. Her body would do this, and her mind would float out on the Endless Sea and be free.

Chi cried out behind her, and Nime whirled. Chi came to a skidding stop in sight of Rem's body, her hands coming up to cover her mouth. She shook her head, staring at the blood and the body. The world shifted, left to right, and Nime realized her head was shaking, too. She couldn't stop shuddering.

Chi was too horrified to put up a good fight. She looked past Nime, shouted the word "monster." She was right; Nime was a monster. But Chi wasn't shouting at Nime, she was shouting at Ira, who moved Nime forward with a nudge in her mind.

Nime had her pressed against a wall in moments, though Chi struggled and thrashed. Her fingers gripped the knife tighter against the blood that slipped through her fingers and brought it down into Chi's chest. One stab should have been enough, but Ira told Nime to keep going. The knife came up again, and down again, and Chi gasped.

"It's not your fault," Chi said, though her breath was short; Nime had to lean in to hear her. She tried to keep her tears out of the wounds, even as her hand continued to stab and stab and stab and stab.

The knife was too slippery to hold onto anymore, and finally, Ira released her, sent her after Miel.

Nime was coated in Chi's blood. It was all she could see or smell or feel, floating on that ocean of blood. How many people had died to turn the Endless Sea red?

But it wasn't all she could hear.

Nime followed the sound of Miel's frantically beating heart to the square, to the temple steps.

Miel was not quick enough. Nime hauled him down by the legs. His hands scrambled at the ground but found no purchase. His feet kicked back at Nime. He was babbling, begging, eyes wild and terrified.

"Nime, please, you don't have to do this. Please," he said, and he kept begging, even as her bloody hands tightened around his neck. His hands scratched and pulled at hers. They tightened and tightened, keeping the blood from his brain until he fell limp. But Ira didn't let her let go for ages, until her hands were aching, and she'd crushed Miel's throat.

When her hands finally released, she collapsed and cried. She cried —loud, choking sobs that shook her whole body—until her throat was hoarse and her eyes stung like her tears were acid. Like the blood all over her was acid. She could not move for shaking.

Nime pressed her traitorous hands into the ground and heaved, bile dripping from her mouth and tears from her eyes, but she still couldn't see through all the blood. Her fingernails scratched at the dirt, weakly at first, and then frantically, digging and ignoring the friction against her skin. She would dig a hole where she, too, could die.

But all that happened was that the Endless Sea of Blood got muddy. Instead of drowning in blood, she floundered in muck. Nime laid down on her side and wept.

17

If I can fix this, I have to.

Past-Navis have paid this price before, and if they could do it, so can I. For some reason, I think of my painting, the storm and the flowers. I'm the Lif; I can make life out of death.

I was so stupid, before. I don't need my hands or my voice to shape. I only have to will it, and it will be. The beat of my heart is the rhythm of the world. My eyes move slowly up to Ira, watching Nime and Miel raptly. He doesn't understand, because he doesn't have his Words. Because this is my valley and my temple, and I am more powerful than him. I search under the stones for a plant that suits my needs, and when I find one, hope lights up in my chest. I might not be able to stop Nime from killing Miel, but I won't let her die, and if there is a way for me to bring the others back, then I will do it, whatever it costs.

I pour creative Potential into the cracks between the stones, and in the space between my heartbeats, I can feel it growing. Ira looks down at me as the tendrils of a red, vining plant start climbing up his legs. He kicks them away, but he can't kick them off faster than they grow. In ten heartbeats, his legs are wrapped in creeping vines and tiny, purple flowers.

Ira pulls my head back again, tugging painfully on my hair, and his lip curls. "You can't stop me," he says. And then he wraps both of his hands around my neck and squeezes. I only get out a squeak before my air is cut off. When I try to twist away, he squeezes tighter.

No, no, I can't die like this. If I die by Ira's hands, I can't fix what he's done. What I've done. If I die here, human life is over. If I die now, the heartbeat of the world stops, and there is no going back.

But I already can't breathe, and the edges of the world turn black.

Nime's still on top of Miel, still pressing down, but he's gone. Nime looks up at Ira; her eyes widen as she sees me.

"Please," she says between sobs.

"Stop," Ira says, and Nime lets go of Miel and scrambles backward. She turns around and gags, scratching at the ground with her fingernails. "Kill yourself, Nime."

If I could scream, I would. This is not how I die, it can't be. For once in my life, I have to be strong enough.

Nime is curled up on her side in the dust, shaking. She stops moving at his words. Isn't it enough? He has killed four people, he has tortured Nime until she's barely recognizable, he's taken everything from her. And it's still not enough for him.

I pour everything I can into my next heartbeat, shaping the vines into hooks to pull him away from me, but all it does is give me one breath and pull both of us backward.

I can't do it. I can't stop him. I'm going to die.

Nime slowly pushes herself up onto her hands and knees. They almost buckle beneath her.

I pull the vines again desperately, and again they give me one more breath.

Oxygen, one of the many possible ingredients for life, gives me a moment of clarity. I can't do it, not on my own. Ira is more than strong enough to overpower me. But I can make something stronger than us both.

My heart uneven, I use what I have left to hastily shape a creature out of stone, out of air. Gray and craggy and towering over us, it roars to life, and I feel Ira jump behind me. His hands only loosen when the stone smacks him to the side with its thick, roughly-shaped arm. I gasp again, and again, until my vision clears and my lungs aren't on fire anymore.

I stop the stone when it pulls back one arm to claw at him with jagged fingers. I need Ira alive for what's next. Before he can speak again, I spin silk across his mouth. Large, heart-shaped leaves grow up over him, and more vines wind around him.

I look at Ira on the ground. He hates me, I can see that now in his eyes. That's alright; I hate him, too. My heartbeat is loud in my ears. Is this how it feels to be furious, to be so mad it fills up every part of you? I have never hated anything as much as I hate him.

But I'm not going to destroy him.

I'm going to consume him, turn him into something new and full of life.

The stone stands watch over Ira while I catch my breath. Nime is still on her hands and knees, shivering, and she falls as I watch. Guilt eats at me from the inside. She's suffering, and I could have prevented it. But I didn't. When I could have stopped the deaths of her friends, I didn't. I didn't think I could. I was following rules that don't apply to me.

I won't anymore.

The stone comes to me when I need it. It crouches down and peers at me with empty sockets where eyes should have been. One hand reaches out and carefully shreds the rope around my wrists. With my own hands, I untie the rope around my face. The stone watches me. I reach out and touch it, the rock warmer than I thought it would be and rumbling quietly.

It lumbers over to where Nime fell and picks her up with care. I need time to think, but there isn't much of it, not if I want to save the others. The stone follows me up the stairs of my temple and lays Nime down in the grass of my sanctuary before going back out to grab Ira. I stand in the hallway, in front of the secret door. I take a deep breath. Be strong, I tell myself. Be brave.

* * *

The box is open in front of me, and the sharp, cold edge in my hands makes my skin crawl. I take it into my sanctuary anyway.

The stone drops Ira in front of the entrance. Not inside, not yet.

I sit in the grass next to Nime, and I think.

There are options. I could back out now and live; I could do my job as Lif and travel through the world spreading creative Potential everywhere I go, like most of my lives. Nime would still be hurt, though. She would still carry the weight of guilt, even though we both know it's not her fault. Not even my sanctuary can heal the trauma she's been through, though it's already fixing her body.

And Ira. Ira will live, too. I don't know if they'll banish him, or imprison him, or something else.

But the world will take much longer to heal, and every death today will be permanent.

Or, I could give the knife to Nime, and I could make things right. It would be hard for her, and it would hurt her more than she already is. I start crying again.

There's only one real option. I sniff and wipe my eyes. After everything, I can't make the same mistake twice. The priestesses from my tower shouldn't have kept their plans from me, but they weren't wrong. It was necessary then, like it is now.

And it's for the best. The world can go back to the way it was before the Fall, before I ruined it, back to growing and thriving and living. My trees will be able to keep growing where they are. This desolation will transform into grasses and flowers and dirt, and animals will live here, that eat and have babies and die and repeat. Anue will fly and sing. People will take naps in the sun, or maybe paint a picture of their love here, in this valley. People who have grown crops, built homes, given birth, sung songs. And the planet will keep turning, back on its orbit, the magnetic field will stabilize. There will be seasons again, like I remember. The water will ebb away and everything, everyone will *live*.

But what about me? I won't ever get to lay in the sun on a grassy hill or fall in love. I won't ever paint again. I'll never get to do *anything*. But would I be willing to sacrifice the world for myself? No. Never again. So this is the only option. I will spend the rest of my life in this sanctuary, and the world will go on.

18

"Kill yourself, Nime," Ira said, and Nime crashed. She couldn't move, couldn't breathe. The world shattered, and all she could see was the red sky, the dark mud walls of the hole she was buried in.

That hole was Nime's whole world, and she awakened into it with eyes wide from horror. She was trapped in hot mud, stinging and burning. Sucking and pulling.

She drowned in mud for what felt like eternity.

The world was only blood and nightmares. There was nothing outside of that hole.

And then Navi reached in and started pulling her out.

It was like climbing out of hell. Clawing hands digging into the walls and pulling, the mud sliding beneath her, getting into her eyes, her mouth, her skin, weighing her down. Nime felt it all around her, soaking in. She would never be clean again, never be able to wash off this filth. She wanted to die, wanted to fall back into the hole and forget, never have to think again, because thinking meant remembering, and remembering meant—

Red, slippery and warm, and all over her, like this mud. But this mud is blood too, isn't it? She'd spilled enough for the hole to be full of it. She was swimming in the blood of everyone she ever loved, and it was her own fault. It was her hands that stabbed and cut and crushed, her legs that chased and her arms that caught. She didn't deserve to climb out, her guilt like a chain around her ankles, around her throat. At the bottom of it all, the pull of Ira, the promise of destruction.

But still.

But still, Navi reached for her, for what was left of Nime. Nime, who was chest-deep in the blood of her friends, in misery, in Ira. He was the mud that sucked her in, pulled her back into the hole, the pit, the blood. He wanted her to stay, to destroy, to be destroyed. His thoughts crowded inside her head. Wasn't that what she wanted? An end to the suffering?

Yes.

No.

He wanted it, but Navi wanted her to climb out, wanted it with her whole being, bright like the sun, blinding Nime's blood-covered eyes from above. Their voices in her head echoed so loudly, they were all she was now. She was nothing, had never been, never would be anything but their voices, their wants, their will. Ira, like water, smooth and numbing, icy and suffocating. Stay, he said, and bleed, and break. Be mine, my Hand. Navi, a rush of warmth, the sound of laughter, a memory of when she was young and someone kissed her forehead, carried her in their arms while she fell asleep. Flowers sprouted from the mud where Navi's light touched it. Come with me, she said, it's not your fault, I love you. You're not a tool for breaking, not mindless.

Nime wished she were mindless.

If she were mindless, this would go away. If she destroyed everything, there'd be nothing to remember. Only the peace of death, oblivion. The hole was so deep, so narrow, it crushed her, pressing her head between its walls.

She would never climb out.

But she wasn't mindless. Not a tool, a person. She could climb out, she could reach up and out, and Navi would help her, pull her free from the mud and the chains. Navi's flowers withered and died and fell apart, just like everything else. Was there anything else?

Yes. There was light and music and warm drinks, hugs and the smell of the sea. There were friends and books and *everything*. If Nime would only climb, dig her fingers and toes in, feel the mud between them. Feel, and climb. There was everything.

A flower slid down, half-dead, deep enough for her fingers to almost touch. She reached for it, but her arms hurt. They ached. Her hands were so heavy, they were made of stone, of metal. Her fingers were so close, so close, the air from them stirred the petals. The chains around her wrists snapped. She was too tired to pull at them, and the flower was dying anyway. She'd kill it if she touched it. The mud clutched her neck like hands tight around her throat.

Just reach a little farther, Nime, reach and pull and be free. The mud loosened; she lifted her arm again and touched the flower with the tip of her finger. It nodded, dipped, bent back again. It was alive. Alive and not dead, not fading and bleeding. It grew in Navi's light, green and yellow and white, strong against the wall of the hole. She touched it again, grasped it around the middle and pulled.

It was strong, and it held as she pulled, though the mud pulled just as hard. But Nime was strong, too, as strong as the flower, and she pulled the hardest of all until another inch of her was free. Her breath rushed shallow and fast. Nothing had ever been so hard. The effort would kill her.

Above, another flower growing from the mud, in the golden light that was so warm it stung her hand when she reached up and grabbed and pulled.

One by one, the flowers made a ladder. Every grab and pull felt like the last she could manage. Nime was so *tired*. Her arms and legs and heart were so sore and heavy, but they moved again, even as the mud rose with her, pulling at every chance to drag her back. They tugged at the chains, but the flowers behind her helped her up, they held her feet and used the mud to grow, and the mud dissolved them into itself.

Navi, at the top, held out her hand. Light dripped from her fingers like molten gold, falling to the mud below, falling on the flowers and on Nime, where it sputtered and soaked in. Each drop was enough for another step, another inch out of the filth that sucked at her skin.

She was so close to the top now that she could see the sun. So close that she could see where the mud turned into grass, could almost touch it, could almost take Navi's hand.

If you touch her, you'll kill her, the mud said, its voice sharp. You will kill her if you get too close. Nime's hand fell back. Only the flowers under her feet kept her from falling back down.

No, your touch isn't death, Navi said. Only if you want it to be. Ira wants it to be. Do you?

No. She didn't want her touch to be a poison, toxic to all she loved. She didn't want that.

What do you want, Nime?

What do *you* want?

She couldn't move, couldn't think. Again there was too much. Too much noise in her head, too many voices that weren't hers. What did she want?

She wanted to be free. To choose. To be Nime. To see the light again. To live. To have nothing but her own voice in her mind.

Her hand came up, grasping, reaching into the light. Navi grabbed it in her own and that, too, burned, but it was cleansing. Nime wilted. She had nothing left in her now, no energy or will. But Navi was strong enough to lift her out, despite the last dregs of mud clinging to her feet, despite Ira's rage and the iron shackles of his will.

Nime landed on the grass and breathed.

* * *

Sometimes the easiest part of a decision is making it, and the hard part is doing it. This is one of those times. Because while there may only be one true option for me, when I look down at Nime, finally resting in my sanctuary, I almost can't bear the thought of waking her, of climbing into her mind and controlling her.

It would be one thing if I had to do it, it's another entirely to force Nime. But it must be done. It must be her. And she won't do it on her own.

So.

It is easy to slip inside Nime's mind, though. Too, too easy. Her poor head is aching from what it's been through, and she has no defenses left to keep me out.

Ira thrashes and yells behind me as the stone carries him into the temple. I'm sure it hurts him to be in here. I don't care.

Ira is all over her mind. He's left marks of his coming and going like it's nothing, like her mind isn't a sacred place. It's hard for me to find her through the mess, hard to hear what is left of Nime. She is deep,

deep inside, trapped by his will. I swallow when I reach her. This is what we make of people, Ira and I. This is what we reduce them to, shivering messes too tied up to move.

I reach in and brush the restraints that hold her. For the first time in my life, I pity her. Nime. I pity Nime, who I have always looked up to and who I believed was unstoppable. That feels like the final thing Ira's taken from her. He holds her tighter, his will all over her. His vines and suckers. I send out my own vines into her mind. I try to be gentle.

It's hard pulling her up and out. She is so deeply tangled up in Ira that I have to peel him off of her like leeches, and each time it hurts her more. A good pain, I hope, like taking out splinters. But she hesitates, she falls back into his poison. Because I'm being gentle. Because I'm not in her mind like he is, bending her thoughts to my will. I blink back tears and force myself in further. I press a thought into her mind. Sunlight, the warmth of love, laughter to counter the death he is filling her head with. Another, this time it's her worth, her humanity. She is not a tool, not something for Ira to play with and use for revenge and then break in a fit of rage. I fill her mind with images of life. I don't leave any gaps for Ira to wriggle through. He does anyway. But Nime is so close; his vines are falling free, pushed out of her mind by my own.

In the end, Nime makes the decision herself. She chooses me over him, and then she's free.

* * *

Navi leaned over Nime, the golden ceiling above her like a halo, like the sun. She smiled through tears. Nime was flat on her back on something soft, and she couldn't find the will to move. Navi smoothed Nime's hair back and held her burned hand, only it wasn't burned anymore. Nime relaxed into the floor. She could hear Ira somewhere nearby, and the memory of death floated in the back of her mind, never far away. But just for a minute, everything was okay. Navi was alive. Navi saved her. Nime was herself again. She was her own.

She smiled back at Navi, and Navi cried harder. She curled over Nime, resting her head on Nime's stomach, her warm tears soaking through Nime's shirt. But then she lifted her head and looked into Nime's eyes, taking a deep breath through her nose. Her other hand came up to rest on Nime, something hard and sharp in it. Nime looked down at it, and her world froze again. Navi clutched a long knife, gold and glass and warm to the touch. Nime looked back at Navi, and she hoped that the knife was meant for her, for her heart that ached. Not for Navi, never for Navi.

Navi's eyes filled with tears, but she met Nime's with determination, with finality. She brought Nime's other hand up to hold the handle and sat back. She helped Nime sit up.

"Nime," she said, and her voice shook. She couldn't speak for a moment, so she closed Nime's hand tighter around the knife. "Nime." Her voice was so full of love and grief that Nime's eyes watered, raw as they were from crying already. Navi pulled Nime's hand with the knife up to her chest, and her hand trembled like her voice. "If you do this, everything will be fixed."

Nime shook her head slightly. No. This wasn't happening.

Navi nodded. "Yes. It's for the best." She paused to swallow. "Everything will be fixed. This will be the end of the Endless Sea. Haven will be able to settle on land and build a new world. Everything will go back to how it's supposed to be. What was dead and destroyed will have new life. You'll be saving the world," she said. Nime pulled back, tried to let go of the knife, but Navi's grip was too strong for her. Navi's face changed; she gnawed at her lip and looked conflicted. "And…I think I can bring everyone back."

"Bring them back?" They were the first words Nime could get out of her mouth. Alive again? The thought was both terrifying and hopeful. And then she frowned. But at what cost? The cost of Navi, little sister, miniature sun? It wasn't worth it.

"But you have to be the one to do it," Navi said, pulling the knife closer so that it pressed into her skin, right above her heart. "I can't do it myself. I wish I could." She started crying in earnest again, clutching at Nime's arm with her other hand. "I wish I could. I wish you never had to do anything like this ever again. I wish you could heal from what's happened." Nime was shaking her head, forcefully now, still too weak to pull away. Navi closed her eyes and leaned her head back so that her tears leaked out the sides and rolled into her hair. "But I have to do this. I have to do this. I'm so sorry, Ni, I never wanted to force you to do anything. But I have to." She sobbed, and Nime could barely see through her tears. When Navi could breathe again, she looked at Nime and gave her a weak smile that quivered with each wave of tears. "I'm sorry. I love you. Please be well."

Nime felt more than heard the order, felt her hand move with the knife and press into the skin over Navi's heart. Saw the blood well up, golden like the rest of her, shimmering and molten as it flowed down her chest and into the ground. It seeped in and began to glow, spreading out like cracks in the ground, quickly moving beyond the walls of the sanctuary, beyond the temple, out into the Dome. Ira cried out, but Nime didn't take her eyes off of Navi, who had stopped crying and was smiling more sincerely at her now. She didn't speak, but her face was peaceful. Nime leaned over and wrapped her arms around her little sister.

19

I close my eyes when Nime sacrifices me, and I open them in darkness.

This is the part of the plan I wasn't sure about. I know that past-Navis have done this to let loose a massive rush of creative Potential. It's a quick-fix for all the big and little hurts of the world. And, theoretically, it should be able to revive the recently dead.

Theoretically. I've never done it before, but that doesn't mean it's not possible.

The only problem is returning their souls to their bodies. I've never done that, either. But I have nothing left to lose, and everything to gain.

Wasn't that what Dad was saying? Isn't that what he meant? If I waste my time doing things that have been done before, nothing new will be gained. And some rules are made to be worked around.

I'm in a good position to work around the rules; I'm the Lif. A piece of the Mother Creator is in me, and if I can't shape the fabric of reality to my desires, who can?

There are things that I know now. I know where the Mothers are; I know the shape of the universe; most importantly, I know the place where souls are, the place I saw a glimpse of when I took a soul for Anue. And I know that I can't truly get there without dying.

So, I am dying.

I look around the darkness. Anue, made from death but full of life, should be able to come here if I call. This line between life and death should be familiar to it.

It flies up to land on my shoulder. It tilts its head and looks at me.

"I need to find their souls," I say. It chirps, short and sweet, and takes off from my shoulder. I follow.

Walking in the darkness isn't truly like walking. I'm not sure how much time passes in the physical world, but I walk for a while, following the spot of brightness that is Anue, its three tails spread out behind.

And then there's a squeezing feeling, an expansiveness, and a hollow ringing, and I am in the Soul Place.

The place where souls are is nothing I could describe with words. It's infinite, it's full and empty, an abyss of light, blinding dark. It's intimate and lonely. I am not meant to be here, but here I am. Between one heartbeat and another, someone appears in front of me.

It's me. The person in front of me is me, in this life. It's like looking in a mirror. I take a step forward, and they do, too.

"Hello again, Lif," they say. Their voice is a similar set of opposing traits: quiet and booming, deep and high. I can hear every emotion in it, layered all over each other. This person isn't one of the Mothers. Those two are distinct in their own ways; this person is everyone and no one at the same time.

"Who are you?" I ask, but it comes out of their mouth.

"Once, at the beginning of the world, there were two mothers of everything: one who created and one who destroyed. They were opposite sides of the same coin, in equilibrium." They sound more like me with every word. "Each one antithetical to the other. They needed nothing, but they wanted a companion. Someone to balance on the coin's edge between them. Someone to be a part of them both." They take another step closer. "And so, they made me." 'Me' is quiet, in just my voice.

And then, half a second later, in every voice again: "US." The person changes, flashes between different faces and bodies, too fast for my eyes to keep track. They walk toward me as they shift. I understand.

"Why are you here, now? I wasn't expecting you." They stop an arm's length away from me.

"Give them back to me, please."

"No one's ever asked for that before."

I don't say anything. They didn't say it couldn't be done. They look at me, tilting their head.

"Anything can be done." They chew on their lip in a gesture so familiar I find myself doing it too. "But why?" I open my mouth. I didn't expect to have to explain myself, but they tilt their head and blink, and they become Remy, then Chi, Sess, and Miel. They change back to me. "I see. Love is a powerful thing. To care so deeply for another being that you would give yourself to see them well is both against human nature and the truest part of it. Altruism is a sign that a soul has matured."

"Nime deserves to be happy," I say.

They sigh and reach out a hand to brush my cheek. "So do you, sweet soul." For a moment, we look at each other. And then they look down. "There has to be balance. It's only right," they say. "Will you take their place?" For a second they shift into Ira. "Lif and Unlif, will you stay here with me?"

"We can, for a while," I say. Whether he wants to be or not, Ira is here with me. With us. Two sides of a coin, and the balance in the middle.

"You'll have to go again, soon. Everyone does." They tilt their head again. "But thank you."

They cup their hands over their sternum, and a moment later, they pull away with a wispy, glowing ball in their palms. I know just looking at it that it's Remy's soul. They hand it to me. It almost looks like a wisp lamp floating about an inch above my skin.

They pull out three more balls of light: Chi, Sess, and Miel. I can see every part of them. I should not be seeing their naked souls like this. But I'm dying and they're dead, and I don't think they'll care too much.

The other me passes them over to me. I hold the souls in my cupped hands like a swirling, luminous nebula.

"Take care of them," they say. A soul is vulnerable without the body to protect it."

"I know." I do; the souls feel like they'll blow away with a breath. I keep them close to my chest. "I'll be back soon."

"I know," they say. I'm not used to that expression on my face: a wistful smile and sad eyes. "When you take them back, give them something to hold onto, something full of life. It's a hard journey to make alone." I nod. I know something that will work.

I turn my head to look at Anue on my shoulder. Its dark, liquid eyes seem to know exactly what I want to say, but I say it anyway.

"Make sure they get back, please," I say. It nods its feathered head, and when I hold the souls out, it picks them up gently in its beak.

I come back to myself, and it hurts terribly, but I won't be here long. I'm in time to help Nime before my body dies and my soul goes back to the Soul Place. She is hugging me and crying, so she's close enough to hear me.

"Fruit pit," I say. It's faint, but Nime lifts her head. For a moment, she looks hopeful. And then she looks down at the knife in my heart, and her face falls again. "Give them each a fruit pit, and listen to Anue."

"Wait," she says, and her voice sounds so broken and sad that I almost wish I hadn't made this choice. And then, without the beat of my heart to support me, I die.

* * *

After she died, Navi disintegrated into fine, golden dust that settled on everything in the room. The giant stone creature that had been sitting just outside the doorway stood with a grating noise and lumbered off, leaving Nime truly alone in the new grove. She sat back on her feet.

For a while, she stayed there, and she didn't think. She tried her best not to think. And then, Nime picked up the knife that she'd stabbed into Navi's heart and held it to her own.

She shook her head and put it down. She couldn't: Navi had told her to be well. She didn't know how, but she would.

That had been the only thing Navi had said at the end that made sense.

A fruit pit and Anue, Nime thought.

* * *

Nime carried her friends back to the temple one by one, and laid them out in the grass, under the trees. That would be a better resting place than the road, and she owed them that, at least. The valley outside grew greener by the second. It was starting to look the way Nime half-remembered it.

The four of them, lying in the leaf-filtered light, looked like they were sleeping. Navi had fixed everything, but they were still dead.

Nime knelt next to Sess and picked a few tiny yellow flowers nearby. She was setting them on his chest when his tablet, peeking out of his pocket, chirped with a new message from his father. *We're on our way*, it said. Nime wanted to throw it against the wall. She looked back at Sess, at his chest moving up and down in shallow breaths. She scrambled backward, as far away as she could get. Anue swooped down from one of the trees and landed next to her. She looked at it.

"A fruit pit," she breathed. A fruit pit and Anue, Navi had said. Whatever Navi had done, if they were alive…

Nime ran over to the first tree, the one Navi had grown herself. It was hidden among a few others, but the golden flowers distinguished it from the others. She dropped to her knees and searched the ground for pits. She almost started digging under the new soil when she thought better of it. Standing, she reached up and grabbed a fruit.

The golden yellow flesh was just as sweet as it had been the first time, but Nime didn't give herself time to enjoy it. She took huge bites until, finding the deep blue pit, she dropped the rest of the fruit and grabbed another. In less than a minute, she had yellow juice smeared across her face and four pits in her hands.

Anue watched as Nime approached her friends. She swallowed and hesitated before kneeling beside Sess again. She stared at him. It wasn't that she didn't want to bring them back—not at all, she wanted them alive so much it ached—it was that she—

She was afraid. What if it didn't work? What if it did?

If they came back, would they hate her? Would she ever be able to look at them without seeing the life leave their eyes? Would they ever be able to look at her without seeing the one who killed them?

Was someone like her redeemable?

Anue squawked and opened its wings, moving the air into a small breeze. Its three-part tail fluttered. Nime looked at it. Right. Fear paralyzed; fear was what caused this in the first place. Still, her hands shook as she took Sess' hand, opened it, and then closed it over a sticky pit.

She leaned back. Nothing happened, except Anue hopped over to Rem and squawked again. Nime tucked another pit into Rem's hand.

The next pit went to Chi—Nime understood what Anue wanted, she thought—and the last she pressed into Miel's palm.

Finally, Anue stopped looking at her. Instead, it took off into the air and circled above them. It was beautiful like this, almost glowing in the light from the window, a moving rainbow. Nime moved over to the doorway. She sat there, knees up to her chest, and she watched. After a minute, Anue flew back to one of the trees and tucked its head into its downy chest.

The temple was quiet. And then—

"Nime?"

Her breath caught in her throat.